THEIR PRETTY LITTLE MONSTER

A MONSTERS NIGHT NOVEL

MILA YOUNG

CONTENTS

Before You Enter	ix
Soundtrack	xi
About Their Pretty Little Monster	xiii
Welcome to Monsters Night	xv
Prologue	1
Chapter 1	11
Chapter 2	18
Chapter 3	28
Chapter 4	41
Chapter 5	52
Chapter 6	61
Chapter 7	69
Chapter 8	75
Chapter 9	84
Chapter 10	89
Chapter 11	104
Chapter 12	113
Chapter 13	129
Chapter 14	142
Chapter 15	157
Chapter 16	177
Chapter 17	192
Chapter 18	213
Chapter 19	227
Chapter 20	238
Chapter 21	247
Chapter 22	262
Chapter 23	271
Chapter 24	282

Chapter 25	298
Chapter 26	306
Chapter 27	329
Chapter 28	342
Chapter 29	358
Chapter 30	367
Chapter 31	374
Chapter 32	392
Chapter 33	402
Chapter 34	414
Chapter 35	424
Chapter 36	433
Chapter 37	444
Chapter 38	459
Chapter 39	477
Epilogue	493
Moon Puffs Recipe	503
Bind Me	505
Their Lethal Pet	507
Their Blood Queen	509
About Mila Young	513

Their Pretty Little Monster © Copyright 2024 Mila Young

Cover art by Sanja
Chapter art by Covers by Aura
Editing and Proofing by Personal Touch Editing and Outthink Editing, LLC

Visit my books at
www.milayoungbooks.com
www.milayoungshop.com

All rights reserved under the International and Pan-American Copyright Conventions. No part of this book may be reproduced or transmitted in any form or by any means, electronic or mechanical, including photocopying, recording, or by any information storage and retrieval system, without permission in writing from the publisher/author.

This is a work of fiction. Names, places, characters and incidents are either the product of the author's imagination or are used fictitiously, and any resemblance to any actual persons, living or dead, organizations, events or locales is entirely coincidental.

Warning: the unauthorized reproduction or distribution of this copyrighted work is illegal. Criminal copyright infringement, including infringement without monetary gain, is investigated by the FBI and is punishable by up to 5 years in prison and a fine of $250,000.

Note: This book does not contain any elements of AI content. All art was designed by real artists, and all of the words were written by the author.

DEDICATION

For those of us who prefer the growl of the beast to the whisper of a prince...

BEFORE YOU ENTER

Their Pretty Little Monster is a paranormal, monster romance and is not a dark book, but there may be triggers for some as it has violence, torture, grief, death of a family member, and dubious consent.

The Devil is the Gentleman
Mercy Raines
Darkside
Neoni
A Little Wicked
Valerie Broussard
In the Shadows
Amy Stroup
A Dangerous Thing
AURORA
Jaws
Lights
Supernova (tigers blud)
Kat Cunning
Devil's Worst Nightmaare
FJORA
Venomous
UNSECRET, Kat Leon
Big Bad Wolf
Roses & Revolution
Devil Inside

CRMNL
Part Goddess Part Gangster
Madalen Duke
Down
Simone, Trella
Kingdom Fall
Claire Wyndham, AG

Listen to the Soundtrack on Spotify - Their Pretty Little Monster playlist by Mila Young

ABOUT THEIR PRETTY LITTLE MONSTER

In their arms, danger becomes desire.

Every year, monsters demand their Offerings—women like me. This year, I thought I escaped. I thought I was safe. Then he arrived.

The Viscount.

Dangerous and ruthless, he declares me a late Offering.

Swept into the deadly realm of the Shadowfen, I realize I'm not here by chance.

They want to rule, and I'm their key. My reality crumbles, and as much as we act like enemies, they refuse to let me go. Their touch ignites a fire I can't resist, fueling desires I never expected.

They call me their little monster.

Maybe they're right.

Because when everything is stripped away, a fiercer side of me no one expected—not even me—emerges.

You see, in the shadows, temptation and peril collide.

So, ready or not, the monster within is about to be unleashed... and these three Shadowfen are eager to claim their prize. Me...

WELCOME TO MONSTERS NIGHT

It started as a curse. A rumor. A hint of superstition.

But then it became *very* real.

Monsters poured out of the portals, their origins unknown, their intentions clear. For one night a year, they roamed the earth, selecting their unwilling brides and dragging them home.

Except not all the monsters went back to their own worlds.

Some stayed.

Power began to shift.

Cities were destroyed.

Humankind reverted.

Villages were created, all the mortals hiding from the dangerous beings that call our realm *home*.

And still, those portals open.

Every. Single. Year.

Allowing more monsters to flood our realm, finding their mortal mates and claiming them against their will.

Or that's the tale we've all been told.

Be good or suffer the consequences.

Follow the rules or your entries into the selection pool will increase.

Every year, sacrifices are chosen. *Sacrifices* that are then dumped into abandoned cities right before Monsters Night commences.

Offerings are what those sacrifices are called. *Offerings* meant to tempt the creatures of the night. *Offerings* put in place to ensure humanity survives this hell.

This is our reality now.

A world filled with deadly creatures and mortal survivors.

And tomorrow is the Day of the Choosing…

Will we survive another year?

Or will we become one of the Offerings for this year's Monsters Night?

Only fate can save us now…

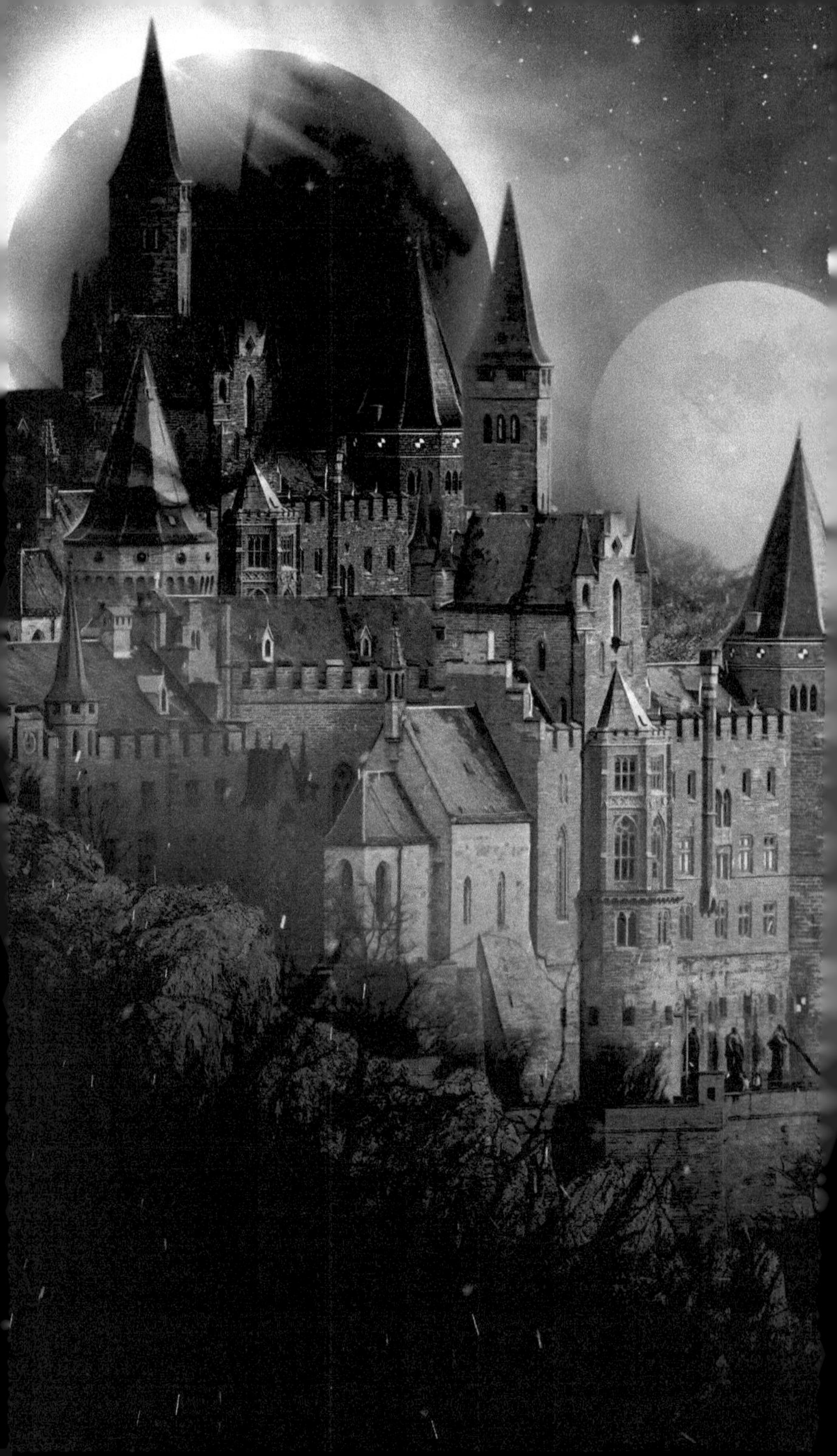

PROLOGUE

MONSTER

Our city melts under the lick of flames. Eyes locked on the window, I can't move, can't breathe. Fear locks me in place, and my knees are close to giving out.

Silvercrest Kingdom is sprawled in chaos. I rub my eyes, unsure what I'm looking at, the shock still startling me.

The ground is cracking open, vast craters marring the once-green land.

All the while, other Shadowfen are scrambling out from their homes, darting in every direction, panicking as houses are swallowed whole by the soil. Entire sections of the land are gone, consumed in an instant. Flames leap from building to building so fast, engulfing everything in orange and black...

Panic thumps against my breastbone as I watch smoke taint the air, swallowing the sun, burning with intensity.

Everything's happening so fast. One moment, I'm cleaning my father's daggers, stuck at home because, at thirteen, I'm evidently too young for the hunt.

My only son will not risk his life. He has a throne to take.

I grind my teeth, furious he left me behind in the castle.

Then, in a heartbeat, the world breaks apart.

Screams pierce the air, high-pitched and desperate. Shuddering, I jerk away from the window and glance at the open door in the parlor. It's coming from deep in the castle, and my thoughts fly to my parents.

"Mother," I call out, bursting from the room into the empty hallway. The floor shakes under my feet, and I stumble, hitting a wall with my shoulder.

"Have mercy on us," I mutter a prayer, the same one I've heard my mother speak so frequently.

Feet pounding against the stone floor, I sprint down the corridors that seem endless. I arrive at her chamber, and my hand trembles as I grasp the handle.

"I'm coming." I shove it open, the door slamming against the wall with a deafening crash. What I see steals the breath from my lungs.

Half the room has disappeared, the stone of the walls crumbling into the abyss below.

Air buffets into me from the world outside, now visible across two walls no longer there. Shattered glass is all over the place, the floor slopes dangerously, and pieces of the wooden panels are missing, others sliding into the gaping void.

My parents' carved wood bed hangs over the edge,

one leg dangling over the broken floor. Tapestries hang in tatters, and the grand chandelier is smashed and swaying wildly overhead from a single cord.

Another scream from down there...

"Mother!" The word tears from my throat, and I'm inching toward the edge of the jagged floor. A cold, hard knot snaps around my heart.

Then I find her.

She's down there, barely hanging onto a loose plank of wood with two hands, far below the broken room. Beyond her is nothing but smoke and a deadly plummet of three stories.

Fear strangles me, the smoke suffocating while ice slips through my veins.

"I'm here," I call out, dropping to my knees, realizing there's no way I can reach her.

She glances up at me—her violet eyes expanding, lips parting for another scream. Silver curls cling to her damp forehead, with the blood from the cut on her temple smearing her face.

My chest constricts, but I'm not going to panic. Father taught me to be brave in the face of danger, of death, of anything. *Show no fear,* he'd say, *and you've already won half the battle.*

"Get your father," she shouts at me frantically, but she knows he's not home and too far for me to fetch. The glassy look in her eyes, the lost expression on her face... she's given up.

"I'm going to help. Hold on!" My arms shake at my

sides as I remain bent over, peering at her, gasping for air.

The walls and floor shudder once more, a loud groaning sounding as the world is being ripped apart. Mother's swinging in circles as she hangs there, her sky-blue gown fluttering around her legs, her whimpers a blade to my heart.

Rubble cascades from the ceiling and rolls over the edge, as does the bed in an abrupt slide.

She screams, flinching, but it misses her. My hands sting from how hard I'm gripping the broken floor.

"Just wait, I'll free you," I shout, wiping at my damp eyes as I retreat. Fire and ice burn in my gut, churning, fighting inside me.

"Save yourself," she shrieks. "Remember, I will always love you, my little howler."

"Don't... this isn't goodbye." I'm up on my feet, frantically checking the room, unsure where to go.

Smoke curls up into the room from outside, and I'm coughing as I lie on the fallen tapestry, its rod no longer attached to it, now hanging nearby. Darting over to it, the floor quivers, a loud croak sounding beneath me, as if everything's going to collapse in a heartbeat.

I stumble, losing my footing. The room suddenly tilts, and I fall over, all while scrambling to hold on to something as I start sliding toward the edge.

Quickly, I grasp onto the wardrobe feet, the piece of furniture made of the heaviest, darkest wood in our forest. My heart thumps in my veins, but I'm not giving up.

By some miracle, the room doesn't crumble and settles once more.

On hands and knees, tapestry rod in hand, I inch closer as more bits of the floor break away, tumbling down into the abyss. The air is thick with dust and smoke, each breath leaving my throat raw, my lungs aching.

"Mother! I have something you can grab! I'll pull you up!" My words are hoarse, barely more than a croak, but I call out, desperation clinging to every word.

Peering over the edge, I search frantically, my heart pounding in my chest.

But she's not there.

The plank of wood is also gone.

My mother... she fell.

Every inch of me shreds.

"Mother!" I scream, the sound swallowed by the roaring flames down below, coming for all of us. Tears prick my eyes, blurring my vision, my chest aching, almost unbearable.

I didn't reach her in time.

She's gone.

Broken, I can't stop crying. I'm coughing, choking from the smoke strangling my throat. I can take the smoke; what I can't do is lose my mother.

The wall behind me cracks with a monstrous creak, a jagged line snaking its way across the stone. I don't waste a second scrambling out of there, my body moving on pure instinct.

I charge out of the room and through the castle, my thoughts on the stone steps, hoping they are strong enough and that I can get out. Each step is a struggle, my body heavy with grief, with fear.

Not a soul in sight... the castle's empty. Please let all the staff have escaped.

Bursting into the main entertainment room, once grand and filled with life, it's now crumbling. Tapestries lie in heaps on the floor, the ceiling gaping with holes. Dust and debris rain down, turning the air thick and unbreathable.

Covering my mouth and nose with my sleeve, I rasp on each inhale as I run through to the main hallway. Destruction lies everywhere. My mother's face flashes before me—silver curls, wide eyes crammed with fear, her last words echoing in my mind.

I reach the stone stairs, hiccupping a tear-filled breath. No time wasted, I descend, taking two steps at a time, slipping on the debris, but I don't stop. I can't stop. On the ground floor, I pivot to the left, to the front entrance.

The castle's coming down around me—fallen ceilings, blocks of stone, a thick puff of dust filling the air.

Desperately, I charge to the rear entrance on my right, just off the kitchen, leaping over fallen furniture and skidding but catching myself before I tumble over.

My heart pounds in my throat.

There it is—the double doors hanging off their hinges.

I burst out into a plume of smoke and ash, following the path I know is there. Screams come from all around me, and I can just make out silhouettes darting through the smoke and chaos. The ground trembles beneath me, and fear smothers me.

Regardless, I press forward.

Before me, two figures emerge, the smoke unfurling around them. I blink, clearing my vision, and recognize them.

My chest beams at the sight.

Father!

He's back from hunting. Broad and tall, the Silvercrest Kingdom needs him now more than ever. The king of our realm.

In front of him stands his vassal, General Bren, in charge of our military.

"Father–"

The ground starts to rattle violently, stealing my words.

Crack!

The piercing sound echoes through the air, the ground tearing apart and leaving my skin crawling.

Terrifying screams flood the air.

With no relief, I catch my balance from the swaying ground, my father and the general blurring in and out of the moving smoke that clings to everything. Each breath grows raspy, my lungs burning.

Snippets of General Bren's deep grumblings to my father reach me.

"Ruined… Kingdom… Change is coming. I will rule." His voice is a low growl, dripping with venom.

I clench my fists, anger rising through me, fury pushing me to take a step closer to the reality of what I'm hearing.

My father has always told me he trusts the general, but as my father bellows back at him, words I can't make out, I notice the curl of the general's mouth.

In that heartbeat of a moment, he wrenches his elbow back, close to his body, then he plunges a blade right into my father's gut, deep and forceful.

I shout, my response lost in the panic around us, in the croaking sound I'm making.

Father slumps forward, a white-knuckled fist grasping the general's jacket. His face is twisted, broken, blood dripping from the corner of his mouth, eyes wide, filled with pain.

Bren shoves my father aside just as fast, and he crumbles to the ground.

"Father!" I shout, my legs shaking beneath me, rage cutting through me.

The sight of him lying there, lifeless, sends me spiraling. I lose all control and lunge at the general, who still hasn't seen me.

Vengeance. It consumes me.

But before I can reach him, a tremendous explosion sounds behind me.

I glance back to see the castle coming down.

Crumbling.

Boom.

The collapse reverberates through my body, shaking everything. A sudden rush of air and dust slams into my side, throwing me off my feet and tossing me aside.

As I'm flung, the weight of death is closing in.

And with it comes my father's words.

Death comes for us all...

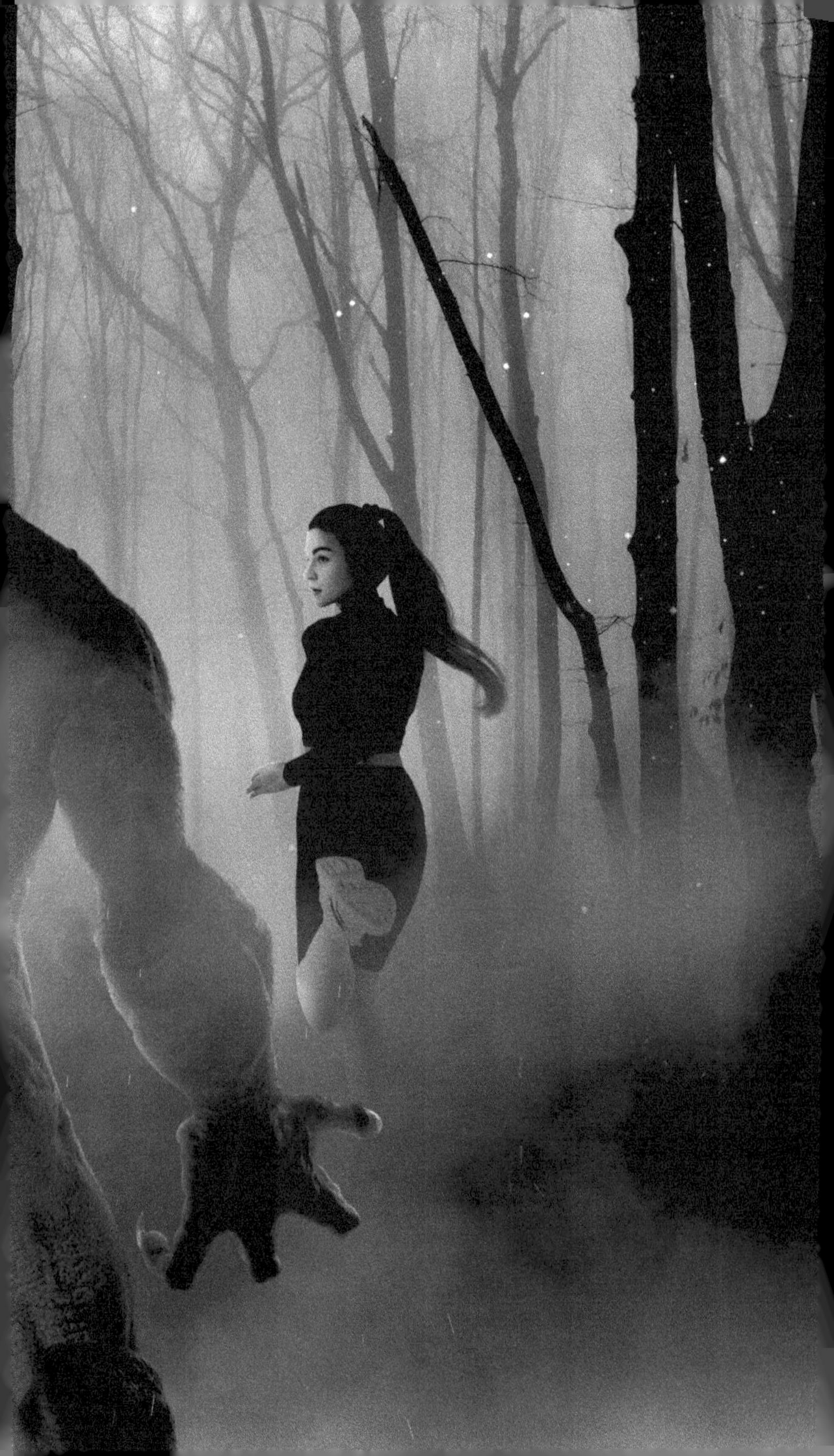

CHAPTER ONE

SAGE

13 Years Later
Earth

I wake with a scream stuck in my throat, the nightmare still clinging to my thoughts.

"Sage, are you all right?" My mother's voice floats across our small cottage into my room.

I manage a laugh. "Just the world ending in my sleep again. Nothing to worry about."

She's all too familiar with the nightmares that haunt me—earth splitting, fires raging, and now the latest joy... my bedroom cracking in half as I tumble into nothingness. It's enough to make me dread sleep.

Feeling *cursed* is the only way to make sense of it.

Grudgingly, I remember the errand waiting for me this morning, so I peel myself from beneath the threadbare blanket and get to my feet. The warm summer air wraps around me too quickly.

Stumbling out of the tiny bedroom across the creaky floorboards, I make my way to the bathroom. A splash of cold water chases away the dream from my mind. Quickly dressed in my burgundy cotton dress and scuffed ankle boots, I catch a glimpse of myself in the mirror as I comb back my silver hair.

A faint violet hue shimmers amidst the silver, and I gasp. "What in the world?" Leaning in closer, I examine the new color, a chill sweeping through me. No one else in the village has hair like this. And despite attempts with my friend, Alina, to dye the silver using beetroot juice and charcoal, it's only become more pronounced—now turning violet. Another reason to set me apart from others in the village.

Heart racing too fast, I pull my hair into a ponytail, hiding the color as much as possible, hoping no one sees it.

In Nightingale Village, differences are dangerous.

Ever since my mother fell pregnant with me out of wedlock and was abandoned by a man she barely speaks of—only mentioning he wasn't from this village—she's been treated as an outcast. Yet, she raised me alone, which is more than some in the village are capable of.

Setting the comb on the counter, I step out of the bathroom. Floors that creak, walls lined with worn wallpaper, and furniture that shows patches of repair—all signs of a lived-in cottage with personality.

I wander into the kitchen, where the sweet smell of

cinnamon porridge fills the air, making my mouth water. Mom stands by the stove in her faded gray dress and cardigan, stirring the pot with gentle precision.

"Morning, lovely. Have some breakfast before you start your day." Her voice is warm.

I lean over the pot, watching the thick mixture bubble, anticipating the moment Mom will add a dollop of raspberry jam.

But I'll have to wait.

"Keep mine warm. I just have to go collect some buckets as my last ones broke," I say. Truth is, I'm behind on my berry-picking quota, so I need those buckets urgently. My sales go to buy smoked meat, which I trade for Mom's medicine.

She glances over her shoulder at me, arching an eyebrow in silent question.

The improvement in her health since starting them has been undeniable. I'll break every damn rule if it means she heals.

She's been struggling with a lung illness for nearly a year, the local medic unhelpful and insisting that her condition is incurable. They won't even prescribe anything to alleviate her symptoms, forcing me to take matters into my own hands. Which is why I've resorted to illegally buying medicine from a Village Protector.

She's suddenly coughing harshly, leaning heavily against the counter to support herself.

"Come sit down for a bit," I urge, guiding her gently to the couch. She settles with a weary sigh. "Have you taken your medicine this morning?"

"There's not much left. I'll take it when I feel worse." She coughs again, her hand pressing against her chest.

My gut clenches and I rush back to the kitchen, turn off the stove, then grab a glass of water. I mix in the last of the herbal medicine—a precious amount—and bring it to her.

"Drink this, please."

She stares at me, her face set in a stubborn expression. Rarely does she ask where the medicine comes from, and I suspect she knows it's not through legitimate ways. Perhaps that's why she's always hesitant to take it, especially when it's running low.

Reluctantly, she takes the glass and drinks it quickly, then lies back, eyes closing as she settles to rest.

"Just relax until I return," I tell her softly, then step outside in the sunlight.

Passing several wooden cottages, I walk past two girls chatting, and I'm reminded of how much I miss my friend, Alina.

Just over five weeks ago, she was selected in our Day of the Choosing as an Offering to the monsters for an annual event. Thing is, names are randomly selected, usually between four to six sacrifices chosen each time, though this year they selected ten, which is unheard of.

For the past two years, since I turned eight-and-ten years old, I've dreaded the Summer Solstice, terrified I'll be chosen, but so far, fate has been on my side.

No one wants to be picked.

Well, except Alina. She was desperate to have her name called out and went as far as to cause as much trouble in the village as possible. Every strike against you gains you an extra entry into the Chalice, and I'm convinced she had gained a couple hundred, ensuring her selection. She'd face anyone who got in her way and collected the medicine for my mom in case she was caught. She defied orders, and I admired her for her bravery.

Then, on her departing day, she told me that she was doing it in the hope of escaping and finding her sister in the Elite City. Mind you, it's a place I'd never heard of before she told me. I pray she's safe, knowing that I'll never see her again.

Once you're selected as an Offering and leave the village, you don't come back.

I shudder at the thought and trudge along a dirt path, which is dotted with water puddles from last night's rain.

A sudden, harsh bump strikes my back, a shoulder slamming into me, sending me stumbling forward. I cry out, falling onto my hands and knees, crashing into the muddy earth. The sting in my knees hits instantly, making me wince.

"Get out of the way," snaps one of the farmers as he brushes past, disappearing around the bend and behind the storage sheds up ahead.

"Asshole!" I yell after him, frustration boiling over as pain shoots through my knees. Struggling to rise, I feel the cold mud clinging to me.

Laughter erupts from my left, and I glance over to see three girls taking amusement in my fall. Heat rushes to my cheeks, and a fire ignites in my chest. I push myself to my feet, wiping my hands on the grass.

"Why bother cleaning up? You'll just end up back in the mud where you belong," one of them mocks.

I straighten up, brushing the dirt from my clothes as best I can. "Thanks for the concern," I grumble sarcastically, meeting their gazes with a defiant glare until they move on.

Breathing heavily, I feel a newfound strength building within me, one I thank Alina for. She would've laughed this off, maybe even taken a bow.

I let the squelch of my boots in the mud provide a small sense of satisfaction. I'm not letting them get to me. Some days are rough, fighting what feels like a losing battle against the village, but as my mom says, *If you can't find a good path, make one.*

Reaching the storage sheds on the outskirts of the farming land, the air is filled with chirping birds and the earthy musk ready for toil. The main shed looms large, housing the village's harvests. I head toward the smaller, quainter shed where supplies are kept. Inside, I find two wooden pails with handles that seem to have survived more seasons than some of the villagers. I note them in the ledger—the good old system where you pay at month's end and hope the numbers aren't fudged to make you pay more.

As I turn to leave, a cluster of elderberries catches my eye. They hug the side of the shed, perfect for our morning porridge. Rare finds, these berries, so I quickly start picking them, dropping them into one of the buckets.

"I hear a new Viscount's been appointed."

Raising my head, I overhear two Village Protectors talking near the shed. The mention of the Viscount has my attention. Weeks after the Day of the Choosing, the previous Viscount and Barons were removed, and we haven't seen or heard from them since. Nobody knows why, but everyone's talking about it, nervous about what's going on.

These newly appointed Village Protectors have recently arrived in Nightingale, watching everyone, too.

I half listen while picking berries until the words *dangerous* and *not local* pierce through their chatter. My hands pause, berries forgotten. "And he's from the Elite City, no less," one of them adds.

I freeze. Wait, that's where Alina mentioned she wanted to go.

"They're saying he's coming to stir things up because the higher-ups aren't thrilled with how this village has been managed," he continues.

Suddenly, I'm up on my feet, buckets in hand, a coil of unease tightening in my gut. Most in the village see my mom and me as burdens.

What if the new Viscount rids the village of us? The thought of being made to vanish sends a shiver down my spine.

CHAPTER
TWO
KILLIAN

Two Days Later

Muscles tense, I scan the recorded footage of the girl on my wrist-piece screen. Her hair catches the sunlight, shimmering with an almost violet hue—a rare color on Earth, but back on my home world of Blight, it's more commonplace.

Yet here I am, observing a human girl from Earth at the most recent Day of the Choosing Ceremony in Nightingale Village. Even with her back turned to the camera, her face hidden, there's a tenderness in her posture—her head slightly bowed, shoulders curled as if bearing the weight of the world.

As the newly appointed Nightingale Viscount, I'm here to fix the village while secretly discovering if she's the one we've been searching for all these damn years.

It's pure fate that I even happened to notice her in the first place. But a recent incident involving Gods from another dimension drew my attention to this village and the inhabitants within it.

Because if one of those humans could be the fated mate of a God, maybe the key I've been searching for is here as well.

So I reviewed the tapes from the Day of the Choosing, studying the mate in question—Alina.

Which is when I noticed her focusing on another woman in the crowd. A violet-hued pixie.

When Cain, the Elite City King, mentioned needing a replacement Viscount, I offered to take the position. Primarily so I could have a chance to learn more about this woman, but also to help this village leave the dark ages.

As King, Cain rules the Elite City of Chicago. Despite his monster origins, he controls the Elite families in his region. Each family rules over one village. And in each of those, a Viscount takes charge over the villagers. He's the only one in each village aware of the Elite families and the structure controlling this world.

I do find it most fascinating to have learned that Elite families are the humans who didn't run when monsters first invaded Earth. Instead, they offered a collaboration, one of governing and controlling humanity for all our benefit.

To avoid the extinction of the human race while appeasing the countless monster worlds, they had proposed that humans be placed in remote villages, monitored by the Elite families while ensuring the collection of human Offerings for the monsters annually.

In exchange, these Elite families were offered boons for providing ideal monster mates for the Monsters Night. After all, powers and gifts, with the ultimate promise of immortality, are tempting rewards to pass up for any human.

So now, one night a year when monsters enter Earth through portals, they can take the chosen human Offerings back to their worlds for breeding, marriage, or whatever the fuck they desire.

And me…I'm here to set things right in Nightingale Village for the future of all involved in my new role as temporary Viscount.

But first, I must secure the girl I've been searching for and take her back to Blight to address our issues. My first priority remains my world back home.

Which is why I'm watching this tape yet again, needing to memorize every detail to track her down.

I reach over, sliding my finger over the video screen where she stands, hoping she'll turn around to show her face, but she never does.

"Are you the one?" I whisper, my breath forming a mist in the cool air.

One touch and I'll know it's her, then there's no time to waste.

Voices nearby pull me from my thoughts, and I lift my gaze, switching off the footage to find a curious group of half a dozen children watching me. With a forced grin, I push back into a walk, surveying the village for her.

Farmland stretches before me, with humans tending

the fields and several women loudly chatting as they pick red globe fruit from trees. The longer I've spent on Earth, the more I detest it. This place, so starkly different from my realm, Blight, only increases my homesickness.

Nothing here feels right—the temperamental weather, the tasteless food, or the convoluted politics back in the Elite City.

Striding along the dirt path, I meander toward the small cottage homes.

"Your Grace," greets Village Protector Edwards, that sycophantic fool, stepping out in front of me from behind a small cottage, interrupting my thoughts.

I study the man who has white wisps of hair at his temples, standing in my way now.

"I thought it suitable to notify you that supper will be served shortly in the main hall. I have personally selected the nobles and families to join us. Many have questions about your appointment." He wrings his hands in front of him nervously.

"Right, of course."

"It's been a long time since we've had true leadership, so your arrival couldn't be more imminent for all of us."

He refers to the last Viscount, who fucked up his mission, taking advantage of his position in this village, claiming three of the girls as his brides, so this man's comment is an understatement.

Edwards regards me intently, and already I'm exhausted from his presence.

"My plan isn't to keep men who, for all I know,

harbor the same doctrines as the previous Viscount. So, time will tell."

Fear behind his eyes darkens his gaze. "Of course, Your Grace. Change is inevitable, and I am yours to do your bidding. Shall I escort you to the hall?"

"I'm capable of seeing myself around. I require no escort. And I'll join you when I'm ready."

His smile falters slightly but quickly recovers, and he moves out of my path.

I stroll past him, continuing my journey through Nightingale Village.

Locals keep their distance, hurrying back into their homes as I pass, yet I catch the weight in their stares and the faint whispers about me. Sunlight dapples the field as I leave the farmland behind and follow the winding paths between homes.

A couple gives me a wide berth, hastening their pace as I approach. As I round the corner, a breeze carries the sweet scent of berries to me. While most human food is barely tolerable to me, providing little of the sustenance I need, berries have always found favor with my taste.

Ahead, in front of a worn cottage, a young woman sits on a log, her back to me, busily sorting through a harvest of red berries. Her fingers are stained a deep red.

The breeze picks up again, tugging at her simple brown cotton dress and fluttering through her silver hair, which flashes with a faint violet hue under the sun —just like in the footage I've studied.

My feet stop of their own accord.

Chest tightens.

It's her.

Though I need more confirmation that she's truly the girl we've been looking for, the odds seem promising. After searching for so long, it feels inevitable that she must be the one.

Just as I'm about to step forward, another young woman in a more vibrant blue dress emerges from another path. I retreat into the shadows, observing, waiting for a moment when she might be alone again.

"Sage, you still haven't finished the berries for the feast? It's about to start," the newcomer says, her tone sharp and somewhat condescending. "Haven't you heard? The new Viscount, Killian, expects perfection."

The girl on the log, Sage, shrugs and rubs her berry-stained fingers with a nearby rag. "I don't care who he is, Lany. As long as he leaves me and my mom alone."

"Hush, are you missing part of your brain? Don't say those things so loud," Lany hisses, glancing around nervously. "I hear he's watching everyone, taking notes on who needs punishment."

That's news to me.

Sage drops her rag into the large bucket of berries. "Well, you better take the ones I've finished." She points at the smaller wooden pail, where the fruit is free of twigs and leaves.

Lany hurries over to collect the bucket. "My family got invited to the feast tonight, you know. I'm guessing you weren't?" she sneers.

"I wouldn't want to attend," Sage bites back

instantly, voice almost deflated, yet beneath it, I hear a spark of her frustration.

Lany's laugh, laced with mockery, echoes around us.

"Sure, you wouldn't. Everyone knows those selected might end up in good standing with the new Viscount," she answers sarcastically. "The Protectors even selected the Jonas family to attend. I mean, they clean the animal stalls for a living, so that says a lot about you and your mom not being chosen." She scrunches up her nose, eyeing Sage with such disgust.

Sage lifts her head, her gaze locking on the girl. "I hope you gain all the attention you crave from the Viscount. We all remember how well our last Viscount *cared* for girls...Perhaps the new one is just as... attentive."

Lany's glare hardens in response, her smile quickly fading as she clearly understands the warning in Sage's words. Her lips pinch.

Something inside me ignites on Sage's behalf, impressed by her response. It's evident that the villagers are aware of the turmoil the previous Viscount had caused. Feeling the weight of her words, Lany abruptly turns and storms down the path, her bucket of berries swaying angrily.

Meanwhile, Sage gets to her feet, grasping the second wooden bucket firmly in her hands and swinging it toward the house, momentarily facing in my direction. She doesn't see me, but finally, I get a clear view of her face.

My pulse thumps wildly—fuck, she's devastatingly

beautiful. High cheekbones, soft porcelain skin, and mesmerizing icy glacier eyes are framed by long, dark lashes. Full lips are tight, and her brow furrowed. Even in her simple brown dress, her curves are undeniable. She must be about twenty or twenty-one years old.

The mission of taking her to Blight suddenly seems like it might be more intriguing than I had initially anticipated. She vanishes into the house, and I find myself whispering under my breath, "I'll be back for you."

Turning on my heel, I head for the village mess hall. I need to blend in and give them something to remember, considering I plan to vanish for a few days soon.

As I enter the expansive, dimly lit hall, it's buzzing with the murmur of voices and the clatter of dishes. Everyone's head turns as I stroll in, their conversations falling into a hushed silence. They know change is coming; they just don't know what kind yet.

That's when I spot Lany again. The girl in the blue dress rushes into the room, joining what appears to be her parents at a table near the back of the hall. Seizing the moment, I nod to the Village Protector who has been watching my approach.

"Your Grace," he mutters as he leans in close to me, his voice barely above a whisper.

In a low tone meant only for his ears, I instruct him, "Have that girl in the blue dress, Lany, and her parents removed from the mess hall. Make sure everyone sees the commotion."

He pulls back at first, taken aback, but recovers

quickly, nodding in understanding. "At once, Your Grace."

I take a seat at the head table, picking at a bowl of fresh berries bursting with flavor. As I watch, he quietly instructs two of the other Village Protectors. They stride purposefully through the hall, stopping at Lany's table.

"Turner family, rise and stand," commands one of the Protectors in a firm, authoritative voice.

"What's the meaning of this?" Lany's father demands, his voice rising as he stands, followed reluctantly by his wife and daughter.

"The Viscount has ordered your removal," the Protector states flatly. "You are to leave the hall immediately; your invitation is revoked."

"But we've done nothing wrong!" The mother's face is a mix of confusion and fear as she clutches her daughter's arm.

"It's not up for debate. Move now, or we will remove you," the Protector insists.

A heavy silence falls over the hall, every eye fixed on the unfolding drama. The father's face reddens with anger, but he leads his family away from the table, not daring to meet my gaze. Lany, however, looks directly at me, her face pale with shock and embarrassment.

"Out. Now!" the Protector's voice booms again, echoing through the hall.

As they are escorted out, the tension in the room thickens, and I can't help but think I could have made things much worse for her. Yet, she's not a true villain—she received the punishment I deemed fair.

The Protector scurries to smooth over the ruffled atmosphere, welcoming people and lifting the heavy energy with practiced ease. I let him ramble on, my thoughts drifting back to Sage and the mission at hand.

Announcing my need to travel for urgent business, I finally inform him once he returns, "I will require a villager to accompany me to carry my supplies and assist with various tasks. I'll only be gone for a few days at most."

He nods eagerly, ready to facilitate. "Of course, Your Grace. We will find someone suitable immediately."

"There's no need," I interject with finality. "I have already chosen someone."

As the meal progresses, my mind remains consumed with thoughts of Sage. With her by my side, the balance of power in Blight will shift.

She has no idea yet just how important she truly is.

CHAPTER THREE

SAGE

Tonight, the shadows seem heavier.

With hurried footsteps that echo softly on the street, I've managed to slip out of the house without my mother noticing—a chore that's becoming alarmingly routine these days.

Wednesdays. Ten p.m. South Street by the cornfield. He'll have a flashlight in his left hand, not his right. And he only accepts smoked meats.

With Alina's words always at the top of my mind and the payment for my mom's medicine in my bag, I hurry toward the farms.

Peering over my shoulder, I catch nothing but the whisper of the wind rustling through the trees. I've been doing this for a couple of months now, and still, every noise, every shadow, has me panicking. Skulking through the night never gets easier.

Even dressed in my black cotton pants and shirt, my hair tied up, I feel exposed.

Up ahead, the cornfield looms near, its stalks swaying in the breeze while the moonlight gives the field a ghostly hue. I navigate quickly to South Street, passing darkened homes with no lights, every rustle of leaves, every owl hoot leaving me jumpy.

Finally, I spot him.

Jason, one of our Village Protectors, is standing at our previous meeting location, cloaked in darkness, his face hidden beneath a hooded cape. Despite the couple of times we've met like this already, the sight of him concealed and waiting still sends a shiver down my spine.

Breathing faster now, I move toward him, my eyes fixed on the flashlight he holds in his left hand.

"Evening," I say softly as I approach. "Do you have my medicine?"

"Like always," he groans, glancing around almost nervously. Has he spotted someone nearby? His reaction has me instantly on higher alert than earlier, ears listening for any sounds. "Let's do this quickly. I have somewhere to be."

I nod, grabbing the paper-wrapped package of smoked meat out of my bag.

He shoves a hand into his cloak's pocket and produces a small parcel swathed in white fabric, then pushes it into my hand, already reaching for the smoked meat.

Except, his parcel feels smaller, lighter than the last order.

"Wait, this is less for the same payment." I raise my

voice slightly, but he shrugs, snatching the meat. But I tighten my grip, refusing to let go.

"Then no exchange," he growls.

"Why is it less?" I demand, needing to ensure we don't run out of medicine. The last batch lasted barely a week, and meat isn't cheap. And by the weight of tonight's medicine, it may last a couple of days if we're lucky. Plus, I've had to pick and sort through several buckets of berries to pay for this bag.

He's silent, his grip on the meat tightening. I squeeze mine as well, unwilling to let this slide when it's about my mother's health.

"You can't just give me less. When will you deliver the rest?"

"It's all I have," he groans.

I narrow my eyes. "I'll have to reduce the payment, then." The fire inside me flares up. I'm not backing down, not now.

He hesitates, and for a moment, I think he might relent. But then he yanks the parcel harder, and I stumble forward, my grip loosening just enough for him to pull it free.

"Hey!" I shout, but he's already retreating into the shadows, vanishing fast, leaving me with half the amount of medicine I need and anger that burns hotter.

"Jason, you owe me!"

Grinding my teeth, my pulse races, my chest rising and falling faster.

Placing the medicine into my bag, I retreat, anger and fear mingling through me.

His betrayal stings, and the worry for my mother gnaws at me. Tomorrow, I'll find him in the village, and I'll make him give me the rest.

Twisting around, I push in the opposite direction to Jason, picking up my speed as every shadow feels like a potential threat. With the moon sliding in behind thick clouds, darkness spreads over the land. Eeriness runs up the back of my legs as I run. My footsteps echo on the dirty path, crunching against the tiny rocks.

I can't bear to think of getting caught. Of being punished for having illegal medicine brought into the village. The last things I need are additional entries put into the Chalice for breaking the rules, increasing the chances of me getting chosen as a Monster's Bride at the next Choosing Ceremony.

That's when snapping twigs pierce the silence behind me.

Fear skates down my back, and I sprint faster, not daring to even look back. My breaths come in quick, panicked bursts. Careening around the mess hall, something dark and fast whisks out in front of me, moving as swiftly as the wind. Something... something huge.

I gasp for air, my chest squeezing as terror swallows me. Stumbling backward, I stifle a scream.

Then it's gone.

I run quicker now in the opposite direction, finding myself in a garden, having no idea where I am. Checking over my shoulder, I don't look where I'm going, and my foot catches on something.

Tripping forward, I barely catch myself, noticing I'm trampling over vegetables.

Another sound, closer this time, something like the rush of air.

What's going on?

I whip around, recoiling until my back hits a tree. A small wincing sound drips from my lips, my gaze searching the darkness frantically.

Was it a bat? Large owl? They swoop down on small animals at night, and Gods know, we have our fair share of rats in this village.

Around me, shadows seem to move, and the darkness feels alive, pressing in on me.

My breaths come too fast, fear strangling my lungs.

Then, I notice someone standing across the garden, someone who wasn't there seconds earlier, holding on to a lantern by his side.

A shudder sinks through me down to my soul.

"Who goes there?" I hiss, my fingers digging into the tree behind me as though I need its strength to remain upright. I blink, clearing my vision, thinking it's the Protector. Is he making me pay for standing up to him? For challenging him?

The figure almost glides forward, making a soft humming sound that sings on the breeze. He's raising his blinking lantern to reveal his face.

It's the Viscount.

Bile rises to my throat, and I'm going to be sick. Fates, this is so much worse.

Did he witness my exchange with Jason?

My legs aren't working anymore.

His eyes are on me, vibrant blue with hints of gold, like the sky at twilight, unnaturally bright. He saunters closer, still making that unnerving humming sound.

Shaking, I can't bring myself to move, feeling more prey than girl.

He won't hurt me, right? He's the new Viscount of our village, our guardian. I almost snort a laugh. Right... as much as the last one was protective of us.

Tonight, the Viscount wears a charcoal-colored warrior's shirt that embraces his broad chest and shoulders, bronze buttons running down the front fashioned into emblems I don't recognize. A matching metal band encircles his thick forearm over the sleeve, and a belt cinches his waist, revealing muscles straining against the fabric. Black trousers hug strong, long legs and end at sturdy boots. One could easily mistake him for a warrior rather than a Viscount.

He appears much younger than when I first saw him upon his arrival. His square jawline, sharply chiseled cheekbones, and parting lips are hypnotic. I catch myself staring at his mouth, and my cheeks heat up when he notices.

His long, dark hair tumbles messily around his striking face, stirred by the breeze and cascading over his shoulders. I've never been this close to him before, and he's not what I expected. There's a wicked sensation curling through me in his presence, one I don't fully understand but that burns deeply—a dangerous feeling that I know could lead to trouble.

The blade at his side glints under the moonlight, heightening my anxiety.

"Are you going to punish me?" I manage to ask, my mouth dry and palms sweating. Is this how it feels to speak not only to a Viscount but also to one armed with a weapon?

He stops just a pace away, his intense gaze never leaving mine. The silence between us is thick, making it hard for me to keep my breathing steady.

"Why are you out at this hour, Sage?" he asks, his voice low, eyes darkening.

I swallow hard, trying to mask how much I'm trembling, but he knows my name. Why does he know my name?

"I was... collecting herbs for my mother," I answer, striving to conceal my nerves. If he believes me, maybe he'll let me return home.

He raises an eyebrow, a flicker of curiosity crossing his features. When the breeze wafts through again, it carries his scent, overwhelming my senses and nearly buckling my knees. He smells like the deep forest, mingled with the embers of a fire and the sweetness of freshly cooked caramel.

"You know you're not permitted to be out at such a late hour on your own," he says in a low, commanding voice. "It's dangerous for a girl like you..."

"I-I'm sorry. I was thinking... I needed to get some...

some herbs." I glance around the garden, pretending to search for them.

"You're not in trouble, Sage, but I should get you home," he confirms, his mouth quirking up at the corners. He reaches out, his hand grasping the back of my arm firmly yet gently, enough to pull me away from the tree.

His touch sends a sharp jolt through me, reminding me of the accidental burn from a flame. I wince, shuddering as the sensation, rather than stinging, turns strangely comforting. Confused, I look up at him; his eyes are wide, and a smile is beginning to form.

His gaze remains fixed on me. My heart pounds, urging me to lower my eyes, but the view of his chest right in front of my face isn't any less disconcerting than the fiery sensation spreading between my thighs.

"It's you," he whispers, his words cryptic yet causing something deep within me to stir—a pulse that starts in my stomach and radiates lower.

Then, his grip tightens, and suddenly, we're moving quickly across the garden.

"Viscount," I utter, alarmed by the abrupt intensity of the sensation in my stomach.

"Call me Killian," he insists. "I've been searching for you, Sage."

"You have?" I ask as I fail at easily matching his brisk pace, looking up at this daunting Viscount who confuses me.

The rest of our walk is shrouded in silence, his hand

firmly around my arm, the reality that he's been searching for me echoing in my mind.

Relief washes over me when we reach my front door, allowing me to feel a level of safety. I turn to face him, my back against the door, and he steps closer, his warm breath brushing my cheek as he leans in.

"I have been in search of an Offering," he whispers.

"Wait, what?" I blink, pressing my spine against the door, my hand frantically reaching for the door handle. I'm breathless, heart slamming into my rib cage. "I'm sorry for being outside late into the night, but I'm not interested," I plead, finally pulling my arm free from his grasp.

There's no surprise on his face, only a thin smile. "Head inside, Sage, and say your farewells to your mother. We leave tonight."

"What?" I gasp. "No, I-I can't..." I feel the medicine in my pocket, knowing it will only last a few days at most. Then what? "My mom's sick. I can't leave. Please..."

He tilts his head to the side, studying me, and there's that unusual glint in his eyes.

"This isn't negotiable, Sage. You are needed."

"But my mother..." I start, desperation clawing at my throat.

"She will be cared for," he says, his voice softer. "I give you my word. I will return in a few days to ensure her safety."

His words mean nothing to me, and it's not as if I can tell the Viscount I'm buying medicine snuck into the village to guarantee he ensures she has a constant supply.

He studies me in silence, and my head hurts with how much everything spins. With how the truth that he's not going to let this go settles into me like I'm carrying a mountain on my shoulders.

"And me? I'm not returning to Nightingale Village?" I murmur, a tremble starting deep in my chest and spreading through me.

There's softness sweeping across his face, but there's something else there, too. *Danger*. When he doesn't respond, I have my answer.

I'm being dropped off with monsters.

Tears well up in my eyes, my throat thickening.

"Quickly now, go inside. We have little time."

I blink at him, hands trembling. "But—"

"You have been chosen." He's grinning again, while I'm feeling nauseous.

Pressing down on the door handle, I hurry inside, my heart shattering at the thought of leaving my mother behind.

The Viscount follows and pauses in the doorway, filling the space and watching me. I want to run, to escape, but where will I go? Leaving the village is impossible, and I have no one in the settlement who will hide me.

The warmth of the cottage feels bitter. I move to my mother's side on the couch, watching her fragile chest rise and fall with each breath. Tears roll down my cheeks while my thoughts still haven't caught up. I've heard stories of the previous Viscount taking other Offerings in the dead of the night, of them vanishing.

I choke on a breath, hugging my middle. Is that my fate?

"Love you so much, Mom," I whisper, covering her with a blanket. "I'm going to find a way to come back."

The words feel hollow, but I need to believe them. I wipe away the tears, not wanting to wake her, worried about what the Viscount might do. Instead, I hurry into the kitchen and sneakily get a pen and paper, scribbling on it in the dark.

Mom,

Please don't be upset with me.

Tonight, I went out to collect your medicine, but the new Viscount found me. Now, he insists I've been selected as an Offering, and we must leave this very night. He says he'll return to the village and help you, but I don't trust him.

I promise that I will come back somehow.

Just remember, when you run out of your medicine, visit Jason Pines; he will sell you more for smoked meat. He'll be on South Street by the cornfield every Wednesday at 10 p.m.

I'm sorry I didn't wake you before I left, but I don't want the Viscount to put you in danger. It's better he doesn't know I told you.

I love you to eternity and back, Mom.

Sage

. . .

I place the note with the medicine on the kitchen counter when the floor creaks behind me.

Ice forms in my veins, and I freeze.

"Ensure you add in your note that your mother is not to speak with anyone about our departure." There's finality and firmness in his voice, a strong warning.

So, with shaky hands, I add a line at the bottom of the note.

His footsteps retreat, and I move into the living room, shaken.

It's dark, and the Viscount's in the hallway now, studying me. I can't see his features, yet somehow his eyes still glow.

"Are you ready?" he asks in a deep voice that leaves me trembling.

"No," I answer truthfully, but I step forward reluctantly, knowing he has the final say in our village. Opposing him would bring far worse consequences to me and my mother.

Luckily, Mom has one friend, her neighbor, who sometimes aids her. She's a woman who hasn't been able to bear children. Many in the village look down on her for it, and I guess she and my mom bonded over that.

The Viscount walks out of my house.

I take one last look at my mom, her mousy-blonde hair draped across her forehead, her eyelids twitching, clear she's in deep sleep. Tears well in my eyes, and my chin trembles, unsure how to say farewell. I'm terrified I won't find my way back, scared for my mom's health.

I drag myself outside, wondering if this is how all the

Offerings from previous ceremonies felt as they walked out of their homes.

Each step away from my home feels heavier, the weight of my promise to my mother pressing down on me. I try to stay strong for her sake, but fear and uncertainty gnaw at my resolve.

CHAPTER
FOUR
SAGE

Standing by the village lake, I stare into its darkness.

The Viscount has extinguished his lantern, and even with the moon's help, I can barely make out anything but its reflection shimmering off the surface. Trees around the water's edge sway, their leaves rustling in a soft, haunting whisper.

"Is this the right place?" I ask, glancing around. "The front gate to the village is in the opposite direction." I squint into the darkness, trying to make sense of his motives, but I can't even see his face.

He gives a light laugh, which surprises me—I've only heard dreadful things about him, but evidently, he can also laugh.

"This is exactly where we need to be. Now take my hand," he commands.

It's really impossible not to panic when you're brought by the Viscount in the middle of the night to a lake, hardly being told anything but that I'm to be an Offering. Each breath sharpens, aching in my chest at how fast they're coming. I keep imagining myself about to be shoved into the water... Is there a monster portal down there? While I can swim a bit, I'll end up drowning.

I take a step back, every inch of me icy cold, but the Viscount has my hand firmly, tugging me alongside him.

"You don't need to be scared."

"Oh, I have plenty of reasons to be terrified," I reply, the edge of panic sharpening my response. "Viscount, please tell me what's going on?"

"Told you, call me Killian." When he cuts a glance my way, his eyes are emitting that strange glow again. If I wasn't about to start screaming from fear, I might have taken a moment to consider what it meant.

Suddenly, he starts mumbling something under his breath, but his voice rises, and it's a language I don't recognize. I was taught the basics about monsters, including the portals they can open and close with magic or incantations. Mom also told me that those selected as Bride Offerings won't know how they will be treated until they arrive, but she suspected it'll be more like a sacred duty we're performing.

Except, wait... I don't understand what the Viscount is doing as his gaze locks on the lake in front of us. Is he summoning the monster to collect me?

The water ripples outward from a spot in front of our feet as if someone dropped a pebble into it. And right in the middle, there's a purple glow, growing brighter.

The Viscount's incantation continues...

My thoughts die as a sudden splash of water sprays us in the face. I squeak out of shock, pulling on his hand to free myself, but he's not releasing me.

"I'm not ready for this," I murmur through chattering teeth at the sight in front of me.

The lake at our feet has morphed into a gaping hole, its edges glowing a sinister violet color while the heart of it yawns open into a black abyss. A mouth ready to swallow up everything... including me.

I recoil instinctively, fighting against the Viscount's iron grip.

"It's time to go," he insists.

I'm shaking my head vehemently. "No, I can't do this. I'm going to die." Panic seizes me, squeezing my chest.

"There's no other way and no going back now," he states matter-of-factly. I hate his calmness.

He hauls me by the arm closer, his other arm wrapping around my lower back, forcing me to the edge of the lake.

"Please, I don't want to do this. Just tell the monster I ran away. No one needs to know the truth."

He laughs, a sound that sends shivers down my arms. "I promise it won't be so bad."

"That's really not funny," I protest, but my objections are cut short when he shoves me forward, right into the gaping maw of the portal.

A scream rips from my lips, echoing the terror of my recurring nightmare—falling into nothingness, just like when the room in my dream cracked in half, and I fell into it.

Flailing about through the void, I scream wildly.

As abruptly as the fall began, I'm shoved out into another place where natural light blinds me momentarily, and relentless rain drenches me. I stumble on unsteady feet, my head spinning.

Where in the hell am I?

Wiping my face of rain, a cry lodges in my throat as I struggle to process what's happening.

Around me is a large expanse of land, patches of grass and scattered stone under my feet, with a massive cliff looming ominously behind me and a savage ocean before me. Waves beat against the shore with ferocious intensity, the water churning.

Desperately, I glance left and right, searching for shelter from the rain, but there's nothing. I'm drenched, drops finding their way down the back of my shirt and skating down my back like frozen fingers.

I have no idea what I'm supposed to do. I spy a massive vessel shaped like a glass globe balanced on a platform farther out at sea. It's enormous, bobbing on the rough water.

I move toward the stone wall, praying for some semblance of cover from the relentless rain. The brooding sky suddenly bursts into a brilliant golden and purple color, throwing dozens of lightning bolts crashing down simultaneously, not too far from the sea vessel. The sky overhead glows like a cracked earth, more lightning spearing out, striking the water. I've never seen anything like it.

Almost immediately afterward, a tremendous boom

explodes, so loud that the ground beneath me shudders. I cry out, teeth chattering, as fear grips me wholly.

Just as I lose my footing, beginning to fall, strong hands catch me around the waist, lifting me back to my feet.

Terror slams into me, and I scream in panic, whirling around to face what I instantly assume is my monster coming for me. I shove against him frantically, but it's not a monster—it's the Viscount.

"Wh-what... Why are you here?" My breaths come out raspy against the howl of the storm.

Rain runs down his face, his hair is plastered flat, and his clothes are thoroughly soaked as he stares out at the ocean.

"They're not going to make it to shore in this weather. Fucking storms."

"Are we meant to get on that thing out there? Is that where my monster is?" I'm shouting over the heavy sheet of rain drowning us. "It doesn't look safe at all."

"We need to go." He grabs my arm and drags me into a fast walk. "We're not safe out here like this."

"Why? What's going on?" Part of me is starting to wonder if I hit my head and I'm imagining all of this.

When a great splash sounds behind us, I glance back to discover something black is pulling itself out of the water, close to where I stood moments earlier.

What the fuck is that?

The creature's as big as a horse but has six short legs with webbed feet. It half drags itself on its belly over the rocks. Spikes stick out around its frilled neck, and a long snout protrudes forward, two long tongues flicking in and out. Disgusting drool seeps out from the sides of its mouth as four beady eyes fix on us with unsettling interest.

Its mouth gapes open to rows of razor-sharp teeth, and it unleashes a hiss that has me whining and bumping into the Viscount.

"Oh Gods," I practically scream.

The Viscount–Killian–glances around to see what's turning in our direction. "Fucking Tidecreepers."

"What?"

Then we're both running the length of the rocky wall, him holding me tightly. Suddenly, he swings left into a narrow cave, steering us away from the storm's fury. He doesn't slow down; instead, we're hurrying faster into the depths of the cave.

As we navigate the passage, he brings us to a stop. I sense him bending to pick something up—and in an instant, a warm glow comes to life from a small sphere that fits perfectly in his hand.

"That's unusual," I remark, using the time to catch my breath, watching the light flicker against the shimmering cave walls. They glow a pale blue hue as if they're made of sparkling ice crystals. The ground beneath us crunches of loose, compact soil.

He nods, glancing at me momentarily with a tight smile that worries me, then we're moving again. "The transfer to the ship doesn't always go smoothly. The storms in this world are relentless, so there are always emergency items left here for such situations. It's not the first time."

How many times has he visited this world?

By the time we rest again, my lungs are stinging, and I'm panting.

He retreats a few steps the way we came, checking if we've been followed.

Still wet from the storm, I stumble about, curiosity drawing me toward the walls of the cave. Despite it being darker with the lantern away from me, there are sparkles all over the wall. My hand reaches out, needing to understand what I'm looking at.

"Don't touch that!" The Viscount's voice cuts through the dim cave abruptly, causing me to flinch. "Everything here will try to kill you. The walls are poisonous, and those shiny points you're drawn to are pin-sharp and will cut through your skin the moment you touch it, injecting toxins into your bloodstream. You'd be dead within minutes."

My mouth drops open, and I yank my hand back as if the wall itself was a burning flame. "What in the world? We need to get out of here."

"Not possible," he replies, just as a deep, menacing growl echoes from somewhere closer to the entrance to the cave.

My stomach drops, and a cold dread washes over me. The sound isn't just threatening; it's a promise of danger or something sinister waiting in the shadows.

"Please tell me it's not that creature out there

following us?" Shaking, I hold myself still, not trusting myself not to fall against the walls.

His silence tells me everything.

He has the light orb pointed back on the curved passage of the cave that leads to the entrance, and I'm behind him in the dark again. Around me, the poisonous points on the walls sparkle like a starry night.

It's always the prettiest things that are the deadliest.

"What kind of world is this? Why would anyone live here?" I scan the floor for anything I can use as a weapon, but all I see are small rocks, and I don't want to touch them.

"Shh," he says, heading back toward the entrance. The light from his grip drops to the ground, then clicks off, plunging us into suffocating darkness.

Oh, hell, did he do that on purpose or...?

Surrounded by danger, now robbed of my sight, I feel every shadow might hide the lizard-like creature. And who in the world is the Viscount, really?

Then, a large hiss slices through the silence, closer this time. I stiffen, the panic chewing its way up from the pit of my stomach. I hate how vulnerable I am, how exposed. The fear is like acid, eating me alive. The cave erupts with an explosion of more hisses and growls, a cacophony of threats converging into a thunderous boom.

A small cry falls from my lips, and I back away.

A deafening sound from outside suddenly shakes the cave. Footsteps, fast and heavy, echo through the corridor of the tunnel, and I hear Viscount shouting something indistinct.

Is he in danger?

The sound of a fierce scuffle floods the air next—punching, thumping, growls of pain.

I hug myself tighter.

Is the Viscount fighting the creature? The noise is horrifying, and I can't exactly sit back and hide. What if he needs my help? Because if he loses, I'm a sitting snack for that two-tongued beast.

A maelstrom of violence intensifies through the cave, and I can't see a single thing. Clenching my fists, I fight the urge to panic and run.

The cave seems to hold its breath with me as I decide at the last minute to find the dropped light orb, hoping that gives him an upper hand.

Deciding that seeing is better than trembling in the dark, I start creeping forward, painfully aware that I can't touch the walls for fear of getting poisoned. The fighting noises—snarls, snapping of teeth, and a strange whistling sound like something slicing through the air—continue to echo around me.

"Please tell me you're winning!" I ask, my words quivering.

All I get back is a grunt—a deep, menacing sound that I desperately hope belongs to the Viscount.

On my hands and knees, I slowly move forward, patting the ground in search of the light. My fingers are tentative, and I'm worried about what else they might find in the darkness. Dread weighs heavily on me as I inch to where I last saw the Viscount drop the light.

Finally, my fingers close around the warmth of the orb, the exterior feeling squishy to the touch. I exhale a sigh of relief, a small victory in the suffocating darkness.

Giving it a small squeeze out of curiosity, its light flicks on, and just as I do, a monstrous gaping mouth with strings of drool comes flying right at me.

I scream, flinching backward, the edges of my vision blurring as if I'm about to pass out.

The creature is suddenly wrenched backward by a figure both immense and daunting. Pale blue skin, marred with scratches and etched markings, stretches tightly over bulging muscles. The same ones that strain the seams of the clothes he wears—clothes that, moments earlier, the Viscount wore. Now, they are ripped to fit his larger, more formidable form.

Long white hair flows halfway down his back, and his arms, visibly more muscular, flex under the skin as he tightens his grip on the twin swords he wields.

Standing tall, his head nearly brushes the ceiling.

In a fluid motion, he pivots to confront the charging beast, his blade sweeping through its body like he's slicing through air—no piercing, no blood, no visible wound. The creature unleashes an ungodly screech as if mortally struck and stumbles backward. Despite the apparent lack of injury, it recovers and charges again, unmarked by the encounter.

The beast lunges once more, and the blue man's swords vanish into thin air before he charges. They clash with a thunderous force that sends vibrations through the ground beneath my feet.

I flinch, a cry caught in my throat. With deft strength, he wrestles the lizard into a chokehold, exposing its pale underbelly, then heaves it powerfully against the wall. The creature thuds heavily, clearly stunned but not defeated—its hide perhaps too thick even for poisoned spikes.

At that moment, the blue man turns toward me, and our eyes lock—those deep blue, familiar eyes now glaring from beneath thick, furrowed brows, his upper lip curled back over sharp-edged teeth, revealing a menacing snarl.

It's definitely the Viscount, transformed and… monstrous.

"Turn off the fucking light," he growls. "This damn beast can't see in the dark."

"You're…" My voice trembles, my heart racing as reality blurs into a nightmare. The edges of my vision darken, the weight of revelation too heavy to bear. The ground seems to tilt around me, and I collapse into darkness.

CHAPTER
FIVE
SAGE

Warmth coats me, and for a brief moment, I believe I'm back in my bed, waking from another insane nightmare about the world falling apart. Along with the warmth, there's the sudden reality of my bed never feeling this hard and the unmistakable crackling snap of fire—something distinctly absent in my bedroom. Couple that with a smell, rich and meaty, and the tearing sound of something chewing on food, and I flip my eyes open, pushing myself to sit upright so fast that my head spins.

I'm greeted by a small fire that blazes in front of me, its tongues licking upward, casting ominous shadows on the glittery cave walls. With it comes a knot in my stomach, tightening—the one that tells me this isn't a dream. I'm really here, in this monster world, and the reality of it crashes through me with such force it nearly rattles my bones.

The Viscount sits nearby in human form, knees bent,

his arms resting on them as he gnaws on some kind of cooked meat, tearing at it like a beast with his teeth. More of it hangs at the side of the fire, speared on the ends of sticks.

His shredded midnight-black shirt and pants still cling to him and cover plenty to not be flashed by him... Maybe a result of the lizard or him busting out of his clothes when he transformed into his monster form. In all honesty, I'd seen it in a flash and paid no attention to his clothes to remember.

My own clothes feel only slightly damp now from the storm. His dark hair, cascading around that strong face, is slightly damp, telling me I've been passed out for a while.

Those vibrant eyes are on me, studying me, and when I look at him, all I see is that large blue monster fighting with swords.

Or had I imagined him that way? I'm not entirely sure what to trust about my mind.

"You're finally awake," he states, smacking his lips.

"I saw you... you're a monster... blue." My attempt to laugh comes out like a strangled sound. "Isn't this the part where you tell me I was hallucinating?"

He chuckles, and it vibrates oddly against the cave walls. "I could tell you that you were hallucinating, but I doubt that would help your current state of disbelief."

My mind twirls with an overload of information. The scent of meat wafts to my nose as I watch droplets drip from the cooking meat. My stomach betrays my confusion with a grumble. At home, having meat was a luxury, and what little I could buy was used on medicine for Mom. Just thinking of her has my breathing quickening again.

"Hey," he says, his voice pulling me back to the present. "Take a deep, slow breath, or you'll make yourself pass out again."

I draw in a shaky breath. "It's... it's just so much. Nothing prepares you for all of this."

"That's true," he replies nonchalantly, taking another massive bite of his meat and chewing thoughtfully.

Watching him eat, there's something unsettling yet fascinating about his intensity. Something primal and animalistic. I'm breathing heavily again.

Meat juices drip down his chin, and he casually wipes it away, the sight somehow making my mouth water despite my brain screaming that it shouldn't.

"Wh-what are you eating?" I finally manage to ask, my curiosity piqued despite my fear. I involuntarily lick my lips.

"Want some?" He's already grabbing one of the sticks with a sizzling piece of meat on one end from the fire and leaning closer, handing it to me.

Accepting it, I sniff it hesitantly; it smells gamey and rich. He couldn't have hunted something ordinary like a rabbit out in this storm, could he? I doubt bunnies exist out here.

"You've cooked the lizard creature, haven't you?" My voice is barely above a whisper, my skin crawling at the thought, especially remembering the creature drooling.

"I saved you the best part... pieces of its heart," he declares, almost proudly in how widely he grins.

Bile hits my throat, and I pull it away from my mouth. "I can't eat this."

"Why? He was about to rip you apart as his meal, so instead, *you* enjoy the spoils of our win."

"Right," I say, the sarcasm dripping. "Because none of this is weird. You being a monster and eating lizard hearts after you slay them." My words are precise, aimed with purpose. "And you're no Viscount, are you?"

He chuckles, wiping his mouth again with the back of his hand. "The truth is, I am what you call a monster, though in my world, like you call yourself human, we are Shadowfen. And I am a Viscount on your planet, recently appointed as Nightingale Village's new leader after the last Choosing Ceremony."

I toss his words around in my mind—*Choosing Ceremony, monster, Viscount*—implications of something sinister. Does that mean Alina isn't safe? It leaves me shuddering, but there's nothing I can do about it when I have my own set of problems.

I picture him fighting the sea lizard and now eating it like a caveman. Yet, when I look at him, I'm reminded of how scared everyone in Nightingale Village was of him.

My thoughts bounce back and forth in my head.

"Many things aren't what you think in your village," he murmurs. "Your previous Viscount and those foolish Barons withheld information from everyone in order to control you. But that's fine. Things in the village will change."

"So, monsters rule the villages?"

"Well," he pauses for a moment as if determining what to tell me. I suspect he's holding a lot of secrets from me. "Cain, a monster, is the Elite City King who rules over the Elite City and all the humans who live there. These families are Elites, or royals, you could say, and each of the villages, like Nightingale Village, reports to them. You have a right to know as you are not returning there."

I swallow hard at his certainty, except he has no idea how hard I'll fight for my mother, the only family I have left.

"How will you do this, if you're here? I had no idea monsters still remained in our world after the Day of the Choosing, or could even become Viscounts."

He shrugs. "In some rare cases, we can step into positions of human authority, and as I mentioned earlier, I will return to your village soon enough. They'll barely notice my absence. Time works differently here than in your world. One of your days is a month for us here."

My mouth drops open, unable to comprehend how that works, yet I'm instantly thinking of my mom and how I have more time to work on getting back to her without her being alone for too long. I'll be back before she has time to miss me...

He continues, explaining how monsters come and go through their own portals on the day of the ceremony to collect their Offerings—humans like me—before taking them back to their world.

"Most humans view us as Gods," he says, the corners

of his mouth curling upward, clearly enjoying the idea of being revered.

He takes another animalistic bite from his meat, and never in my wildest dreams would I have imagined a God devouring a lizard so savagely. An extremely handsome God at that, but still savage.

"I-I don't know what to say." There's a torrent of information in my mind, feeling as though it's going to explode with all these revelations.

"But enough for now. These aren't matters you need to worry about anymore. Now eat. You'll need your strength," he instructs, his tone softening slightly. "The rain's eased outside, and the Howler is making its way over to pick us up."

"Howler?" I echo. Reflexively, I nibble on the meat skewered on my stick. My reaction is immediate—I flinch, pulling it away, but not before I've bitten off a piece and swallowed it. A sigh escapes me because, much to my dismay, I love the taste. It's sweet, salty, and fatty. How can a drooling lizard taste so good?

"Sea vessel," he clarifies, pulling me from my musings about the surprisingly delicious meat.

"Oh! And the... Howler is taking us to your home?" I ask, my curiosity spiked.

He pauses, a strange expression crossing his face, a slight crease at the bridge of his nose.

"The vessel, Howler, is my home. We live on the sea, for now, anyway."

I blink at him, processing this new information.

"So, like pirates." I offer a lopsided grin, my mind

conjuring up images from one of my mother's storybooks.

"I guess, if that's easy for you to picture it," he answers nonchalantly, then bites into his food.

I watch him for a moment, only to realize when I glance down at the stick in my hand that I've eaten mine without really paying attention. He hands me another meat stick, and I shake my head, but he insists. Reluctantly, I take it, admitting to myself that I'm weak for lizard meat, no matter how absurd that sounds.

Compared to what I've gone through today, I'm not even shocked anymore.

"So, then, what about you? You're delivering me to a monster in your vessel, then returning to the village to act like a God?" I fail to keep the sarcasm from my voice. It must be that I've already faced my death a couple of times today that I'm speaking so boldly to the Viscount... except he's Killian, a monster.

He pauses mid-chew, his expression unreadable for a moment before a wry smile curves his lips.

"It's a bit more complicated than that," he admits, setting down the half-eaten skewer he started on. "My role as a Viscount isn't just a facade; it's part of a larger effort to help humans, to ensure things run as fair as possible. If the current structure of villages and ceremonies falls apart, monsters will take over Earth, along with as many Offerings as they want. And it won't be long before your kind is extinct."

I swallow the meat in my mouth, almost choking on it. "You're joking, right?" I sputter out.

He shakes his head, his expression serious, lips taut at the corners. "No, it's the truth. It's what the Elite family has implemented to prevent chaos—by having regulated Offerings once a year. The sacrifice of a few saves an entire race."

I try to digest his words. The idea that a few should suffer for the many is an idea that sounds logical in discussion, but when you're one of the few, it feels terrifying and unfair.

"And me? You never answered my question," I press, needing to know where and who I'm being delivered to.

Just as he opens his mouth to respond, a sudden, blaring sound erupts from outside, cutting him off.

I flinch, my heart leaping into my throat. "What's that?"

"The Howler's here. Quick, we need to move," he says urgently as he jumps to his feet and begins extinguishing the fire by kicking dirt onto the flames.

I hurry to assist, scattering earth over the remaining embers until the light winks out, leaving us in semidarkness. He's got his orb light on as I chase him out of the cave. Once I reach his side, his hand grips mine firmly. But I'm trembling about what will happen next to read too much into his behavior.

We pass the carcass of the lizard, its body sliced open and disturbingly still. I avert my eyes, focusing on the cave exit as my stomach churns with unease.

The blaring sound continues, and Killian moves faster, dragging me alongside him.

As we reach the mouth of the cave, daylight floods

my vision. The rain is still falling, but it's eased to a trickle. I'm momentarily blinded by the natural light. When my eyes finally adjust, I'm staring at a massive globe vessel.

The Howler floats on the water a fair distance from the shore, and I can't for the life of me see how we get on board. It's enormous, its surface opaque like mist, making it impossible to see inside, yet the balconies that curl around the outside are clearly visible, suggesting the vessel has over a dozen levels, maybe more.

Killian's hand squeezes mine lightly, and I glance up at him. The overwhelming explosion of constant surprises makes me lightheaded once more. He looks at me with a smile, one that's disarmingly kind, and my heart flutters despite my better judgment. I remind myself he's a monster, yet I find myself drowning in those sharp blue eyes.

"To answer your earlier question," he begins. "You're here because I've chosen you as my bride."

I gasp, instantly pulling my gaze from his.

He chuckles.

My stomach plummets as if I've stepped into thin air, my body trembling, and I think I might pass out again.

CHAPTER
SIX
KILLIAN

Turns out, fate *can* fuck you up when you least expect it.

My mission had been clear from the start. Bring the girl into Blight, then do whatever the hell it takes, including sacrificing her to the enemy King, to reclaim what's rightfully ours.

The Silvercrest Kingdom.

Yet I'm foolishly grinding my teeth at the thought of doing that. Since collecting her from the village, her scent has been heavy in my nostrils—raspberries, cedar, and the delicious perfume that is all her. Her touch has brought out the beast inside me, roaring for escape to do more than destroy those fucking Tidecreepers.

When I revealed to her that she was to be my bride, it was supposed to be a strategy to gain her trust until we revealed her true reason for being here and the role she'd play.

Except a savage hunger now grows within me that

perhaps this girl is not just our key but something so much more.

That she's my *real* true mate.

I take in a heavy breath, fighting the urge to drag her back into the cave, to fuck her until she's out of my mind. Maybe that's what I'm feeling—a pent-up absence of sex.

Yet, a flicker of doubt crosses my mind. My attraction to her is undeniable, the connection intense. But I've been down this path before, years ago, and it nearly fucking destroyed me. The scars remain, a reminder of what I lost, so am I prepared to let myself believe again? To risk everything on the chance that this time, it might be real?

Clenching my hand at my side, I glance down at the girl.

The same girl who should mean nothing to me.

She's standing so close that her breasts are pushed up against my arm. She stares up at me with innocence in her icy eyes, and even the way she tugs on her lower lip between her teeth isn't helping me.

It's impossible to look away with the twin beasts of lust and fury battling in my chest for control.

My gaze raked down her body as she slept in the cave, and the temptation to strip her, taste her, inhale her scent drove me mad. The savage hunger to bite into her skin, to spread her legs, to fuck her, left me pacing like a beast. I always get what I want. And if I didn't want her scared out of her mind, needing her sane for what's coming, I would have claimed her in that cave.

That's how things work in Blight.

Hunt down your mate.

Bite her.

Fuck her brains out.

Then she's yours for life.

There's something troubling about how I react to her. I'm fucked because I shouldn't be drawn this much to her, especially since she's only a half-Shadowfen. She doesn't even know she's not fully human, yet I'm consumed with thoughts of claiming her.

True mates are real, rare as they are. They bind for life, and as her protector, I'd be committed to keeping her safe, breeding her, and responding to her every need.

She can't be my true mate...

It sure as fuck also isn't my intention to be distracted by thoughts of her full breasts, picturing them free of her clothes and licking them.

"Are you okay?" Her voice pulls me from my thoughts, her eyebrows knitting together in concern. "You're staring at me strangely and haven't said a word."

A spark of anger flares within me at how quickly I've lost control. *Fuck.* I've let her distract me.

Here I am, imagining all the things I want to do to her, desiring her in ways I hadn't anticipated. Her gaze holds mine, and I feel exposed, unnerved by how quickly I've become entangled.

"I'm fine," I manage to say gruffly. "Just keep your attention on the water. There are more Tidecreepers that might come for us." I step away, trying to put some distance between us, but her hand clings to mine, held by her fear.

I lift my gaze to the Howler gliding over the rough sea toward us, not arriving quickly enough. The fresh air helps clear the fog in my head, and I regain some composure. Straightening my shoulders, I refocus on the mission, pushing aside any feelings that have no place in me right now.

Taking a deep breath, I watch the vessel pause about twenty feet from the shore, which is as close as it can get without risking the rocks.

A horizontal protruding platform juts out from the bottom half of the vessel, directly in front of us. It's as wide as my shoulder and immediately shoots out, powered by enchanted technology, its surface gleaming under the stormy skies.

Sage flinches beside me, her eyes wide at the sight. The Howler is unique and engineered by a master of magic and mechanics.

I squeeze her hand, saying, "We need to move fast now."

"All right." She sounds hesitant, but as I charge forward, taking her with me toward the rocky shore, she keeps pace.

We're feet from the water.

The bridge has barely made landfall near us when one of the Tidecreepers lunges out of the water on all six legs, barely ten feet from us on the left. It hisses viciously, its companions mirroring its aggression as they rush at us, venomous drool dripping from their serrated, snapping teeth.

Sage cries out, backing up instinctively, but I tighten my grip on her arm.

"No running away," I instruct. With strength fueled by adrenaline, I snatch her around the waist and, in one fluid motion, hoist her onto the bridge that reaches up to my hips. Without hesitating, I vault over onto the railing, landing solidly in front of her so I can hold her close and force her to run.

The creatures hiss and gnash their teeth, hurling themselves toward the bridge, their claws scraping against the metal as they attempt to climb. Sage screams, and I twist my attention to her as she teeters dangerously close to the edge, flinching each time the bridge shudders.

Fuck me!

In a heartbeat, I grab her hand, pulling her forward. "Run!" I command, and to my surprise, she quickly falls in step behind me, navigating the narrow, swaying platform.

"This is insane," she replies, her grasp squeezing my hand, yet she surprises me by keeping up.

Suddenly, the platform sways violently under us, and Sage's weight shifts perilously to one side. She cries out, her hand slipping from mine.

Darkest hells.

I spin on my heels, maintaining my balance with practiced ease, only to see one of the creatures has climbed onto the platform, its weight causing the structure to tilt dangerously.

Bastard Tidecreeper.

Acting on instinct, I scoop Sage into my arms, her body pressed tightly against mine. Her eyes are wide with terror, fixed on the monstrous figures swarming in the water directly beneath us. I don't let her see the danger for long. In one swift motion, I throw her over my shoulder like she weighs nothing.

She releases an *oomph* and clings to me.

"I knew I shouldn't have eaten that lizard in the cave. I think these ones know and are coming for revenge."

Somehow, I manage to laugh at the situation.

"These beasts' brains are as small as pebbles. I doubt they have the capacity to think beyond attack and eat." With her secured, I sprint the remaining distance to the vessel.

"Shut it fast!" I yell as I lunge across the threshold.

"On it," replies Howler, the vessel, almost robotic in nature, distinctly male. The door closes behind us with a swish, sealing us in the Arrival Pod, shutting out the rain and creatures. I hit a palm against the button in front of the glass doors, and they slide open with a swift, seamless motion. Carrying Sage, I step into the Transition Chamber.

Gently, I set a shaking Sage down on her feet. She's trembling, her eyes bouncing around the room. Like before, she has a doe-eyed, terrified look, as if she might pass out once more.

"What is this place?" She hugs herself, glancing around, turning on the spot.

"This is where we manage everything from gear to preliminary decontamination—kind of a buffer zone before you enter the main areas of the vessel, especially for when we go deep sea diving." I half grin, but she doesn't notice.

She's too busy scanning the stark, utilitarian room, offering a station equipped with the removal and storage of gear and anything we bring back with us from hunts from deep sea dives.

"And... are we safe here?"

"Safe as you can be on a vessel that's home to creatures like me," I explain, trying to offer her a reassuring smile.

"I saw your transformation back in the cave into your monster form, which was pretty terrifying." She glances down at my shredded clothes.

I shrug, not giving it much thought because when we go hunting here, we do so in the nude. Nothing gets in the way.

"Clothes are easily replaced." I pluck a blade of grass from her wet hair. "Now, you need rest first. There's a room prepared for you where you can relax without fearing for your life. It's where you'll be staying. Later, you can ask me all the questions you desire."

Sage moves about hesitantly, her body still shaky. She tilts her head back, meeting my gaze with that vulnerable look.

"This morning, I was at home, and my mother was

making me porridge. Now, I don't even know how to take all of this in. It's like nothing I've ever experienced or imagined in my life."

I walk over to the shelving unit, grab a towel, and hand it to her. She dries her face and hair.

"The place will grow on you. You'll see. Now, come, let me take you to your room. You'll want to get out of those wet clothes," I say, trying to make my tone as gentle as possible. "Later tonight, you'll join us for a welcoming dinner to meet the pack."

She blinks, and I can't tell if she might cry, yet her brow furrows. "And then what? I become your bride?" She holds my stare, the shy girl revealing her brazen side. Then she dumps the towel on a shelf.

"First," I start, placing a hand on her lower back, directing her to the sliding doors that lead into the main hall of the vessel. "There's a ritual you will need to undergo."

She scrunches up her face. "What ritual? Why?"

"More on that later. You've already experienced enough surprises today."

"I really hate your surprises."

"Are they meant to be pleasant things?"

She cuts me a scowl.

Nudging her forward, I feel the tension in her back, and with another look at Sage, the girl who was meant to be just a key to our kingdom, now I fear she might just end up being my undoing—instead of the savior I hoped for.

CHAPTER
SEVEN
WOLFE

Out here, surrounded by the endless expanse of ocean, a monster could easily go mad. Too fucking late for that, I suppose.

Here on the bridge, I recline with my feet propped up on the console, the quiet solitude of the sea soothing my twisted soul. It's the one place on this vessel where I can escape; the captain and crew usually leave the navigation to Howler and they work out of the office, giving me peace... rare and delicious peace.

The door slams open with a force that would startle anyone else.

Killian strides in, his hair slicked back and his clothes crisp, the scent of salt and storm clinging to him—looks like someone's fresh from playing hero, leaving me grinning.

"Thought I'd find you in here," he groans.

"Guilty as charged," I respond with a short grin.

Killian leans his back against the window, hands in

the pockets of his pants, the turbulent sea a fitting backdrop for his troubled expression.

"Found her, didn't you?" I ask, rotating my chair to face him fully. The storm outside mirrors the one brewing in his gaze.

"That I did," he replies, a flicker of something unfamiliar—hope?—flashing across his expression.

"And?" I press, sensing the shift in his mood. It's a marked change from the fury that he usually returns with from Earth.

He chuckles low, finally breaking his serious demeanor.

"Found her all right, and that's reason enough to celebrate. But..." His voice trails off while avoiding my gaze as he pushes off the wall and strolls over to the controls.

"But?" I prompt, already knowing when Killian hesitates it's because the news is more complex than he lets on.

He shoots me a hard look, his jaw clenched. "It went damn smoothly once I found her, which is more than I expected after so long. We should start making arrangements to pay King Bren a visit."

I rise to my feet, his name grinding up my gut, and narrow the distance between us. "What aren't you telling me?"

The nerve under his right eye twitches like it always does when he's holding back information or lying.

With a sigh, he faces me, heaviness etched on his features.

"I think she's my true mate."

The declaration hangs between us, heavy like the storm clouds outside. True mate? That's a twist I hadn't anticipated.

"Well, fuck!" I growl, not expecting this of all things. "Are you certain?"

Killian had been down this path once before. Through hell and back. I saw it firsthand when he thought he found his true mate during a Monster's Night on Monster Island.

And it nearly destroyed him.

Since then, he's been traveling between Blight and the Elite City on Earth to find his intended mate. But just recently, when he heard stories of a human in Nightingale Village being compatible with a God, it caught his attention.

It worked in my favor.

He found the girl we sought for Blight, except now seeing him like this again, claiming that *she's* also his true mate, makes me worry. Is she truly the one?

"This complicates things," I groan.

He nods. "You think?" Fire burns behind his eyes, the tension in his shoulders thickening. He's flicking random buttons on the dashboard on and off, not really paying attention, though I'm pretty certain he's toggling the storm alarm for those down in the lower decks. Those bastards can use a bit of a scare. They've become too damn complacent, taking twice as long to respond to alerts when we hit savage waters.

"Because I can feel it right here." He places his palm

against his chest. "It's unlike anything I've ever felt. The hunger she's stirred in me is insatiable. I can't get her damn scent out of my head, and it's fogging my thoughts."

"Have you considered getting laid? How long have I been telling you to invite one of those four-breasted Shadowfen to your bed? You'd be surprised at the pleasure their split tongues can offer."

"Hell, Wolfe, this is something more than just needing to fuck. And for your information, I just jerked off twice in the shower, and nothing's changed."

I frown, having never seen him like this before. He's always been the unrelenting type of Shadowfen who wouldn't let anything stand in his way. Normally, if he'd found someone, I'd congratulate him, except he's talking about the girl who's meant to finally give us the chance to dethrone that bastard King.

"Because you think she's your true mate?"

He exhales loudly. "We're going to confirm it, for sure. I need to know to be certain. I'm arranging a mating ritual, then we'll see if our true natures emerge or if it's, as you say, me starved for a fuck. If you're right, then I'll fuck until my balls drop off." He gives me a broken grin because we both know he'd enjoy that way too much.

The worry lines deepen across his face, seeming to carry the weight of his thoughts. He genuinely believes this girl could be his true mate. Finding her is rare but not impossible.

While we never intended to sacrifice the girl directly, if something happened to her during our confrontation with King Bren, we wouldn't fret over it. Now this changes things.

But we've faced enough obstacles, and we'll get over this one.

"Agreed. Let's confirm this sooner rather than later."

"On it," he answers, already turning toward the door.

"Speaking of problems, have you seen Nyko recently? If anyone's going to track down the girl on the vessel and give her his own personal welcome, it'll be him. And as much as I love the bastard like my brother, I don't trust him not to break her. We need her intact for this."

Lips pressed tight, he nods and leaves me alone once more. As the door shuts behind him, the quiet hum of the vessel fills the space.

I frown, remembering when Killian had lost Inka, how he could barely go on. And I don't want him to get his hopes up. He's always been the epitome of a take-charge protector among the Shadowfen, my second-in-command—relentless, determined, terrifying.

Tension curls in my gut, and I grip the dash, knuckles turning white.

With it comes the dark memory of the day my father was betrayed flashing vividly in my mind. The cold gleam of the blade as it was driven into his gut, the way his eyes widened in shock and pain—it's an image that has haunted my nights, fueling a fury that no time has eased.

Heaving for breath, even after all these years, the hollowness inside me never ceases.

I have no intention of giving up until I gain revenge.

Killian's sudden depth of feeling for this human girl complicates things. If she is indeed his true mate, it binds her to our cause even more intricately.

I watched Killian struggle to maintain his composure, the muscle in his jaw working as he processed the weight of what lies ahead. I fucking loathe seeing that in him, knowing the suffering we've all endured because of that son of a bitch, Bren.

Ever since the Great Desolation, when devastating earthquakes shattered our world, the balance of power has shifted. Those who didn't align with the self-appointed fucking new King were banished from the mainland, forcing us to make our home in the harshest of places...

The unforgiving expanse of the open sea.

I'm not sure if I can allow anything to get in the way of finally taking back what's mine.

CHAPTER
EIGHT
SAGE

"You have time," I whisper to myself, trying to calm my speeding pulse with the knowledge that one day back home equates to a month here. In that span, so much can change, especially now that the Viscount—who is far more monster than leader—has claimed me as his bride.

A bead of sweat trickles down my back at how quickly everything's happened.

The room I'm given is designed to distract, to awe, and damn him, it's sort of working.

My gaze is drawn irresistibly to the large, circular bed with thick blankets of a muted bluish color. Behind it, the wall morphs into a three-dimensional painted image of a rocky bay under a night sky. The sea churns violently, illuminated by a lone, burning light in a cottage to the left. A silhouette sits on the rocks, staring out at the tumultuous waters. The clouds are dark and oppressive, almost mountainous, with a bright moon daring to peek through. There's something breathtaking about the image.

The ceiling curves overhead, giving the room a cylindrical feel with all the walls stark white, save for the one with oversized double doors that lead to a balcony.

I slide the doors open, and a rush of salty breeze greets me, tugging at my clothes and loose hair. Stepping out, I'm mesmerized by the height at which the vessel sails above the churning sea. We glide smoothly, despite the rough sea with whitecaps whipped up by the gusting wind, stunned there's no rocking motion.

It feels as though I'm on land, which surprises me.

Leaning forward, I grip the high railing, peering down at the waves that crash against the vessel's side. The location we just escaped from shrinks into nothing more than a small island lost in an ocean expanse. To my side, the view extends into a relentless sea, the horizon occasionally lit by lightning bolts, painting the sky in dark violet hues.

Gods, where have I ended up?

Shivering from the cold gusts that whip around me, I step back into the warmth of my room and close the balcony doors with a soft click. My clothes, still damp, cling uncomfortably to my skin, and I want them off.

Curiosity leads me to a door I haven't explored yet, tucked discreetly on one side of the room. It opens into a bathroom. The walls, partially made of glass, reveal narrow chambers filled with lush, vibrant plants and flowers that seem to thrive between layers of glass and wall. They are beautiful.

Nearby stand a fancy toilet and a sink that resembles a pearl in its smoothness and luster. Beyond that, a glass door leads to a shower room. At home, I'm lucky to bathe in a tub once a week to conserve water.

I let out a small squeal of excitement. Stripping in seconds, I step into the shower, where I place my hand on a panel beneath the golden showerhead. Water cascades out instantly to the perfect temperature as though it can sense what my body can take.

"This is incredible." Moaning as the water rushes down my body, I notice water trickling down inside the glass walls, watering the plants, too. Maybe I've finally become delusional, but I laugh at the sight while standing under the hot stream, never wanting to leave this room.

Who would have believed that monsters live such opulent lives, while in Nightingale Village, we struggle for everything? Even the shampoo smells of flowers, and I use it to lather my whole body.

Refreshed, I finally emerge, fingers pruned, and wrap myself in two fluffy towels—one around my body, the other drying my hair. Barefoot, I pad across the smooth floorboards back into the bedroom, not yet ready to put on my semi-wet clothes. I approach the wardrobe, hoping for a robe but discovering an array of clothes instead.

I may have cried a tiny bit because I've never seen so many outfits and beautiful fabrics. Perhaps these are someone else's clothes, but they might not mind if I borrow some. The closet is stuffed, the clothes hanging neatly on hangers, in all kinds of colors. I reach over, gently running my fingers across the materials, enjoying the textures against my touch.

Pulling out something that's almost cushion-soft in my hand—a black bodysuit with long sleeves and a V-neck that feels warm to the touch. Curious, I step into it, dragging it up over my bare skin, surprised to find it actually fits like a glove, is comfortable and, thankfully, not transparent when I glance at my reflection in the glass. Why aren't there any mirrors in here?

Sure, it hugs my body, but considering I haven't seen any underwear to put on, it leaves me feeling covered. I tug at the low V-neck, which shows a bit too much cleavage, and as I rummage through the wardrobe, I don't find any small tops I can wear underneath.

This will have to do.

I'm clean, warm, and refreshed.

Next, I track down a pair of black flats at the bottom of the wardrobe. Slipping them on, I run my fingers through the tangles in my hair and stand there with my thoughts turning back to being married to a monster.

Everything inside me rears up to protest, to fight it. My gut hurts at the fear that I won't find a way out of it. I mean, I'm stuck on a vessel surrounded by monsters. What will stop them from overpowering me?

Fear wraps around me so fast my head spins.

I'm going to be stuck here for now... at least until I work out a way to return home. So, that means working out how to survive, something I've been doing for so long in

Nightingale Village. Just surviving being ignored by most of the villagers, by looking after my mom, by trying to behave to avoid getting extra entries into the Choosing Ceremony.

And look where that got me.

Killian insisted I was safe here, but he's a monster I barely know, and I sure don't trust him.

Eyeing the door out of my room, I approach it, my hand reaching for the handle. I need to explore and know exactly what I'm dealing with.

"Where would you like to go, Sage?" a male unexpectedly greets me, causing me to jerk back in surprise, searching the room for him.

Except, I'm alone.

"Hello?" I answer cautiously, half expecting a figure to materialize in my room.

"Hello, Sage. My name is Howler, and I *am* the vessel."

"You are?" I've never heard of such a thing.

"I control the vessel, navigating as instructed but also providing guidance. I assist all four thousand six hundred and ninety-three passengers aboard, including you now." His voice seems friendly, but I'm stunned to hear the sheer number of monsters who live on this massive vessel.

"Nice to meet you. I want to explore a bit, I guess," I say, lifting my head, unsure of which direction I should be speaking.

"Very well," Howler responds. "Just outside your room, take the hallway to the end, turn left, and follow it to the transporter. I'll guide you to the top level where the wonders of Blight await."

"Sounds perfect," I say, more to reassure myself than him. I head into the corridor bathed in shadows, lit only by the occasional flicker of lights embedded in the dark walls.

I push into a stroll, taking in the framed paintings on the wall of various creatures, one even of the Tidecreeper, paying more attention to them now that I'm not being rushed into my room by Killian.

As I continue down the dimly lit corridor, the air subtly shifts, growing dense with a scent that tugs at the edges of my memory—a blend of something dusty and sweet, like wild jasmine hanging in the air. It's oddly comforting, and it calls to me.

Drawn by the fragrance, I quicken my pace until I notice the corridor subtly widens, spearing into three directions. I'm swinging to the right, where the smell is stronger and leads me to a grand, ornately carved door left slightly ajar. A sliver of soft, bright light spills through the crack, casting dancing shadows that flicker. The smell intensifies, sweeter now, mingling with the musty odor of something like fresh rain on dry soil.

I push the door open and enter a large, circular room that appears to be a library or perhaps a study. Heart speeding up with excitement I hadn't expected, I take in the lofty room and the thousands of books. I can't believe my eyes. Towering shelves flooded with books of all sizes line the curved walls that have no sign of ladders or stairs to reach books several stories high.

"Is this real?" The books I've read were mostly about farming and nature, with a couple that my mother owned about a fantasy world with elves. But this... I giggle, struggling to understand how this monster world is so bad. Compared to being an outcast back home, being ignored or pushed around by others, have we been scaring ourselves with stories about these monsters?

In the center of the room, a globe the same height as me sits on a golden bracket. It's a world I don't recognize, and as I approach it, the orb slowly rotates, its intricate details absorbing the room's light. I reach out, half expecting it to feel as fluid as it looks, but the surface is hard, solid. Yet when I touch it, the water ripples under my fingers.

Curiosity gets the better of me, and I give the globe a gentle spin. What catches my eye is the vastness of water. One great mass of land hunkers to the north, flanked by a scattering of tiny islands, then there are a few more small ones here and there, but that's it. The rest is an endless blue. It's bewildering, the notion of a world so dominated by water.

There's no beep from Howler, which I find intriguing, as I'd expect him to interrupt and tell me about this globe. Perhaps he isn't always around unless called?

Shaking off the silence, I wander over to a bookshelf, letting my fingers trail along the leather-bound spines. The titles are a mix of English and scripts I can't decipher, unusual symbols I guess belong to the monsters' language.

As I delve deeper into the room, my feet land on a square metal plate unexpectedly.

Instantly, I'm shot upward on the small metal platform.

I scream, wobbling frantically, crouching to avoid tumbling out as it whisks me up at an alarming speed.

The platform halts abruptly, and my heart feels like it might burst through my chest. I desperately clutch the railing that runs across the row of books.

"What the fuck?" I blurt out, gazing down at the dizzying height. Panic flutters through me; I'm not usually afraid of heights, but this is too much.

Swiveling around, I try to spot a way down, but my attention is caught by a movement across the room—something blurry and dark—but when I snap my eyes up, there's nothing there. Just the flickering lights, the shadows, the books.

I'm losing my mind.

"Hello? Howler?" I call out into the stillness, and the silence that follows is suffocating.

Panic mounts as I notice movement again from the corner of my eye. Each time I try to focus, it disappears. Trembling, I glance down and find two subtly raised silver buttons integrated into the base I'm standing on. With a deep breath, feeling the threat of whatever lurks nearby growing, I tap down on one button.

Nothing happens.

Shit.

Desperation clawing at my throat, I stomp on the second button. This time, I'm plunging downward so fast my stomach hits the back of my throat, a scream ripping from my lips. I hit the ground with a thud that rattles my teeth. I tumble out, dizzy and disoriented, shocked I didn't just die.

"This place is a death trap," I mumble to myself, making a mental note to be more cautious. Then, that shadow, the blur—I see it again, darting along the bookshelves and dropping to the floor. I'm not sticking around to find out what it is. I bolt for the door, my heart in my throat.

As I dash out, I crash into someone. A startled scream escapes me as I collide with a solid figure, tumbling backward.

CHAPTER NINE

NYKO

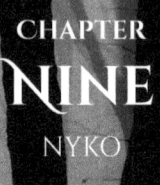

They say change never visits the deep currents of Blight, but the air tells a different story today.

A new scent lingers through the corridors, half human, half Shadowfen—someone Killian has been chasing to bring back for us. The girl who will be our key to removing that traitor from the throne, who we'll use to our advantage and gain back so much that we've lost.

I lurk in the hallway, the thrill of the hunt pouring through me. This newcomer might be the catalyst we need, but for now, I'm driven by a more primal curiosity.

Her scent fills the vessel, sweet and unfamiliar, reminding me of the red berries Killian once brought from Earth. Others on the ship have also been talking about her.

Except she has no idea what's coming her way.

Until then, I can play.

I glide through the shadows as one of them, my form

barely a whisper along the darkened corridor. Killian and Wolfe might sense my presence when I take shadow form—the bastards always do—but to others, I'm just another shade in the gloom.

Her scent is stronger up on this floor, intoxicatingly so, mixed with something wild that tightens my gut in anticipation.

Reaching the Chamber of Tomes, I slip inside, merging with the dimly lit edges of the room. There she is, high up on the lift, flailing as if battling something in the air. What is she doing up there? Silver hair flutters behind her as she swings around on the spot.

I scurry up the bookshelves toward her, my form shifting closer to where the shadows are densest. Inches behind her, I cling to the shelves, my senses overwhelmed by her closeness.

Inhaling, I draw her deep into my lungs, tasting the sweetness of her scent on my tongue.

Berries.

Faint perspiration.

A sliver of bitter fear.

And beneath it all, her sex scent finds me...

I shudder at how intensely it curls through me.

She's dressed in a black bodysuit that hugs every inch of her, following the curves of her tiny waist and the flow of her hips. Where the fabric tucks itself between her asscheeks has me staring, desperate to reach out and lick.

She turns abruptly, and I leap across to the other side of the room, still keeping her in my sight. Something about her stills me, quiets the constant chaos that roils within me. It's just us here, in the silence of this vast room, surrounded by tomes and the hum of the vessel.

Glancing my way, I flick over into a dark corner to not spook her... not yet, anyway.

She fiddles with the lift, calling for Howler. However, he's not permitted in the Chamber of Tomes, not after he went into a frenzy in an attempt to explain the premise of every book in our possession in under a minute. He practically went into meltdown, sending the whole vessel into a blackout.

I blame Killian. The fucker taunted him, got him all worked up to the point that he frizzled.

Wolfe lost his shit, and it took us two days to get Howler back online as we floated aimlessly at sea.

Right now, my gaze lingers on the human girl, the fabric moving with her, shimmering slightly under the intermittent lights.

When they hit her clothes from a certain angle, the black fabric becomes almost transparent, revealing what's underneath.

Shifting closer, she turns, her full tits jumping under her suit, and the light illuminates her, showing me everything.

I freeze.

Round, high-placed breasts.

A small mound of hair between those gorgeous thighs.

I lose my grip, suddenly falling. She glances in my

direction again, and I'm kicking against a shelf, throwing myself higher up to where light won't reach.

Pausing in the spot, it's impossible to flush out the images of me stripping her, giving her my personal welcome to the vessel. Wolfe would go ballistic. He made it clear she's not to be touched or played with because she's our answer to gaining our kingdom back.

But would a bit of play hurt anyone?

She's so much more than I expected, so much the perfect little package needing unwrapping. I assumed I'd just have some fun with her, scare her a bit, but now I've got something else in mind.

The girl's stunning, incomparable to anyone on our vessel. Silver hair tumbles over her shoulders with a faint tint of violet... a sure sign she's coming into her breeding term—a time when her body seeks her mate, where she'll cry for him to fuck her. Most women never find their true mate, and the Shadowfen males are well versed in pleasing a female to sate her during these times.

The idea that this innocent human has no clue about the changes her body is undergoing amuses me. If she needs guidance, I'm here, lurking in the shadows, ready to emerge.

Suddenly, she's plummeting down in the lift, her screams piercing the quiet. Why doesn't she simply tap the lever more softly to control her descent?

As she stumbles out of the cage, disoriented and nearly collapsing, instinct propels me toward her. I swoop down, my form nothing but a swift blur.

Catching sight of me, her eyes widen with unmistakable fear, and she bolts from the room, her screams echoing down the corridor. I pursue her frantically.

When I catch up, she's recoiling from a collision with Killian. His arm swoops around her back, pulling her closer and guiding her away. He throws a knowing glance back at me—damn him, he's always aware of me.

Under my breath, a low growl rumbles, a sound of frustration. I back away, leaving them, knowing I'll get my chance soon enough.

CHAPTER
TEN
SAGE

Killian's hand is a vise on my elbow as he ushers me swiftly down the corridor, while I glance over my shoulder back at the library, convinced I'd seen something.

"I came to collect you for the evening meal," he explains in a low rumble that vibrates through the air between us.

"So, what's the rush?" I pant, fighting to pull myself free from his grasp. It seems as though we're heading back to my room. Are we dining there?

He lets out a long exhale. "First, you're changing clothes for your first time meeting the Pack."

I glance down at the one-piece suit clinging to me, its fabric soft and oddly comforting. "I had no idea I had to dress up in something fancy," I quip.

He stops so abruptly I nearly crash into him. His breath hitches, those azure eyes darkening as they sweep over me again. I pull away, my back hitting the wall, my stomach fluttering. His gaze dips lower, and I instinctively hug myself, suddenly feeling exposed under his intense stare.

"What's going on? You're acting all strange... I mean, stranger than normal."

Killian steps closer, the space between us charged with electricity.

"What you're wearing, Sage," he starts, voice rough, "is usually reserved for nights you want to entice a Shadowfen into your bed. Something I'd entertain in a heartbeat, but I suspect you aren't aware of the impact your outfit will have on anyone."

My eyes bulge, my mouth dropping open in shock. "What, th-this jumpsuit?" I stammer, my face scrunching in disbelief.

He licks his lips, his hand grazing the underside of my jaw, tilting my head back. His touch leaves a trail of heat that zips down my spine. Since our encounter in the garden back in Nightingale Village, I've been irresistibly drawn to him, my body responding in ways I've only read about in the hushed corners of my bedroom with my mom's elf books.

"It is when it's transparent under bright light."

I gasp, covering myself with my arms, and he chuckles—a dangerous sound.

"It's too late for that, Sage, but unless you want to offer the same privilege to everyone else, I'd suggest changing into something else. All the clothes in your wardrobe were chosen to fit you."

"Well, maybe don't put a transparent outfit in there next time," I say, irritated.

Killian clears his throat, the sound rough like gravel. "Let's get you changed."

As he guides me into my room, I pause and press a hand to his chest. "You wait for me out here."

The corner of his mouth curls upward. "I like this stronger side of you. And this one time, I'll abide by not coming into the room." He leans a shoulder against the wall, staring at me, and his cockiness is out of control.

I enter my room and shut the door with a bang. Even from inside, I hear his laughter.

Rolling my eyes, I make my way quickly into the bathroom, staring at my reflection in the glass wall, not seeing any transparency. Then again, it's not especially bright in here.

Quickly, I peel off the comfortable jumpsuit, then stand in front of the wardrobe again, butt naked and afraid of what the next outfit will do to me. As I rummage through the wardrobe again, finding mostly dresses, I finally pull out something that feels a bit more modest than the jumpsuit—black wide-legged pants paired with a pale green long-sleeved shirt.

I hold the shirt up to the light, ensuring it's not revealing. Satisfied that it's not, I dress quickly. The fabric is soft and stretchy, clinging in ways that emphasize every curve. Though the shirt's low neckline and the way the elastic cinches just under my bust make me a tad self-conscious, it's comfortable.

I'm not sure why every outfit has to highlight parts of my body I'm not trying to showcase.

I check my reflection once again; everything looks normal. With a deep inhale, I step out to meet Killian, who hasn't moved from his position against the wall.

"Better?" I ask.

He lifts an eyebrow, his lips tugging into an amused smirk. "Perfect."

I tug at the elastic under my chest, adjusting the fabric that insists on curling under my breasts.

He grins and gives me a slight nod, then we're on the move. The awkwardness between us stretches out, and I still have so many questions, like...

"Why isn't the portal on the boat? Would have been so much easier to get here."

Killian's lips twist into a half smile. "Thinking of returning home?"

"Of course," I admit truthfully. "I worry about my mom, and I want to see her again. Plus, I asked a real question, especially after nearly dying outside the vessel."

"I always keep my word, Sage." He leans in, his voice a low rumble, and I catch my breath every time I'm in his space, inhaling his fresh woods and addictive caramel sweet scent, as well as the embers of fire that's all him. "The constant movement of the ship, the vastness of the water... It makes transporting unstable. We tried once, and it was a disaster with our test subject lost in the middle of the sea."

He draws back, and his muscles bulge against the

fabric. It's impossible not to get lost in their movements. The cords in his neck tighten, too, that strong jawline with the faintest hint of stubble. Everything about this man... no, this monster... fills me with dirty images. I've never been with a man before, never been drawn to any in such a way.

It's bad enough that I'm here to be his bride, but then to feel the fire between my thighs, the moisture that builds up each time we're near, is becoming too much. I keep imagining myself in his arms, his mouth between my legs, just like in the books I've read where the females always scream with pleasure. I never really understood the undeniable pressure in their body they spoke about until now.

It presses down through me, the sensation to be touched urgent, and again, I'm staring at his chest and lower. I once spied one of our Village Protectors naked by accident. No one saw me, but the sight both shocked and intrigued me. The man had a lot of hair, then his dangling—

"If you keep staring at me that way, Sage, we're not going to make it to dinner," Killian promises firmly.

I nearly choke, my mind torn between embarrassment at being caught staring and the growing heat in my body that makes no sense to me.

"You say some really strange things sometimes," I accuse, though I feel my cheeks burning up. A smile tugs at the corners of my mouth.

"I didn't say that lightly," he murmurs, his words a warm caress against my cheek as we move to a set of circular steps made of metal. We pause, and his hand trails up my arm, stopping to rest gently at my collarbone. The touch is light, but it sends a shiver through me.

"Resisting you is becoming more difficult by the second, and I'm trying real fucking hard."

I can't breathe at his confession.

"Do you feel it?" he asks, his eyes locked on mine, searching.

"Your touch?" I manage, my voice barely above a whisper. My body is hyperaware of his proximity, every nerve ending seeming to fire at once. My body sways in his direction, as though it's betraying me.

"And how your body reacts." His gaze intensifies.

I shake my head, fighting the heat between us. "Am I supposed to feel something beyond your hand?" I arch an eyebrow at him.

His brow furrows, and he moves aside, giving me space. Then he's grinning.

"Clever girl. But tomorrow, you won't be able to hide the truth from me."

I blink at him as he pushes me to start climbing the stairs, but I'm still stuck on his words about tomorrow.

What did they mean?

Despite my resistance and fear, I want to respond to his advances, to discover what being with someone as powerful as him would be like. Sometimes, I feel as though I've always been the good girl who never broke the rules, who never talked back, and who tried to be invisible.

Now, I blush at my thoughts toward a monster, which is confusing because I have no idea what I'm even doing.

Killian's presence behind me as we head into the glass elevator and descend in seconds and the way he stares at me hungrily are slightly unnerving.

Once the doors open, we walk into an open dining area that's spectacular, every surface gleaming like glass. The walls, the ceiling, and even the floor beneath our feet appear to be made of this material, but with lights underfoot that glow with each step we take.

Dark purple vines covered with luminous berries are woven from one floating lantern to another, infusing the room with a faint glow.

The space is deserted except for two men lounging across the room on plush couches. Killian gently nudges me forward, his touch adding to the already burning fire inside me.

Reaching them, I'm instantly taken aback at first by the fact that they're in their human forms, not monsters, and secondly... I might fall over from how incredibly stunning they are. Are all monsters this attractive? Muscles and brooding looks, yet behind those beautiful faces are deadly creatures.

There's one who wears his dark hair pushed back, only bringing out the sharpness of his cheekbones more. His eyes are amber, almost burning like fire. Broad shoulders relaxed against the back of his couch, he grins at me, every line of his body strong, powerful, and deadly.

Opposite him is a man who's reclined, a smile

playing on his lips. Long, chestnut-brown hair just grazing his shoulders catches my attention. He runs a hand through it, yet strands tumble over jade-colored eyes. It's the constant smile I'm drawn to, as if he knows a joke and the punchline no one else will understand. He sits sprawled, legs wide, one arm draped casually over the back of the couch. He's in all black, a shirt so tight it pulls taut across his broad chest.

As Killian guides me to a plush couch adjacent to theirs, he says, "Sage, this is the Pack. This is Wolfe, the Leader of the Shadowfen," he says, gesturing toward the man with a glowing amber gaze.

Wolfe gives me a soft nod that somehow manages to look both regal and intimidating.

"Across from him is Nyko, our resident schemer and the one who keeps life interesting around here."

Nyko bursts out laughing, the sound so deep it could be mistaken for a growl.

"Hello," I manage, a tight smile on my lips as I settle onto the cushions.

"Welcome, Sage," Wolfe answers. "We've waited a long time to finally meet you."

He has? I had no idea Killian had been searching for his bride for so long.

Nyko's grin widens. "Welcome aboard, Sage. Consider this your new home."

His words sit with me—*home* is a term that feels too permanent, too settled for this floating glass castle. My home is back in Nightingale Village, the only place where I've ever truly felt safe and loved. The thought of my mom alone hurts deep in my chest. The only reassurance is knowing that with the expansive time difference in our worlds, she's still sleeping on the couch.

Killian shifts beside me, then leans back, stretching out his legs and crossing them at his ankles.

"The Howler is your place to explore," Wolfe explains. "Everyone is aware of your arrival and has been given strict instructions to be on their best behavior." He's wearing a mesmerizing grin, which hardens as his attention swings over to Nyko.

His laughter fills the room, sounding quite wild. "Oh, I'm always on my best behavior," he replies, winking at me. "It's just that my best isn't what most expect."

"Right," Killian pipes in, studying him as well.

"So, have you started exploring yet?" Nyko asks, his jade gaze narrowing on me. "I highly recommend the Chamber of Tomes, filled with books and surprises." He pauses for a moment, the room seeming to freeze in time, and I feel as though I'm missing something. "Also, the fourth floor is perfect for when things become too overwhelming."

A laugh bursts past my lips a bit too quickly, and I shift in my seat under their watchful stares.

"Like right now!"

Nyko howls with laughter. "Yes! It's my hideout. The only place on this ship Killian won't follow me so he can drag me into one of his grand plans."

Killian snorts. "I'm not that desperate for entertainment."

It's strange to see Killian appear less stiff compared

to him in Nightingale Village. Another reminder that beneath the pretty face, he's still a monster, one who will do as he pleases to get what he wants. A predator will always be that, right?

"Thanks, I'll do some exploring," I answer quietly, turning my attention to the rest of them. "It really is unusual to live on such a vessel, but intriguing. I bet it must be awful during storms. Why don't you move to one of the large lands I spotted on the world globe in the library?" I'm suddenly blushing from the explosion of questions that dribble from me.

Killian places his gentle palm on my knee to steady the bouncing.

"The sea keeps secrets better than most, and we've become accustomed to them," Wolfe acknowledges. "Besides, that particular land is currently occupied."

I wait, expecting him to say more, but he never does. None of them do. Strange.

Killian asks Wolfe about the weather we're traveling into, but I'm too distracted by the monster slithering out from the side door to the room. Round, black body, one massive eye, and eight limbs–half of them scuttling on the floor, the others balancing plates.

My stomach flips, my gaze glued to them.

The monster reaches us and hands out the plates. I accept mine, and it gives me a slow wink. I'm sitting here, shaking slightly, thinking that it's going to attack me.

"She's showing her appreciation for taking her food," Killian explains. "And wants to see you enjoy it."

"Um, thank you," I say, glancing down at my plate.

On my plate, there are some pinkish meat slices and a pile of blue, translucent spaghetti, which might be harboring bugs, seeing as one of the black seeds has wriggling antennae. Thankfully, there are also a few raspberries. I pop one into my mouth, grateful for something familiar.

I glance up at her and smile, then try to blink slowly, but she makes a grating sound and scurries back into the kitchen.

"You upset her," Nyko muses.

Stiffening, I say, "I did?" Then again, my food did come with bugs. One is crawling across my plate now.

"You didn't touch the food she cooked," he explains.

"Oh, I-I'm not that hungry," I explain, fiddling with the raspberries, pushing them away from the insect before I flick him off my plate.

"That's Tidecreeper meat," Killian insists. "I noticed how ravenously you devoured it back in the cave, so I ordered it just for you."

"I'm not a fan of it," Nyko asks. "That thing drools too much for my liking."

"To be fair," I begin, noting that Nyko hasn't touched his food either. In fact, none of them have. "I only ate that because I was in shock." It tasted good, I can't deny it, but the idea also makes me gag.

Killian scoops his raspberries onto my plate. "I've arranged for a Veil Ritual to be held tomorrow night, so it will be an early start."

I pause, the fruit halfway to my mouth, remembering

him mentioning it briefly when we first arrived. "What does it involve?"

Nyko leans back, half yawning. "Why are we running that? We had one just a few full moons ago."

Killian's gaze narrows. "Stay out of it, Nyko."

Wolfe's reclined, barely paying attention to them, focusing only on me. My cheeks flush, a reaction I can't control.

Nyko shakes his head. "Oh, is this part of our original plan, or something new you cooked up? Like that time you snuck off to that island without telling anyone and almost died?"

Killian shifts, his expression darkening, like he's ready to leap across to Nyko.

Wolfe still studies me, licking his lips, as if I'm the meal he wants instead of his untouched plate. He has no shame, not hiding that he wants me to quiver under his gaze.

What is he even doing?

The other two are arguing, but I can barely hear them from how loudly my heart thumps in my ears.

It's a crazy sensation, but as the corner of his mouth lifts, I'm convinced I feel his fingers on the bare skin of my arm. My skin ripples, sensitive, as the softness strokes up my arm, skipping over to my collarbone, lingering.

I'm unsure what I'm feeling and if it's all in my imagination.

When the sensation travels down the valley of my breasts, swooping over my breast, then the other, before curling around a hardened nipple, I give a small yelp, flinching back in my seat.

Everyone's staring at me now, and I quickly eat the rest of my berries, convinced I'm losing my mind.

Gasping for air, I shift in my seat, innocently running my arm across my chest, uncertain what's happening to me.

Wolfe's attention never shifts, never taking his gaze off me.

Nyko's on his feet, laughing loudly at Gods know what, while Killian chuckles back, as if they are having a contest on who can make the loudest sound.

But that touch... it's unrelenting, stroking me, zigzagging across my stomach.

Lowering.

Further...

My heart's racing.

Hand gripping the edge of the couch, I'm breathless.

Wolfe's gaze is devouring me.

His fingers dig into the back of the couch where he's got his arm stretched out, the only part of him showing any sign of tension.

Is he doing this to me?

I can barely think straight, sitting here and attempting to act normal when my body's burning up. The heat pouring off of me has me perspiring. Tenderly, it lingers just below my belly button, inching ever so lower.

Squeezing my thighs together, I pinch my lips, feeling as though I'm losing control of my body, every inch of me dictated by a light graze. It's enough to send butterflies through my stomach.

The touch suddenly slips between my thighs, where I'm soaked, where I'm so desperate for release. I jolt to my feet, unleashing the groan stuck in my chest. I blush at having everyone staring at me, at the experience still lingering even after it's stopped.

"Are you okay?" Killian asks, up on his feet with me, his hand firm on my arm.

"I-I'm just a bit overwhelmed and tired," I stammer, unable to meet their stares. "I'm going to head back to my room. It's been a long day."

Killian rises swiftly. "I'll escort you."

I'm already walking out quickly.

"It was a pleasure, Sage," Wolfe says, his voice deep and seductive.

I glance back at him to find he's watching me with eyes that are on fire.

Nyko, on the other hand, winks, saying, "Good night, little human."

I'm on fast feet, and Killian's there opening the door for me. By the time I reach my room, he leans in close, his hand bracing the door frame above me.

"Don't let them get under your skin. Wolfe knows what he wants the moment he sees it, and he's taken with you."

I swallow, trapped under his intense gaze. "And you're okay with... with that?" I must have misunderstood what being claimed as his Bride Offering by a monster meant.

His smile is dangerous, and his fingers move up to my chin, his thumb dragging across my lips.

"You have no idea how tempting you are to us. You smell of innocence, of sweetness."

My heart thuds painfully against my ribs.

"The three of us, the Pack..." His voice drops to a husky whisper. "We share everything."

Fates help me. His implication lights up my body. With it comes the fear that I'm in way over my head.

I shove the door open, hurrying into the sanctuary of my room.

"Good night, Killian," I manage.

His laughter follows me as I shut the door.

Collapsing onto the bed, I try to calm myself. The idea of sharing twists through my mind, alarming, yet it's sparking a curiosity in me I never expected.

I'm left considering the possibility that I no longer know who I've become...

CHAPTER
ELEVEN
SAGE

Sleep still clings to me as I rush down the corridor at an ungodly morning hour.

"Hurry up, girl," the lanky monster grunts, his skin the color of faded purple, almost bruise-like in the dim corridor light. "We can't be late to the Veil Ritual." The monster moves fast on his spindly legs, every now and then glancing back at me as though worried I've fallen behind.

"It's Sage," I correct him, stumbling down the corridor after being woken up by a loud banging on my door. "And did we have to do this so early? I've never slept so soundly in my life." For the first time in forever, I experienced no nightmares—no world ending, no falling to my death—and I wanted that to last.

"Grimm," the monster states as he turns a corner, staring at me with a face that has no nose. It's rather disturbing to look at, but I don't want him to see me cringing, so I smile at him. "Grimm's my name, and you shouldn't grin so much. It will make others think you are weak."

"Oh," I murmur, almost tripping over my own feet in our hurry. For some reason, everyone's always rushing on this vessel. "Grimm," I ask. "Can you tell me what exactly happens at a Veil Ritual?"

He curves around a corner, and I rush after him down the dark corridor with the occasional light fixture on the wall that resembles some kind of shell creature with tentacles. Its cone-like shell shines with bluish light.

"It's a test," he finally answers. "To ascertain if you truly belong to your mate."

Swallowing the lump in my throat, I go silent, trying to process his words. "I'm certain I don't," I answer almost instantly. I'm a human; he's a monster.

I follow him up a set of spiral metal stairs, where he pauses halfway and waits for me to catch up. "Human, I understand you are frightened, but being afraid will kill you faster. Once a Shadowfen has laid claim to you, your fate is sealed."

My heart stutters, hating the sound of that.

"Then why bother with a stupid ritual?" I groan, my hand on the metal railing as I drag myself upstairs behind him.

"Because there's something about you that Lord Killian doubts."

He doubts me? Why? My shoulders pull back. "Am I in danger?"

"You *should* be worried," he continues. "Those who aren't of interest to our Lords don't remain with us for long. The best way to hide a body out here is in the ocean."

I gasp, leaning in closer. "They kill brides?" How many other brides came to this world or other monster realms and died? Fear spreads through my chest at what I'm getting myself into.

He shrugs, and the space on his face where there should be a nose scrunches up. "It's been known to happen."

My legs weaken beneath me as I force myself to keep moving. Suddenly, I don't want to be here or attend the ritual. An overwhelming panic tightens around my chest because so much remains confusing, like why he selected me as his Bride Offering in the first place.

A suspicious side of me tells me his decision has nothing to do with making me his bride. Why else would they all keep saying they've been waiting for my arrival?

And now, this ritual terrifies me.

Breathless, I rush after Grimm, and soon, we're standing near a set of double metal doors that look large enough for a giant to fit through. My thoughts fly to Killian in his monster form, and terrifying concerns pop into my mind that this ritual involves me and actual monsters.

Grimm claps, and the doors swing outward. I'm left breathless at the sight before us.

How is a jungle growing on a ship?

We're on the top floor, the cool breeze wrapping around me, tugging on my dress and hair.

Tall, lush greenery stretches upward, disappearing

into the sky. Trees I don't recognize, in shades of blues and violets, have leaves as large as my face. The forest stretches outward as far as the eye can see, and by the looks of it, it takes up an entire floor on the vessel.

Stepping inside, I take in the expansive forest that somehow exists on a ship. In front of us runs a stone walkway with exotic flowers blooming in vibrant colors that pulse in the dim light, dotting the land, along with grass up ahead of us in an open area easily large enough to fit over two hundred people. To my right is an explosion of woodland.

I draw in the refreshing, crisp air. As we step along the path, I start to realize there are so many monsters to my left, staring at me. It's startling at first to see the wide array of creatures living on this vessel. Most are built as if made for war. Round, tall bodies appear to have armor as skin. Tusks, horns, claws...

Glancing around frantically, I have a horrible thought that these monsters are somehow involved in the ritual with the woods.

Then I spot the three monsters from last night's dinner. Killian's already marching up to me, dressed in a pair of loose black pants. No shoes, no shirt, and I'm unsure where to look when I'm drowning in the sheer number of muscles he has. His stomach is ripped, his biceps bulging, and his pants sit dangerously low on his hips.

"Good, you're finally here," he says, as if whatever is going on is ordinary.

"Wh-why are you dressed like that? All of this is really scaring me."

He glances down at me, his hands cupping my face. "Deep breath, Sage. I promise this isn't a means to torture. The Veil Ritual is a rite of passage that will confirm we are destined to be together."

The chatter around me seems to escalate, and I feel like all eyes are on me, the human, the person who doesn't belong here.

"Come, let's get ready."

I'm glued to his side as I make my way across the stone path, heading to where females are either going into small capsules or coming out. They are in human form and appear to be around my age. They all wear similar white dresses that hang loosely from their shoulders, cinched in at their waists, and fall to mid-thigh. They're wearing white enclosed shoes.

Before I know it, Killian is ushering me into a booth, too, handing me clothes and shoes. "Quickly, get changed so we can begin." He's in the doorway, grinning, offering me a smile that melts me.

Then he shuts the door, and for a moment, I just stand there, trying to catch my breath.

I keep going over Grimm's words that if I don't fit in with my monster mate, I could end up dead. That terrifies me when I promised my mom I would return to her.

So, death is out of the picture.

I change my clothes, and by the time I'm out, I'm collected by Killian and brought to stand next to him and Nyko. He's glancing over at me, his lips curling.

"I'll give you a hint," he whispers as Killian speaks with Wolfe.

"What do you mean?"

"When it starts, run. Don't lose one precious second. Make Killian work for you because you are the one with power over him."

My head hurts as confusion comes over me.

Run. Nyko said to run. I glance at the other girls, who are all stretching and smiling. They keep taking glances at a group of men dressed like Killian, also in human forms.

I'm no fool... we're going to be chased, aren't we? This isn't about seeing who runs fastest in the woods...

"Welcome, everyone," Wolfe announces abruptly, his voice projecting across the open space.

The murmurs from the gathered crowd fade as Wolfe steps forward to face everyone. He's wearing a warrior outfit similar to the one Killian wore when he found me in the garden in Nightingale Village... a memory that feels like a lifetime ago.

"Bringing together true mates has been crucial to our lives, and the Veil Ritual has been the foundation of our society for generations." He pauses, ensuring the full attention of every monster present. "True mates are rare, but there are times when destiny generously provides us with a pulsing star in the sky. It's a bond that brings forth strength, unity, and sometimes, the salvation of our kind."

Wolfe's eyes gleam as he looks around, his stare

pausing on me a few seconds too long before he continues.

"Today, we gather to celebrate the possibility of such an occasion. May the participants find their true mates today and reveal the path that destiny has laid out for us."

Everyone breaks out into a hooting sound, the noise loud and warming to see their people uniting.

"May the ritual commence."

In a flash, the girls, half a dozen of them, hurry forward, taking a line in front of the woods, facing them.

Behind them, the men move in, standing in a row.

Killian ushers me forward while Nyko calls out, "Don't make it easy for him."

I glance back, unsure what he means, and suddenly, I'm in the line with the other girls, all of us dressed similarly. Killian steps back and joins the men, all bare-chested, looking ready to wrestle bears, except their eyes are all on us.

Killian winks at me, and my stomach twists.

"Rules are simple," Wolfe begins. "Brides get a head start. The moment you are captured by your mate, you are his, and the true magic of the ritual will reveal itself if destiny has blessed you."

I lean in next to the girl near me, who's trembling, appearing as shaken as me. "I'm so nervous I could cry."

She grins at me, her yellow eyes squinting, and it's nice to have a friendly face. "It's all theatrics, really. We'll each get selected, but there's an off chance that the ritual magic will awaken our true mate connection. My mother told me that it's so powerful, once established, they will die for one another."

"That's intense." The more she tells me, the more this ritual frightens me. "And once they catch us?" I glance over my shoulder at Killian, who's watching me like a hawk.

"I'm Joa. You're Sage, right? Everyone's been talking about the new girl."

"That's me," I say, nervously.

"Hey, it's not too bad here. The males love it when you're rough with them in the ritual."

"Rough?" I must have sounded panicked.

She grins at me, leaning in closer, and slips into my hand a short blade.

"Here, I have three on me. You can take one. Maybe cut them a bit, be fierce."

I swallow hard, and I half choke on a laugh. "You've just described the complete opposite of me."

But she's already glancing back at the line of men farther behind us, blushing as she stares at a man with wild blue hair and matching reptile eyes. "That's the fun part, refusing them at first," she whispers. "They mark you."

I stiffen. "Wait, mark us... how?"

An abrupt hissing noise grabs my attention, and I twist toward the woods, watching as pink mist unfurls from nozzles mounted on the sides of the rooftop walls, pumping it into the forest. It seeps between the branches and trees, weaving through the woodland.

"What's that?" I murmur, shaking and struggling to pretend I'm not panicking.

"The Essence of Ethros, a flower grown only on our vessel and known for its potent scent that will draw out the true nature from us and our mates. You have to inhale a lot of it to be effective."

A piercing siren instantly goes off, loud and deafening, and I flinch.

The girls bolt into the woods.

"Run, Sage," Wolfe's yelling.

Ritual.

Mating.

Potent mist.

Fuck!

This is not going to end well, is it?

I throw myself into the woods, running like a mad woman.

CHAPTER
TWELVE
KILLIAN

Sage disappears into the woods, her short dress fluttering high across the back of her thighs, and my cock's already throbbing. Adrenaline pumps through me, muscles flexed, unsure how much longer I can wait. I shudder with the anticipation to track her down fast.

Hunger tears through me, the beast in me demanding we rush after her, catch her, and mark her at once. Never in all my years have I been so consumed by a woman, so fucking obsessed.

Seconds tick by, and I'm itching to run.

Glancing over my shoulder, Wolfe and Nyko are on the sidelines with the crowds, both breathing heavily, chests working overtime, most likely wishing it was them in my place. I see the savagery in their eyes, just as I'd witnessed it last night at dinner. If left alone with Sage, they would have made her theirs... and fuck, I don't care if they want to share her, but I'm sure as hell not missing out on my chance.

Heart thundering, I'm not the only eager one. Others in the lineup alongside me are pacing in a small circle, shaking their arms, stretching...

My gaze locks on the woods, the same shadowy path Sage took.

Ready.

So fucking ready.

The siren rings, loud and piercing.

Like a beast unleashed, I bolt after her, driven by the need to pursue, to claim.

Behind me, the air fills with the raucous shouts of the spectators, but their noise fades into nothing against the rush of blood in my ears.

Shadows darken my paths, trees everywhere, and thick bushes that I leap over. I dart left and right, ducking under branches. No sight of her yet, but I'll find her.

Pink mist drips into the woods around me, and I inhale deeply, letting the magic seep into my lungs, spreading through me. Knowing it will come into effect once I have her.

Thundering footsteps, war cries, and growls resonate around me from the others, each set to catch their prey. While most coming into this might have their sights set on someone specific, they have a right to claim any female participating in the ritual.

That thought alone pushes me faster, and I quicken my pace.

Thick with the scent of damp soil and old growth, the branches around me sway from the wind. The combination of sea and forest air is something I've grown accustomed to. Something that feels like home.

Twisted branches and shadows hide her from me, and considering I have yet to catch sight of her, it starts to worry me.

Taking a deep inhale while my feet shove against the ground, I propel myself forward, but I don't pick up her scent.

Fury slams into me.

That's when a blur of motion to my left catches my attention. My heart hammers with the hope that it's her, but no, it's another competitor, his form monstrous, barreling through the underbrush on all fours, tail slashing through the air, spikes like jagged knives trailing down his back. Behind him and farther to my left, a few others pound the ground, also in their monster forms, knowing they're faster this way.

The last thing I need is to terrify Sage more than she is, charging after her in my true form.

So, where is she?

Knowing Sage, she'd want to be as far from the others as possible, and seeing most are on my left, rushing in that direction, I pivot my direction to the right in a wide swing.

Pulse surging, legs pumping, I move like the wind.

Suddenly, I catch the flick of silver hair dancing between trees up ahead amid the shadows, and there she is.

The girl moves fast... admirable.

My cock hardens at the promise of marking her. I run full speed directly toward her.

The little thing glances back over her shoulder, and for a split second, our gazes clash.

Wide eyes.

Her mouth falls open.

Grinning, I charge ahead, driven by her fear.

But she moves just as fast and darts right into shadows, vanishing from sight.

I'll find her; she won't get far.

When I hear the distinct sound of her cry, anger crashes into me. I'm suddenly careening to her like a tornado, my mind going to a dark place—warped, raw anger at the thought of anyone touching her.

Skidding around a thick tree, shoving aside a low-hanging branch covered in leaves, I practically ripped it out of the ground to get past. There in front of me, the snorting asshole on all fours straddles over her as she frantically crawls backward to get away from him, kicking him in the face.

That's my girl.

Every muscle in my body coils, and I lunge at the fucker, anger lashing at my insides.

Reaching him, I snatch him by the back of his neck, squeezing and wrenching him back with such force that I throw him into a tree. I pounce on him, anger blinding me, and my hands are around his spiny throat.

"You dare fucking touch what's mine?" His eyes are bulging, his claws swiping at me, but I feel nothing. It's all part of the ritual—if you want a girl someone's claimed first, you have every right to challenge him to fight to the death.

"Lord, I'm sorry. I didn't know she's yours."

Liar! This fucker knowingly turned his attention to the wrong female.

A hard smack abruptly collides into my back. Enough for me to release the fucker and swing back around, half expecting another asshole wanting to claim Sage.

But instead, it's her, standing there with a branch gripped in two hands, shaking.

"You don't need to kill him!" She lifts the branch with anger, and from the corner of my eye, I notice the man I challenged is scrambling away.

It's his lucky day that I don't chase after him, not when my sights are set on my beautiful human.

"Would you rather I let him rut you?" I reach for the branch and rip it out of her grasp, tossing it aside. Then I go to grab her, but she shoves against my hand, recoiling. Her face is red from running, her breaths rushing, and I love seeing her so worked up.

"No, but... You can't just kill someone." She suddenly twists and bolts away from me.

I laugh, adoring everything about her.

Adrenaline has me charging madly, my pulse pounding because I'm racing right behind her. With the wind blowing in my face comes her sweet nectar scent pouring all over me.

The Essence of Ethros in the pink mist is coming into play, bringing out our primal hunger, our savage needs to rut. She has no idea why she's so wet... but I inhale it so heavily in the air that it calls to me.

I quickly dart to the right and come around to intercept her, arriving directly into her view.

She screams, then backpedals and swings around, but I'm moving too fast, and I have no intention of stopping. I crash into her, my arms looping around her, my movement pushing us both forward in a moment where there's nowhere to go but down.

I twist, placing myself underneath her, taking the brunt of the fall, her on top of me. She bounces against me, that soft body, those breasts so full, so delicious, that my cock strains in my pants.

But she's fast, and in a flash, she's straddling my chest, those temptress thighs tight against my ribs, the slick of her cunt wet against my chest. She's got a blade, holding it to my throat.

"Enough," she states, baring her teeth.

Oh, she's showing her Shadowfen side, and I fucking love it.

"Where'd you get that knife from?" My cock is so hard when all I can think about is shuffling down and under her skirt, taking her into my mouth, tongue-fucking her hole until she melts for me, screaming my name.

"Does it matter?" she exclaims.

I'm convinced one of the girls must have given it to her, as weapons are encouraged in the chase.

"I've got the upper hand, which means I won, and this is over."

I laugh, obsessed with how adorable she is. She presses that blade tighter to my throat, the bite pinching my skin.

"That's not how it works." I'm shaking under her with lust, loving her being on top. The smell of her slick reminds me of the raspberries from her world. A growl rips out of me, my hips rocking slightly at how fucking hard I am, how desperate I am for her.

"Look around. There's no escape for the women. And you, Sage, are mine. So, unless you behave, I'll have you begging for me."

She chuckles, even if her cheeks blush a bright pink.

"Well, you found me." Her voice is quivering, and all of her is shuddering. "So, you won. Happy now?"

With my hands on her thighs, she arches her back, giving out a moan. Taking that moment, I snatch her hand with the blade and swiftly move it away from my neck. A small squeeze of her hand and she drops the knife.

"Ouch," she cries as I snatch the fallen blade and throw it somewhere over my head, out of her grasp.

But she's too fast, already scrambling off me, then rushing after it on hands and knees, as if she's not listening to me that the blade won't help her.

I hadn't meant to be too rough with her, but she left me no choice.

Rolling onto my side, I'm up on my knees in no time, grabbing her ankles as she attempts to get to her feet, and I haul her back down. The motion not only has her falling forward onto her stomach but pushes her dress up to her waist as I drag her closer to me. The sight has my cock strangling for release.

She cries out, wriggling to get up, one arm stretching out for the blade but it isn't close enough.

With her ass bare for me, I lower my body on top of hers, pinning her down before she escapes. Cock cradled against those cheeks and only the fabric of my pants between us, I'm not sure how much longer I can hold back. I'm not a strong man when it comes to Sage.

"Get off me," she cries, bucking against me.

"I wouldn't do that if I were you." I chuckle in her ear, my hips already grinding against her, her scent so much stronger now.

She moans beneath me, and there's a growl in my throat, an involuntary sound.

"You smell delicious, so sugary."

The gorgeous girl writhes beneath me, her muscles quivering. Her ass arches upward, wanting me, despite her protests.

Fucking beautiful.

I lean forward, my lips on her ear. "That's it, Sage. Follow your body."

"I've never been this hot before, this aroused... like I might die. What have you done to me?"

I lift myself off her and sit back on my heels, staring down at that firm, round ass and the slick that covers her inner thighs. She quickly turns over to face me, sitting in front of me and pushing her skirt down to hide herself.

Her scent is so strong now that it fogs my head.

Around us, the cries and screams of being claimed fill

the woods from the other contestants, but I only have eyes for Sage.

"Are you going to fuck me now? Is that how you'll claim me?" She's quivering, staring at me with that doe-eyed gaze. Close to her, I see the flecks of violet in them starting to come through, her Shadowfen side pushing forward in her body, just like the color of her hair deepening in mauve.

Her perfume intensifies in my nostrils.

"Is that what you want?" I ask, my hand resting on her knees. I'm wrecked, barely holding on, but I'm under no illusion that this girl has never lain with a man. It's in her scent, so ripe, so delicious.

It drives me to insanity.

She tugs her lower lip between her teeth, biting down on it, the fight on her face clear. The Essence of Ethros might have brought out our carnal pleasures, but it's only drawing on what's already inside of us.

"I-I don't know." Yet she thrusts her breasts forward and parts her legs for me in a move I didn't see coming.

"Let me show you," I murmur, my sight lowering to the sweetest cunt bared to me. Pink and swollen, her pussy is quivering. "My Sage, you're so very wet for me, aren't you?" I trace my fingertips down from her knees, following the curve of her inner thigh, her scent like euphoria, like berries, like fresh water.

She whimpers, spreading her legs wider for me, and all I can think about is driving my cock into her, balls deep. It jolts in my pants, pushing for release, but perhaps I've spent too much time in the human world, developing a conscience, to think that her first time shouldn't happen here.

Instead, a finger drifts over to her cunt, the heat from her body sliding up my arm. Tenderly, I run the back of my knuckles across the length of her, then slip a finger between her folds.

She's gasping for air, her eyes closed, and her innocence has me at her mercy. So silky soft, I press down on her swollen clit, and she winces, her hips rocking forward. Giving her what she craves, I slip a finger into that tight little cunt.

Her cry is the most beautiful sound I've ever heard. She's trembling against me.

I work my finger into her and back out, moving faster, seeing her lose herself before me.

My hunger billows, the ache painful to the point that I'm seeing double vision. I won't be able to hold on much longer.

"Is this what you want?" I ask.

"Um." She nods her head.

Fingering her is not enough for me, not when I keep breathing in her scent.

Her eyes are hazed over when she opens them, and those nipples push so hard against her dress.

"Have you ever had a man lick you?" I shuffle back before kneeling in front of her, praying to my Goddess, to her sweet cunt.

She's breathing quickly now, her cheeks rosier than before, which I'll take as a no.

Without pause, I bury my face between her thighs,

the flat of my tongue over her offering, devouring her sweet taste. I trace her from her clit to her hole, going slow at first, savoring her.

"Please don't stop," she whispers.

I almost die hearing her pleading. As though madness has me possessed, I lick and suck on her offering, plunging my tongue into her hole. Control is a strong suit of mine, but at this moment, I'm fighting a losing battle. My cock aches, the monster in me pushing to the surface, but I don't relent. I eat her cunt like a ravenous beast.

Her cries echo around us, her body arching as she fists the grass around us. She's close, and I need her all over me. She shamelessly grinds herself against my face while I reach up her body, tearing at her dress, the rip loud as I free her breasts. I grope one, squeezing its softness, the hardness of her nipple in the palm of my hand.

Her moans sing in my ears, her body sensitive to my touch.

It's been so long since I've fucked, so desperately long.

Never releasing her, I push my tongue into her again and again, my nose on her clit, and she bursts into the most alluring scream. She's shuddering under me, but I don't release her, not yet, not until I've had my fill.

Lapping her up, I take it all as she comes so hard it's fucking beautiful.

In an instant, the building intensity buzzes inside of me, the spark on my skin, the reminder of the Veil Ritual.

Releasing her, I move my mouth to her inner thigh, teeth extending, and bite down into flesh.

She screams, a different sound now, but I don't release her. I sink my teeth into her skin.

A growl rips from my throat, the coppery taste of her blood still fresh on my tongue.

She fights back, shoving against my shoulders, clawing at my head. I hold her down, my body trembling with a violent shudder that racks through me.

It's not just a physical intoxication toward her... I feel it seeping deep down into my soul.

The pink mist thickens around us, or perhaps it's blurring my vision. I lick the bite, wiping away the blood on her skin, when a forceful blow strikes me in the chest.

An invisible strike right in the solar plexus.

I snarl, struggling to rise, my limbs faltering, and I collapse next to Sage, who's also convulsing.

Clasping her hand is the last thing I remember before darkness swallows my vision.

The air's knocked out of me as I flip open my eyes to find I'm standing on a cliff's edge, overlooking a landscape I recognize from my childhood.

Homes dot the countryside, families move about their daily business, and from my vantage point, the grand, lofty stone palace stands majestically.

It's strange that I'm brought to the old kingdom in Blight.

Movement beside me draws my attention. Sage is here, gazing out over the land, then at me, confusion etched across her face. I smile, a reaction to her I no longer control. And with it comes the answer of why I'm here... because of her.

Because of us.

Seeing her comes with a sharpness in my chest again, along with an explosion of warmth, with possessiveness, with the strength drawn to her.

I've never felt this way before, even with my first love, Inka, who I had assumed was my true mate, but I never tested it. What I felt for her wasn't the same. She was never my intended mate.

Unlike Sage.

This... it's like the first time I saw Sage—the deep rush of emotions, the connection crashing over me, overwhelming, heart-thumping. Like this whole time, I've been living in a cave, and only now I've stepped out into the sunlight, experiencing real warmth.

I'm a warrior, a hunter, and nothing stands in my way, so how is it that when I look at her, I become someone else? Someone who craves a future that isn't filled with only revenge, with hatred, and with fury for everything I've lost.

She stares up at me, blinking, as if she's had her eyes opened up, too... staring at me as though I'm her everything. Fuck, that's everything to me.

"*I feel strange,*" *she murmurs.* "*I'm so drawn to you, but I barely know you. And then this place... I swear I've seen it before.*"

"*You have?*" *I reach over, pushing her silvery violet hair behind an ear, her skin gentle under my fingertips.*

She blinks, casting her glance over the land. "*I think so, but it's never been this perfect, not this beautiful. I remember the castle over there, in ruins, in flames..."*

Is this her Shadowfen side calling her to its origins?

"Where are we? What happened to the woods?" she asks, glancing around and hugging herself.

Her expression carries innocence, but behind her gaze, I know there's a strong woman needing to emerge.

"This is Silvercrest Kingdom, or what it once looked like. The place was destroyed a long time ago during the Great Desolation, a time of unimaginable earthquakes that ruined our world."

She breathes heavily, just staring at the castle.

I slide my hand into hers, turning her attention to me.

"There's a reason we're here, sharing a vision," I begin. "This is what the Shadowfen call the Veil Ritual. It's where the veil lifts, and we find each other in the same vision. It's the mark of being true mates."

Blinking rapidly, her eyes wide, she shakes her head. "No, that can't be right. I'm imagining this because I don't belong in this world," she protests, pulling from my grasp.

As she does, a great thunderous growl sounds in the air, the ground shivering beneath us, and instantly, the cliff behind her crumbles, leaving us stranded on a shrinking ledge.

She hurries to my side, glancing around, shuddering.

"Destiny disagrees." I chuckle, drawing her even closer, an arm tight around her back. "You're exactly where you're meant to be."

"I don't believe you," she murmurs, her gaze darting around us. "We're different races. I don't..." She trails off, her

attention searching the kingdom down below for answers. Her fingers tremble slightly in mine. "All my life, these dreams... seeing places crumbling, feeling lost. If this is all true, then..." Her voice cracks, and she's shaking harder now.

"Sometimes destiny hides the truth from us until it's time."

Her gaze locks with mine again, desperation behind that glassy stare. "If I'm here in this vision, if I've seen it all before... what does it mean?"

I hold her gaze, steady and unflinching. "You know what it means, Sage," *I say softly.* "Deep in your heart, you've always known the truth."

Her breath catches. "No, you're lying..."

Just as fast, the vision is ripped away, and we're both lying on the forest ground, gasping for air.

I draw myself up, my head still fuzzy. Next to me, my true mate's scrambling to her feet, tears fresh in her eyes.

"Sage," I reach for her with my hand, a darkened pain in my chest tightening for her agony.

"No, you're wrong." She pulls away from me. "I'm not your true mate because I'm not like you. I'm not a monster. I hate this place, so how can I belong here? My mother..." Tears fall down her cheeks, then she darts into the woods, away from me so fast that I'm still stumbling on my feet from the vision, from her reaction to a truth I hadn't intended to reveal to her.

Not yet, anyway.

Well, fuck!

CHAPTER
THIRTEEN
SAGE

My whole life, I've been fearful of being selected for a Bride Offering. No one explained what to expect, so of course, I expected the worst.

Now, I find out that maybe I'm part monster.

This has to be some cruel joke.

My breaths come faster as I charge straight out of the ritual forest, clutching my dress where Killian tore it across my chest, making a beeline for the stairs in the hallway.

Noticing a large, insect-like monster coming down the stairs, I teeter on the spot, not wanting to deal with that, while at the same time tying up the loose, torn fabric of my dress into a knot in the middle of my chest, covering myself up in case I end up flashing anyone.

I make a rash decision to head downstairs instead of up to where my room is.

Right now, I just want to be alone.

Away from everyone, especially Killian, knowing he'll try to find me. I can't cope with the ritual I experienced, how desperately I wanted to give myself to him, or the reality of what the vision revealed.

Me as his true mate.

Me as a half-monster.

Fuck!

Shaking my head, I wipe away the damn tears, wishing more than anything to be with my mom, to ask her for the truth. I'm shaking with anger at her for keeping me in the dark. Maybe she did it to protect me, seeing we're already outcasts in Nightingale Village, but that doesn't explain why she never told me more about my father.

I keep running, not ready to face it all. My calves ache as I descend the stairs, my breaths coming in sharp gasps. I finally stop on a random floor when I spy a set of open doors that lead to what looks like a glowing lake. I have no idea how this vessel carries such luxuries, but it's like its own tiny world.

I hurry toward the doors since I can't see anyone else in there and step inside. It takes my breath away. The air is warm and humid, like a hidden paradise. In front of me lies a small rock pool, with plants in deep purples and reds growing around the perimeter, along with large-petaled flowers floating on the water's surface, glowing a golden color. They are the only light in this room, giving off enough brightness to chase away the complete darkness. The water shimmers, reflecting the glow, and it's spectacular.

Without another soul inside the room, I push the doors shut, needing me time.

Removing my shoes, I crouch down by the water's edge, the pond not deep as I can see the silvery glitter bottom. I dip my feet inside the cool water, watching it for a moment, ensuring nothing's going to attack me. When nothing does, I settle down, swishing my legs around, enjoying the coolness.

The tears I attempted to hold back flow more freely now, mixing with the sweat and the humidity of the room. I'm not just crying because of discovering a truth about the heritage I'm struggling to accept, but because of how lost I feel, how alone, as though I truly don't know where I belong.

I don't fit on Earth, I see that clearly now, but is this place my permanent home? Where it feels like I'm walking around in a nightmare?

Forgotten by a father who either knows nothing about me or refused me in his life, I keep circling back to my mom. Did she lie to protect me, or was she ashamed? I consider the idea that she had no idea my father had been a monster... then why refuse to talk about him? Why play down the strange silver hair when the rest of Nightingale Village noticed it?

She had to know the truth.

I lean forward, closer to the water, my reflection distorted by the ripples. For a moment, I don't recognize myself until the water settles and turns mirror-still.

My eye color has changed from that pale blue to violet.

Staring back at me is a girl I barely recognize. I gasp as a cold chill runs through my veins. My gaze darts to the ends of my hair, noticing the stronger, more pronounced violet hue that covers the bottom half of my strands. It falls down my back and around my shoulders, shimmering under the light of the glowing flowers.

I lift a trembling hand to my face, tracing the lines of my now smoother skin and the more defined cheekbones. My reflection shows someone I barely recognize, someone transforming before my very eyes. A wave of panic hits me, and I wonder—will I turn into a monster, too? What will I look like?

Goose bumps rise on my arms, and I rub them, trying to ward off the cold fear feasting on my insides.

The crunch of foliage behind me crackles, my heart leaping into my throat. I half expect it to be Killian, but it's someone else entirely.

I scream at first, seeing the creature that drags itself into the room. Uncertainty climbs to my throat, terror choking me.

The figure is lanky, with thin legs and arms that seem more like wings. Its face is pale white, and darkness sweeps from his hairline back, merging with his clothes, making it difficult to tell where he starts and ends. Its hands are stark white like his face, long feathers dancing underneath the length of his arms.

"No need to be scared," he murmurs in a gravelly voice that leaves me startled. I start to pull back, but he adds, "You don't need to leave on my account." Nothing about his voice matches his appearance.

"I'm s-sorry. Is this your room?" I stammer.

He shakes his head. "This is a communal room for everyone to share. Everything in here is made to calm you—from the air temperature to the pond to the soft sounds of trickling water." He walks with long steps toward the far edge of the water, at least eight feet from me, and climbs up on the ledge. Planting his feet on it, he crouches down, bony knees sticking out on either side of him, his feathery arms dipping forward, sinking into the water just as I've done with my feet.

"Ahh, that's better. Something about this water always settles me. Please, stay. I've had a shit day myself and could use the company."

I settle back down, my feet dipping back into the water. "Of course, you're welcome to join."

The monster's not large, maybe five-foot-eight or nine. As he sits there, I keep telling myself not to scream again. He is a thing from horror stories. When he glances my way, his mouth partly open in what I think is a smile, with crooked teeth showing, I tremble.

Except I'm like him now, right? And if this is where I'm going to be until I work out how to go see my mom and check on her, ask her about who my real father is, I have to try to fit in.

"So, what brought you here?" he asks, breaking the silence again.

"Running," I admit with a smirk. "From a lot of things, but mostly from myself."

He nods as if he understands completely. "We've all had those moments."

I sigh, my gaze drifting back to the glowing flowers. "I think I've been doing it most of my life."

After a long beat of silence, he clears his throat. "You're the new human," he says, more a statement than a question, and just like the girl at the ritual said, I'm the talk of the town on the vessel.

"That's me," I answer softly, unsure what else to say as I'm still trying to make sense of it all.

"I'm Clay," he states, his birdlike head twisted, staring at me. "The captain of this vessel."

"Wait. I assumed that Wolfe…" I'm stunned.

"Ah yes, he is the leader of the people on this vessel, but the ship belongs to me. Something I built with my team long ago for the King to explore the world, for easy travel, and for war. The Queen named the ship Howler, after her son. Though today, the vessel resembles very little of what it once looked like, carrying an army, weapons, but now…" He shrugs, staring back down into the water.

"It's your home," I finish for him, remembering Killian telling me in our vision that the kingdom was ruined. The dreams I had my whole life—were they flashes of what this world faced? I still have no idea why I was privy to the past, but I'm hoping those nightmares have stopped as they did last night.

"We lost our home thirteen years ago," he explains in his gravelly voice. "The Howler is temporary until destiny brings us a new opportunity." He glances at me again, his eyes staring into me strangely.

"I get it because I grew up never feeling like I fit in

back in the village, and now that I'm here, I don't feel I belong either."

"Belonging is a journey, not a destination," he answers, then dips his attention back to the pond. "We all find our place in time."

I can't help but feel slightly bad for him. "So, what actually happened in this world? I keep hearing bits and pieces like the world wasn't always like this."

"It wasn't," he explains. "Once, it had more land, a world ruled by a kingdom, the royal family of Silvercrest. Then we experienced devastating world destruction... a natural event that shook the world and broke it apart. Fires spread, then rain came... so much of it that it flooded, and the oceans and rivers rose, stealing land. It was at this time that the royal family was betrayed by another, claiming himself as the new King. His supporters were in far greater numbers than those who opposed him. He promised them a dry home, while the rest of us who knew he stole the kingdom were banished into the waters."

"Oh, fuck," I whisper, the gravity of what he's saying sinking in. My heart aches for what they've been through. To lose everything, to be cast out into the water—it's heartbreaking.

"What happens now? Everyone's trying to get the kingdom back?" I think of Killian, Wolfe, and Nyko, the leaders of these people. Is that their goal, too?

"That's the intention," he answers, glancing my way with that intensity that leaves me shifting uncomfortably on the edge of the pond.

I'm not sure what to say as I feel the weight of his words pressing down on me. The future of a broken kingdom, a world submerged, and I'm now trapped in the same plight.

"But on brighter topics," he begins. "I hear you've been matched as a true mate with Lord Killian. That is rare. You must be ecstatic."

I laugh, unable to control myself at his statement. "Not sure that's the word I'd use for it."

Clay's face remains impassive, the shadows on his face darkening. "I was once the King's navy chief in command," he begins, his voice carrying the weight. "Now, I'm reduced to ferrying people around the seas." There's a bitterness in his tone, anger simmering beneath the surface. I can't blame him; just hearing his story makes me tense and furious for him, for all the monsters on this vessel.

"Do you know much about the new kingdom?" he asks, tilting his head to the side.

"Not really," I admit. "I had no idea about Blight either."

"So, before you came to our world, Blight, there was nothing? No visions or dreams about it? Sometimes, that happens when you are far away from your true home." His gaze deepens, almost as if he's searching for something in my eyes.

I shake my head, trying to keep my voice steady, not trusting his intentions to reveal my nightmares. Unsure why, but something about him makes me not trust him.

"No, nothing like that. Why do you ask? If I experienced those, does it mean something?"

He tilts his head, his birdlike eyes narrowing. "It's just rare for a Shadowfen to not be matched to another true-blood Shadowfen. In the old kingdom, such unions were forbidden, carrying a significant punishment."

I shift uncomfortably, pushing out a fake laugh. "Well, lucky that's not happening now."

He holds my stare for a moment too long before he gives me one of his creepy smiles. "Yes, very fortunate."

Why's he so interested in me? Before I can ask him why, another monster bursts into the room. He's a barrel of a creature with deep brown skin and spiky hair all over his body. And he's naked, something dangling between his legs. His gaze locks on me.

I instantly look away, blushing, staring down at the water. How can he walk around like that?

"Captain," the monster states urgently. "*He's* changed course again, demanding *he* wants to go to land immediately."

Clay stiffens, his demeanor shifting to anger in an instant, his brow pinching together, shoulders bunching up. "It's too damn early," he snaps. "We have to build up our defenses more. When did he change his mind?"

"Early this morning, before the ritual. I missed it, sorry." His head bows forward pitifully.

I keep my gaze low, pretending I'm not in the room. The tension in the air thickens. Clay huffs, clearly perturbed, and excuses himself from me with a curt nod.

"I must attend to this. Enjoy the calmness I've now lost."

I watch as he marches out of the room, leaving me alone once more. My heart is still racing from the barrage of questions and the unexpected confrontation.

That was strange... right?

I can't shake the feeling that something is off. The way Clay was interrogating me, the urgency in the first mate's voice, the sudden change in plans—it all feels too coincidental. I splash my feet in the water, trying to calm myself, but my mind keeps racing.

And who was that monster referring to, wanting to go to land... Wolfe or Killian, perhaps? I found it strange to hear him not even mention a name, but Clay knew instantly who he spoke of.

The glow of the flowers in the pool reflects off the water, casting eerie shadows on the walls. This place is beautiful, but now it feels tainted. I don't move, not wanting to leave the silence just yet.

I'm still not ready to face my truths.

Wolfe

Dual moons hang low tonight, casting a bright glow over the waves, making them shimmer like liquid silver. My hands grip the railing, the cool metal grounding me as my mind focuses on the results of the Veil Ritual between Killian and Sage.

Surprised? Fuck, yeah. Yet I shouldn't be.

Nyko's lounging on a chair on my balcony, feet propped up on the railing, hands behind his head, in his own little world.

"Any sign of Killian?" I ask, considering he charged in here after I asked him to track down my second-in-command.

"Not since this morning when he charged out of the ritual after Sage, mumbling something about her now knowing she's part Shadowfen."

I shrug. "She was bound to find out soon enough." Preferably not during the Veil Ritual, and in hindsight, we could have handled that better over the course of dinner the other night. But I assumed we had time, and I hadn't expected Killian to rush into the ritual like a fucking madman possessed.

Here I hoped her arrival would be straightforward with no complications. Yet I can't believe my own damn body's reaction to our little human. This beautiful girl with innocence pouring off her messed me up, and guilty as charged, I've been obsessed with her ever since.

"And now," Nyko states, distracting my thoughts. "He's either fucking her, or he's sulking somewhere for pissing her off. Though, I have to admit, she's been on my mind since she first arrived. Her scent is a fucking enchantment, and I've had a raging hard-on since she got here."

I groan seeing he's had a similar reaction to her arrival.

"I'll be honest, I didn't expect her to be his true mate."

Nyko chuckles softly. "Something's wrong with me. Earlier I paid the Abyss Room a visit, and none of the four-breasted girls down there held my interest. My damn cock went limp as fuck." He punches up to his feet, growling. "Sage has fucking broken me. I have no hatred or jealousy toward Killian, but hell, I barely held back during the ritual. I craved being the one to chase her down, to sink into her sweet pussy."

I growl under my breath, shaking off the hunger for Sage clinging to me.

"How about you keep it in your pants, and let's see how things pan out before making things worse? She's here for a mission, not for you both to lose your heads."

Nyko gives me a deadpan stare. "Right, and you felt nothing for her back at dinner, using your shadow to feel her up? Think I didn't notice or smell the arousal you brought out in her?"

I shake my head, exhaling and breaking into laughter. "Fuck, I'm just as bad as you two."

Nyko's chortling. "So, what now? We all have one big fuck party and get her out of our systems?"

I shudder. The image has my cock hardening. I turn from him, deeply inhaling the night air. We didn't search for Sage this long only to end up tripping over our feet for the girl.

"Earlier today, I notified Clay that we're changing course and want to pay the kingdom a visit ahead of schedule. Now, I'm worried we're moving too fast," I state, my anticipation wavering.

He's frowning my way.

"With Sage being Killian's true mate, and what happened to him and his last lover, he's not going to let us hand her over. And I won't force him to."

Nyko runs a hand through his hair. "Fuck! I've been ready from the second we first set foot on Howler all those years ago. But this is going to turn into a fucking storm now, isn't it?"

I groan, hands fisting at my side. "Leave it with me," I state.

"Whatever works." He's already marching out of my quarters, never showing his emotions, unlike Killian. Yet I've seen the way he stares at Sage, too, how she's impacted him as well.

My thoughts linger on her, on the strength of the attraction she holds over me. But as much as I fight the urge to fall prey to her, the complication with her being Killian's true mate and using her with King Bren... Fuck, this cripples our plans.

CHAPTER
FOURTEEN
SAGE

The day's been a struggle.

It's later in the night, and nothing I do helps me sleep. I've been tossing and turning in bed for hours. Since spending half the day in the pond room, then grabbing food from the dining restaurant, mainly consisting of berries, I've been hiding in my room.

Killian hasn't barged in, and I hoped alone time would help me calm down, along with getting another good night's sleep.

Except it hasn't.

My stomach's growling for food beyond berries while my head's been replaying the events of the ritual.

Not only is Killian my true mate...

But I'm half-monster.

Since coming to my room, a burning heat has been roaring inside my body. No shower will cool me down, and I have that strong feeling wash over me that it's Killian's touch I crave.

The sensation pushes through me.

Flames.

Guilt.

Fear of how quickly I'm losing control. How back in Nightingale Village, I kept my distance from the villagers who bullied and pushed me around. Remaining hidden from them gave me the temporary salvation I sought.

But evidently, there's no running from the inferno consuming me.

I close my eyes, and I swallow the thickness in my throat, squeezing my thighs together from the building sensation, the tingling that refuses to leave me. Rolling onto my back in bed, I exhale loudly. The growing sensations are rattling me.

Killian touched me in a way no one ever has, not even me. His mouth... I whimper at the buzz curling between my thighs. That tongue on my pussy... I had no idea what a real orgasm felt like, but his mouth was electric.

Rolling around, teasing myself, isn't helping, so when my stomach growls once more for food, I climb out of bed and decide I'm not getting anywhere.

Dressed in a pair of leggings I found in the wardrobe drawer, along with a loose shirt, I decide there must be food being served somewhere on this ship. With no clock, I have zero idea what the time is.

With one glance outside the balcony doors, staring at the two moons hanging high, I assume it's around midnight, so I slip into my shoes and head out into the hallway.

Eerie silence.

Shadows stretch across the wall from the dim lighting, and only the sound of my footsteps echoes around me.

At the top of the spiral metal staircase, I pause. Voices float up from below, faint but unmistakable. Maybe there's a kitchen down there or a different dining hall where I can find something normal to eat. Just as I start to descend, a dark, wolflike creature is coming in my direction from a few floors below, and fear has me freezing up.

The sight of it makes my stomach churn with terror. The spiral staircase stretches endlessly downward, making me dizzy just to look at it, and I quickly recoil, backing away.

I find myself rushing right past the elevator doors, where I pause as the doors slide open for me. With a shaky breath, I step inside, and the doors close silently behind me.

For a moment, I'm enveloped by a faint light.

"Where would you like to go?" Howler's voice fills the small space, and I flinch at the loudness of his question.

"I'm hungry," I admit. "Is there anywhere that serves late-night food? But nothing too... wild, please."

"Of course," Howler replies smoothly. The elevator starts moving, but I don't feel it. Instead, I see the floors flashing by rapidly on the display through the glass doors. I have no idea how far we're descending, but my stomach's churning with where I'll end up. There are no buttons to press.

Finally, we stop, and the doors open. I stumble out into a hallway where the walls and floor are all made of wooden paneling. Glittery stars dot the walls, casting the area in a gentle light.

Instantly, a comforting scent of freshly baked bread finds me, and I swear my mouth's watering. My stomach growls in anticipation, with desperation.

"If you go into the kitchen straight down the hallway," Howler explains. "We have a baker working into the night that might appeal to you."

"Thank you."

I approach the doorway, my nerves building, but the enticing smell of baked bread gives me the courage to knock. Before my knuckles touch the door, it swings open to reveal a brightly lit industrial kitchen. It's a large room with counters running the length of two walls, and at the rear wall stands an oversized, oval-shaped wood-fire oven. The wave of heavenly baked smells draws me inside.

"Hello," I say to the woman who's just pulling out a tray of something from the oven with her bare hands. She's stocky, with four arms, purple horns, and a pixie-like, cute face. Her smile instantly eases my discomfort.

"Sorry to interrupt," I add. "But Howler suggested I might find something to eat in your kitchen."

She sets the tray on the counter and turns to me, her completely white eyes blinking. "You're a hungry girl, and you've come to the right place." Her voice is soft, slightly high-pitched.

I nod. "Very much."

When her smile widens, revealing fangs that slip out past her bottom lip, I don't back away. There's something warming about her presence, something that reassures me I'm safe here. She wipes the flour from her hands on the apron she wears over a mauve dress, her feet actual hooves. I try not to stare.

"Come, take a seat, and I'll bring you a selection." She waves for me to follow her through the kitchen, and I hurry past the random baskets lining the middle of the floor. Each holds different ingredients—rainbow-colored flours that could be made out of anything, really. One is filled with what appears like apples; that's until I notice one is bruised and leaking with blood.

I cringe on the inside, worrying about what I'll be served. In one basket, there are wriggling worms, but thicker and longer than the ones I've seen back home. My stomach turns at the sight. When I see a few of them diced up on the counter, I start questioning my decision.

"It's not often I get anyone coming for a midnight meal anymore, not since Night Rush opened a few floors down," she explains begrudgingly. "Seeing as they serve heavily fried food and drinks, most go there now."

"I prefer the idea of something quieter," I reply as she leads me into a long room with arched seating areas. Midnight blue walls glow under lantern-style lights hanging everywhere. Red tablecloths cover the two rows of tables with a narrow path down the middle. Right at the end is an oversized semicircle booth and table, but I take a seat at the closest table.

"I won't be long," she explains, crossing the room to the kitchen.

"Thank you," I call out after her. "Nothing fancy, please. Like, I'm not into worms."

She laughs, and I'm left alone in this gorgeous room. Before long, she emerges with a large wooden tray she holds with all four hands and places it down in front of me.

My eyes widen at the selection of various bread rolls, all different colors, along with a bowl filled with a blue kind of paste and a cup of something steaming.

She sits across from me, and I smile.

"This looks and smells divine. Thank you."

"Enjoy. Everything here I've made. The tea is from a special herb that we grow on board, and each bread has a different center. Nothing with worms, I promise." Grinning, she reaches for one of the buns, rips it in half, tips part of it into the blue paste, then takes a bite.

I salivate, watching her, and select a purple bun. Tearing it, I take a small nibble only to find it's sweet, and there's a honeyed middle that has the consistency of mashed beans.

"Oh, this is heavenly." I take a large bite, unable to get enough.

"Try the butter. It comes from a special butterfly larva that, when cooked and whipped, turns out creamy."

I swallow the mouthful, staring at the larva butter, and I feel compelled to at least taste it.

I lightly scrape the corner of my bread into the butter that's soft on my tongue, instantly reminding me of the flavor of popcorn.

"Wow!"

I might have just found my favorite new food. Look at me, eating lizards and insect larvae.

Finishing the first roll in no time, I reach for a yellow one.

"I might be coming here to eat from now on."

She claps all her hands. "I welcome it."

As I eat, she watches me, especially as I moan about how fruity the yellow bun tastes. I wash it down with the tea that is slightly bitter and deep green, but it's drinkable.

"My name's Kiri," she says softly, and I realize how rude I've been.

"Oh, I'm so sorry. I'm Sage. I was so hungry I didn't even introduce myself."

"It's been a long time since someone has shown so much passion for my food," she responds, still smiling as she watches me eat. "I have a few loyal customers who come after hours, so I welcome you as well."

I laugh. "I might even take some of the buns with me to my room. Back home, my mother used to make these delicious milk bread rolls. You could eat them with every meal or even plain. They were so good." Just talking about her makes me miss her deeply, and as much as I tell myself barely any time has passed back home compared to here, it doesn't lessen the sting.

Kiri's expression softens, her lips pulling into a smile. "I learned all my cooking from my mother, who died in the Great Desolation along with so many others. If you wouldn't mind, I'd like to try your milk bread recipe. We have some milk suppliers on the ship."

Something about the way she says that leaves me feeling slightly nauseous, imagining terrifying monsters, maybe spider creatures being used. I shudder on the inside, but I just nod to Kiri, saying, "Of course."

Then she breaks into telling me about her daughter, Rina, who's already learning to bake. We talk for what feels like hours, and it's the first time I've felt semi-normal on the vessel. I also eat every last roll on the table.

I finish my second cup of tea, the warmth of the drink soothing me. Just as I'm about to savor the last sip, the door opens from the kitchen.

Something tall and blue enters, and at first, I flinch. It takes me seconds to realize that it's Killian in his monster form. An excitement flutters through me at his presence. White hair falls halfway down his muscular chest. The top half is pulled back from his face, some loose strands tumbling over his eyes.

Skin a faint blue hue, he stands about two feet taller than his usual height, broader and more imposing. Darker blue markings snake across his exposed torso, arms, and neck. Some are healed scars, while others form intricate patterns I don't recognize—tribal flames and diamond shapes of thorns and blades.

Two leather bands circle around his biceps, seeming to strain under the pressure of his bulging muscles. Hands are tipped with sharp claws, like nails that glint under the light.

Regardless of what they mean, they ignite an inferno inside of me, a raw, animalistic attraction I have no chance of ignoring.

I'm practically drooling as I stare at him.

My gaze trails over all those muscles, at him wearing loose black pants, the elastic band sitting low on his hips, and no shoes. At least he's wearing clothes, considering others don't seem to bother.

Then again, the obvious bulge in his pants, seeming to move, dancing down against one thigh, has me gasping with shock.

I straighten in my seat, attempting to appear unfazed by his arrival, even if my insides are doing somersaults. His face is still his, those piercing deep blue eyes boring into me, yet everything else about him screams warrior.

His blue gaze finds me, and there's a glint behind them as he strides over. The room seems a lot smaller with him in it.

Is it wrong that I'm becoming badly infatuated with a monster?

His powerful presence heats up the air, wrapping around me.

Kiri's instantly on her feet. "My Lord, it's so good to

see you tonight. Seems you're no longer the only lone midnight snacker. I'll bring you the usual?"

Killian nods, thanking her, then strolls over to me. My stomach is full, yet part of me feels empty just looking at him. There's something about his presence that always leaves me wanting more, yet he's brooding tonight, with darkness behind his gaze. He stops in front of me, scanning my face as if searching for an answer.

"Sage, I'll join you," he states in that deep, smooth voice that sends shivers down my spine.

"Okay," I answer, trying to keep my response steady, but I can hear the slight tremor in it, feel the quiver deep inside me—the one that has been keeping me up all night, remembering the things he did to me in the ritual. The seduction of his lips on me, his face buried between my thighs—just the thought has a delicious quiver fluttering deep in my stomach.

He pulls out a chair and sits across from me. He seems barely comfortable on it and might fit better on two seats, but he stays there.

"Couldn't sleep either?" he asks.

"Something like that," I admit, unable to stop staring at him in his monster form. At the intricate tattoos on his body, at how his muscles flex with each movement he makes. "I needed some normal food, and Howler suggested this place."

"Kiri's bakery is my go-to," he admits. "I struggle to sleep most nights and end up here."

She soon returns, placing a plate of assorted pastries, double the size of mine, and another cup of tea in front of

Killian. "Enjoy, my Lord," she says with a smile before leaving us alone.

Suddenly, it's just him and me again, and my breaths come too quickly.

He's looking at me, seeming to forget about his meal. His deep blue gaze lingers on my stronger violet hair, then focuses on my matching eyes... and I curl a lock around my finger.

"I'm guessing these changes are somehow related to the ritual?" I taunt, well aware that the ritual changed me.

"It's your Shadowfen emerging," he admits. "Being here in Blight, having the magic of the ritual in your body, your true self is finally showing itself." He pauses for a moment as though waiting for my response, but I'm slightly panicking on the inside, my heart going too fast. Then he continues, "It's beautiful. And I know it's a lot to take in, but—"

"Yeah, it is," I interrupt, shifting in my chair uncomfortably. "And I'm changing. I feel it inside me, too, and it's scaring me. You should have told me this would happen."

"Would it have made a difference?" he asks nonchalantly, which annoys me.

I blink at him, my heart pounding. "Well, yes."

He leans forward, his presence overwhelming and intense. "You don't want to understand who you really are?"

I hate the way he says that. It's too much, and maybe I'm not ready.

"I grew up my whole life being different, being ridiculed for it, bullied. Maybe I just want to stop being different."

Killian leans closer, the table groaning under the weight of his elbow resting on it, his stare dark and intense.

"You're not different, Sage. You're extraordinary. And extraordinary people face extraordinary challenges. You are coming into your strengths and abilities. It's exciting."

"Is it?" I exclaim sarcastically. His words hit me hard, making my heart beat faster.

His large hand reaches over, covering mine completely on the table, and the room seems to tilt. That single touch has butterflies twisting in my stomach, my gaze falling to his mouth, to his lips, that tongue that devoured me.

I might be swooning.

"And it's not fair to praise me when I'm mad at you," I admit, my insides tangled, my breaths speeding up the longer I stare into his dark, dangerous eyes. His gaze consumes me, the stroke of his fingers on the back of my hand teasing me.

A curl on the corner of his mouth has me hypnotized.

Breaths tear from my lungs, savage and fast.

"Maybe you should stop staring at me that way," I say, repeating something he said to me when I first arrived.

He breaks into a loud chuckle, the sound addictive. "We're way past that point, my pretty little monster.

We're true mates, and that means the craving for each other becomes insatiable if left ignored."

I gasp. "How long will the craving last?"

He shrugs, a predatory gleam in his gaze. "Varies on how much you're longing for me."

I burst out laughing.

He reaches over and cups the side of my face with a hand, his finger on my mouth, pushing his thumb past my lips and into my mouth. Something comes over me, something so primal that I draw him deeper into my mouth, sucking on him, my tongue running over him.

The lingering heat bursts through me, and I flush with shame at how much I enjoyed having him in my mouth.

"Tell me that you feel nothing right now," he teases with a low growl.

My body reacts before my mind can catch up, my lips closing tighter around his finger, my breath hitching. The taste of him, the feel of his skin against mine, sends tingles along my pussy.

I can't lie to him. I don't want to.

But admitting it, giving in to this savage hunger I feel for him, scares me more than anything else. Because once I do, there's no turning back.

I pull away slightly, his thumb slipping out. "I... I can't."

His eyes darken, something almost possessive taking over his expression. "You can't deny what we are, Sage. And you can't deny that you want this as much as I do."

He gets up swiftly, towering over me. Before I can

react, he lifts the whole table away from between us as if it weighs nothing. My heart thunders, and I scramble to my feet, suddenly nervous. One stride, and he's stolen the distance between us, the hunger on his face mirroring the arousal that's driven me crazy all day. Before I can take a breath, he has me in his arms, off my feet, his lips crashing down on mine.

The kiss is fierce, possessive, my body wavering against his, my hands clasping the back of his powerful neck. He holds me effortlessly, walking us to the rear of the room, where I remember the circular booth is, while never breaking our kiss. The room spins around me as he sets me on the table, not releasing me, his hands gripping my waist firmly.

I'm scared, trembling, but there's a thrill in it, a dark excitement that courses through me.

He breaks our kiss, but he's glued to me, his breath hot against my skin.

"You're mine, Sage," he growls. His voice is a low rumble that coaxes a purr from my chest, a sound I've never made before in my life.

What is going on with me?

"You've always been mine, and I'm never letting you go."

I swallow hard, my hands clutching his neck, trying to ground myself. The room feels too small, too hot, and all I can focus on is him, the lust in his gaze, the raw power in his touch.

"Maybe we're going too fast," I murmur.

He leans in, his lips brushing against my ear. "It's not

fast enough," he teases, his large hands roaming up my sides, leaving a trail of fire in their wake. "I've waited too long for this, for you. For years, I haven't lain with a woman, and now I know it's because I've been waiting for you."

I'm unsure what to say. I've never been with any man, but to hear that he's not slept with any other for so long draws me to him even more.

I know where this is going, yet I can't bring myself to stop it. The attraction between us is all-consuming.

He pulls back slightly, his gaze locking on to mine.

"I want everything from you." His tone is possessive and commanding. "I want it all, Sage."

"And what if I say no?" I challenge.

He grins, a dangerous, predatory smile. "You won't," he says confidently. "Because you feel it, too. This pull, this need."

I bite my lower lip, my heart slamming against my rib cage, hating that he's right.

He leans in again, his lips just inches from mine.

"And soon, you won't have any doubts."

His mouth claims mine again, his kiss like fire.

I'm lost in the passion... in him.

I know I'm falling into the abyss, just like in my nightmares, but I never thought it might be something I would enjoy so much.

CHAPTER
FIFTEEN
SAGE

"Did you think of me today, Sage?" Killian whispers in my ear, leaving me quivering. "About me licking your sweet little cunt? How perfectly my finger fits into your hole? Did you wonder what it'll be like when I fuck you?"

I shudder while fear and arousal steal my breath.

"Killian..."

He's in his monstrous blue form, towering over me, pushing himself to stand between my thighs. I part them for him easily, sitting on the edge of the table in the bakery.

I tell myself to drive him away, but he knows I won't... I see it in his smirk. I keep thinking about the inferno he awakened in me in the woods, the flicks of euphoria, and the lust coursing through my body might be the end of me, considering how desperately I now crave him.

"I asked a question," he commands, running that

wicked tongue along my neck, feeling somehow longer in his monster form.

Clawed fingers trace up my inner thighs, and a moan slips past my lips.

"Yes, I thought of you, too." My response comes rushing out.

"I missed you today," he teases, his body overshadowing me as I grasp his strong arms. "It was unbearable, giving you time and staying away."

"I-I... needed time after that ritual."

His touch slides higher, and I'm breathing quicker, lost with the idea of him being my first. It both scares and excites me. Then those claws brush across the apex of my thighs, coaxing a guttural noise out of me, a sound I've never made before.

My body's on fire under his touch, and I'm completely consumed by him.

His mouth is on mine again, and the kiss is magic... I'm floating, taking his tongue into my mouth, but something about it feels strange. When he flicks mine, I understand he has a forked tongue.

Gasping, I pull back.

His gaze locks on mine as he drags that forked tongue slowly over his lips. His tongue is long and slightly curved where it splits in two. I shake all over, not out of fear but because I'm horrified by the undeniable attraction I feel.

I'm throbbing for him, yet my head screams to run away.

"Don't be afraid." His blue eyes change to a midnight

sky. "This is just the beginning." His words are a dark promise. "The things I'm going to do to you..." He pauses, a visible shudder rolling over his powerful monster body. His hands slide up to my hips, and before I know it, I'm leaning in to meet him.

Our lips graze just as the sound of fabric ripping startles me. The leggings are being tugged down my hips. I gasp, pulling back slightly to see his claw rushing down on the side of the fabric, tearing it.

"Killian, what are you—"

He's relentless, stripping away the remnants of my leggings so fast it leaves me shaken as he yanks them off. I'm left bare-assed on the tablecloth, blushing like crazy, the cool air hitting my bare skin.

"You can't just—" I start, but his lips crash against mine, silencing my protest.

His kiss is fierce, possessive, and against my better judgment, I melt into him. His hands, rough and commanding, roam over my body. Slipping under my shirt, he finds my breasts and squeezes them. His claws flick my skin every now and then, not enough to hurt, but with just the right pressure to leave me moaning. His touch slides down to my thighs once more, parting my closed legs. His fingers trace deeper and deeper until I feel the graze of his talon.

"Please don't hurt me," I murmur, holding on to him for dear life, my body humming for him.

"Oh, my pretty little girl, I would burn down this world three times over before I let any harm come to you." Kneeling in front of me, he stares at my offering, grinning wickedly.

My face is on fire at the way he studies me, the flick of that long, forked tongue darting out, taking a stroke of my drenched pussy.

I moan instantly, the sensitive touch an explosion of sensations.

"This is what you do to me," he growls against my spread thighs, his breath hot against my skin. "You make me lose control."

Groaning, my hips give an involuntary rock, the bakery table wobbling beneath me. Every inch of me pleads. I protest and regain some level of sanity, but my body betrays me, and I lift my bent legs, balancing my heels on the edge of the table, giving him all the access.

His growl of approval vibrates through me.

"So pretty, so pink." He takes more licks, that tongue feeling so different from the last time, stronger and thicker. When he pushes into me, I cry out. I feel it wriggling against me, and I know I shouldn't be allowing this…

"I should be running…" The words pour out more to myself than to him.

"But you're not," he replies seductively. "You're right here with me, where you belong, with your cunt on my face."

The raw hunger of his words does something to me, unraveling the last threads of control I'm holding on to. I give in, knowing it's too late. I'm already being swept into his fire.

He presses in closer... Gods, that wicked tongue goes back inside me so deep that I feel it while his talons are on my clit, pinching it.

I cry out, shaking all over, and the battle of right and wrong about what I'm doing rushes over me.

The deeper he tongue-fucks me, the more he teases my clit, leaving me gasping for air. All those fears and doubts are forgotten. There's only him and me.

I hold my breath, listening to the wet sounds he makes as he devours me, my own cries escalating. The pressure deep in my stomach is a storm, growing while I try hard to muffle my screams.

It's impossible to hold on, and the moment his talons pry open my lips, giving himself more access, an explosive orgasm crashes through me. The scream I've been pushing down comes rushing out of me savagely. I convulse, my pussy quivering in Killian's mouth.

There's no stopping his hunger, and he licks me relentlessly while I close my eyes, fisting the tablecloth, riding the most beautiful climax. I'm flying through the heavens, never wanting this sensation to end. As if Killian can tell, he's now moved that devious mouth to my clit, sucking on it.

I keep on bursting, sparks of electricity jolting through me, and when I finally collapse onto the table, breathless, I smile.

"That was insane," I murmur to myself. When Killian rises to his feet from between my legs, my fear climbs through me once more at how easily I gave in to him.

That I let him do that to me in Kiri's bakery crashes over me with guilt.

He's standing before me in his monstrous form, and his pants barely contain the real monster bulging to escape. I shiver at the sight of his size, at the tip already sticking out from the band of the pants, blue and coated in slick.

Reality slams into me hard, and genuine fright rattles me down to my bones.

Am I ready for this?

My hands tremble.

I scramble off the table, the tablecloth slipping away as I slide down. Snatching it, I wrap it around my waist as I pull away from Killian, my heart banging loudly in my ears.

"No, we can't, not here," I whisper, glancing nervously at the kitchen door, using that excuse as my way out. My head starts to clear, and all those feelings I forgot come back like an avalanche.

His eyes darken with amusement and something more primal.

"Such a human response." He chuckles, a low, menacing sound. "In Blight, we embrace the union of two mates without shame."

I'm still gasping for air, trying to steady my speeding pulse.

"Well, I'm half-human, right? And that half isn't ready."

"The only reason I concede is that I know this is our first time." He stares at me darkly, that bulge in his pants not going down. "But after tonight"—he exhales, his voice a dangerous promise—"there'll be no pauses."

His words annoy me, and I want him to know that he's not in control of me. When he takes another step closer, I turn and bolt. Not my best move, but I know exactly where this will end, and as much as my body craves him, craves that huge beast pushing to escape his pants, I'm scared.

In the kitchen, I spot Kiri kneading dough, her head jolting up to me with surprise, no doubt at my abrupt entrance.

My face burns with embarrassment. "I'm sorry for..." I blurt out, then sprint out of the kitchen, rushing to the elevator.

Inside, I gasp, "Howler, take me to my room, now, fast."

"As you wish, Sage," Howler's calm voice replies.

As the doors shut, I swear I spot a blur of shadow dart out of the bakery kitchen door. The elevator zips me up, and I rub my arms, heart hammering in my chest, shaking uncontrollably. I teeter on the spot, unable to stand still from the nerves dancing under my skin.

The doors open, and I lunge out onto my floor just as I notice movement coming up from the circular stairs in the opposite hallway.

Killian!

Pivoting, I run for my life to my room, away from him, adrenaline chasing me.

"Sage, this isn't going to end how you think it will

just because you run to your room," he calls out in that dark, almost crazy voice.

Just like in the woods during the ritual, I charge ahead, my feet hitting the floor hard. At my room, I shove the door open and lunge inside, swinging around to shut it, but a massive blur of blue comes right on my heels. I recoil, having no chance to shut it. A small cry escapes my lips as the backs of my heels hit the bed, eyes huge.

Killian stands in the doorway, flicking on the lights, not breathing as heavily as me but lingering there casually.

"You can't keep running from me," he says, walking inside and kicking the door shut behind him. "I'm starting to worry that you're not interested in me." His grin is enchanting, doing its trick to unfurl the fear that tells me to back away.

"As I already said, you don't need to fear me," he explains softly. "But what you need to know is that with our ritual, the Shadowfen have a need to release their pent-up arousal. Otherwise, that deep hunger where you're dying to be fucked will soon turn into pain."

I blink, trying to unpack everything he just said, the word *pain* at the forefront. It leaves me wondering if he's attempting to trick me.

"So, you're helping me, then?" I smirk despite the fear knotting my stomach.

He tilts his head to the side, a slow, predatory smile spreading across his lips. "You could say that if it helps you."

As he moves closer, it's difficult to focus on

anything but the way his muscles shift under his skin with every step. He's not wearing much, just those loose black pants hanging low on his hips, his bulge still as huge as ever. And here I am, staring at it longer than I should be.

He strides closer, and I scramble onto the bed, bringing myself closer to his eye level. I press my hand against his chest to stop him, and his skin is a furnace under my touch. The move might have been a mistake, considering that single connection has my knees wavering. His hand cups over mine, then he lifts it to his mouth and kisses it tenderly.

"For my first time," I say with a shaky voice, fully aware of where this is heading. I'm not fooling myself into pretending I don't want it because I do. "I can't take you in this form." My gaze lowers between us.

His smile is beautiful and captivating, then he kisses my knuckles.

"You'd be surprised what you can take."

"Killian," I whisper.

"I'll take care of you, Sage." He grins, his eyes crinkling at the corners.

I'm quivering. His words are meant to comfort, but they only make the anticipation more intense. He leans in closer, his breath warm against my skin, and I shiver harder.

Then, it's me who leans in closer, my lips capturing his in a kiss that I embrace.

His hands wind around my middle, unwrapping the tablecloth from around my waist and tossing it aside.

Next, he wrenches my shirt up and over my head, breaking our kiss.

There's a tenderness in his movements and behind his gaze. Standing naked in front of a monster should terrify me, and it does slightly, but there are other feelings involved. Something so much deeper in the way I react to him, how he drives me crazy with his obsession over me, how he shows me those snippets of absolute tenderness that have me swooning for him.

I reach up and cup his strong blue face, so much larger against my palm, and he leans in. This powerful Shadowfen, soft under my touch, is beautiful.

At that same moment, I sense him shuddering, and instantly, he's shifting before my eyes, the blue vanishing from his skin, his size reducing, those scars on his body remaining, but not the tattoos. In a heartbeat, he's back to the Killian I first met in Nightingale Village. A Viscount, I feared at first. Now, I'm naked and pulling him closer.

Our mouths clash, and he kisses me with untold passion. My stomach tickles, and I can't ignore how desperately I desire him. He knows it, too, and I don't have to say it. The words are confirmed in my actions. It feels right, even though I'm so nervous I could cry.

In moments, he has me in his arms and off my feet, then lays me on the bed. He vanishes into the bathroom for a moment, then returns with a long strip of fabric, or more like a tie from a robe, which begs the question… there's a robe in my bathroom?

Before I can ask him, he's standing at the side of the

bed, weaving the fabric into the intricate holes of the headboard carved into waves.

"Should I be worried?" I ask, twisting around, but he's already returning and gently taking one hand.

"I won't let you run away from me again. I can see it in your eyes that you will." Grinning, he has my wrist wound in seconds before I can wrench free from him.

"Killian, this isn't necessary."

He reaches over, taking my other hand with more firmness as I resist him. In seconds, my arms are over my head, tied up.

"Really?" I ask, pulling against my restraints.

He grins, staring down at my body. "You're too captivating to be real."

Then he drops his loose pants, and my response flatlines.

His hidden beast pops out.

I gasp in response to the thickness of his erection, the bulging vein, the head so bulbous it's never going to get inside me. Based on the one I've seen before in the village, they don't even compare. How in the world is Killian's so huge?

"I'm slightly terrified now," I admit truthfully, while he palms that creature between his legs, takes a seat on the edge of the bed, and buries his face in my neck.

"I can sense the monster in you, the darkness we all have." His tongue strokes down to my collarbone, and he continues down my body, not rushing.

My heart's in my throat.

"You can tell from kissing me?" I stiffen, staring at

him, but he never pauses kissing me. His mouth clasps around a nipple, and I moan, writhing against him, the earlier euphoria still there, as though it lives permanently in my body.

"From your scent," he confirms. "She's there, a real darkness that lingers. You just need to be patient until she comes out."

I clear my throat. "I don't think there's any rush."

He gets up and climbs on the bed near my feet, pushing them apart, and that fierce stare traces over my body, his lips curling upward.

"I want to meet that side of you, to know all of you. To understand the Shadowfen side of you."

Unsure what to say, I can't imagine what to expect, but having him press my legs wider, his hand reaching down between them, my body trembles.

"You're so wet and ready for me." Clasping his large cock, he leans his whole body over me, pushing his tip against me and rubbing it over my slick lips.

I feel like I can't breathe as he stares into my eyes, one hand perched on the bed alongside me, the other guiding himself into me. He presses his lips to mine, so faint this time that it leaves me dizzy.

"Sage, I am a Shadowfen who is commanding, in control, savage, but we are more alike than you realize. And tonight is about giving you a memory you will never forget."

We're kissing again as he guides his cock to my entrance. I wriggle beneath him, pulling against the restraints on my wrists. He holds me there for a moment, breaking our kiss, then he pushes into me.

Forcing my breathing to remain even, my mouth falls open, and I pant. He's focused on spreading me, pushing deeper. His fingers are on my clit, rubbing it. I release a cry, driving my breasts up against his chest. His mouth moves to a nipple, tucking it between his teeth.

Carnal pleasure thumps through me, taking up residence where he's plunging into me. Gasping for air, I'm convinced I might pass out. He's going slowly, pulling back out, then pushing in again, the strain of spreading me leaving me moaning for more.

"I love how tightly your cunt squeezes my cock." A low growl echoes from his chest. "Fuck, Sage! I'm going to fuck you so hard."

I writhe, my chest rising and falling. He covers me in kisses while pushing deeper, as if fighting something. Then, in a moment of gasping, something tight inside me unfurls, and he's driving into me.

A scream of pure pleasure washes over me. I've heard stories that a girl's first time is more painful than pleasurable, except this is the opposite for me. The pain only adds to the arousal I've been feeling from earlier.

"How are you feeling?" he asks, pausing once more, buried so deep inside me I've never felt fuller.

"Like I'm about to come again, like nothing I've ever felt before."

"My good girl," he says.

Those words shouldn't elicit excitement in me, a

desperate need to please him, but they do. I need this more than I ever thought I would.

Killian's blazing stare is on me, watching my every reaction. He pulls out of me, then drives back in.

I bite down on my lower lip, mostly to stop from screaming endlessly. He pushes back in and out again, the motion picking up in pace. Each time he plunges back into me, spreading me wider, a delicious ripple courses through me.

Never in my life have I imagined that I'd need a cock inside me so fiercely.

But I crave this.

I'm needy.

Desperate.

He's moving faster now. I pant, my body rocking as I hold on to the tie keeping me prisoner for him.

"You're mine, Sage, and I'll take such good care of you."

I press back into the mattress, feeling the real stretch of his cock driving into me again and again. Whimpering spills from my lips while Killian's face is one of concentration, his gaze hazed over as though he's lost himself to me.

His mouth is down on my neck once more, that tongue licking me, and he's picking up speed. The whole bed shudders, slamming into the wall with each thrust into me.

Writhing and crying out, he buries himself so deeply into me, keeping me pinned down. Moisture floods between my legs, and I feel it seeping out each time he pulls out.

His mouth curls around the meaty part of my neck and shoulders, teeth scraping my skin.

He's owning me, fucking me, dominating me, and when he bites down into me, sharp teeth breaking into my shoulder, I scream out. With it, my body shatters from how fast he's going now. Thrust after thrust, he takes me, his tongue licking at my bite, sucking on it.

I hate myself for how much I love it. That grip I've had over myself now unleashes, and I'm coming, cries rushing past my mouth. Shuddering under him only seems to make him wilder, picking up his speed. Pulling back from me, he licks the blood from his teeth.

I'm shaking, coming for longer than I expected.

He's on his knees, hands around my thighs, lifting my ass off the bed. The growls from his throat echo around us, the tightness on his face as he never stops fucking me.

I'm tied up, his captive, and he's making me his. I wasn't expecting this... in truth, I had no idea what to expect. But I'm moaning, trembling, sweat covering my brow as the intensity never wavers.

Lust coats his expression, his snarls loud now, fingers digging into my thighs as he holds me to meet his every thrust as he drives in deeper.

I've barely come down from my orgasm when he lifts one leg up by the ankle with both hands and twists me onto my side.

Quivering against him, I'm hungry for more, and when he pulls out of me, I whine.

His hands stroke my ass, squeezing as he flips me onto my stomach, my hands still secured. I'm face and chest down, ass high, as he pushes himself between my thighs.

"I'm going to fuck you until you come again," he promises, his fingers sliding along the slickness of my pussy, replaced by his trunk-like cock.

"Killian," is all I manage as I struggle for air, my body shuddering with arousal.

His cock is pushing back deep into me, his hands gripping my hips, guiding me. Moving to give him easier access, I still can't believe how desperately I need him.

"Oh Gods!"

"Do you like this?" he purrs, then breaks into a dark laughter as he drives into me. This time it's different. He's fucking me like a damn animal, thrusting, with my ass rocking back against him.

My cries grow louder, full of explosive need. I feel the pressure building with each thrust, the overwhelming sensation that I'm so full that I'll explode. The grip of his hands on my hips is stronger, bigger, as something sharp digs into my hips.

I glance back, which is difficult to do as I'm breathing so hard, my arms tied up, and seeing Killian in his blue monster form leaves me startled.

"I knew you'd take me easily," he coos while he buries himself to the hilt inside of me, balls slamming into my pussy.

"Fuck!" Lava consumes me, and I feel a slight trepidation that I'm being fucked by a monster. The sensation of his shaft feels different, too, almost as though there are bumps on his cock, the friction of him parting my lips, driving into me and flooding me. It's painful but sweet, and already that delicious tightness in my stomach rises, building up to another climax.

"You're such a good little monster." He rails into me, sending waves of pleasure through my body. "So responsive to my cock."

I jerk against the binds around my wrists, the licks of my screams pouring from my mouth, the kind that leaves me burning up.

"Please," I exhale, wanting my hands free so I can move closer, to touch him, to explore.

"I'm going to come in your cunt, Sage." He's making those hungry, growling sounds again. "Then next time, I'll come in your ass and your mouth."

Wait, what did he just say?

Panic rises through me as I remember some of those elf books I read back in the village, how they intended to breed the woman they captured.

"You're going to breed me?" My question is a jumble of words and my rushing breaths.

"You are mine now, Sage." He's grunting, claiming me endlessly. His fingers move down to find my clit. They press down, teasing me as he continues to fuck me.

Fear, mingled with a desperation to climax again, twists into a confusing mess inside me. The more he strokes me, plunging that massive cock into me, the closer I reach the edge.

I can't hold back, and I'm shuddering, my breaths coming out in ragged pants as my body shakes.

Snarling, he slams into me so hard my whole body jolts, the bed jostling beneath us. Suddenly, he pauses inside of me, roaring. His cock pulses inside of me, the warmth of his cum pouring out.

We're both on a high, my throat raw, and that pressure of him filling me to the brim, the orgasm tearing through me as the room begins to tilt.

I'm struggling to breathe with the intensity of my climax, coming harder than before, so much longer, too.

"Take it all," he snarls. "Milk my cock."

When he finally releases me, drawing his cock out, he swings me around onto my back so fast the room spins with me.

Thick, blue jets of cum spurt out of his big cock, more of it pumping across my chest, my body, more splashing over my face. He growls, stroking his dick. I smell the muskiness of his cum, taste its saltiness that finds my lips, and lick it out of curiosity, still floating on a high.

I'm burning up as I float down, collapsing on the bed, exhausted.

Leaning back on his heels, there's a mess of cum between us, mostly on me, and he's staring down between my legs, smiling. He reaches down, running his fingers along my inner thighs and seeming to push his cum back inside me.

Watching him, I say nothing, still shocked by the

whole ordeal, still buzzing from the elation. The grin on his lips widens.

"Absolutely beautiful to see your cunt covered and dripping with my cum. And I'm happy I was your first."

I attempt to speak, but I'm completely exhausted, and as though he picks up on it, he's getting off the bed.

At that moment, I take true stock of his monster cock, and I almost choke at the sight, knowing why I already feel the soreness between my thighs. Thicker and longer than his human cock, it's pale blue and ribbed all the way down the shaft. How did he even force that into me?

"Let me clean you up." His hands gently remove the restraint from my wrists, and there are pins and needles in them as soon as he frees me. He leans down, kissing the skin that's raw. "I will kiss them until they heal." Then he scoops me into his arms and walks us into the shower. He holds me under the water's spray, never taking his eyes off me.

"The years I've waited to fuck someone were worth every second," he purrs. "I want to fuck you, again and again, all night."

"Aren't you exhausted?" I'm convinced I'll pass out.

"Not tonight. It's your first time, so we'll rest now." He sets me down on wobbly feet, and I hold on to him as my shaking legs refuse to hold me. "I've got you," he whispers.

I'm staring at him, my thoughts racing with what just happened, asking, "So, you came inside me. You want me pregnant?"

He's grinning like that would be the most amazing

news in the world to him. "My dream is to have a large family, so yes, but don't worry for now. Pregnancy for Shadowfen is a long process of teaching your body to accept us before you will release your eggs."

I'm slightly hyperventilating. "I-I'm not ready for a family."

He runs his large palm down my body, cleaning me of his cum, even between my thighs. "There's nothing to worry about. Some females are known to take years of breeding before they are with child."

"I'm really not a fan of that word."

He laughs at me.

Perhaps it's exhaustion or pure adrenaline, but when he leans down to leave a gentle kiss on my brow, then my lips, I grip him tighter, unsure at what stage I found myself staring at Killian as if I can't bear to be away from him.

Yet my chest squeezes impossibly hard each time I meet his gaze.

CHAPTER
SIXTEEN

SAGE

I lie in the darkness of my room, Killian pressed tight against my back, his breath warm on my neck. His fingers gently stroke my wrist, where it's still slightly sore from being tied up.

I can't believe I just had sex. With a monster, no less.

"Did I hurt you too much?" he asks.

"Is it strange if I admit that I enjoyed the pain?" I murmur, curling in on myself, while he draws me closer to him, embracing me with his body.

His lips brush my ear. "Pleasure is never enjoyed without a sliver of pain."

"You know what else is strange?" I say, turning my head slightly to look at him, where he still holds his monster form. I should be scared, but his appearance is becoming a real turn-on. "You're not like the Viscount I first met in Nightingale Village. I mean, you look like him in human form, but you don't really behave that way anymore. Even the way you speak is more relaxed."

"Do any of us really show our true selves when away from home?"

I think about his words, about how, in the village, I always put on a mask around others to avoid gaining attention. Alina had seen more of the real me than anyone else there... well, except for my mom. Now, I wonder about both of them and if they're safe. I suspect Alina would be cheering for me if I told her I just lost my virginity.

"I have appearances to maintain on Earth," Killian continues, drawing my attention back to him. "The Viscount is who you first met, who had a role to play, but the Shadowfen you're with now, that's who you're going to fall in love with."

A laugh escapes my lips, but he's not laughing with me.

"That's very forward," I admit, glancing back again at the hard expression on his face as he studies me, something I'm becoming more accustomed to—the healed scar that runs across his brow, the curls of deep blue ink reaching up along his neck and collarbone. Next to him, I'm tiny, yet my fear has transformed into something more profound, something that resembles an attraction I never expected.

"I'm a Shadowfen who always looks *forward*," he says sarcastically. "The past holds nothing for me."

We lie in silence, his response toying with my mind while he tightens his hold around my middle, his leg draping over mine, giving me zero opportunity to leave if I tried.

"What happened in the past?" I ask out of curiosity.

Silence.

I assume he's not going to respond. Part of me guesses he may have lost many loved ones during the Great Desolation on their home world.

"For a long time, I traveled to other worlds, searching for my intended mate, as she wasn't on my home planet. Then I thought I found her... someone who swept me away so fast that I stood no chance to doubt anything," he begins. "I foolishly believed she felt the same way."

Silence stretches between us, impatience getting the better of me.

"Did she hurt you?" My throat is tight at hearing him speak of his attraction to someone else.

"She passed away, and only after that did I discover she was going to break up with me." He pauses, and my insides clench at his pain. "It took me a long time to come to terms with the hurt and grief. I honestly believed she was the one, and when I lost her, I threw myself into hunting or fighting anything and anyone who stood in my way. Nyko wasn't much of a help as he encouraged me, joining in alongside me." He chuckles as if remembering the moments.

"It's only in more recent years that I tried to find my true mate again. And I had to be certain she was the one when I found her." There's hardness in his voice, as though he's worked out how to separate his emotions from such a heart-wrenching experience.

"I'm so sorry you went through that." Draping my

arm around his, I draw his hand up to my face and kiss it, then glance back at him.

"I guess that's why you insisted on the ritual with me, to make sure?"

He nods, then kisses the top of my head while holding me possessively, as if he has no intention of ever letting me go. There's something painful in knowing he suffered, that his heart was ripped out, his feelings not returned.

"The past is just that, Sage. My focus is you and our future," he says with strong conviction. Does he assume I'm going to run away from him?

In all honesty, I'm taking it day by day, still dealing with my own changes that I can't even think about what the future will bring. Let alone what having a true mate really entails.

After a long pause, I ask, "How would I find out who my father is? To discover if he's still alive and maybe... if he'll even want to see me?"

He stiffens against my back and swallows loudly. "We have a whole section in the Chamber of Tomes listing everyone before the Great Desolation."

I frown, figuring I may not know his name, but maybe Mom took his surname? Do monsters have them? "Hmm, do the Shadowfen have surnames? I don't even know my father's name."

"It's not a common practice," he confirms. "So, for me, I am Killian Venator, while Nyko carries no surname. It depended on our ancestor's positioning in the kingdom. Only those close to the royal family were permitted to choose a surname. These days, it's not much of an issue as most go by first name only. Our identities are easily revealed by our blood now."

"Perhaps I can have mine tested, see if there's a way to match it with others in your records," I ask, hopeful.

"That's possible." He says nothing more, as if the topic bores him. But it gives me direction, knowing what I'll search for tomorrow on the vessel.

"Thanks, I'll do some investigating."

After a while, he says, "Sleep now."

I shut my eyes, trying to push away the pity, but it lingers in my thoughts. His grip on me is firm, and I find a strange comfort in it.

For the first time in too long, I let myself drift into a deep sleep, feeling safer than I ever have.

I wake up with a gasp in my throat, disoriented and momentarily unable to remember where in the world I am. The darkness of the room presses in, memories rushing back, and I call out softly, "Killian?"

No response.

I sit up, the cool sheets slipping off me, and my eyes catch the faint sliver of moonlight coming through the slightly ajar balcony door. Faint voices drift into the room.

Rubbing my eyes, I push back the covers and swing my legs over the side of the bed. The floor is cool beneath my feet as I pad softly over to the balcony. Grabbing a shirt I'd left on the chair, I drag it down over my head and body. The closer I get to the door, the more distinct the voices become, though I can't make out what they're saying.

I step out onto the balcony, the cool night air washing over me. My gaze is drawn to the railing, and I glance down at the scene on one of the lowest balconies near the water.

Killian stands there, unmistakable even in the dim light pouring out from inside the vessel. His blue skin seems to absorb the moonlight, making him appear almost magical.

Across from him is Nyko, elbows propped up behind him against the railing. His wild, chestnut hair flutters in the breeze, and even from my vantage point, it's impossible to ignore those sharp angles of his face, the heavy eyebrows, the perfectly shaped lips with a dimple in his chin. I may not see all the details from up here, but I've memorized him from our first meeting.

He's ridiculously handsome, yet he gives off a crazier vibe than Killian, which worries me, especially with the butterflies fluttering in my stomach at the sight of him.

"Think she knows?" Nyko asks, the wind carrying his voice to me.

Killian shrugs. "Doubt it, but I think we should tell her."

"Wait, didn't you just say she hates the idea of being one of us? So, you don't think it's better to tell her once we get there?" Nyko's tone is incredulous, straightening his posture.

Are they talking about me?

Killian doesn't answer right away.

Nyko turns to stare out across the dark water. "Wolfe said he's worried if she knows the truth, she won't go through with it."

My heart clenches, and my stomach knots. They're talking about me... I just know it. What are they hiding from me?

"Fuck that. I don't feel right keeping this from her. She's asking questions, and it's gutting me to hide things from her."

Ice fills my veins. What are they talking about? I need to know.

Nyko barks a laugh. "So, what's your plan? For all of us to keep floating on this damn vessel for eternity?"

Killian huffs, gaze lowering, hands curled into fists. "You think I don't know what's at stake?"

"Maybe you're right." Nyko changes his tune. "We tell her, let her know what she's getting into. I guess she has every right to know who her father is, so we go in with her, knowing what she's walking into."

My breath catches, and I gasp, pulling back from the railing instantly in case they look up.

My father?

Why the fuck would they keep such a secret from me? And when I asked Killian about my father, he said nothing. Asshole!

Shaking from anger and fear that snaps around me, I

glance down once more, but now it's only Killian on the balcony alone, grasping the railing.

Their words hang over me, suffocating. They know who my father is, and they're hiding it.

A sudden movement next to him catches my eye. Emerging from inside is Nyko, the blades he's tucking into his belt catching the light. Killian is busy fiddling with something in his hand. He presses his palm to the side of his neck, sticking something white to his flesh, which vanishes into his skin almost immediately. He turns to Nyko and does the same. Nyko tilts his head aside, accepting the gesture, then unleashes a howl and suddenly leaps over the railing, disappearing into the dark waters below.

I gasp, gripping the balcony railing. Moments later, Killian follows suit, diving into the sea with the same fluid movement. They vanish from sight, leaving only ripples in the water.

I stand there, feeling the cool breeze tug at my hair, trying to process what I've just witnessed, what I've heard. The boat appears still, not traveling, the night eerily calm.

What are they doing?

A sick feeling stirs in my gut as I turn to go back inside. I catch sight of my reflection in the glass doors. Violet eyes glow back at me.

My violet eyes.

I pause and stare at myself, freezing in place.

"I'm changing too quickly."

It's the same hue that's deepened the color of my

hair. I run my fingers through the strands, unable to ignore how much darker they are now.

How long before I turn into a full monster? It shouldn't scare me, but losing control does. There's no way I can ever return to Nightingale Village with how different I've become, and that hurts.

Fear grips me as I stand there, staring at my reflection, while the weight of what's coming for me presses down on my shoulders.

Exhaling loudly, I turn away from the door and head inside, yet my reflection stays with me. That same reminder of how out of control my life really is. I slip back into bed, curling up under the blankets, feeling more lost than ever. I don't think I can sleep, not when I'm worried about what truths are coming my way.

Whether I want them to or not...

Nyko

The great sea of Nerya swallows me whole, its chilling embrace snapping around my body like a thousand tiny needles. Named after the first Queen of Blight, these waters are ancient, powerful, and treacherous. And why we're going hunting.

Most of our land is now submerged, but the course

Howler's on keeps us over the original ocean, a vast abyss beneath us.

Muscles taut, my senses heighten, the magic gills on my neck start to pulse. The first breath of water I suck into my lungs always feels like drowning. My body rebels against the intrusion, lungs seizing up. A few moments later, the sensation regulates, and I breathe easily underwater.

An explosion of water surges past me as Killian zips by, a blur of blue against the dark ocean. His powerful arms slice through the sea, legs kicking with incredible speed, propelling him forward effortlessly.

He'd wanted to hunt tonight, and I haven't seen him starve for a kill in years. When he came to my room, he'd been bouncing on his toes, pent-up energy radiating off him in waves.

"I'm ready to fucking destroy something," he'd said. "I feel like I could carry the damn ocean on my back."

Never one to turn down the chance for a fight, I leapt at the chance to join him. Now, I pump my legs and arms, catching up to him.

Killian's different, moving faster underwater than usual. I typically leave him behind, eating my dust. Tonight, I'm fighting to keep up with him. *What the fuck, Killian?*

With the light strapped to my head, the beam carves through the darkness, as does Killian's, making following him easy.

He fucked Sage last night; that thought is massive in my thoughts. I smelled her on him the moment I opened the door to him. Jealousy still burns inside me that he got to that sweet girl first, and here I am, craving her like a damn fool. After inhaling her scent on him, I knew without a doubt what I had to do—make her mine as well. She just doesn't know it yet, and that was part of the reason I agreed to go hunting in the middle of the damn night.

Fish glide around us, translucent bodies, making it easier for them to hide from predators. But they're not what I'm searching for tonight. I dive deeper, Killian right ahead of me. The adrenaline coursing through me is intoxicating, yet that nagging jealousy beneath it all drives me to move faster. Chest pumping, I scan the ocean for my prey. Tonight, we're the apex predators in this ocean.

The water around us is alive with movement, the pressure deepening around me. Long serpentine fish swish below us, along with small and fast flickering underwater fireflies.

A dark shape emerges from the depths, and before I can make it out, Killian's already diving toward it. I stare down, my light revealing a mossy green fish as thick as our bodies, its mouth gaping open, filled with arm-long incisors. It's coming right for Killian, mouth agape to devour him whole.

I pause for a moment, assessing if he needs my help, but Killian is a force of nature, his movements precise and deadly as his swords manifest in his hands. I've always thought of them as cheating in battle. He wields them like they're part of his body, moving with precision.

With swift, calculated strikes, Killian decapitates the creature, the water clouding with blood. He grabs the severed fish by the tail, tying it to a rope from his belt with practiced ease. He attaches a float to it—a device that expands automatically with oxygen and drags the carcass up to the surface. We don't waste kills; everything goes to feed our people.

As he turns for his next kill, my attention catches something lurking in the shadows, watching me. It starts to circle me, and a grin spreads across my face.

It's a Derokar, exactly what I'm after. These bastards are tough, territorial, and will shred anything apart in their way.

What a good day for you to die.

I charge toward the creature, drawing the blades from my belt, aiming for the beast that comes at me from the pitch-black depths. Its teeth glow with an eerie light, razor-sharp and ready to tear me apart. A sharp fin runs along its back, jagged spikes down its sides carrying toxins potent enough to paralyze.

The Derokar jolts closer.

I dodge to the side, my legs kicking ferociously, slashing the blades through the water, aiming for its exposed flank. It's fast, but I'm faster, my movements a blur as I strike again and again. My knives rip through its tough hide, but it retaliates, a spiked tail whipping toward me, slamming into me, sending me tossed aside through the water.

Fuck.

Finally stopping myself, I twist around to find the

Derokar's charging this way, its body wriggling in its fast approach. I duck under it at the last second but not before its teeth drag across my arm. Pain shoots through me.

I jam my blades upward, tearing through its underbelly. Blood fills the water quickly, a dark cloud that will soon attract a swarm of other beasts. This one convulses, snapping out of the way, but I don't let up. I dart after it, my legs and arms working overtime, sinking my knives deeper into its underbelly wound, tearing into it with ferocity.

It bucks violently, but it doesn't last long.

Tucking the blade into my belt, I thrust my arm into its lesion, past ribs and organs, until I feel its heart, still under my fingers. With a swift yank, I tear the small bag these creatures produce, right next to its heart. For something so ugly, they are highly prized for the beauty they create. I wrench it out, shoving the creature aside, and feel the small parcel in my hand with two pearls inside.

Killian appears beside me, his eyes gleaming with the thrill of the hunt. He gives me a nod, and I know it's time to head back. We can't stay here much longer with all this blood in the water. I clutch the pearls in my fist and shove myself upward.

When I glance down, I spot the swarm of at least a dozen Derokar circling. They'll come after us. Shoving the sack with pearls into the pocket of my pants, I swim frantically, pushing myself until my head breaks the surface. The boat's farther away.

Hell.

"You had to kill a damn Derokar, didn't you?" Killian growls.

We swim wildly while snatching the ropes tied to floats and his kills, dragging them with us. I dive in and help him snatch them up.

"Says you who bloodied the sea so heavily tonight that one dead Derokar would barely be noticed. They're predators and come at the smell of blood."

He grins at me, knowing he regrets nothing.

I don't either, so we push on, swimming like maniacs to reach the boat with our haul.

Just as we scramble out of the waters back up near the balcony, throwing ourselves over the railing, the swish of the sea behind us shows it's swarming with creatures.

"Like hell," he growls, desperately hauling in the catch, one hand after another, dragging on his catch.

I rush to help. Some of the dead fish are already being chomped on by those bastards. The water's become a frenzy of fins, tails, and blood as the monsters of the deep fight to reach their meal. While we pull out half of what Killian killed, the rest is lost.

"That was damn close," I mutter, stabbing my hand into my pocket to collect the pearls still in their milky mucus bag. I rip them open, collect my perfect mauve pearls, and toss the rest into the ocean. These are rare, and once upon a time, only royalty was permitted to own such beauty.

Killian chuckles, a dark sound that rumbles from his chest. He glances at the pearls in my hand, his eyes narrowing with interest. "Nice catch. Worth the trouble?"

I grin with triumph. "Always worth it," I reply, curling my hand around them. We move indoors, and Killian orders Howler to call for help to fetch the catches. I turn to watch him begin to haul the massive fish inside from the balcony, his energy endless.

"Are you all right?" I ask. "You're acting stranger than usual tonight."

"Never been fucking better," he snaps back, tossing the fish inside through the open balcony doors like they weigh nothing, and those bastards weigh ten times our weight.

"Well, seeing you're high on fuck knows what, I'll let you be," I grunt at him, not sure what's gotten into him. Sure, he spent the night fucking Sage, but since when does using all your energy during a fuck feed your adrenaline to crazy heights?

Killian doesn't respond, lost in whatever frenzy he's in, and I shake my head.

I stroll back to my room, my mind wandering. Staring at the two mauve pearls in my palm, I think of Killian and Sage, wondering how soon it'll be my turn to impress her.

CHAPTER
SEVENTEEN
SAGE

The morning sun filters brightly through the windows of my room, and I've been up for hours, washed and dressed, and enjoyed fresh fish in the hall upstairs for breakfast. My thoughts are still jumbled with the memories of last night after having the best night of my life with Killian. Then things went downhill.

Killian and Nyko's conversation consumes my thoughts, all coming back to them knowing who my father is.

They've been keeping secrets from me. Anger pricks along the back of my neck. I naively took them at face value, but that's my fault, isn't it? I should be used to everyone taking me for granted.

Stepping out of my room, I say, "Howler, take me to Killian's room, please."

"Morning, Sage. Unfortunately, he's at a meeting and can't be disturbed."

Groaning, I suggest, "Okay, what about Nyko?"

"He's attending the same meeting. They will be available later in the day."

Sighing heavily, I go with my final option, figuring, based on the conversation last night, he might actually be the best person to talk to.

"Please tell me Wolfe isn't with them, too?"

"Lord Wolfe is running late, so you might be able to catch up if you hurry."

"All right, let's go." I rush ahead down the corridor before he's even given me instructions.

Howler guides me through a part of the ship I haven't seen before. The walls are pristine white, with more windows offering views of the vast ocean outside. I hurry up a set of grand stairs, complete with red carpet. It's all fancy, so out of place for this vessel, and it makes me feel even more of an outsider.

Eventually, I reach a set of double doors. I hesitate for a moment before knocking. It opens, and there stands Wolfe, looking ready to walk out. His burning amber eyes widen, then he grins, melting my knees. His presence is overwhelming, and for a moment, I forget why I'm here, lost in being so close to this powerful Shadowfen. He's in his human form, dressed in dark clothing, including a button-up deep navy shirt with a metal band around his thick bicep, just like Killian wore back in Nightingale Village.

"Sage, a pleasant surprise." That dark, husky voice of his isn't helping me.

"Can we talk, please?" I ask, trying to steady my voice.

He nods, that grin widening. "Of course, but we will have to do it walking. I'm late for a meeting and have something I must drop off up in the woods first. My assistant, Grimm, has the day off, leaving me in disarray."

"Of course, and thank you," I add quickly. "I know where the woods on the vessel are, if you want me to drop something off for you instead, so we can talk?"

He pauses, studying me. "You would do that?"

I nod while he seems taken aback by my generosity. It can't be too hard.

"You continue to surprise me, Sage." He puts his hand into the pocket of his pants, takes something small out, and then places a black stone in my palm. As he pulls away, his fingers graze mine, just enough to send a buzz right through me. Fast and all-consuming, I draw in a rapid breath.

His hand grasps mine, closing it over the stone, and he holds me for a long pause, staring at me, his gaze dipping to my mouth.

"Th-That was kind of strange," I say.

A grin quirks his mouth, and I want to kiss him, press myself against him, and discover if he tastes as delicious as Killian.

Wait. What in the world? Where did that come from?

I think of how he made me feel over dinner when I first arrived, so is this him manipulating me again? Caution spears through me, knowing I need to be careful.

He's licking his lips, and I'm clearing my throat, fighting the urge not to forget why I came to see him.

"It's all right," he explains. "Your body's going through changes."

"Oh." Is that what I'm experiencing? "I thought it might have been you influencing me again."

He laughs, though his gaze holds me captive, glimmering under the lights.

"You know, every Shadowfen has a level of ability to control shadows. Most can move shadows, create puppet shows on a wall, but some are really powerful. Like transforming into a shadow completely, or like mine, I can manipulate it to do my will, allowing me to touch others from a distance or move objects, to mention a few." He reaches over and strokes my cheek, his touch as tender and sensual as his shadow had been the other night. "What about yours, Sage?" He offers me a soft look and takes my elbow, leading us into a walk.

I shake my head, still coming to terms with his reveal about shadows, racking my mind if I've had any encounters with shadows.

"I haven't experienced anything."

Then we're walking quickly, and I'm speeding along just to keep up with his long strides.

"Do you know who my real father is?" The words blurt out, but he's rushing me, and I'm tired of being kept in the dark.

His expression darkens slightly, glancing over at me as if it's something he wasn't expecting me to ask.

"This is a much larger discussion to be had, and I

can't do it justice in a few moments. I will come find you after my meeting, all right?" His words are final, his face slightly pale. Then, with a final squeeze of my elbow, he strides ahead, vanishing down a dark hallway.

"That went terribly," I mumble to myself. He couldn't run away faster.

Frustration bubbles up inside me. He's going to avoid me, isn't he? What annoys me the most is that next to him, my body reacts in ways it shouldn't. I'm drawn to him, and I hate that I find him so attractive that I forget my thoughts.

But he's a monster, and I need to remind myself where I am—a dangerous world.

I grew up my whole life believing I'd never find out who my father was. Now that I have the chance, I'm not going to give up on it. He *will* tell me.

By the time I'm up on the top floor, knocking on the heavy wooden doors that lead into the ritual room, my stomach knots return. There's no response, just the eerie silence, and I glance down at the stone in my hand.

What the hell are you, and why should I bother delivering you for Wolfe?

Yet, here I am, pushing the door open. I guess it's because I'm honest to a fault, even to a monster.

A soft breath behind me makes me pause.

I turn, but there's no one there. I recall Wolfe's explanation about Shadowfen possessing a shadow ability, and my skin suddenly creeps.

Entering the vast room, I call out, "Hello?" My voice

is swallowed by the whistling breeze swishing through the rustling branches, a chill rushing up my arms.

The woods stretch out before me, their eeriness amplified by the stormy sky visible through the open roof overhead. I stick to the stone path passing the forest, glancing at the flowers that seem out of place in this space. Farther to my left, I notice huts—offices, perhaps, or maybe living quarters?

With Wolfe's hurried departure, my hand in my pocket, gripping the stone tightly, I hurry along.

The wind picks up, rustling the leaves and crashing into my back.

I knock on the first door. No answer. The second, the third—nothing. Irritation dances through me.

Finally, at the last door, I spot a metal latch on the door. Opening it, I discover a compartment with a couple of other stones and two scrolls all the way down where I can't reach. A makeshift postal box, I guess. I slip the stone inside, hearing it clunk against the metal base. As I turn to leave, the breeze becomes stronger, the trees swaying wildly.

Strangely, I feel the sway of the vessel for the first time since boarding, and glancing over through the glass walls reveals the roughness of the sea, the white peaks, and the dark curtain of rain in the distance.

Time to get out of this area.

I quicken my pace, my eyes darting to the shifting shadows amid the trees.

Then, I see it—a shape in the forest, something that looks like an animal but darker, more sinister. My heart skips a beat. This can't be right. It's a trick of the light, and as another gust of wind blows, the shadow vanishes.

I pivot toward the exit, only to find the door closed. Panic surges through me. I left it open, didn't I? *Stop panicking. It had to be the wind from the open ceiling to the outdoors.*

Something slithers out of the woods near the doorway, blocking my path.

I know I shouldn't be scared. But my skin crawls as I watch the creature that's easily six feet long—slithering on its belly, then rising on its back legs. It has an elongated face, sharp and reptilian, like a snake. I hate snakes. Memories of the few I saw in my village flood my mind.

Fear strangles my lungs, and I start backing away, knowing there's no one else up here with us. The creature comes at me fast, falling to the ground, slithering toward me, and I scream.

I twist and run into the woods, the only place I can think of. The forest closes in around me, shadows thickening as I push through the underbrush.

That hissing follows me.

My breath comes in short, frantic gasps, and I trip over roots and stumble but keep moving. The trees seem to reach out, branches clawing at my clothes, my skin. The stormy wind picks up, howling around me like it knows I'm in huge danger.

I find a large tree and press myself against it, trying to control my breathing, to hide. My heart pounds so loudly in my ears I'm certain I'll pass out. Will that creature snake thing try to eat me?

Gods!

Fear's almost paralyzing, locking my legs in place.

That terrifying hissing grows louder, closer. I flinch, shaking uncontrollably.

So, I peer around the trunk, seeing it slithering through the underbrush, searching at least fifteen feet away. My hands tremble.

This can't be happening. I thought I was safe here, and why the hell did Wolfe send me up here if it's dangerous?

All I feel is terror.

I need to move, need to find a way out.

In a heartbeat, I rush forward, heart pounding in my chest, the cold air burning my lungs. The eerie silence is broken only by the sound of my feet crunching on the forest floor. I keep frantically glancing over my shoulder, terrified that the creature's going to catch me.

Every rustle of leaves makes me jump, but I've lost sight of it.

A branch snaps to my left, and I flinch, changing direction in a panic. I dart faster, branches tearing at my clothes and scratching my skin. The darkening shadows are disorienting, and I have no idea where I'm going. My only thought is to escape.

Brighter light ahead catches my attention, and I push harder, desperate to reach it. I keep looking back, my fear growing with every glance. Suddenly, my foot catches on something, and I tumble forward. I hit the ground hard, pain shooting through my knees and palms.

I scramble to get up, only to realize I've tripped over a bunch of metal boxes and devices, metal tubes rushing into the ground and snaking up the side of the glass wall that overlooks the great ocean down below.

I'm at the edge of the woods with no way out!

Terror surges through me as I untangle my foot from the cords, pushing the stuff away. One of the devices releases a hissing sound, but I don't care. I just need to get out of here.

Pivoting, I rush in the direction that will bring me out of the woods... I see the flowers far in the distance.

The snake creature emerges right on the path up ahead, not glancing my way.

I startle, backpedaling, my heart about to rip out of my chest. It's still not looking my way, and I'm cupping my mouth to stop a scream.

So, I dive back into the woods but trip over a tree root, falling hard to the ground. Shit!

Fear grips me as the crunch of leaves and twigs sounds closer. Scrambling to get up, I frantically scan the woods, spotting a massive tree with a hollowed-out section in the trunk. I sprint forward, and I'm squeezing myself into the dark, cramped space inside the tree. My knees press tight, against my chest, my breath shallow as I hide in the shadow, praying I'm concealed.

Outside, the crunching footsteps grow louder, closer.

I press my hands over my mouth, stifling the urge to gasp. I need to stay silent, stay hidden. The creature—or whatever is hunting me—is too close. The very thought of it finding me squeezes my chest tight with terror.

As the footsteps continue, they seem to head in the direction of the door, to my right. I wait, counting each heavy step as it moves away, letting the silence stretch, my anxiety mounting with each passing second. Finally, when the sound fades to a distant echo, I dare to peek out.

The coast seems clear, but my body shakes as I ease out of the tree's hollow. Every instinct screams to run, to find another exit, anything that might lead away from this nightmare. I set off in the opposite direction, hoping against hope there's another way out of the room.

And that means crossing the woods to the other end.

I move as quietly as I can, my steps light on the forest floor, barely breathing. I'm listening for the slightest hint of movement or sound.

Something suddenly whips through the air. The rush of it is so close that the heat of its passage brushes my cheek.

I recoil in shock, stumbling over a protruding tree root, but I never fall. I twist around to see a dart slammed into the tree behind me.

"What the hell..."

Panic claws at my insides, urging me to move faster. Without thinking, I sprint into the dense part of the woods where the trees grow close together, their branches weaving into a thick canopy overhead that blocks out most of the light. Underbrush and more roots cover the forest floor, making every step risky.

I dodge between the trees, my breath ragged, heart pounding. Every rustle of leaves, every snap of a twig underfoot spikes my anxiety—am I still being followed?

Glancing back, I find nothing but the green and shadow of the forest. Could I have lost them? The thought barely registers before I spot a thick cluster of bushes with a dark, inviting gap beneath them. It's not much, but it's enough to conceal myself.

I push my legs harder, gasping for breath, the fear like ice in my veins as I sprint in that direction. The underbrush grabs at my ankles, trying to slow me down, but desperation gives me speed.

A whizzing sound zips right past me, the whack of a dart in the tree right in front of me, inches from hitting me. I whimper, pivoting away from the shrubs, staring over my shoulder, trying to catch a glimpse of my pursuer, but the forest is too thick. How are they seeing me?

In an instant, I collide with someone. And I'm screaming, throwing punches in a desperate attempt to escape.

"Sage, it's me... it's all right. You're safe."

I glance up and see the most beautiful man—Wolfe. Around him, a trickle of pink dust floats in the air. It tastes almost like fresh rain, just like the first time I was in the woods with Killian.

My head swims, my heart thundering for a very different reason now.

He tilts his head, squinting at the tree behind me.

"What is that!" He leads me to the tree, inspects the weapon, then sniffs it. "Poison. What the fuck!"

"Someone's trying to kill me!" I'm quivering. "And that just missed me." I shake my head, trying to clear the lightheadedness.

Wolfe drags me into his arms, his protectiveness surprising me.

"No one's going to lay a finger on you. I'll destroy them," he promises, glancing around, then looking up at the heavier fall of pink mist being shot out across the forest. "Who turned on the Veil Ritual machine?"

It had to be me when I tripped over all those boxes and cords. Those fuzzy thoughts I experienced at the last Veil Ritual wash over me, along with that deep heat in my body. Fear rises because the last time I felt that way... I gasp at the things I did with Killian.

Wolfe's suddenly staring at me like I'm his meal.

A snap of twigs breaks the silence, slicing through the thick desire building between us.

"Stay low and hide," he commands, his voice urgent. "I'm going to get this fucker."

"No, don't go," I whisper, dread seizing me. But he's already sprinting into the woods, swallowed by the shadows. I huddle by an overgrown bush, trying to make myself as small as possible, feeling so vulnerable.

Bang.

I flinch at the front door shutting loudly.

Wait, did Wolfe leave me here? He wouldn't, would he? Trembling, I wait, ears straining for any sound.

Footsteps echo closer.

I hide lower behind an overgrown shrub, my pulse raging in my veins.

"You can come out now," Wolfe's voice calls, deeper and huskier than before. I peer out, seeing him standing a few trees away, glancing around, even looking right at me but not seeming to notice me.

I'm too busy staring at him in his monster form.

Glowing eyes are more pronounced now, his hair wild and dark as night, horns curling out from his head, skin tanned. He's wearing nothing, just him, all those muscles, fingers tipped with black claws, and a massive cock.

It hangs low, and I swear I'm seeing two things dangle there, but I could be imagining things because I'm going to pass out from the constant surprises coming my way.

His attention suddenly swings in my direction, and I shoot to my feet, but he looks right through me. That's strange.

He turns on the spot, and my attention tumbles to the long black tail whipping at the shrubs behind him. My mouth falls open at the sight, at the muscles rippling across his back. He's tall but not as big as Killian in his monster form, yet still large enough to tower over me, to intimidate.

"Sage," he growls, black smoke rising from around his body, darkening wherever he goes. He's snarling, brow creasing, and I notice cracks appearing on half his face, glowing amber as if he's about to detonate.

"I'm here," I finally answer, and his gaze lands on me, blinking. I step closer to him.

He struts forward, finally seeing me, taking my hand with his clawed one, dragging me into an embrace.

"I thought I lost you." The way he says that sounds almost genuine, almost caring.

I can't find my words at first, not when I'm pressed up against a naked Wolfe. His skin is an inferno, and those dangling cocks are hardening and pressing against my lower stomach.

"I-I was here the whole time." I can't concentrate on anything but his body, too afraid to move in case I accidentally touch... them.

"You must have been deep in the shadows," he states, sounding more like he's convincing himself than me.

His hand rises to my face, and a claw tips under my chin, lifting so I glance up at this monster who's every bit as terrifying as Killian. Yet, there's something darker behind Wolfe's eyes, as if he's capable of the most heinous of acts and wouldn't bat an eye at his actions.

"Did you see who was chasing you? I didn't get to the bastard in time, then heard the door slam, but I wasn't going to leave you here alone," he explains, his other hand sliding up my arms gingerly, leaving me quivering with unexpected need. "Did they hurt you?"

"It was s-something slithery. A gross snake creature. It only hissed, didn't say anything."

His wide brow furrows. "A Sylar, kept as fucking pets by many of this vessel because they can be trained to do your bidding, including hunting down someone, eating them, making them disappear. Never liked those things, but I would never make anyone get rid of their pets because of my own personal tastes."

I gasp, hating the sound of those things. "And they throw darts?"

"Well, not the creatures," he murmurs, while his gaze drops to my lips and lower, both hands now on my hips, fingers digging into me as if he can't decide if he's going to complete his sentence or have his way with me.

I draw in a breath, my hands on his chest, and I don't remember moving them.

Around us the mist is still pumping out, falling around us like snow.

I blink, trying to shake my head to clear the fogginess.

"The Sylar," he says as if struggling, and I don't even remember what we were talking about. My touch slides up his chest, resting on those flexing pecs, and I giggle.

Fates, did I just giggle at him squeezing his muscles?

Wolfe's gaze narrows, and he suddenly asks, "Howler, who was in the room with us a few moments ago?"

"A Sylar," Howler replies.

"Who else?" Wolfe presses.

"Sorry, but I didn't detect anyone else."

"The fuck!" he mutters under his breath. "And who did the Sylar belong to?"

"I cannot detect."

Wolfe's snarl is low and feral.

"What does this mean?" I ask, my head so foggy I'm struggling to keep up.

"Someone's using magic to cloak themselves from Howler," he explains, exhaling loudly. "Something I thought we had Howler programmed to overcome."

Wolfe's gaze hazes over and he suddenly pulls me closer, scanning the surroundings as if expecting the creature to reappear. His grip tightens protectively around me, the fear around us, though, quickly giving way to something more primal as his hands skip down my sides and slide under my skirt.

I gasp at his rugged touch, yet I don't push him away, knowing there's something we need to remember, but it slips my mind.

Instead, a moan spills past my lips.

"Sylar," he starts, staring at me so deeply, so closely, I don't think I can take another breath. "It's a distraction. The real killer was with it, watching you, waiting to strike." He gives my ass another grasp, and I cry out with unbearable pleasure from the way his claws press into my flesh, bringing me the pain I desire.

"My head feels blurry."

"Sage." His husky voice is filled with lust.

I lick my lips, and his whole body stiffens. Maybe it's the closeness of our bodies, the protectiveness he offers, or the pink mist... but I feel brazen, aroused, and the way he stares at me is as if he's daring me.

Sucking in a breath, I trail my hand down his stomach made of muscles, holding his stare. This isn't me, yet it feels exactly like me. A girl buzzing with arousal, who's just discovered how incredible sex can be...

My touch tenderly slides over the trimmed hair above his groin. Then they're there, my fingertips running over one, then the one underneath it, so long, so hard.

He growls under his breath, his breaths coming harder, faster.

I'm rolling my hips from just touching him. Then I wrap my hand around them both, unable to completely touch my fingers.

He snarls, his hands moving to my hips, and he has me pinned to a tree, and his mouth is on mine.

His hands are all over my body, driving up the skirt of my dress while I curl my legs around him. I'm wearing nothing underneath because, evidently, no one in this world bothers with underwear. Part of me is horrified at how desperate I am to hump him. I kiss him back with a savagery that surprises me.

We're together, bodies pressed, the urgency in his kiss dominating me. He adjusts himself, the scorching heat from his cocks snuggling up against my spread pussy. I take that opportunity, desperately rocking against them, rubbing them.

His hands are on my ass, guiding me up and down, stroking himself with me, while I'm thinking about one thing... how in the world he's going to fit those into me. Especially seeing as I'm still slightly sore from Killian's monster cock.

He slides his kisses to my neck, the light stubble on his face scratchy against my cheek. He licks me, biting.

"Tell me, Sage," he growls in my ear. "Are you mine?" He thrusts against me as though we're having sex.

I groan, holding on to him, losing my mind, my breath.

For a split moment, a rush of fresh, cold air washes over us, the mist pushed aside, clarity claiming me.

With it comes the reminder of the danger I've just faced, the attempt on my life, and that now, we're sitting targets.

Wolfe's licking my neck, and I manage to somehow untangle myself from his kiss.

"We shouldn't be doing this."

His gaze meets mine, fire blazing behind them, a deep, guttural growl in his throat in protest.

"Yes, agree. Not here. Back in my room."

"No, that's not what I mean."

He's instantly crossing the woods with speed, me coiled around him, his mouth back on my neck.

"Why do you taste and smell so delicious?" he whispers. "I want to eat you up."

I cling to him, unable to stand being away from him, my head growing dizzy again. He grunts the more he licks my neck.

We barely emerge from the woods, greeted by the light, when suddenly my vision pulses in and out, just like the last time I was in the woods with Killian. Then it all goes black...

· · ·

My eyes snap open, and I'm standing in a dark place, slithers of light streaming down on me from gaps in the ceiling. I must be underground, and I'm rubbing the chill from my arms, well aware that I'm in a vision, just like last time.

I turn to the surroundings around me of old stone buildings in ruins, relics... hard to tell really what this place is, but there are homes underground, broken, destroyed. Remnants of a life once existed wherever. Half a door on the ground is covered in dust, and someone's random shoe lies between two stone walls.

A shadow falls over me, and I twist around to find Wolfe there, both of us staring at each other, aware of what this means.

My heart's galloping in my chest because I can't fathom how this can be.

"You're my true mate as well?" I gasp.

"I didn't expect this," he answers, yet his arms embrace me, drawing me against him like there's no doubt in his mind who I belong to. The warmth from his monstrous form engulfs me. He kisses my face, and I can't stop smiling. "But it's everything I could have wished for. For too long, I believed I wouldn't find my intended mate. Not when my mission had me focusing on anything but."

With him holding me tightly against him, the smile in his eyes, the excitement in the way his hands stroke down my body, I'm left torn between pulling away from him to make sense of it and following the urgent fire burning inside of me, giving in to my craving for Wolfe.

But I remind myself he's kept secrets from me, yet the way he treats me so tenderly makes my head hurt with confusion. I think of Killian...

"So, two true mates are possible?" I ask, not really understanding the concept, except for the overwhelming sensations that consume me when I'm near these monsters. The hunger I feel for them, the arousal, it turns me into someone else.

"It's rare in our world, but it has happened before."

"So, what now?" I ask, watching him staring up at the ceiling for a bit too long as if the news startles him more than he admits.

"Now, you're mine. And you're Killian's." His lips come down on mine, and the fierceness in his kiss spreads over to me. My hands are on his huge biceps, and I'm wanting more... "It means that there's so much I need to tell you, to explain." He sighs heavily... and I suspect it has everything to do with my father.

He's glancing at our surroundings, and I follow his line of sight.

"Where are we?" I ask.

There's pain on his face as he glances around. "A place I once called home. This is the old Silvercrest Kingdom," he murmurs. "Turned to ash and ruins."

I can't even begin to imagine how hard it must be to see his home destroyed, laid forgotten somewhere underground. I lean closer and slip my hand into his, drawing him to glance down at me.

"Focus on me," I say. "You don't need to see all of this."

His hand trembles in mine, and my gut twists in on itself.

"I never wanted you to see this," he admits in a soft voice.

"But you're my true mate, a Shadowfen, so you should see the ruins of the world we once knew."

We stand in the dim light, the weight of the old kingdom, the uncertain future.

Once beautiful and captivating, the place is now broken and buried.

"Did my father die in the Great Desolation?" I ask, turning to meet Wolfe's gaze, but he's shaking his head.

"I wish I could say he had," he admits, his response startling. "The son of a bitch is very much alive."

An ache stabs into my chest, and just as fast, darkness inhales me once more.

CHAPTER
EIGHTEEN
WOLFE

I'm grasping Sage by the hand, rushing us out of the Chamber of Rituals.

The heaviness of what I lost all those years ago bears down on me from the vision I just experienced, the images of my mother hanging from the edge of broken flooring in her bedroom haunting my thoughts. The ache still sits inside me like a permanent blade in my heart, and revisiting the past twists that knife deeper and deeper.

But we can't stay in the woods, not knowing Sage is in danger, and our bonding as true mates distracts us to the point of making us vulnerable.

Sage stumbles alongside me, but I can't slow down. Not when I'm desperate to get her alone, to know she's safe. Right now, my brain is fucking me up, wrenching me in so many directions that I'm about to lose my shit.

I can't leave her side. And despite everything, I can't help but want to finish what we started.

"Wolfe," she says, pulling against my grasp.

"I want you away from this room," I explain, rushing us into the elevator.

"You think I'm in *real* danger now?"

Hearing her voice tremble undoes me. I had no fucking idea, none at all, that she'd be my intended mate. I had one mission for her, and that meant not getting close to her. But from the moment she arrived, my head's been screwed over.

I glance at those delicious tits, her nipples pressing against her dress, her intoxicating scent screaming for me, those deepening violet eyes looking up at me with fear, with lust. Matching hair, starting to lose more of her silver hair, frames her face, falling to her waist, and I picture wrapping it around my hand, holding it tight as I fuck her.

Growling, I take slow inhales to settle myself.

That deep ache pulses inside me, reminding me that as a true mate, our connection would be unbearable unless I fuck her again and again. That my insatiable desire for her won't fade away.

Heart hammering, I face her, my hands on her tiny waist, and she stares up at me, a quirky smile on her lips.

"So, it's normal to be running around the vessel, naked and all?" she teases, glancing down at me in monster form.

I fucking adore that she makes light of a moment that's drowning me, that should scare her halfway to the Seven Hells. So, I appreciate her attempt to lighten a heavy mood.

"Are you finding it difficult to concentrate?" I quirk an eyebrow, pushing a few strands caught in the corner of her mouth off her face as she breathes quickly.

Her blushing cheekiness has my cocks throbbing, and I push them against her, so desperate to have her legs spread and wound around me.

"You're distracting me," she whispers, while I'm leaning in and taking a lungful of her scent that has my balls pulling up tight with need. Berries. Vanilla. Sex.

She's mine.

That's all I can think about.

I'm about to instruct Howler to take us to my floor, but I stop. Sage is staring at my cocks again, and I'd be a real fucker if I didn't allow my mate to explore what I'm packing.

"Get on your knees," I order.

Her gaze flicks up to me, a lost breath on my lips.

"You heard me."

She's watching with her narrowing gaze, her tongue dragging over her lips. That look absolutely breaks me.

Then she calls out, "Howler, please take us to Lord Wolfe's room."

My gaze drifts to her smirk, the lava inside me bubbling.

"You think that will stop us?"

And her hand is on my cocks as we start moving, gaze riveted on me, tugging on me gently first, her touch tender. "They're so hard, but soft on the outside."

"I give you all of me." I place my hand over hers, tightening her squeeze, tugging me harder, faster.

"Fuck," I grunt, slamming my free hand to the wall. "Howler, stop the elevator."

"You're so big." She works me with two hands, those thick veins running down my bulging shafts, throbbing. Sparks shoot through me, and I grind my teeth, snarling, needing this more than breathing itself.

"Taste me," I demand. "Sweet girl, you're going to break me if you don't."

"I've never done this before."

"Just take it slowly and I'll guide you." My pulse burns, staring down at her fisting my girth, then she gets to her knees in front of me, a cheeky grin curling on her face. She takes one tip into her mouth, her tongue teasing.

I hiss, unable to look away as she pushes the second one into her mouth, her lips spread, and when she glances up, they throb harder. The most beautiful sight in the world who didn't need any help with sucking down on my cocks.

The deeper she takes me, the more purring sounds she makes. Those moans telling me she's enjoying herself.

"You want more, my sweet girl?"

She bobs her head lightly and slides me deeper. It surprises me how much of me fits into that beautiful mouth, now with bulging cheeks.

She takes a few more strokes with her tongue, with her sucking on me, leaving me weak and at her mercy. Then she abruptly pulls out, licking the juices from her lips.

"You taste so sweet and salty." Up on her feet, she smirks at me while the agonizing ache of the buildup leaves me crippled.

"My cocks are yours, but you're not finished," I state the obvious.

"Howler, open the doors," she instructs, then glances my way, wiping her mouth. "And I am done."

She ducks under my outstretched arm, still on the wall. I twist around as she hurries out of the elevator onto a floor that's neither hers nor mine. She stands there with her chin high, and I can't help but admire her confidence. She's not going to win, but I give her points for trying.

I follow her, and she backs away.

"You've been holding secrets from me, and first, you're going to tell me everything about my father. Then, if you're a good boy, I'll give you a treat."

I burst out laughing as she spins on her feet and lifts that skirt, flashing her ass at me, then darts down the hallway. She has no fucking idea what a sex-starved monster will do...

We're on the training floor, half dedicated to residential homes and the rest to classes for fighting and weapon lessons.

My girl's walking toward the main doors that lead straight into the room where they practice death moves. As much as I'd like to watch her walk in and see Shadowfen strangling each other, I prefer to have her concentrate on me at this moment.

I march after her, snatching her around the waist and

twisting her around, then throwing her over my shoulder. She writhes and fights me.

"Put me down."

But I laugh. "First mistake you made was thinking you could stop me. Second was challenging me." I shove open a door to an unoccupied suite not yet furnished. Fine by me.

"Release me," she yells, hitting me in the back.

I slap her soft ass, and she bucks against me.

Once near the balcony, I let her down to her feet, grabbing her dress in the process, ripping it up and over her head. The material rips easily, slipping off her naked body.

She gasps, covering herself.

"This is fair, no? Now, we're both naked," I state with a smirk.

"You asshole!" She's glaring, and I adore her resisting me.

Her bare skin glistens in the dim light filtering through the window. I take a moment to appreciate the sight before me, her beauty raw and all mine. She stands there, trembling, glaring at me.

"You think you can just—"

I cut her off, pressing my lips to hers in a bruising kiss, my hands dragging down her curved waist to her ass with possessive hunger. She moans into my mouth, yet she's pushing her hands against my chest.

Heat between us ignites, about to erupt.

"Wolfe," she gasps when we break apart for air, her voice defiant. "You can't just take what you want."

"So, you're saying you don't want this?" My lips are on hers again, my hand falling to between her thighs, finger pressing between her soaking lips. "Those purring sounds in your throat tell a different story." I pull back from her just enough to make sure she sees me smiling, my thumb tracing her swollen clit. "You'll get your answers after I fuck you."

"Wow!" She goes to slap me, but I catch her wrist, kissing her fingers.

"You'll enjoy this more if you don't fight me."

With a thrust, she jerks her hips away from my hand, her eyes darkening, and I can see the internal battle she's fighting. Her scent is intensifying, and I sense her agony of holding back, see it scribbled over her face.

I don't give her time to overthink it, going after her until she's pinned to the glass door to the balcony.

"Wolfe," she warns. She has her palms against my chest again.

I lower my head, trailing kisses down her neck, biting and sucking at the sensitive skin right below her ear. She arches, pushing those tits against me, a soft whimper escaping her mouth.

"We belong to each other now," I murmur against her, my voice rough with desire. "And I'm not letting you go."

Her hands claw at my arms, drawing me closer as if she can't stand the distance between us but hates herself for desiring me. Lowering my hands to the back of her thighs, I have her off her feet in seconds, pulling her beautiful legs around me.

Her eyes lock on to mine, a challenge burning in their depths.

"What if I don't want to belong to anyone?" she whispers, her voice trembling. "What if these urges I feel where I can't control myself have everything to do with the magic in my body from the mist?"

"Such magic won't work unless deep down you possess those desires and feelings. Just because you don't admit to yourself what you really want doesn't make it fake." My grin widens. "Let me show you exactly what it means to belong to a monster like me."

I capture her lips once more. Despite driving me away, she kisses me with fury, her tongue pushing into my mouth, tangling with mine. I suck on hers, and she moans, pressing those full breasts against me, teasing me.

Sharpness suddenly bites down on my lower lip. Pain flares instantly, and I flinch. It's enough time for her to drop from my grasp and rip away.

"Sage," I growl, tasting the metallic tang of blood on my lip. She just bit me, and I'm grinning. "You're going to have to try harder than that."

There she is, across the room, raising an eyebrow and staring at me.

That daring gleam in her gaze intensifies, but she has no idea of the dangerous hunger inside me. Trying to cast it aside is impossible, and she feels it, too, as she stands there, squeezing those delicious thighs together.

"Don't fight it," I state, my savagery raging with emotions for her, taking in her naked body—fucking perfect tits with tight, dusty rose nipples, the small patch of dark hair with a hue of mauve.

"What fun would it be if I'm too easy on you."

She's devious!

I spear my fingers through my hair, cocks throbbing harder just as she takes a run for the front door, her steps hitting the hard floor.

Hell, she's going to fucking ruin me.

Heart pounding, I go after her. Whipping my tail out, I snatch her around the waist and haul her back. Her legs tangle, and she trips, but I'm there to catch her in my arms.

She cries out, shoving against my hold. "Let me go."

Falling back into me, she stares up at me, those damn angry eyes, my weakness. I'm like a beast around her, my nostrils flaring with each inhale of her sweet perfume.

"You're only going to hurt yourself."

Desire burns in her gaze. "Then release me, and *you* won't hurt me."

I chuckle, even if her words are a slap to my face. I'd never hurt her.

"Once you've started your fever, your body will hunger for my cocks. That taste in the elevator was just the start of appeasing the monster inside of you."

Her nose scrunches, not liking that at all. "Then tell me how to stop it."

Silence pulses between us.

Hell help me, but I'm inches away from taking her, tired of playing these games. Lowering her to her feet, hands around her, my tail snaking up her leg, I whisper, "Only one way to do that... with my cocks."

She searches my face as though I'm lying while my tail lingers at the apex of her thighs. "Don't lie to me."

I burst out laughing. "Tell me, Sage, what do you want me to do?" My hand slides over to her breast, squeezing it, my own desperation barely holding on.

Quivering in my arms, she's making those beautiful purring sounds in her throat, the ones that tell me she's ready.

"Wh-what does being in *fever* mean?" she whispers, parting her legs for my tail.

The moment I move it up to stroke her, she shakes violently.

"It's your body changing, acknowledging that we are true mates, preparing to be rutted."

She blinks, her lips thinning and her jaw clenching. "That sounds very animalistic."

I shrug. "Aren't we all animals?"

She arches an eyebrow at me.

Beautiful. I stand there, my cocks aching for her, my tail already pushing past her drenched lips.

Her hands are suddenly on my arms, digging in, holding on.

"I hate that you are making me want this, that I can't stop thinking of having your tail inside me. That I'm desperate for it."

"Fuck." I shake at her words. I can't hold back. I can't resist. I drag her up against me, in my arms. She snaps her legs around me, the fierce arousal between us an inferno.

"I would never make you do anything you don't already want, sweet girl." I plunge my arm down between us, my fingers on her swollen cunt. She's drenched, dripping with lust, ready for me.

She's shuddering, crying for me already.

Guiding my cocks to her entrance, I push into her slowly.

She's tense yet clawing at my shoulders, moaning for more.

I press into her, and fuck, she's tight.

"Please," she cries. Writhing against me, she adjusts her hips to accept me more easily. She's tiny, and I'm huge, but her hole grabs my cocks, sucking them in.

"Gods! They're so big!" She's singing my praises, and I push deeper, burying myself.

Her breaths come as quickly as mine because squeezed into that tight space, constricting them, is both euphoria and torture.

I growl, but she's bowing her head, breathing heavily as I have her completely full.

"Look at me." I walk her to a wall, giving her something to lean against.

Her face flushes, lips parting.

"Fuck me, I'm yours."

I grin. This is what I've craved, what I've starved for.

"Hold on to me. I'll give you anything you want."

I bury myself deeper into her, down to the hilt. Her legs

quiver as she tries to hold on, but I'm carrying her weight, hands on her ass. The tip of my tail slides between those gorgeous round cheeks, finding her puckered ass, and I feel her tighten around me. She's soaking wet, and I slip into her.

"You wanted him inside you, and I'm here to fulfill your every wish."

"Yes," she says shakily, and I'm losing my mind.

She's so fucking beautiful.

A snarl rips from my throat, and a pulse charges through me, the darkest of my desires, the deepest parts of my hunger awake.

I pull out, then thrust back in, the flames inside my body licking at me. The sweet pain of her constricting my cocks consumes me. I fuck her, fast, violently, unable to stop myself.

She tilts her head back, taking it, those pretty tits bouncing, my hands squeezing her cheeks. Wriggling, grinding herself against me, her gaze is filled with lust. Mouth open, she's panting.

I can't get enough of how her breasts jiggle, how her cunt tightens every time I pull out, trying desperately to hold on to me. Those violet eyes flicker up to mine, hazed over, and the sheer line of perspiration on her brow glows in the light from outside. Slick drips from her, coating my balls.

The harder I claim her, the more she whimpers, the more she rocks against me.

I've never experienced such a powerful need to fuck any woman, never had this overwhelming urgency to protect her from the world.

"Wolfe," she cries, her body shuddering.

I work into that tight pussy, tail teasing her ass, pushing in and out. My own arousal surges forward with ferocity. Leaning forward to claim her lips, I plunge my tongue between them, desperate to have as much of me inside her as I can. For her to know she's mine. I want to fuck her on the floor, on the balcony, in the rain starting outside... every damn place.

She groans out louder, clawing at me as I rut her relentlessly. I have no self-control, which is becoming obvious, transfixed by her moans and her scent.

Kissing me back, she embraces me harder, rubbing herself, and I'm on the verge of losing myself.

"Wolfe," she whispers. "I'm—"

Then she's screaming, convulsing in my arms. Her pussy squeezes my cocks like a vise, my tail slipping out as she ferociously comes all over my erections.

I hiss...

Heart twisting in my chest, I never stood a chance to hold back. With her warm body against mine, her moans in my ears, I come just as hard, buried in her down to my balls. I pulse, flooding her with my seed.

Howling, I'm pumping while she's riding me. She has the side of her face on my chest, exhausted but shaking, still coming as I fill her. We stay that way for a long moment, neither of us moving. I don't want this to be over.

She shivers against me as I walk her into the bathroom, finding several towels neatly folded on the shelf. I grab one and place it on the counter, then set her ass on it and pull out of her, much to her groans of protest.

Her legs won't hold her, not with how exhausted she appears. I glance down to where her inner legs are slick with her and my cum. Her eyes flutter as if she's going to sleep.

"I'll take good care of you," I tell her.

She glances up at me, blinking.

"Can you help me back to my room?" she whispers.

I lean in, pressing my face to her neck, inhaling her, then whisper, "I'm going to clean you first."

She leans against me, and when I pull back, her body follows, her breaths heavy. I grin at seeing her already asleep.

"Sleep tight, my sweet little girl," I say. "You're mine now."

CHAPTER NINETEEN
KILLIAN

Wolfe stands in front of me in his human form, his eyes burning with fire.

"Are you certain she's your true mate as well?" I groan, a snarl behind my words. All of me adores the idea of Sage belonging to just me, so it's taking me a moment to accept that she's his, too.

He stares at me deadpan, as if I haven't been listening. Except I damn well heard every word, especially the part about him fucking her. We've shared everything since we were children, and I grind my teeth that this includes my true mate... *our* true mate.

I peer over at the door leading into his bedroom, knowing she's in there.

Wolfe crosses the main living area, picking up several towels from the floor, tossing them into the bathroom, and buzzing around the place, completely unlike him.

Around me, the walls of his quarters are covered with weapons and ancient artifacts, paintings, golden coins, and jewels from what we managed to salvage from the old kingdom. A heavy oak table sits in the center, covered with maps and scrolls.

My attention swings back to the bedroom door, eager to take a peek inside.

"Is this why you called me here? To fucking brag?" I ask, moving closer to the bedroom, my voice dripping with sarcasm.

"It's to discuss what we're going to do about her father," he replies, his voice steady but filled with underlying urgency.

"She needs to know," I state instantly, turning away from the door, ready to do it myself. "As much as we fucking hate the idea, we have to do this sooner than later."

Wolfe's lips pinch tight, but he doesn't protest for a change. Of course, he sees clearly now that she's his true mate.

"Good," I say, trying to inject some finality into the conversation. "We tell her the truth, then we work out new plans to take *him* down."

Wolfe opens the door slightly and glances into the room. Even from out here, I hear the deep breathing of her sleeping, a sound that's oddly comforting. The idea of joining her is clawing at the back of my mind.

"She might hate us once she finds out, but it needs to be done," he murmurs, his voice barely above a whisper.

"We'll deal with it, and we'll make her see that we'll tear the world apart for her," I growl, stiffening.

I get it, all our plans are now compromised. But I

have no damn intention of releasing her, let alone sacrificing her to her bastard father. We might have intended to use her as a bargaining chip initially, but not now that she's ours. I'm falling so fast for her that I'm drowning, so our plans will fucking change.

The intensity behind Wolfe's stare darkens every time he glances over to the bedroom. "We need Nyko to join us to confirm how we're handling this." He sighs deeply. "Why does he always fucking disappear when we need him?"

I chuckle, knowing Nyko vanishes often but never tells us what he's up to.

"We'll speak with him tonight." I suck in a deep breath, trying to steady my racing thoughts. I cross the room, unable to resist, and peer into the bedroom, too.

There she is, lying on the bed, completely naked, the sheets tossed aside, and she's flat on her back, fast asleep.

My breath catches in my chest, my cock twitching at the sight.

I slip into the room. Wolfe follows, both of us sitting on the large, engraved box at the end of the bed, an object he rescued from the bottom of the sea and restored.

Her bare feet are within arm's reach, my gaze traveling up to where she has one bent outward, giving us the perfect view of the sweetest cunt I've ever seen. Glistening lips, slightly parted, reveal a slice of her pink offering. My cock's growing harder at the sight, at the memory of my mouth wrapped around her clit, my tongue piercing her hole. A small tuft of hair shows deeper violet hues now. My attention slithers up over her soft stomach to those delicious breasts, her scrumptious nipples tight. It takes every ounce of strength not to climb closer, spread her legs, and devour her.

"She's beautiful," Wolfe mutters, distracting me. I glance over at him, and he's staring at her just as obsessively. "She needs to move in with one of us in our quarters."

"Mine," I respond instantly, earning a grin from him. I stare at the rise and fall of her chest. "She's shown her feisty side more recently," I explain. "Revealing her true Shadowfen side. She's going to change soon, so it's best we're with her."

"Someone tried to kill her in the Chamber of Rituals," he states, his tone serious.

"What the fuck?" I whisper as a surge of anger explodes within me, my fists curling, a growl rumbling in my chest. "Why didn't you start with that?"

She stirs, twisting onto her side, and we both step out of the room, shutting the door behind us to avoid waking her.

I take a deep breath, trying to control the rage boiling inside me.

"I found her terrified in the ritual room," he explains quietly. "She mentioned a snake creature, a Sylar, I'm guessing, chasing her. Its handler must have been there because a poisonous dart just missed striking her." He paces in the living area vigorously, suddenly lifting one of the sword weapons on display off the wall. He's studying it like he's seeing it for the first time.

I'm taken aback. What the hell is he doing? I shake that off and focus on this madness.

"Who the fuck would go after her? I haven't heard any grumblings among the Shadowfen about her arrival." My thoughts filter to her father, that he's somehow involved. "Shit, you think her son of a bitch father heard she's here and is trying to kidnap her for himself?"

Wolfe's expression darkens, his body visibly shaking, and he's pacing again.

"We can't dismiss that idea," he snarls. "It's exactly what that bastard would do." He's practicing with the sword, cutting through the air, looking ready to go into battle, exerting himself.

"Wolfe, what the hell is up with you?" Yet, I recognize this behavior almost immediately as I question him, remembering he's just fucked Sage. After I claimed her, the adrenaline rush was burning me alive. I had to go hunting just to shake it off... and now I watch Wolfe struggling with the same intensity.

He glances over at me, shaking from adrenaline. "I can't help it. There's something..."

"You're feeling it, too, aren't you?"

He growls, as though just standing still is killing him, and after a few more swings, he puts the sword back up on the cradle on the wall.

"Claiming Sage did something to you, just like it did to me. After I took her, I had an explosion of energy, so much that I needed to hunt before I went mad. And I see it in you now."

He blinks, his brow furrowing.

"It feels as though she's filling us with energy, like a battery, charging us to the maximum."

His eyes widen. "You think she..."

"I do. Her powers are coming forward, and fuck, if this is a taste, she's going to be a lot more powerful than any of us expected."

My heart thumps faster just thinking of her ability, how easily it can hurt her if she's not prepared.

"More reason to keep her protected with one of us at all times," Wolfe states my exact thoughts. "But right now, I'll fucking go insane if I don't release this energy." Pacing, he rubs his palms down the sides of his legs as though he has no idea what to do with them.

"Go!" I laugh, remembering very well the hyped-up intensity.

He's already on his way out of the door. "You remain here with her," he states, then he's gone.

Thinking of Sage, my pulse pounds, and the staggering need to shield her from danger has me just as damn overwhelmed as Wolfe.

Wolfe

I march out of my quarters, not wanting to be away from Sage's side. Yet, the adrenaline surges through me so fiercely I might go ballistic if I don't expend the energy. And I sure as fuck don't want to lose my shit in front of the other Shadowfen who are already questioning my ability to gain us back our kingdom.

My heart slams against my rib cage, muscles taut, insides tense—reminiscent of the times I've faced off with beasts. And now, I need to beat the shit out of something.

My thoughts spiral around her... as a half-Shadowfen, she should be weaker, her powers diluted, yet she carries an energy that impacts others in ways I've never seen before. All of my kind are born with their own level of shadow abilities, but this is something so much more. It's as though she's a conduit, transferring power into others.

That's fucking unheard of.

There are tales of Shadowfen with unusual abilities from the past, tales of someone born with such strength that they possessed control of others' shadows. It was so dangerous that they ended up locking her up in isolation. She carried the power to make others kill themselves, to turn against anyone, to manipulate the shadows as if they were her own limbs. She had the power of a God.

The thought churns deep in my gut, telling myself we won't have that problem with Sage.

I rush toward the training rooms, passing Shadowfen staff, who glance at me, bowing their heads in respect. I take the back corridors to the elevator, not in the mood to deal with anyone.

"Wolfe," a whiny voice calls from behind me, and I recognize it at once. Clay.

I roll my eyes, tensing all over as I twist around to find the captain coming at me like a Tidecreeper, his posture rigid, movements jerky. He's seething, eyes burning with an intensity that makes his birdlike frame even more imposing.

"We have to talk," he groans, the long, black and white feathers running the length under his arms fluttering in his approach.

"I'm busy," I snap. "But if you insist, you can join me in the training room, and I'll listen."

He grumbles, clearly displeased. The Shadowfen isn't a fighter, not with his frail appearance. He peers at me as if I'm joking.

"I've been trying to get hold of you, but you've been elusive."

"Okay, you have me now. Talk, as I need something from you, too." My annoyance rumbles behind my words at his persistence.

"You've commanded us to change course to the kingdom, and I've gotten all the weapons ready. Howler is ready for a full assault. We need to confirm our plan of action."

I cut him a sharp stare, but he doesn't look away. Yes, I changed course once Sage was on board, but that was before I knew about her being Killian's true mate or mine. Still, I haven't worked out our new plans, but it sure as fuck won't line up with Clay's destructive plans.

"As I've explained previously, we're not going in there to destroy the kingdom. Only the false King," I state flatly, my impatience tightening around my chest.

He exhales loudly, almost making a squawking sound in the process. "After what Bren and all those betrayers who followed him did to you... to all of us! They should be slaughtered."

I shake my head, exhaling slowly to keep my fury in check.

"Those who followed did it for the safety of their families, and I won't punish them for wanting to offer them protection. My goal is to remove the fucking murderer of a King, not decimate our Shadowfen. Have you forgotten our mission—bring the kingdom together as one, not divided?"

Clay glares at me, his feathers ruffling with irritation. "It's because she's Killian's true mate now, isn't it?" His voice drips with accusation. "I suspected the moment she arrived, with the way you all chased after her, that things would change."

Fury plays on my mind, muscles tensing. Sure, Clay is the captain of the Howler, who offered us a home after the Great Desolation, but this vessel belongs to the old kingdom, to my family, and he needs to remember his place.

"Watch your mouth, Clay," I growl. "Right now, you need to trust me, not question me."

His eyes narrow, the tension between us thickening.

"Maybe you should put your focus on why Howler couldn't identify who else was in the Chamber of Rituals when Sage was attacked. Something glitchy's going on, or perhaps someone hacked into the system," I snarl.

His eyes turn into round orbs, fright scribbled across his expression. "That's impossible. Howler's systems are impenetrable."

"Then explain why it couldn't detect the intruder?" I snap, shoulders curving forward.

Clay swallows hard, his usual composure slipping. "I'll look into it immediately. This puts us all in a very dangerous position. Perhaps someone on board is feeding information to King Bren?"

The darkness of his suggestion presses down on me but reminds me of a similar conversation Killian and I had just discussed.

"First, let's find out what the fuck is going on with Howler, and inform me at once."

"Of course, my Lord."

"And delay our approach to the kingdom by a few days. We're not ready yet."

A vein in his throat pulses, then he nods once.

I move past him, exhausted from this conversation, my fists refusing to unfurl. If I don't walk away, he'll be wearing them.

"Your father would never go soft on his enemies," he accuses behind me. "The traitor slaughtered him in cold blood."

I swing back on him, rage simmering just under the surface.

"My father isn't here," I hiss. "I am, and I know exactly what I'm doing."

He squares his shoulders, meeting my gaze head-on. "Do you?"

Tension ripples, and I'm moving toward him before I can think straight. Energy speeds through my veins, adding fuel to my anger at being pushed by this asshole. Captain or not, he's crossed the line.

Fear flickers behind his gaze, and he recoils. When a small group of children rush down the corridor, the gutless swine jumps in alongside them, escaping my side.

Turning, I slam a fist into the wall, leaving a crater of a hole. I don't lose fucking control of my emotions, but Clay's picked the wrong time to play fucker with me. He's always been the devil's advocate, that's nothing new, but today, I have zero patience for it.

Heart thundering in my chest, I pivot and storm toward the training rooms, furious at his damn persistence to destroy everyone in the kingdom. It's not the first time he's brought it up, and each time, I shoot him down. But he's starting to worry me...

He's angry; I get it. We all fucking are at what happened to our kingdom. But my father brought me up to do anything in my power to resolve a problem before resorting to war.

And I sure as fuck won't let anything—or anyone—stand in my way to achieve that.

CHAPTER
TWENTY

NYKO

For fuck's sake! I march toward Wolfe's quarters, a storm brewing in my thoughts. Just spoke with him about being Sage's true mate, about her attack in the Chamber of Rituals, about her power, yet all I can think about is... Are you fucking kidding me? Those two asses are her true mates, and I'm here obsessing over her but get nothing? Well, that's not going to work.

I burst into Wolfe's room without knocking. Killian jolts to his feet, looking like he's been caught jerking off.

"What the hell?" he snaps, glancing at me as I shut the door behind me. "What are you doing here?"

"Wolfe gave me the rundown of what's going on. It's my turn to watch over her."

His shoulders shoot back. "Like fuck it is. I just started."

I smile, calm as shit, strolling across the room. "You

want to be exhausted tonight when you take over watching her? That's why I'm here."

He glares at me, and I stop myself from chuckling, attempting to keep my voice low, figuring she's asleep in Wolfe's bedroom. I throw myself down on the couch, feet up on the small table in front, reclining.

"Off you go." I smirk, waving him off.

Killian throws me death glares. "You think I trust you alone with her? Last time we left you in charge of a shipment, it ended up at the bottom of the seabed."

I snort, crossing my arms. "Hey, that wasn't my fault. How was I supposed to know the damn crates were poisoned? And besides, Wolfe needs your help."

Killian's jaw tightens. "What's so important?"

I shrug. "Just some recon. I think with the scouting team, our path to the kingdom is clear. Can't have any surprises, can we?"

"Recon, my ass," Killian mutters, but he's wavering.

I can see it in his eyes. I might be lying about taking over from him as Wolfe's suggestion, but the recon is hand-on-my-heart true.

"Come on, Killian. You know I've got this," I say, leaning forward on the couch, trying to appear nonchalant. "Besides, you could use a break. You're wound tight as hell."

He stares at me, lips thinning. "If anything happens to her—"

"Yeah, yeah, you'll rip me to shreds," I interrupt, waving a hand dismissively. "I've heard it all before. Now, go. I'll keep her safe." I chuckle. "All under control."

His fists clench and unclench, his eyes darting between me and the bedroom door. Finally, with a muttered curse, he says, "Fine, I've also got a few people to interrogate about the Sylar, so I'll get that done." He shoots me one last warning glare, then strides out of the room, tension radiating off him in waves. "I'll be back."

"Yep, I'm sure you will," I call after him, smirking.

The door closes behind him.

I glance at the bedroom, my heart pounding. Time to check on our little princess.

As I approach her bedroom, I unfurl my shadow, my monster side rippling down my body, feeling like water washing over me. In a flash, I become a complete shadow, slinking forward and slipping under the thin gap beneath the door and into the room.

Sage stirs on the bed, clearly disturbed by Killian's loud insistence on staying behind, though Wolfe had told me he gave her a sleeping tonic to help her sleep soundly. So no surprise, she hasn't woken up yet.

And now she's mine.

I float in as she settles onto her back, her eyes moving behind her eyelids as if she might still be asleep, but I'm too preoccupied with her being completely naked.

My breath hitches, shallow and uneven, as I take in the curves of her round breasts, the thin waist, and the round hips that call me to the patch of hair between her thighs. Fuck, I can smell her in the air, the fragrant perfume that screams berries and sex. My cock pulses, taking shadow form... The soft rise and fall of her chest and the way the sunlight caresses her skin leave me captivated.

My heart slams in my chest, and I close the distance between us. Her body is intoxicating, and it pulls me to her.

It's unbearable, impossible not to touch her. I float over the top of her, inches above her body, staring down at her face. Her features are delicate, her violet hair fanning across the pillow. The same hair that shimmers like a violet flame, catching the faintest glimmer of sunlight.

Her lips, slightly parted with deep breaths, draw my attention.

Those two bastards wanted to keep her to themselves. Otherwise, why not invite me to see if she's my true mate, too? Never mind. Like most things, I'll do it myself.

My hand reaches out, fingers just a whisper away from her cheek. The warmth radiating from her skin is intoxicating. I hover there, torn between the need to touch her and the fear of waking her.

Every detail of her is etched into my mind—the gentle curve of her neck, the delicate lines of her collarbone, her hourglass figure. I drift lower, my gaze traveling down her body, over the gentle slope of her chest, the curve of her hips. The sight is mesmerizing, and I'm powerless to look away.

The urge to touch her becomes overwhelming. At this moment, she is everything, the only thing that matters, and I will not be denied.

Lowering myself, holding my shadow off her body, floating there, my mouth closes around a hardened nipple. I'm not a Shadowfen who can resist temptation. The vibration of her nipple in my mouth shudders through me, and I can't stop the growl that slides over my throat. Drawing her more into my mouth, sucking on her, I crave her sweetness.

She groans, her eyes still closed, her breaths heavy, so I move over to her other nipple, calling for my attention. Fuck, she's beautiful. The sensation of her in my mouth feels as real as skin to skin, even in my shadow form.

Releasing her, I slide lower, positioning myself between her legs, pressing them wider with my hands, slow enough so she doesn't wake.

Arousal hits me at the view of her pink lips, her scent so vibrant it leaves me hard to the point of pain. It's bound to all my senses, and I'm blinded by her beauty, unable to control myself.

Just one kiss.

One taste.

The anguish of pulling back tugs at something inside me. My mind fogs on the ripe scent of her sweet, berry and musky scent. It's something forbidden, something I'll fight to the death to capture.

Never one to waste a perfect moment, I move in closer.

My shadow tongue pushes out past my mouth and licks the full length of her. The arousal from earlier kicks me so hard I'm lost. My cock is so thick as I wrap my lips around her, unable to stop if I wanted to. And fuck, I don't.

Her chest rises and falls quicker, her violet hair shifting over her face as she tilts her head back, unleashing a beautiful moan.

Shudder after shudder of arousal tightens my stomach and my balls. Moisture seeps out, and I lap it up. My muscles tense as I push myself closer, fucking desperate to be inside her.

My hard-as-fuck cock stands upright, and fire sweeps over my body. I admire how beautifully her tits move with each breath she takes. I flatten my tongue, running it between her lips, tasting all of her sweetness while she's heaving for breath now, writhing on the bed.

Fuck, she's stunning, losing control like this. She moans, her legs spreading wider for me. Her body wants me, craves my dick inside her.

Part of me wants her to wake up, almost to have her fight her instincts as I know she would, for me to push her, to show her why she needs me. But it doesn't stop me from devouring her dripping cunt.

She's breathing heavily now, her hips rocking, and I fucking love her against my mouth. I need so much more. My fingers pull at her hole, stretching her just enough for me to draw back to see the small channel gaping for me.

I smile, my dick hardening, my pelvis bucking forward. Shoving my tongue into her, I taste her deeply, my nose pressed to her clit, rubbing her. My hands cup her ass, lifting her to meet me.

Her moans and my grunts tangle together. Those

wicked cries on her throat, hands moving to her breasts, squeezing them, hold me captive.

She smells of the most desirable flower in the world. I'm an animal, eating her savagely while her beautiful sounds escalate, her inner thighs, my face, covered in her juices. I need more... Fuck. I can't stop. I'm completely lost and have never felt this way toward anyone.

She has a pull on me that turns me into a savage... Her body tenses, and suddenly, she springs up into a sitting position, a beautiful scream escaping her throat. The sound pierces the quiet room, raw and filled with pleasure.

In an instant, I pull away, fading back into the shadows. My lips curl into a dark smile as I lick them, savoring the taste of her. The shadows embrace me, hiding me from her sight, but I watch her shuddering from her climax, dripping with her excitement, trembling, her chest rising and falling rapidly.

Her eyes dart around the room, almost fearful. She clutches the sheets, drawing them to her chest, closing her legs, and catching her breath. Even in her fright, she's captivating.

Blinking, she sits there curled up, seeming lost. When she finally gets to her feet, I dart through the sliver under the door, already transforming into my human form. I hurl myself onto the couch, noticing my cock is tenting my pants. Just as the door opens, I snatch a cushion, covering my erection. Acting nonchalantly, though my heart races from the encounter, I glance up at her with an innocent smile.

"Hello, sleepy."

She's wrapped in a blanket, her violet hair cascading over her shoulders messily. She startles at seeing me, pausing midstep.

"Where am I?" she asks, glancing around, sleep still tugging at her eyes.

"In Wolfe's quarters. Apparently, you fell asleep after he brought you to orgasm."

She stares at me incredulously, her cheeks flushing a deep crimson. "Oh... and you're here because?"

"Well, since your incident in the ritual chamber, we're going to keep a close eye on you to ensure no one hurts you again. Consider me your protector."

She blinks, clearly processing my words. "That's kind of sweet, I guess, but also a bit restrictive."

I chuckle, leaning back on the couch. "Sweet, huh? I guess that's one way to put it."

"So, what now? We just stay here?"

"Nope," I state, licking my lips, still tasting her in my mouth. "You are going to shower and get changed. I'm certain Wolfe has some clothes for you in there. He's nothing if not beyond organized. I'm taking you out to get something to eat. Plus, I have something I want to show you."

She doesn't move but stares at me, confused.

"Look," I say, softening my tone, "I know this is all overwhelming, but we're here to keep you safe. I promise we won't let anything happen to you. We're going to find out who attacked you and fuck them up."

She wraps the blanket tighter around herself. "And we'll be safe?"

"Trust me. With me, no one would dare lay a finger on you. I have a rather lethal reputation on the vessel. I don't always play nice."

She nods slowly, her stare never leaving mine. There's a flicker of something there—hope, maybe, or curiosity. It's enough for now.

She hurries back into the room where the bathroom awaits. And I'm left behind, lifting my pillow and staring down at my erection tenting my pants...

Fuck, you better go down, and fast.

CHAPTER
TWENTY-ONE

SAGE

"What *is* this place?" I ask, glancing around the long hallway Nyko and I are strolling through. Chandeliers hang overhead, their crystals scattering the light across the arched ceilings, the stone walls lined with tapestries. Lining our path, there are carvings of lifelike beastly heads on podiums. It's terrifying, yet I can't stop staring at the collection of severed animal heads.

"The Beast Hall." His voice deeply echoes around us, a wicked grin curling on his mouth as he stares at me like he's in his favorite place in the world.

Since waking up in Wolfe's room, Nyko's been determined to show me around, and I welcome it, as I haven't had a chance to see more of the vessel.

Besides, it takes my mind off the reminder that I'd woken up with the most beautiful orgasm rocking me awake. I swore I had dreamed of one of the monsters going down on me, and I couldn't stop him... I didn't want to, to tell the truth. Because I wished I'd woken up and found one there, to put out the flame that's constantly burning me up.

Of course, I blame it on all the talk about true mates, about my body going weak around them, and the ridiculously wicked sex I've had with Wolfe and Killian. Still slightly sore, I feel it with every step I take, reminding me of how much I enjoyed them.

Yet, here I am, also stealing glances at Nyko alongside me in our stroll.

"That's a Braucor," he states loudly, sticking his chest out, staring at a two-headed goatlike creature with curled horns. "I single-handedly destroyed that asshole. Look at him now!" He's chuckling.

I scrunch up my nose even more to think these *are* real heads. He points to a particularly large one with fangs jutting upward from its lips, a squashed nose, and bulging glassy eyes. It's freaky.

"That one took a bite out of me." He lifts his shirt, revealing his toned stomach and the low hang of his pants on his hips. As I trace the contours of his muscles, I spot the healed scar on his side—large teeth marks.

"Oh, hell! That would have hurt!"

"Like a damn bitch." But he's smiling, proud of his war wounds, studying another grotesque head, smiling to himself. He wears his human form again, dressed in a long-sleeved shirt that has metal bands across his biceps and dark pants that hug powerful legs, while he keeps raking a hand through his hair. Except, it's his jade eyes, how they glint behind his long lashes, that leave me breathless.

I have yet to see his monster side. Though, for now, I'm beyond content with him being less terrifying. There's actually something deeply captivating about him but also slightly scary.

He catches me staring and grins, showing perfect white teeth, well except for the two canine teeth, much longer and sharper. Since when are monsters so beautiful?

At the end of the hall, we swing left, where against one wall are lofty windows revealing the sea. For a change, the golden and purple sky's bright, the water settled.

Sunlight illuminates Nyko's hair, revealing strands that look bronze and gold, hair that sits messily around his face. It's as though he rakes his hand through it most mornings and declares it done. That rugged look goes with his constant brooding appearance when he's not smiling. There's a dimple in his chin, a heavy brow, and tanned skin telling me he spends lots of time outdoors... fighting beasts, no doubt.

He remains close to me, almost touching, especially as we begin to pass more Shadowfen strolling by. He ensures he places himself between me and them, seeming to study them with such intensity that they avoid his stares and lower theirs, moving past us quickly.

I appreciate it since the recent attack has me constantly glancing over my shoulder.

The room opening up ahead of us is peppered with

round tables and seats, and one wall is completely made of glass... well, a tapestry of colored shapes mounted to create a window. It throws a rainbow across the room.

"This area is gorgeous."

He just nods, studying me constantly. "So very beautiful." Then he winks my way, releasing all the butterflies in my stomach.

I blink away from him before he has me blushing.

We pass several tables full of monsters chatting, coming in all kinds of forms.

Some are completely covered in hair; others have claws and tails. A few stares come in my direction, including a young girl with three eyes who smiles my way. I give her a small wave back.

Before I know it, Nyko and I are heading down a set of stairs at the rear of the room, two floors to be precise, where the sound of chatter reaches me, and the smell of spices and foods has me sniffing the air, stomach rumbling for food.

"We're going to eat at one of my favorite spots," he tells me, giving me a sneaky smile.

"I could eat whatever I'm smelling." It's savory, spicy, and delicious. I might be drooling.

He leans into me playfully, his breath on my cheek, his words in my ear: "Have I mentioned how delicious you smell?"

"Hey," I gasp. "Don't distract me because I'm starving."

He chuckles, guiding me toward a set of lofty double doors that open on our approach. Inside spreads out an indoor market, but unlike anything I could have imagined. Stall after stall lines the wide pathway, filled with all kinds of items for sale. Jars filled with tiny creatures floating in a blue liquid, baskets with dried meat, and I don't care to know what animal they belong to. Another table displays bowls of strange, long purple fruit, another with potted plants where the leaves grow faintly. And one vendor has a dead Tidecreeper strung up from its hind legs, with its head off.

I cringe.

Above the narrow walkway, there are strings of lights giving off a glowing effect, lighting up the area even brighter. Something small rushes past my legs. I might have yelped and bumped into Nyko, regretting it instantly as the store girl nearby laughs at me. I look back to see it's a bright magenta-colored, bunny-looking animal.

"You're safe," Nyko tells me. He automatically loops an arm around my lower back, drawing me against his side. "It's only going to gnaw on your ankles."

"Haha." I untangle myself from him, while he's giving me his mocking smirk.

As we continue through the market, he subtly guides me with a protective arm, ensuring no one gets too close. Despite his playful demeanor, there's an edge to his movements. We pass a vendor selling strange, twisted roots that seem to pulse faintly with light. Another stall displays intricate tiny carvings of creatures I can't even begin to name.

Nyko turns us down a narrower path until we stop in

front of a stall filled with jewelry. I'm in awe at the glittering they release from the lights—necklaces, bracelets, earrings, rings, and even beautiful brooches made of metal with tiny colored stones.

"Anything catch your eye?" he asks, his voice soft, leaving me buzzing. His closeness has me leaning into him.

"Are you sure?" I ask, glancing up at him. "These look expensive, and I—"

"Absolutely." He's giving me his brilliant smile, full of charm today.

I might have just swooned, but I quickly drift toward a brooch of something that resembles a butterfly with tiny stones in its wings. While I study it, Nyko's talking to the stall owner in a language I don't understand, and in no time, he has my piece paid for, and the man behind the stall hands me a small paper bag, which I take and hold close to me.

"Thanks." I glance up at Nyko. "I've never owned any jewelry, and no one has ever given me such a gift. Thank you." I pause, fighting the tightness in my chest. "Why are you being so nice?"

He takes my hand in his, swallowing it with his own.

"No reason needed, unless you want me to make one up?"

I blink at him, smiling, unsure if I've experienced a day of being spoiled in my life. Back home, I have errands to run daily, to look after my mom, to collect berries. And now, part of me feels guilty for taking it easy, for being bought a brooch when my mom's at home sick, without me. As much as I remind myself she might not even be awake yet with the time differences, I still miss her terribly.

"I'm starving. Come on, let's grab some food before I start snacking on you," Nyko teases, winking at me, and I somehow wouldn't put it past him. His large hand squeezes mine lightly, and we move quickly until we end up in front of a stall that smells heavenly, like roast. I'm salivating. There's a bowl filled with oversized drumsticks on a small fire, roasted, coated in spices, and continuously turned over. As tempting as it looks, the notion terrifies me of what animal it could be.

Nyko starts ordering, and I lose track of what he's selected. We move quickly behind the stall, where there's a tiny courtyard-style area with lights and lofty plants in pots, giving the look a fairy-tale vibe. It's gorgeous. He guides me to one of the empty tables in the corner near a glowing plant. A soft song plays around us, blocking out some of the chatter from the market. I can't stop glancing around, really liking the location. The people we pass bow to Nyko, showing their respect, I assume.

"Wow, this place is wonderful." I place the paper bag on the table, reaching inside, grabbing out the brooch, loving how it glints in the lights, and pin it to my shirt.

"This really is so pretty. Thanks." I pick up the bag to throw it when I feel something else jiggling about in the bag. Curious, I tip it out into my palm, revealing a bright silver necklace. The chain is a long strand with intricate floral patterns on the ends, each holding a mauve pearl that glints and reflects a pearlescent shine.

"Whose is this, because it's beautiful?"

"I got it for you." His eyes are sparkling, and I'm about to cry.

My mouth falls open, excitement flaring through me.

Nyko nods, leaning forward with that intoxicating smile. "In Blight, it's said that such necklaces show a connection between two Shadowfen... the person who gifts it and the one who wears it, which is why there are two pearls. And I want you to wear something that will remind you of me. Plus, that metal is a white blood-gold, a rare material."

"Do I want to ask what blood-gold is?"

He's laughing but still holding my stare, and it's odd as I haven't yet seen this calmer side of him yet, and we're just getting to know each other, so why's he gifting me a necklace? I'm no fool and know he likes me, I see it in the way he stares at me, so maybe he's a lot more romantic than he lets on.

"It's a fusion of white gold and my blood."

My throat chokes up at the sentiment, his gesture beautiful... though the part of a pearl being each of us feels slightly obsessive. The blood part is a bit disturbing.

"Your blood?" I ask, my voice slightly squeaking.

He grins, his gaze darkening, and that tells me everything. "Blood-gold is known to have protective energies."

"Now, that I like." I glance at the piece, not seeing any hooks on the ends to latch it, and it's not as if I can tell him I won't put it on when he stares at me like he's never been happier.

"It's gorgeous. Will you help me put it on?" I ask, not

even freaked out as much as I should be, but I adore his gesture.

He's already on his feet, coming over to me.

"So, how do I wear it? I can't see where to loop it closed."

"It doesn't latch," he states, standing and moving closer to crouch next to me. He takes the necklace, saying, "Lift your hair for me."

I do as he asks, and he threads it around my neck. The metal molds softly against my skin, but not tightly, and the two pearl endings drop in the middle of my collarbones, one sitting slightly lower than the other.

I reach up, my fingers shaking. "It's stunning. Are you sure about this? It looks really expensive."

He reaches over, straightening it, the tips of his fingers grazing my skin, leaving behind a path of tingles. But he's gone just as quickly back to his seat. He stares at me with those hypnotic jade eyes, his smile having a way of making me swoon and forget my thoughts.

"It's made for you and now you'll never forget me." He's smirking, leaving me laughing.

I sense the necklace settling, its weight comforting yet cool against me.

"It's a really special gift. Thank you." My cheeks are burning up as I keep smiling.

That's when a waiter appears at our table, delivering a large round silver platter brimming with food. She sets it down, almost taking up the whole table. My stomach is growling with hunger at all the delicious roast and spicy fragrances.

The oversized drumsticks coated in herbs and oil glisten under the courtyard lights, alongside bowls of vibrant salads and an array of dipping sauces. There are skewers of what looks like grilled vegetables and cubes of meat, but their colors are more vivid than anything I've ever seen, almost glowing in the light. There are also buns similar to the ones I ate the other night in the bakery.

"This looks incredible," I gush.

"Dig in while it's warm."

I reach for a drumstick, its size and weight much larger than I'm used to. "What kind of meat is this?" I ask, slightly afraid.

Nyko's laughing already before he's said anything. "It's a Pluckar. A large birdlike creature. I've hunted a few in my time. The bastards are fast, super aggressive, and territorial. Catching one is a challenge as they often turn on you in a flock."

"Sounds like turkeys, what we had back on the farm. I've been chased by them in the past, and it's terrifying." I take a tentative bite, and the flavors explode in my mouth. I moan instantly, eyes widening. The spices and salt blend perfectly, and I can't help but groan in delight. This can pass for turkey meat. "I love this." I take another large bite.

Nyko watches me while grabbing his own drumstick and tearing into it. Juices run down his chin, and he catches them with a napkin. The sight makes my stomach growl even louder. I take another bite, then another, until I'm left with a bone that's easily as long as my hand.

"It's the most delicious thing I've ever tasted." And it's not some weird creature that slides on its belly or drools or shoots poison from its saliva. Just normal meat. I pray I'm right.

As I set down the bone, I notice Nyko watching me with the same hunger I just showed the food. Embarrassed, I quickly grab my napkin, wiping my mouth.

"I love watching you eat so excitedly," he coos.

"That comes from not eating for what feels like forever." I reach for one of the buns. It's a pale cream color, and when I tear it open, it reveals a bright yellow center with small pieces in the jam-like sauce. Nearby is a small bowl with blue cream... the butterfly larva, if I remember right. No hesitation, I dig right in.

"Noted," Nyko murmurs, grinning at me as he leans back in his seat. "Make sure to always have food for you."

"Where do you raise these animals, anyway? On the vessel?"

He's shaking his head. "We have a regular Day of the Chase at various islands where we stop for supplies." He nods, leaning in closer, pushing the plate of drumsticks closer to me.

"Last time we went, Killian was cornered by the Pluckars. The fuckers surrounded him, and he was there with his swords out, ready to battle, shooing them away." He's chortling at the story.

"And what did he do?"

"Well, while he killed some, he ended up climbing a tree until they left him alone."

I giggle, trying to imagine Killian scared of anything, let alone cooped up in a tree from birdlike creatures.

As I keep eating, my thoughts drift to Killian and Wolfe and how they still haven't been truly honest with me. I take a deep breath, studying Nyko, deciding it's time to get some answers.

Putting the second half of my bun down on the platter, I ask, "So, Nyko, let's talk about something serious."

He nods. "Hit me."

Taking a quick sip of the table water, I ask, "Do you know who my father is?" I hadn't expected to shake this much from asking one question.

He pauses for a moment, his expression unreadable as he wipes his mouth before lowering the napkin.

"Your father is the false King in Blight," he answers directly, no hesitation.

My mouth drops open for the second time today. "You better not be damn joking."

Except, his expression is dead serious.

"That son of a bitch took over the Silvercrest Kingdom after the Great Desolation, and it's why we're now fucking stuck living on this vessel." Frustration and anger ripple behind his voice.

The food in my gut churns. I can't find my words, and I'm struggling to breathe. My father destroyed their lives and took over a kingdom!

"You deserve the truth," he adds with a low voice. "I

know Killian and Wolfe want to tell you but are worried about how you'll react."

"Why?" My shoulders shoot back at his comment. "I have no allegiance to my father. I've never even met him, so what difference would it make?"

"Because we're planning on going in to remove him from power... by any force necessary."

I'm fully aware of what he's saying.

They're going to kill him.

It's difficult to have feelings toward someone I've never met, someone who abandoned my mother and me, who left us ostracized in a village that ended up hating us. My whole life, I've desperately wanted to know who my father is... to ask him why he never returned, never wanted to meet his daughter.

Yet, the unsettling sensation that I'm now with a powerful Shadowfen who intends to kill him dawns heavily on me. I frown, my hands shaking in my lap.

"It's a lot to take in, and why we've taken our time to tell you."

"But I had a right to know," I answer curtly.

"Yeah, you did. But your father's actions have impacted us all, so it's not that straightforward."

"Then why not just summon a portal and pop into his kingdom and get your revenge when he least expects it?" Anger simmers in my veins.

He sighs. "It's not that simple, Sage. A portal can only be summoned to take you out of our world and back, not across Blight. And we tried having Killian transport himself from Earth right into the kingdom, but it backfired. They have magic around their island, and Killian was thrown back into Earth."

The reality hits hard, and part of the sting is that if he'd wanted to visit us, he couldn't have.

Thoughts fly in every direction, dread squeezing my gut at his revelation about Wolfe.

Shifting in my seat, I ask, "So, Wolfe is the true heir to the kingdom?"

"Yes, he is now the rightful King of Silvercrest Kingdom."

I swallow hard, trying to come to terms with the news, with everything I've learned since arriving in this world—the reason for them living on this vessel, why Wolfe and the other two are in charge. My thoughts spiral on what Killian had said to me in Nightingale Village... that he's been searching for me. That I'm needed.

He's watching me intently. "Are you all right?"

I blink at him, my words pouring out, "Why was I brought to Blight?"

He doesn't respond instantly, and his face is stoic, blank of any emotions. But when he doesn't answer, I do it for him.

"You were all planning on using me to get to my father, weren't you?" My voice trembles with a mix of anger and betrayal. "That's why you brought me here—to use me as bait or have me convince him. Whatever it is, you three were going to use me to your benefit!"

"Sage, it's not that simple," Nyko replies, his face

blanching, that serious expression confirming my worst fears.

So, all those things about Killian and Wolfe being my true mates, them bringing out emotions in me... was it all fake? Did they trick me? My heart's galloping, the courtyard tilting, and I feel like I'm going to be sick. Pushing my chair back, I jolt to my feet.

"You've all been using me this whole time."

"Sage," Nyko states, reaching for me, but I flinch away from him and dart across the courtyard, bursting into the busy marketplace. I glance back to see him coming after me.

Betrayal churns in my gut, and I hate that I feel anything for them. I turn and push myself into the crowds and down a path on my left to get away from him.

At that exact moment, something sharp jabs me in the side of the neck.

I cry out as my knees buckle.

Dizziness comes so quickly that I have no time to react before my world darkens, and I fall.

CHAPTER
TWENTY-TWO

SAGE

I gasp for air, startling awake, convinced I'm back in Wolfe's bed, having slept an entire day after the strangest dream of spending a day with Nyko. Opening my eyes, yawning, I roll onto my back, the bed rock-hard and cold.

Wait, this isn't right!

That's when a horrifying hiss fills the room.

Heart in my throat, I jolt to a sitting position. And it all comes back quickly—the day with Nyko, the market, the truth about my father, the realization of why I'm really in this world. But right now, none of that compares to the immediate terror of *where* I've woken up.

Around me spreads out a strange room with polished stone floors, no furnishings, and the walls and ceiling resemble a cave. Grooves are etched into the walls, jagged stone hanging from above, and the small lights embedded in the rock steal enough of the shadows to show me I'm in really big trouble.

Where the hell am I?

"H-hello?" I call out, assuming I'm still on the vessel, not on some island, based on the spotlights in the room. Turning on the spot, taking in the large enclosure, I can't see a way out, not from where I'm standing, but there has to be a way out, maybe in the shadows.

I rub the side of my neck where I was jabbed, fear tumbling through me as I realize that whoever attacked me in the woods has to be responsible, right? I was barely a few steps out of the courtyard when they struck. My skin shivers—they've been watching me the whole day?

Scanning the room, I start walking around, searching for a door... I entered the room somehow.

Then that hissing comes again.

I flinch hard, my heart slamming into my rib cage. Whipping around, across the cave-like room, something shifts in the shadows.

It slithers out, and the fear, the shock—it all crashes into me.

My scream rushes out involuntarily as I see the same creature from the woods. It's here and has me trapped. I back up, hugging myself.

"Gods, this can't be happening."

An elongated body covered in black scales glistens in the dim light with six long legs with webbed feet. Being so much closer to it is terrifying, but I can see the details more now—the fangs from lips peeled back over them. It lifts itself on its hind legs, towering, and its long face with gleaming eyes pierces right through me.

Fates, I don't want to be swallowed by the snake creature.

My breath hitches, my hands shaking as they search for anything to defend myself with. I have empty pockets, and there's nothing around me. Shit!

"No, no, no," I whisper, my voice trembling. I keep backing up until my back hits the cold, jagged wall. The thing hisses again, its forked tongue flicking out, tasting the air, tasting my fear, no doubt. Its eyes are locked on to mine.

"Stay back!" I shout, but my voice wavers, betraying my terror.

The snake beast doesn't seem to care, dropping back onto its belly, those limbs bent and coming toward me. Its movements are slow and deliberate, as if savoring the moment.

I try to think, try to find a way out, but my mind is a jumble of fear and panic.

Glancing around desperately, searching for any possible escape, I come up empty. My heart's pounding so hard it feels like it might break a few ribs. That's when I spot a small dark opening in the far left corner of the room, barely large enough for me to squeeze through. Seeing the snake slither from the right, deeper in the cave, maybe that's my way out. Not overthinking, I dart toward it, my legs shaking, praying I can make it before the creature reaches me.

The hissing escalates, and my skin is covered in goose bumps. I don't dare look back, fearing it's right behind me.

Frantically, I drop to my knees, scrambling through the opening, spotting a light at the end. It's narrow, but if that snake thing can slither through it, so the hell can I. The rough stone scrapes against my arms and back.

Hisses echo behind me.

I'm moving desperately, terrified out of my mind, not caring that walls are catching and pulling on my clothes. I tug against it, needing to escape.

Just as I think I'm there at the opening where a beam of light greets me, a sharp pain shoots through my ankle, and I'm yanked back. I scream, clawing at the floor, trying my best to pull myself forward.

"Help, someone help me," I bellow, hoping I'm heard, but the creature's grip is relentless. I don't want to die here.

"Let me go!" I shout, twisting onto my back, kicking my other foot into its leg, the one latched onto my ankle.

Golden eyes glint in the dark passage, and it unleashes another hiss, then drags me back into the cave so fast that I stand no chance of stopping it.

The rugged walls scrape across me, burning sharply and feeling like they're tearing me to shreds. I cry from the pain, but there's no time for pity. I kick it again viciously in the face and yank my ankle free.

Scrambling up, the pain shoots up my leg where it jammed its damn claws into my ankle.

"You shithead!" I cry out, feeling just as angry as scared. Realizing no one is going to save me, I know I have to do it myself. I didn't come this far to die by a snake. A new surge of energy pours through me, something I put down to adrenaline.

I back away as it hisses, long green fangs bared. My whole body is shaking. If I get behind it, maybe I can strangle it. The idea of touching it terrifies me, but what other options do I have?

The sting on my shoulder and jaw burns from the cave's scratches. I rub them, my hand coming back bloody from where I got scratched up in my escape. I gasp. My arms have scratches, too. Glancing down quickly, I see the tears in my shirt and pants, blood staining them. Then I spot a few drops of blood on my new necklace, on the pearls. Somehow, my brooch is untouched.

As much as I'm pissed at being trapped in here, I'm also annoyed that the beautiful necklace is tainted. I never receive gifts, so this means a lot to me.

"You're going to pay for this," I sneer at the snake. I have no idea where my newfound bravery comes from, but maybe deep down, when it comes to facing life or death, I'm a fighter, not weak like most in the village assumed.

Another hiss, and this time, the creature strikes fast with bared teeth.

A whimper spills from my throat as my body darts into action. I shove myself out of the way so quickly I'm left confused by my strength, yet I feel invincible, stronger, faster. There's no time to think about it. I'm buzzing all over, and I welcome this new part of me.

I hurl myself to its side again, knowing this is my

chance. As I leap toward its back while it's twisting around, I crash against it, bringing us both down, me on top of it.

It's a strange sensation to be cringing and screaming at touching its scaly body while forcing myself to throw my arms around its neck. I know this isn't me, but all my terror and facing death must be affecting me.

Inside my chest, my heart's on fire, my head screaming, but my body... it's floating on an energy I don't understand. I embrace it, knowing this is the only way I'll survive.

The snake convulses, and in a sudden thrust, it bucks me off. I fly across the room, hitting the wall with a thump, the air expelled from my lungs.

"I'm going to die," I gasp, pushing myself back up.

"What the hell am I thinking? I can take that on."

Lifting my gaze, I watch the creature beneath the lights, and I swear I must have hit my head because I see two of them now. Well, not quite—the second one is a shadow of the first, with a mauve hue. It's not mimicking its actions but lingering there, staring at the creature.

I blink, trying to clear my vision, but the shadow remains, watching. The snake hisses again, its attention diverted to the strange shadow. Taking advantage of the distraction, I push myself up, every part of me aching. I have to find a way to use this. I have to survive.

The creature lunges at the shadow, but it passes right through it. The serpent slams into the wall from the momentum, then spins around, shaking its head.

The shadow is staring at me now, and for a moment,

I swear it's waiting for me. Eyes glowing, its mouth isn't gaping open, and it's not in a striking pose. It's strange to say, but it doesn't feel threatening.

I press my back harder against the cold, rough wall of the cave.

In the eerie silence of the cavernous room, the shadow serpent and I stand frozen. The actual snake creature, realizing its shadow counterpart poses no threat, turns its attention back to me.

This is just great!

Panic claws at me as it slithers toward me, body tight as if preparing to strike.

Trembling, I'm trapped.

"Do something! Help me!" I shout at the shadow, desperation tainting my voice, figuring if it's here, there's a purpose, right?

The real danger approaches, its forked tongue tasting the air, and it lunges at me.

I instinctively dodge to the side, the buffet of air from his attack shoving me farther away. I snap around fast, and that's when I spot the shadow sliding rapidly across the floor in a fluid rush toward the snake. Heart pounding in my ears, I watch the shadow serpent lunging at the snake, throwing itself at him, knocking them both over.

Wait, it's taken a solid form now?

I dart out of the way, wanting to be nowhere near them. In that same heartbeat, the shadow slithers away, then it stands there again, staring at me once more from a few feet away.

My chest's pumping so fast now as terror consumes me.

"What the hell is going on? What are you doing?"

I swing my attention to the fucking snake, arching up, dripping venom from its gaping mouth, eyes huge and clearly furious. It rushes at me, and this time, it's as though I'm ready, the overwhelming energy in my body shoving me forward to duck and weave out of its path.

I'm terrified.

That's when I realize my movements are being echoed by the shadow.

Frustrated, I shout, "Attack it! Don't just copy me!" I thrust my fist forward in a commanding gesture.

The shadow lunges at the creature, its shadow fangs bared and sharp.

They clash, their bodies entwining in a terrifying tangle.

The two serpents locked in battle.

Wait... if it's copying my actions...

As they roll across the floor, the shadow seems to gain the upper hand, its body somehow finding purchase on the serpent's slippery scales. I'm glued to the sight, my fists curled tight. I drive my fists into the air in front of me as though it's me fighting the creature.

They're both a blur of speed and savagery. The shadow coils itself around the real snake, tightening its grip before sinking those long black fangs deep into the neck of our enemy. It thrashes wildly, its body convulsing in a desperate attempt to free itself.

I cringe, staring at it struggling, and can't look away, terrified yet wanting that thing eliminated.

Slowly, life fades from its eyes, its movements growing sluggish, then stopping altogether.

As the shadow releases its hold, the limp body of the beast thuds heavily onto the stone floor. The shadow then glances over at me, its form flickering slightly. I lean against the wall, my breath coming in ragged gasps.

"I don't know what you are, but thank you, and please don't attack me now."

Exhaustion and shock threaten to buckle my knees when I catch movement from the corner of my eye—a hidden door in the rock wall sits open with Killian and Wolfe standing in their monster forms, Nyko nearby, mouths all hanging open, eyes huge.

My heart skips. How long have they been there?

Nyko suddenly stumbles on his feet, moving more into the light.

I gasp at how pale he looks. Before I can even process everything completely, he sways on his feet, a hand clutching at his chest, and then collapses with a heavy thud that reverberates through the still room.

It's the same moment the shadow serpent crumbles into a cloud of dust that drifts away into nothingness.

"Nyko!" I cry out, rushing over to him. The distance between us closes in seconds, but each step feels agonizingly slow.

CHAPTER
TWENTY-THREE

SAGE

Tears blur my vision as I grip Nyko's hand tighter, my fingers intertwining with his limp ones. The sterile smell of the medical room fills my nostrils where he lies motionless, his skin unnaturally pale against the white sheets of the medical bed. Tubes snake from his arm and neck, connected to machines.

The moment he collapsed in the cave room, Killian lifted him and ran up here. Wolfe clasped my hand, taking me alongside him in a rush. No one said a word, but the fear, the panic, coiled around me because if Wolfe and Killian were scared, then Nyko was hurt bad... really bad.

Now, I look up at them, searching their faces as they stand on the opposite side of the bed.

"Please." My voice breaks. "Tell me he'll be all right."

Silence stretches, heavy and suffocating.

"He's strong, and this won't keep him down," Wolfe

says, and I know he's trying to be comforting, but I don't miss the hardness in his voice, the worry in his furrowed brow.

Killian attempts to give me a weak smile. "He'll be fine in no time. You'll see."

His words leave me shaking because I suspect I know... Truth is, I have no damn idea how, but I'm certain it has something to do with me and the shadow serpent back in the cave room.

The doctor, a monster resembling a stick insect with long, slender limbs and an elongated torso, moves with swift precision around Nyko. He adjusts the vials connected by thin, clear tubes to Nyko's veins. He has a small round head, and its large, green oval eyes study Nyko, making a grinding noise as if he's rubbing his teeth together.

"What's wrong with him? Please tell me," I plead with the doctor, who's holding a metal coil attached by a black handle, the machine emitting a low hum. He's looking at all of us instead of just me.

"You will need to vacate the room now, please." His words are devoid of warmth, but he's not unkind.

I blink at him, not wanting to leave Nyko's side, but Wolfe has his arms around me, ushering me out of the room. "Let's go. We'll be just outside."

One glance back and he's placing the coils against Nyko's chest. They instantly turn fiery orange, causing his whole body to convulse.

A whimper spills from my lips as I'm rushed out quickly, the door closing behind me. I barely remember moving, but I'm sitting on a chair in a long white hallway, Wolfe and Killian on either side of me I see their distraught expressions.

"Why are you being nice to me? I'm responsible. I don't know how I did it, but he's hurt because of my power. The shadow vanished just as Nyko collapsed." My throat's thickening, tears sting my eyes, and I can't stop replaying the scene over and over in my mind—Nyko collapsing just as the serpent shadow fell apart into thousands of particles before vanishing.

Wolfe grips my hand a bit tighter. "Every power is beautiful but can be a double-edged sword, Sage," he explains in a calm voice. "You didn't hurt him intentionally."

I shake my head, the tears spilling over. "It's not beautiful," I state. "I hurt Nyko. How can something that causes so much pain be good? And how did you even find me?"

Killian, sitting next to me, frowns deeply. "We finally found a stall owner who happened to see you being kidnapped. Tell us what happened in the cave."

Clutching the handles of the chair, the hard edges bite into my palms. I recount the terrifying events with the snake—the attack, my failed escape, the surreal moment when the shadow obeyed my desperate commands.

"I don't understand much of it," I admit with a trembling voice. "There was this rush of power through me. I didn't feel like myself, yet it was as though I could fight that stupid creature. I could have died." I'm gasping for air.

Wolfe's expression darkens, his brows furrowing, studying me, listening. "Powers like that... are rare and often a sign of deep connection to another's shadow essence."

The silence that follows sharpens with the distant hum of the soft whir of medical equipment from inside the infirmary.

"Give me a moment," Killian says, getting up and hurrying down the hallway.

I stare at Wolfe, murmuring, "It felt like I could take on the creature on my own, which is absurd. And that shadow, it moved with me, following my instructions. Well, sort of, as I really had no idea what I was doing." I give him a wonky smile, then glance at the door where we left Nyko, my insides turning into knots. "Do you think he'll heal?"

"I hope so," he answers, which leaves me feeling dreadful on the inside.

I curl in on myself, but he's hugging me, and I appreciate his tenderness more than he'll ever know.

Killian returns, his grin a welcome sight as he hands me a transparent cup filled with something milky orange. And when I sniff it, it smells like dirty socks. I scrunch up my nose.

"Drink it. It will help calm you down," he assures me.

Despite the odd aroma, I trust him enough to take a sip. To my surprise, it's sweet, almost like warm, spiced orange juice, comforting me more than I expected. I take a few more sips, letting the warmth seep through me.

A different doctor rushes past us and heads down the hallway.

"I'm still trying to work out your ability. It seems to need to draw energy from someone to work. And why Nyko? Why not me?" Wolfe asks. "Why not one of us? Why not someone else at the nearby market?"

"Maybe because we'd spent time together beforehand," I suggest, remembering our last discussion, the revelation about my father, the reality of why they brought me to Blight. Nyko never corrected me when I asked him because he knew I was right. I'm here to serve a greater purpose that benefits them in reclaiming their kingdom... and that's hard to swallow. Perhaps I'm being unrealistic, believing their feelings are true, and now I struggle to accept that they are. And what happens once they get what they want from me?

My stomach hurts, and I'm torn at the heartache I feel for Nyko because I did that to him, yet I'm angry at them...

"What did you do together?" Wolfe persists.

I'm hyperaware of their hands on me, while irritation is starting to fill me. But I remind myself this isn't the time to get into that argument, not until I know Nyko is safe.

I sip the warm drink. "We wandered through the market, then had a huge meal, during which I put on the brooch he bought me." I look down at it, still pinned to my shirt, unstained. "And then he gifted me this necklace."

Reaching up, I touch the pearls cradled in the small curve just below my neck, noticing the dried blood stains on them, and a wave of guilt rattles me.

Wolfe's focusing on my necklace, running his fingers along the silver chain.

"Do you know where he got this from?" he asks.

"A vendor in the market. Why?"

Wolfe glances over to Killian, also looming over me. He tilts his head, touching the necklace, too, leaving me slightly claustrophobic.

"What's going on?" I ask.

"Is that chain made of blood-gold?" Killian quips, staring at Wolfe, not me.

I watch them both. "Nyko said it was crafted using his blood."

Wolfe nods his head. "That explains why you were drawn to Nyko's energy. The necklace connected you to him, and the blood in the metal had your power reaching out to him."

"Wait, how is that even possible?"

They both stare at me as if they're having the same thought, and the darkness behind their gazes worries me.

"Such powers are rare. I've only heard of them connected through true mates," Killian explains. "It's why when you mated with Wolfe and me, we were supercharged with unimaginable adrenaline. We were both buzzing around for hours afterward."

"You were? I had no idea," I state, feeling like it's a thing for them to keep me out of the loop, and I fucking hate it. "Wait, so you're saying Nyko's my true mate too?" My head's spinning. How many mates can a girl have?

I'm trying to take it all in, unsure how I feel about three intended mates, but then it does make sense, seeing how attracted I've been to all of them.

"So, if I understand correctly, when I have sex with any of you, I fill you with a burst of energy, but when I use my power, I draw on yours, almost draining you to death?" I'm shaking all over. "This is too much. I simply won't use my ability ever again." I gulp the orange juice down. "Aren't those red flags to you?" I ask. "Or is this where you lock me up and use me for my energy?" I'm unsure why I even said the last part out loud.

Their expressions wear their gravity—the same heartache breaking me.

"We've only read about such abilities in history books," Wolfe explains.

"On the bright side, now that we have a handle of your shadow side," Killian suggests with a small smile, "it means we can help you tame it, learn how to control it."

I'm slightly scared. "You make it sound easy, but my ability didn't feel simple back in the cave." My knees are bouncing, my anxiety rising.

Wolfe's expression softens as he places a comforting hand on my thigh. I flinch, pushing his hand away, feeling a surge of irritation.

His brow furrows at me.

Caught between the frightening potential of my newfound powers and the unnerving plans the three Shadowfen had for me, I'm left feeling edgy and on guard.

"It's going to be all right," Wolfe reassures me gently, but his words don't soothe the angst burning up inside me.

"I'm not so sure," I murmur, skepticism heavy in my voice.

Just then, the door to the infirmary swings open, interrupting us. The doctor steps out, his expression somber, a slight grin on his lipless mouth.

"Lord Nyko is stable," he announces, and relief washes over me. "He was drained close to death, but with rest and proper care, he should recover in a few days."

"Can we see him?" I ask immediately, moving to the edge of my seat.

"Yes," the doctor responds. "He's on a strict regimen of medications and will need constant monitoring for the next few days. We can transfer him to his quarters in the morning, but he will need constant supervision for the first twenty-four hours."

"I'll do it," I interrupt swiftly. Taking care of Nyko feels like the least I can do after everything that happened. "I need to be the one to do this."

"Perfect," the doctor retorts, while Wolfe studies me with curiosity.

"Very well," the doc agrees. "Come inside with me, and I'll show you what needs to be done."

Getting to my feet, I glance back at Killian and Wolfe, still in their seats. There's a haunted expression on their faces, as though they suspect something else is going on with me, and they aren't wrong.

Right now, focusing on Nyko is a necessary distraction and a chance to maybe right some wrongs.

The thought that the affection these three Shadowfen have shown me is part of their strategy to use me against my father leaves my gut twisting into knots. A bitter taste of betrayal rises in my throat, leaving me sick to my stomach.

Killian

"She's on edge. Nyko told her about her father. I saw it in her eyes." Wolfe's gaze sharpens, his voice a low growl as he leans against the cold metal hallway wall.

I nod, looking toward the infirmary where she's with Nyko, my fingers itching to go claim her. To bring a smile to her face because that last glance she gave us screamed her fury.

"I want to wring Nyko's damn neck to find out what happened. At least give us a heads-up." I clench my jaw. "But the power Sage unleashed, it's fucking impressive. That wasn't just a burst of shadow. She manifested a damn replica of the Sylar. I've never seen anything like it."

"Me, neither." Wolfe groans under his breath, his features set hard. "I need to speak with Sage. Come clean."

Arms tight against my side, hands curling from tension, I nod.

"She's really taken us off guard. I didn't expect her to be our true mate, so that fucked up our plans. All I want now is to steal her away to be with me. Yet if we don't get her to control her power, how long before she drains us all to death?" I'm not frightened of her, far from it. I'm more worried about her safety and her dealing with the risks. Fucking concerned she will do something stupid if she's angry, as a lot of our shadow powers are triggered by emotions.

Wolfe swallows hard. "A power we shouldn't mention to others. Remember the fear that spread in the old kingdom when everyone discovered my father's assistant's ability? They imprisoned her for life in a magic-encased cell because the city started revolting with fear that they weren't safe."

"Fuck them," I snarl under my breath. "Sage's energy should only impact us."

"Try telling that to the terrified Shadowfen, already feeling trapped on this vessel."

The girl I'm utterly obsessed with has the power to

eliminate us, and our enemy is her father. Yep, this is getting really fucked up.

I pause for a moment, staring down the corridor that feels colder than usual.

"So, how much are we going to tell her about our original plans?" My response is low, not wanting the couple passing us to hear.

"Everything. She needs to know it all—the real reason she was brought here, what her father has done, and even our intentions with her." His face is stiff, eyes steely.

"Fuck!" My voice trails off, knowing she won't take it well.

"We're way past the point of half-truths and shadows. She's part of this now, whether we planned it or not. And she's not just a piece on the board. She's our true mate and will rule alongside us."

I smile at the thought, but worry still burrows through me that she'll push against us.

"And if she decides to side with her father?"

His lips are thin. "Then we did a shit job of convincing her how much she means to us."

CHAPTER
TWENTY-FOUR

SAGE

In the dim light of Nyko's bedroom, shadows stretch long and deep across the walls. They're carved from dark wood to resemble a dense, shadowy forest. It's beautiful but slightly terrifying. Above, the ceiling is painted to depict a dense canopy of leaves with glimpses of the pinkish sky peeking through. The smell of medicinal herbs fills the space.

I've been sitting beside his king-size bed for several hours this morning, watching over him, caring for him. My entire body's shaking as he still hasn't woken up.

I did this to him!

I might have finally stopped crying from the guilt eating me up, yet I feel like shit on the inside. Fear crowds in my chest, breaths coming so fast, that I destroyed something inside him. Combine that with the possibility that Nyko's also my true mate, and my life's becoming an utter mess.

I somehow managed not to lose my mind and have

been focusing on Nyko, gripping the small bowl of salve in my lap.

"Well, I need to paste you now. Doctor's orders," I whisper into the stillness of his room, my words a terrible attempt at lightness. The medicine is meant to somehow help regain his energy while he's sleeping.

I cringe on the inside every time I remember the doctor's words—*you almost drained him to death.*

So now, Nyko lies motionless, his skin ghostly but thankfully less death-like than yesterday when he passed out.

Perspiration beads on his forehead, and each shallow breath he takes seems like an effort. The blame I'm feeling keeps churning in my gut. Because my life wasn't becoming brutal enough, now, of all the monster abilities, I had to get one that could kill my true mates. I sigh.

Staring at him, I follow the perfect lines of his cheekbones, the strong jawline, his thick eyebrows, and long lashes. My attention dips to his pale lips. He's perfect in every way, kindling awake the need I have for him deep inside of me.

Even lying in bed sick, his muscles are impossible to miss. My gaze traces the thin line of light brown hair running down the middle of his stomach, vanishing under the blanket around his waist. I'm teasing myself, torn between the guilt and an attraction I can't ignore.

Gently, I scoop some of the clear salve that's cool against my fingers and apply it to his chest, smelling slightly like freshly cut grass, and the cream is sucked up by his skin almost instantly.

Apply it every hour to his chest, the doctor had said, so I've done just that. His skin is warm under my touch, though it leaves me wondering why he's always in his human form. I struggle to believe he'd be so hideous that he avoids transforming.

As I finish rubbing in the salve, I pull back and go wash my hands in the bathroom. The room feels colder now, or maybe it's just the chill seeping from the walls into my bones.

Sitting next to him again, I fold my hands in my lap, the silence of the room punctuated only by his labored breathing and the distant rumblings that darken the sky. A storm's brewing. I twist in my seat to glance outside at the black clouds heading our way, when a soft knock at the door grabs my attention.

"Come in," I say, just as it opens.

Wolfe strolls inside, his presence commanding yet gentle. He's wearing a white V-neck shirt that hangs loosely around his waist, yet it's impossible to miss the muscles pressing against the fabric and those powerfully broad shoulders. He's in his human form, and still, he's so tall and strong.

"How's Nyko doing?"

Wolfe stands on the other side of the bed, staring down at him, and despite everything, butterflies are beating their wings wildly in my stomach in his presence. Then he lifts his head in my direction.

"I know you're upset, Sage, and you have every right to be, but I think it's important we talk." The ache behind his gaze wells in the pit of my stomach.

I breathe heavily, hands curled in my lap, and he watches me with a devastating expression.

"Start, then. Explain why you all kept me in the dark. I want to know your real intentions for me being here."

Wolfe exhales and pulls up a chair across the bed from me, making himself comfortable.

"It wasn't meant to be this way, Sage," he begins, leaning back in his seat while my mind's spiraling. "Our Shadowfen have grown exhausted from living on this constricting vessel, our resources dwindling, and everyone's demanding a solution to reclaim our kingdom. I don't blame them. I've spent my life trying to do just that."

"Have you attempted to speak to my f—*him*—to see if he'll compromise?"

He nods, the corners of his mouth creasing. "We endured three battles with his army, and in each, we lost good Shadowfen. Your father's a fucking asshole who'd rather see us all dead before he gives an inch."

I swallow the thickness in my throat, detesting my father more than I thought possible. And I have yet to meet him.

"Then we discovered he's been trying to find a way to summon a portal to Earth to find his daughter. That's when we decided if we could collect you, we'd have an advantage over him. Especially since he doesn't know the magic to open a portal, unlike me. I taught it to Killian and Nyko only, just like my father had taught me." He pauses, watching me intently, as if he's judging my expression.

I gasp, imagining the discussions they would have had about me being just something they could use. That ache digs deep down inside me because, like most in the village, that's how I'm seen—as someone they can use.

"Wh-why would *he* care who I am?"

Wolfe shifts in his seat. "Your father is a ruthless bastard. I learned from an insider that he wanted to discover your shadow power. Many in his bloodline are known to have unusual abilities, and he hoped you'd be an asset in his battle to secure his reign over the stolen kingdom. To use against us."

The more I listen, the more anger flares inside me. Now, I'm beginning to understand why my mother told me nothing about him.

"So, you decided to get me first, and what? Sell me to him? Use my ability against him?" My heart's hammering, waiting for his response, needing to understand exactly who my true mates are.

He leans closer against the bed between us, exhaling loudly, and for a moment, I stare down at Nyko. He's still passed out, and I wonder what he'd say if he was awake.

Lifting my attention, Wolfe's flaming eyes appear tamer today, which surprises me, considering I'm shaking so hard.

"Sage, you need to understand. Our intention *had* been to use you in our plan, so I'm not going to hide that from you. A decision born of desperation. But never in a million years would we have guessed you'd be our true mate. This changes everything because we will never hurt you!"

My hands curl tighter, fingernails digging into my palm, stinging.

"But you ripped me out of my life, made me leave my mother behind. You were going to give me to my father, even if he could have harmed me."

Lips thin, he nods, and something dangerous swirls inside me, something angry, vengeful.

"You had no right!" My voice rises, and I'm on my feet, pacing, unable to hold back the anger. My insides are torn between the truth and knowing I can't exactly ask them to take me back home now. Not with how much I'm changing, with how I won't fit back in the village. If I was an outcast before, how much would I be after word spreads that a monster returned me?

I'm looking out at the storm, my eyes stinging, a sickening pain deep in my chest.

"Sage," his voice grows tender, coming right behind me.

I twist and find him there, staring down at me, his brow furrowed, while a flare of violence swirls through me.

He reaches for me, but I step away.

"I can't, Wolfe. You lied to me. You were about to barter me off to a brutal man for land? Or was the whole plan to use me as a distraction while you attacked him? Was I your entry into the kingdom he banned you from?" I gasp and blink away the tears, hating that I want to cry instead of being strong.

But the frown on his face, the way he swallows hard

tells me that was exactly his plan. I was their way to reach my father. Nothing more than a key. Assholes!

"And what about now?" I state. "What's your new plan?" I'm shaking, arms tight at my sides, and I want to throw something at him. I'm not a violent person, but right now, I'm trembling with anger.

They brought me here, not because Killian picked me as his bride. I was their way in to get to my father.

"I'm so sorry, Sage." His words are barely a whisper, wavering and carrying on a long exhale. "The blame is on me, my sights so deeply set on giving my Shadowfen a permanent home, on getting revenge on that fucking bastard, that it clouded my judgment."

"No, it didn't," I snap. "You knew exactly what you were doing." I hold his gaze, and there's a flare in his jaw.

My whole life, I took all the insults, the pain of being invisible, and that coldness courses through me once more. The past surfaces like a reminder that nothing will ever change for me. It thumps my insides, and I'm close to screaming, to crying at always being the one others toss aside. I'm crumbling on the inside.

Silence pulses inside my chest while Wolfe stares out at the oncoming storm, shadows falling over his expression.

"I was thirteen when the Great Desolation destroyed our kingdom," he murmurs, drawing my attention. "It was on this day that many Shadowfen perished, that my home came crumbling down. It happened so fucking fast I had no idea that would be the last day of the world I once knew." He stares out at the lightning show across the ocean in the distance, his posture stiff, hands balled tightly at his sides. "I was running for my life to escape the crumbling castle when I saw them... Bren, your father, arguing with mine." He pauses, taking sharp inhales.

"What happened?" I ask, caught up in his story.

His top lip curls. "While the world was breaking apart, Bren plunged a blade into my father's chest."

I gasp loudly, hugging myself.

"And I still dream of Bren's last words... *Ruined... Kingdom... Change is coming. I will rule.*"

"Shit!" The shred of bravery I'd been holding on to falls away as I stare at a man who's lost everything.

My head hurts.

My heart burns.

He twists to face me, and the slightest touch of his hand on mine leaves me breathless.

"We didn't expect you to mean anything to us, and I fucking loathe even saying that. I don't blame you for hating us for it, but I can't regret the decisions I made. If Killian hadn't found you and brought you back, we would never have discovered you as our true mate. I would never have experienced the racing pulse of my heart every time I walk into the room with you, the longing that tears me apart, the hunger to have you in my arms, to see you smile."

"You have no right to say those things while we're arguing." I glare up at him, tears rushing down my cheeks. Especially when I'm wondering what they would have done if we weren't true mates. Then I think of our strong attraction from the beginning, even before the Veil Ritual.

I shake away the thoughts.

Wolfe wears a thin grin, but his eyes are drowning.

I suck in a strangled breath, my inhales coming too fast, yet I'm melting on the inside at his words.

He steps closer, and I pull away, shuddering in my shoes.

"I watched your father kill many Shadowfen in cold blood when he forced those who followed the old kingdom off the land. Families, loved ones, friends, and neighbors. For them, I'd risk throwing myself into a pit of flames if it brought back a fraction of what they lost. If I could remove all their grief, I would." He pauses, breathing quickly now. "I never said I was a good guy, Sage, but I'm a fighter for those who need it. Then you came into my life like a damn earthquake, ripping us apart. Your presence turned everything we'd planned on its head."

I blink at him, feeling helpless, angry at everyone, sorrowful for all the wrongs... all because of my father.

"I feel things for you, Sage, things I never expected to. I'm broken, but I won't put you in danger, and I'd die before I let your father have you. So I'll work on a new plan to find another home for us all, no matter how long it takes."

My heart's splintering, the pain swallowing me, teetering between fury and grief. The atrocities these Shadowfen faced, living with those memories, make it hard for me to blame Wolfe for his decision.

"I don't know what to say. I'm still torn, but I'm starting to understand why you did what you did." I'd do anything for my mother, so am I any different? Maybe I should just go to my father's side, bring the Shadowfen some relief, discover a way to overpower him... but just as quickly, I stiffen, shoving aside the pity at myself, the absurd thoughts.

Instead, a new anger rampages through me, one that is white flames aimed at my father.

"I wish I could take away your pain," Wolfe coos.

Everything he said feels like a blur in my head. The sharpness in my chest comes from how strongly I'm drawn to him, and I guess that's why it hurts so much.

"I think the part that tears me apart the most is that you kept it from me. And I'll be honest, it stings knowing that I came here to be sold off."

He stares at me like a man barely holding it together, deflated, with no response, while my insides are a mess.

Wolfe grabs my arm, holding me firmly.

"What do you want me to say to make it better?" He drops to his knees in front of me. "I'm not ashamed to beg for forgiveness. I can't sleep, worrying myself sick with how I'm going to sort out his fucking mess. You're pure of heart, and it's destroying me that we drew you into our chaos."

I stare at him, unblinking, unsure how to answer, but I'm crying.

"I can't bear to lose you," he says, his fingers still grasping my arm, and I feel the tremble in his touch. "You know that, right? You are mine, Sage. And I'll prove that like I should have from the moment you arrived."

"I'd like to not feel like I can't trust you." Shaking, I find myself drowning in his gaze, the invisible connection between us pulsing stronger. His rise of desire for me is so much more than just physical attraction. He wouldn't hurt otherwise, wouldn't have glassy eyes when he looks into mine, wouldn't shake as he holds me like this might be the last time.

His hands fall to my waist as he climbs to his feet, his gaze on my lips, and before I can get any words out, he's cupping my face with two hands, his thumbs wiping away my tears.

"I don't want you to cry. You're ours now, and we might have fucked up how we first found one another, but going forward, that changes. As my true mate, I will bring the world to your feet and show you that you are my goddess."

We're staring at each other, our bodies pressed close, and I'm buzzing with a need for him.

"You don't say those things, but I like them."

"I'm hoping you can forgive us," he whispers, not letting me go.

If I thought I was angry at him, my body had other ideas because he makes me weak, and I lack control. I push myself up on my tippy-toes, and our mouths clash instantly.

We kiss ravenously, starved, his hand sliding to the back of my head, curling my hair around his hand, keeping me pinned to him, his other hand sliding down to my ass, squeezing. He grinds against me while kissing me so wickedly, making me whimper.

Fisting his shirt, I hold on, knowing exactly what I crave, blinded by emotions that consume me. The rest of the world fades, leaving behind a raw, intoxicating carnal desire that drives me to insanity.

In seconds, he has my dress up to my waist, his hand between my legs, and I'm moaning at the perfect way his fingers rub my clit. I groan at his assertiveness, my nipples hard, the buzz building deep in my stomach. I'm drenched so fast it's not fair how my body betrays me.

"Maybe we shouldn't." I glance at Nyko across the room, still unmoving in bed, but Wolfe's not backing off.

He holds me close as he moves out onto the balcony, where he takes a seat on one of the seats and drags me down to sit on his lap. The wind's blowing, tugging against my clothes, but I barely feel its cold when I'm burning up.

We're kissing again like we can't stay away from each other.

I draw his tongue into my mouth, and I'm floating on the beautiful way he growls. He's fiddling with his belt, and I reach down between us, pulling at his pants. Breaking our kiss, I glance down to his cock popping out. It's thick and hard, and there's only one in his human form, but I swear it's as thick as his two monster ones put together.

"Are all monsters so huge?" I ask.

He smirks at me with a knowing look that tells me they are.

"Tell me how much you want me inside you, stretching that pretty little cunt."

I swallow, but instead of shying away, I whisper, "I'm dripping wet, hungry for you to fuck me." My thoughts are clouded, funneled to one thing... Wolfe inside me.

His fingers are on my chin, raising my attention to him, and we're kissing, his tongue pressing into my mouth, claiming me. Then, just as fast, he releases me and turns me on his lap, so I'm facing away from him. He draws me back against him, his fingers digging into my skin as he lowers me onto that huge cock.

I feel slightly dirty, being outside, exposed, though he doesn't seem to care.

I straddle his lap, and he spreads his legs, in turn yanking mine wider. I'm drenched from the things he does to me. It never crossed my mind to be fucked on the chance that Nyko might see or hear us, but it undoes me. The heat between my legs is an inferno, pooling into liquid lava.

He growls as his strong hands lift my skirt, then he rubs me with his dick, guiding it into me, and plunges in with a merciful thrust. Clutching the chair's handle, I cry out from the assault as he goes deeper, stretching. Barely able to breathe, I gasp for air, whimpering.

"You're doing so well, Sage."

I groan with him fully nestled inside me. "I can't seem to ever say no to you."

"Do you want to?" His lips are on my shoulder as he reaches across my front, tugging down on my dress, freeing my breasts. He grasps them as his hips grind into me. I moan, the exhilaration of being fucked in public, being exposed, more thrilling than I expected.

"I want you screaming." Gripping my hips once more, he starts to thrust, lifting me up and down on his dick, and I'm rocking myself, moving with the motion of how quickly he's fucking me.

Our breaths escalate, and he's moving so quickly now, my body shaking, my breasts bouncing crazily as I hold on. The friction between us is a blaze, and I can barely see straight from how fast and hard he claims me.

He dives into me, over and over, the monster who had me brought here as a sacrifice. Who fell to his knees for me, who promised me the world, but am I ready to trust him?

He unleashes a feral snarl. Sharp teeth bite into my neck as he fucks me wildly. I scream, the pain and the carnal pleasure destroying me.

The buildup rushes through me, ripping me up. I'm thrashing, crying out from the orgasm that keeps coming and coming.

Floating... that's how it feels.

The delicious ache inside me.

That's when I know deep inside that not only am I his, but he belongs to me, too. The ache in my heart turns into an unbridled lust, his brutality, his obsession. A desperation to never leave him.

I know what's happening to me...

I'm falling hard for him, the kind of falling where my heart will shatter into hundreds of pieces if he ever lets me go.

It terrifies me.

But I'm shaking, breathless, my body throbbing.

He's relentless and only fucks me harder. Looping an arm across my stomach, he's on his feet, taking me with him.

"Hold on to the railing," he commands as he lowers me, and my feet find purchase on the balcony.

"Don't you dare stop," I warn him.

He laughs, squeezing my ass. "I wouldn't dare."

My fingers curl around the cold metal, and he presses against my back, pushing me forward, while he steps back, taking me with him, essentially forcing me to bend over.

There's no pause, just him hammering into me, our bodies slamming together. I moan each time he thrusts, shuddering.

"Wolfe!" I cry out as sparks of lust soar through me again so quickly after the last climax.

That achy need in my body owns me, and despite my sore limbs, I grip the railing. I feel the power of his strength as he rams into me, those lustful sparks lighting up behind my eyelids.

It crashes through me so dramatically that my vision is blinking in and out. With it comes Wolfe's thunderous growl as he slams into me, then comes to an abrupt stop, roaring his own orgasm.

Each breath is heavy, and I can't speak, my body barely holding me up. If it weren't for Wolfe, I'd be on my hands and knees, already collapsed.

Warmth coats my inside as he pumps into me, and I

cry out the second orgasm I'm riding, squeezing him, unsure how long it takes to float back down. When I do, he collects me into his arms, raising me off my feet. I'm dripping, I feel it between my thighs, but he only grins at me cradled in his arms.

"I will never let your father take you from us. But now you need to rest."

With those words, a newfound fear trickles across my chest... a reality that hasn't surged through me until now. The pure danger that if my father discovers I'm here, wouldn't he do anything in his power to take me?

CHAPTER
TWENTY-FIVE
SAGE

I slump down in the chair next to Nyko's bed as Wolfe exits, leaving us alone. He had a meeting he was running late to. I guess neither of us expected to end up having sex on the balcony, and after he filled me in on everything—the awful mess they're all in—my head's spinning.

My father's a psychopath. Everything I've heard about him makes my skin crawl, and deep down, I wonder if he's aware of my presence here. The thought of him harming others to get to me sickens me.

Fingers twisting in my lap, I'm torn about what to do. The knot in my gut tightens. I stare at Nyko, noticing a slight improvement in his color.

"Please get better soon," I whisper, dabbing his brow with a towel. "I feel guilty as hell for doing this to you." And with everything else going on, I can't live with having injured one of my true mates.

Pulling back to grab the bowl of salve from the bedside table, a grip tightens around my wrist.

I flinch, glancing over at Nyko holding on to me, his eyes half-open, his grasp weaker than his usual firm one.

"Nyko, you're awake." I shuffle closer to the bed, smiling, never happier in my life. "Thank the fates. How are you feeling? Can I get you anything?"

"Why does it smell like sex in here?" His voice is groggy as he scans the area, staring at the open door leading into the living room.

Heat lashes my cheeks. Flashes of Wolfe and me on the balcony play heavily on my thoughts, my pulse speeding through my veins at how desperately I craved him.

"Is that the first thing you notice?" I murmur with a half smirk, trying my best to mask my embarrassment.

He's staring right at me, and he might be sick, but he's not one to miss anything.

"Who was it? Wolfe or Killian?"

I shift in my seat uncomfortably. "You must be feeling better," I half joke. "And Wolfe paid you a visit earlier."

"Better," he admits, still holding my gaze. "But I think your scent helped wake me." He grins, then scrunches up his face as though that movement brings him agony.

"I doubt it's me," I say. "You've been out of it since yesterday. Should I get the doctor?"

I move to get up, but his fingers tighten around my wrist, and that jolt of warmth I'm familiar with from him sweeps through my body. A sensation so overwhelming that a single touch renders me completely distracted by him. It makes sense after discovering that he might actually be my true mate.

"No, don't go. I want it to be just you and me. When I touch you, the world isn't so dark."

"I never knew you were so poetic," I tease, though his thoughtful words affect me to where I'm swooning on the inside.

As if to prove his point, he pulls me a little closer. "If I weren't still feeling half-dead, I'd have you all over my face as I'm convinced tasting you will heal me fast."

I shouldn't be shocked by him anymore, yet he always has me blushing hard. "How can you just say that?" I murmur.

He chuckles, then winces, his laughter turning into a cough. "It's the least you can do after almost killing me." He raises an eyebrow.

The guilt digs into my heart, yet his grip on my arm sends warmth up my arm, a strange comfort when I want to hide from the world. I didn't grow up with such freedom, not when I had nowhere to hide in the village. Not when I had duties to perform to help my mother.

"I'm joking," he rasps, his hand weak against my arm. "Don't you dare hold back on using your power on my account. From what I saw, you're incredibly powerful, and if you need to drain me to use your power, then I willingly offer myself to you."

"Don't say that," I respond instantly, except he's serious. I see it in his jade eyes. "I almost killed you, so how can you be so calm about it?"

The edges of his mouth curl upward like even that action is a struggle for him.

"Because you didn't kill me, Sage. You acted to save yourself, and that's what matters."

"I've been a mess of guilt, fear, and anger at myself." My words tremble.

He pats the bed next to him. "Want to crawl under the blanket with me, and I'll spoon you?" He gives me the sweetest grin, and I burst out laughing.

I'm starting to see two very different sides to Nyko, and I'm drawn to both. The dominant, reckless monster who has that wild look in his gaze where you know he's about to do something crazy. Then the Nyko who can be sweet as honey, makes me swoon, and gives me gifts like necklaces. Is he even aware of his dual personality?

He's coughing again, wincing in pain, and a sickening sensation comes over me, that guilt I can't escape.

"I'll be right back," I tell him, starting to stand up, but he's not releasing me.

"No, you're not going to get the doc. Stay by my side, tell me what you and Wolfe spoke about, what you did together while I lay in bed, passed out." He raises an eyebrow again at his dark humor.

Settling back in the chair, I share with him everything Wolfe revealed about the chaos surrounding us with my father, my fury at being lied to, and even his apology.

"I'm trying, but I'm still dealing with my anger at the

hidden truths, at myself for hurting you." My voice cracks. "It's like I feel cheated somehow at how fast I was torn from my life. And now, I doubt I'll ever be able to live there again. Not with me changing into a monster."

His thumb tenderly strokes the inside of my arm. My knees are bouncing at coming to terms with everything.

"Yesterday, after our meal, if you hadn't been kidnapped, I'd intended to take you to the Chamber of Rituals."

My shoulders draw back at his admission. "After everything?" I'm shuddering.

"I'm fucking blinded and fuming that Killian and Wolfe have both confirmed you as their true mates. I know you're mine, and I want to prove it, too. I'll do anything to show you that we belong together."

The room warms up, or perhaps it's just me and my whiplash of emotions swirling inside me, from frustration to internal blame to gushing over Nyko.

"Let's agree that you don't take me to that room ever," I murmur, heart racing at the thought. "But I have a confession for you. You know my shadow ability isn't just rare but apparently intricately tied to my true mates. And I draw power from *them only*. I mean, let's not test that theory any further, but that means—"

He's howling, laughing, then coughing viciously. "Best news I've ever heard!" He chokes the words out.

When he finally calms down, I let out a relieved breath.

"All right, no more excitement for you. But you know, the reason I drew on your energy and not Wolfe's or

Killian's is because of this," I explain, my hand reaching up to my neck, fingers running across the blood-gold chain. "I think your blood in the necklace connected us deeper."

He cracks a weak grin, eyes twinkling despite the glassiness from exhaustion. "Knowing I helped you makes me feel incredible, my princess."

I smile back, just wishing it hadn't cost him so much.

"So, true mate"—he tugs my hand to his mouth and kisses the back of the palm—"what else can I entertain you with before I seduce you into bed with me?"

I laugh, adoring him the more time we spend together.

"How about finally showing me what your monster form looks like once you're feeling better? A girl's curious."

He smirks, that devious glint in his gaze worrying me. Suddenly, I regret asking him.

"Once I'm healed, you won't hold me back."

"That slightly scares me," I tease, though part of that isn't a lie.

Thunder rumbles outside, louder, closer, and he tightens his hold on my hand. He draws my palm to the side of his face. We stay like that as he leans into my touch, eyes slowly drifting closed, his breath ragged and worrisome.

The room's soft light casts shadows around him. The storm outside rages as he slips open his eyes once more.

"Did Wolfe tell you about his mom? About the Great Desolation?" His question slices through the quiet, his tone no longer playful, more exhausted, more serious.

I nod slowly, my throat tight. "He mentioned... that my father killed his," I whisper. Even saying it buries me under guilt because he's my dad. "It's horrifying to think I'm related to someone capable of that."

"When Wolfe escaped the crumbling castle, he tried to save his mother but never reached her in time..." His response falters. "She plummeted to her death as her bedroom tore in half during the castle's destruction."

My hand flies to my mouth, stifling the gasp escaping. "Oh, shit!"

"He's struggled with the loss of his parents for a long time." He yawns.

My heart aches fiercely for Wolfe, imagining him as a young man facing such brutal losses. I recall his words, how he'd do anything for those who believed in him. He might claim he's no hero, but in my gaze, he's nothing short of one.

"I feel so awful for him," I whisper.

Nyko shifts, grimacing from the movement.

"After the destruction, your father imprisoned a lot of Shadowfen, including Wolfe, kept in a damn dungeon for months until we managed to escape. Clay was with us, too, and it was his idea to steal Howler." He pauses, catching his quick breathing.

The horror of his words chills me to the bone. My skin crawls at the thought of what they faced, being trapped and tormented.

"I... I had no idea," I stammer.

"Just... just so you know." His gaze drifts to the ceiling. "Wolfe's been through a lot. He can be an asshole sometimes, but he's suffered immensely and never stopped fighting for his people. Try not to be too harsh on him. So, if you want to take your anger out on anyone, I give you permission to try killing me again." The corner of his mouth lifts, and he lowers those grinning eyes.

I roll mine. "And what about your family?" I ask softly.

"My father was the King's physician, taken during the Great Desolation. My mother... I never knew her. She died during childbirth with me." His words fade, and his eyes close once more, the confession seeming to drain what little energy he had left.

As I sit there, absorbing his words, my heart beats with sorrow, not just for Nyko but for all of them. They've all lost so much, endured unimaginable pain, yet they found a way to keep fighting toward the goal of finding a new home.

Not much time passes before Nyko slips back into a fitful sleep, and I slip my hand away from him.

I sink deeper into the chair, my thoughts working overtime as the storm outside intensifies, almost mirroring the mess I'm in—scary, dangerous as hell, and looking like there's no way around it.

CHAPTER TWENTY-SIX

SAGE

"Maybe I should just stay with Nyko," I suggest, looking up at Killian. His hand is warm and engulfing mine, holding me a little too tightly, as if he's afraid I might slip away. He towers over me, the blue of his skin almost glowing under the dim lights of the hallway, his muscles bulging, and his presence feels both comforting and overwhelmingly powerful.

"You need to eat something, stretch your legs," he insists. "Besides, Wolfe's there with him now. They're going to do another checkup with the doctor."

The intensity in Killian's deep blue eyes softens, and he leans a little closer, his long, silver-white hair cascading over his shoulder and down his chest. He's wearing pants, at least, which is less distracting than Wolfe, who goes full commando in his monster form.

"Did you miss me?" he teases, a playful smirk tugging at the corner of his lips, a twinkle in his gaze. He impresses me with how he can switch from fierce to charming in a heartbeat.

I smile in response because I can't control myself around him. "Maybe a little," I tease him back.

Laughing, he draws me closer to his side, his lips on my brow, his breath on my skin. I inhale the strong woodsy, masculine scent tinged with a hint of saltiness, just as I remember his cum tasting when he splashed himself all over me.

"Don't lie. You've been hungry for me. I can see it in the way you stare at me. I smell your arousal the instant I touch you."

My legs tremble, a flush of heat burning between my thighs.

"There's my pretty little monster." His lips curl into a wide smirk.

"You know, you don't need to always say the obvious. Sometimes, less is more."

Walking down a long corridor, the area looks familiar to me, as though I'm starting to get used to the vessel.

Killian's laughter rings out again, piercing through the hallway with a devilish charm. Every time he does that, I feel a little weaker around him, as though I don't stand a chance.

As we round a corner, the crowd thickens in the hallway that spreads out to the main area I'd visited before with Nyko. We pass the rainbow-colored window, though with the storm moving in, not a lot of light is streaming indoors.

I spot a hulking monster with dull orange skin strolling

in our direction, edging into my path. He's covered in scales that shimmer under the overhead lights, eyes a piercing yellow that seem too focused on me. Instinctively, I inch closer to Killian, trying to get out of his way.

Killian's hand suddenly shoots out, grabbing him by the throat.

I startle, my heart bouncing against my rib cage.

"Are you blind?" Killian snaps in a dangerous growl. "You can't see her walking here?"

The monster gurgles, clawing at Killian's grip, his gaze widening in fear. After a tense moment, Killian releases him. The scaly guy rubs his neck, coughing and avoiding my gaze.

Others nearby stare at us, and I feel extremely subconscious about causing a commotion.

"S-sorry, my Lord," he stammers. "I just didn't..." He scurries past us and vanishes around the corner.

"What was that about?" I whisper, my pulse racing in my ears from the sudden confrontation.

"Some on board aren't sure about you yet," Killian explains.

"No, I mean, you didn't need to be so rough with him," I say, but then it hits me. "Wait, some of them don't like me?"

He sighs, his expression softening as he looks down at me. "You're new, and with everything that's been happening..." His words trail off, and he shakes his head. "Let's just say not everyone is convinced you should be here."

"That's hurtful, but I guess I get it. Who would want their enemy's daughter on board?"

"Not that," he corrects me, turning to face me and pushing a curl of hair off my face. "Most don't know exactly who you are. It's your human side."

"Oh," I murmur. "That's just fucking mean and racist."

"Many are fearful of change or newcomers, but I've heard rumors of some females being jealous of you spending so much time with us." He raises his eyebrows, seeming proud of that.

My gaze narrows. "Really now?"

"Don't look surprised. You have no idea how many marriage proposals I've received over the years."

"All right, I didn't expect you to say that, but they're going to have to keep their hands off now!"

"Wait, was that a possessive growl in your voice? Are you jealous?"

"As if," I scoff. I push to keep on walking, having no idea where we're going, but I need to stop him from seeing that deep inside, I'm burning up with so much jealousy I want to paint the words *He's Taken* on his chest. No idea where that came from, but evidently, that's the new me around these monsters.

He's at my side, his hand slipping into mine. "We can't be too cautious until we find out who's trying to hurt you, so until then, anyone comes next to you, I'll deal with them."

I feel the weight of all the stares in my direction now,

and thanks, Killian, for making me paranoid, knowing some Shadowfen dislike me.

Reaching the elevator, Killian commands Howler to take us to the third floor, and we're there in seconds. Stepping out into a less crowded hallway, Killian keeps his hand on my back, guiding me through the sprawling corridors. Arriving at a set of open doors, my anticipation grows.

Stepping through, I'm struck instantly by the breathtaking view. The walls curve into massive glass panels, revealing the dark, turbulent sea. The vessel is submerged beneath the ocean on this floor, and exterior lights pierce the water, illuminating the occasional creature darting past. The upper part of the windows shows the water sloshing against the glass and how rough the sea is.

Circular couches are scattered around the dimly lit room, each centered around a table and filled with monsters.

"This place is amazing."

"Wait until you taste the food," he murmurs.

"I love it already," I admit.

The floor beneath us shakes slightly, and instinctively, I grip Killian's arm tighter.

"It's all right," he soothes, holding on to me. "Sometimes, during large storms, the vessel feels the sea's movements, especially when we're hit by large waves. Normally, the vessel is stabilized by powerful rotors, and with a touch of magic, they keep us steady, but tonight might be a bit bumpier than usual."

"Should I be worried?" I ask, trying to hide the tremor in my response.

"Not at all," he replies confidently.

A young woman approaches us, carrying what appear to be menus. Her skin is a deep pink, matching her flowing hair, and she wears nothing but a short, thin skirt, her four breasts exposed with green nipples. I try to keep my gaze averted, my cheeks heating up at the sight. She doesn't seem to notice me, focusing all her attention on Killian.

"My Lord, what a pleasure to have you join us tonight," she purrs, and I instantly dislike her.

She guides us to a table, chatting with Killian as if they're old friends and I'm nonexistent. A sharp pang of jealousy slices through me. She keeps giggling, shaking those small breasts deliberately.

Killian, however, seems oblivious to her advances, his focus alternating between the path ahead and back at me. By the time we're seated next to the window, she's leaning in close to him, practically pressing her chest up against him.

What the hell? She's meant to be offering him the menu, not herself.

I frown at her, shifting in my seat uncomfortably.

Killian suddenly groans under his breath and lifts his chin in her direction.

"You can leave us now. I'll call you over when we're ready." He shoves the menu into her face, and she stumbles back, shooting a glare my way as she retreats.

"Damn," I mutter under my breath, unable to hide

my surprise at her blatant flirting. "She didn't even try to hide it."

Killian looks at me, a flicker of amusement in his eyes. "I approve of your fiery jealousy," he grunts. "But I barely notice the flirting because I'm not interested in them."

His hand scoops around my waist and drags me to the side of the circular leather couch, our sides pressed up real close. I giggle at bumping into him.

My attention is instantly caught on the monstrous creature swimming right past our window, close enough that I can make out its razor-sharp spikes trailing down its back. Its mouth is bristling with jagged teeth, hanging open as if it's permanently poised to kill. A shiver jolts down my spine.

"That's exactly why I'll never go into that water," I remark, genuinely intimidated by the sea and the beasts living in its depths.

Killian chuckles, his gaze following the creature as it disappears into the rough, shadowy water.

"It's not too bad, really. It's like those fluffy kittens you have back on Earth," he says sarcastically.

"Kittens?" I scoff, staring at him incredulously. "Are you kidding? Yes, if they had rows of sharp teeth and looked ready to rip your face off. Sure, they're similar."

His laughter fills the space between us, rich and deep.

Another fish monster, most like the ones I'm used to from home, glides by, its skin shimmering with golden scales that reflect the artificial light from the vessel.

"Now that one is kind of beautiful."

"Maybe I'll make a diver out of you yet."

I almost choke on my breath. "Not in that ocean, not in this lifetime. Let's not get ahead of ourselves."

"Fair enough. But you know, there's a lot to be said for facing one's fears."

"In the past few weeks, I've faced fears I didn't even know I had, so no, thanks. You can keep all the swimming beasts to yourself," I say, giving him a lopsided smile.

He nods, his hand reaching over to my necklace, his fingers tracing the pearls.

"That beast you just saw? Nyko took down a similar one the other day. He actually gutted it to extract these two little pearls on your necklace."

My breath catches in my throat, my fingers instinctively also reaching up to touch the smooth, cool surface of the pearls. "These came from that terrifying thing out there?" Shock shudders my question. "He fought one of those?" Nyko's lying in bed after almost dying, and earlier, he was still making jokes with me. Does nothing scare that Shadowfen?

"We've been hunting for most of our lives."

Since I arrived in Blight, it has been an endless ordeal of surprises, fear, and adjustments. Maybe if I stay here long enough, I'll start to feel normal and not freak out on a daily basis.

The waitress returns, her gaze lingering a bit too long on Killian, leaning over to him as she offers the menu to him again with a flirtatious smile.

"My Lord, may I take your order?" Her tone is a tad too sweet.

Killian, who doesn't even accept the menu, begins to order effortlessly, as if from memory, listing off items with ease. I have no idea what he's ordering, but the waitress is nodding rapidly, then she excuses herself.

"Wait, fuck! Forgot to give her our drink orders." Killian frowns, twisting around to search for the waitress. But when I twist around, she's gone. He signals to someone across the room, and I turn to find Clay, the captain of the vessel, making his way toward us.

"Clay, good timing," Killian greets him with a nod. "Take a seat with Sage for a moment while I go sort out our drinks."

"Oh, no, that's not necessary—"

"I insist." His words leave no room for argument.

Clay nods and slides into the booth on my other side, his feet up on the seat as he sits perched like an oversized bird, feathery arms by his side. He truly is terrifying.

"You got it." His presence is oddly disarming—feathery fingers drumming lightly on the table, a friendly grin lighting up his face.

Once Killian shuffles out and vanishes, Clay glances at me with an awkward smile.

"You're going to like the food here," he begins. "They only serve seafood. It's a favorite of the crew."

"Are you here with your family?" I ask, feeling uncomfortable about being dumped with the captain as my babysitter. I get Killian is paranoid about leaving me alone for even a few moments, but I'm the one who has to face the uncomfortable conversation.

"Friends," he answers, glancing over my shoulder at the room as though he'd like to be anywhere else. Yes, I feel the same way. There's a scrunch of feathers on the bridge of his nose. "I hope you're starting to fit in well here. Any kind of change can be... disruptive. Not just for you, but for everyone else on the vessel." There's an edge to his tone, a sharpness that makes me sit up straighter.

"You mean my being here?" I think back to Killian's words about some Shadowfen who are not happy with my presence. Is that what Clay's hinting at? It's not as if I asked to be brought here.

He smiles, which just looks strange on his white face with darkness sweeping from his hairline and back, but it's way too creepy. Leaning back in the seat, he's inspecting his fingernails on his hand, long talons that could easily tear into flesh.

I suddenly feel uneasy in his presence.

"I mean the movements of the vessel, our course adjustments, our stops, they don't go unnoticed. Even in the deepest waters, eyes might watch, ears might listen."

"You think there are spies on the vessel?"

He twists his head toward me. "Someone like you needs to remain vigilant because in such turbulent times, if you don't make the first move, it gives the enemy a chance to do it."

I blink at him, swallowing hard as a chill races down my back. He's talking about my father; he has to be. "Clay," I start, just as Killian returns.

The captain rises to leave as Killian thanks him. Then he's gone, and I'm left with my insides twisting.

"Everything all right?" Killian asks, shuffling closer to me and taking me into his arms.

I smile at him, nodding, then I shake my head.

"Do you think my father knows I'm on this vessel? Could he have spies on here?"

He exhales loudly, his brow deepening. "Why do you ask? Did Clay say something? We've had no new additions to our population for over a decade, so I highly doubt we have spies. But everyone has different agendas, so I can't rule it out. But I promise that we're going to keep you safe and protected. No one will touch you."

I shrug, half grinning up at him. "I know you will. I'm paranoid, I guess."

Embracing him, I soften against his side, my hand resting on his chest, unable to let go of Clay's words.

Was it a warning? Could my father already know where I am? Is Clay hinting that waiting here, hoping to stay hidden, is a mistake? A knot tightens in my stomach. Maybe it's time I stop just reacting. Maybe I have to make the first move. If danger is coming, I should help Wolfe ensure we meet it head-on, not hide from my father.

The room seems to suddenly sway with the rhythm of the ocean that sloshes and slams against the windows.

"Whoa," I mumble while Killian tightens his hold around my middle.

"Nothing to worry about," he reassures me, smiling.

Around us, the other diners are chatting loudly, unaffected by the boat's movements, and the tight knot in my chest softens just a bit.

The waitress arrives with our drinks, a lighthearted grin on her lips, but for a change, she doesn't make any small talk or flirt, aside from letting us know the drinks have arrived. Mine's a tall glass with lots of greenery, ice, and a pale green liquid.

I take a sip, reminded of apple and mint. "Oh, this is delicious."

Killian doesn't have eyes for anyone else but just watches me as though I'm the most entertaining thing in the world for him.

Soon enough, the food arrives, and the table is covered in an assortment of dishes. I take them all in, unable to identify a single dish. One plate is teeming with thick tentacles, their tips still twitching as steam rises off them. There's one dish with dark, curled leaves, which are glossy and slick with what I hope is a cooking oil. The skewered meats look normal, except for the meat charred at the edges, oozing a vibrant green juice. Why does this food have to look so intimidating?

I hold back from gagging to not be rude and offer Killian a smile, seeing he's studying me for my response.

"Let me serve you a bit of everything." He's already busy scooping food onto my plate.

"Please, just not the skewers."

He glances at me with a comical frown. "That's the best dish on our table."

I shrug. "Maybe next time. I'm not sure I'm in the mood for oozing meat today."

He chuckles, placing a full plate in front of me in moments. Once he's got his plate heaped, he digs in. So, I do the same, and surprisingly, they aren't so bad. Like most of the things in Blight, they're the opposite of how they appear.

"Tell me about Nightingale Village," he prompts, twirling something that resembles a fork but with too many prongs around long strands of a green vegetable. "What's life like there on an average day?" He picks up a piece of something crunchy-looking and pops it into his mouth.

I pause, spearing a small, tentacle-like morsel on my plate.

"It was tough," I start. "The people there... they weren't exactly kind to my mother and me. Always whispering, always staring. It's like they blamed us for every bad thing that happened just because we were different."

He reaches over, placing his hand on my thigh. "They had no idea how lucky they were to have known you."

I laugh. "Yeah, right."

I dive into talking about the village, the lack of resources, the hardship, but also the great times I had with Alina and my mother. With no idea how long I've been talking, I find my plate's completely empty, and Killian's already filling it back up for me.

"I'm going to change things when I return," he explains before taking another big mouthful of a purple root vegetable that looks like a potato.

The ship tilts beneath us, shaking me in my seat, and I grasp the table, my drink sloshing in the glass.

"Okay, that one was scary," I say, trying to ignore the flutter in my stomach.

"We're perfectly safe here." He's enjoying his meal while plates wobble on the table. "Anyway, I have grand plans for Nightingale Village when I return."

"Do you think… will I get to see my mother again?" I watch him, needing to know because just the thought of her has me tearing up.

He pauses and twists his head in my direction. "I give you my word, I'll make it happen," he promises sincerely.

"That means the world to me," I murmur, quickly wiping away a stray tear. "If she wasn't so sick, I wouldn't be as worried." I go on to explain how I've been secretly getting medicine for her from one of the Village Protectors and how it's improved her health.

"You love her so much; she's lucky to have you," he observes with admiration behind his words.

"She deserves everything," I reply, feeling a weight lift at sharing this with him. "Anyway, with your plan to head back to Nightingale Village, you're coming back here, right?"

"And if I decide not to return?" He's using that sexy tone that has me squeezing my thighs together.

I lean in. "Well then, I guess I'll have to send out a search party and drag you back fast. I know you use the pond in the village to summon the portal! And I know the two Shadowfen who can operate them." I raise an eyebrow, challenging him.

A slow grin spreads across his face, his eyes glinting.

He leans in, his masculine scent with a hint of fresh wood and the sea washing over me.

He smells so sexy...

"Why would I run when I have someone so captivating to come back to?" His husky whisper stirs something wild inside me, making my nipples harden, and the ache in the pit of my stomach awakens.

I blush but hold his gaze, the air between us electric. I have my hand on his chest, not even remembering putting it there.

"Sounds like you've got it all worked out," I whisper.

"You have no idea," he purrs, his mouth on my neck, taking a sharp inhale. "I can almost taste your arousal, and it's fucking intoxicating."

I breathe heavily as his hand slides up my thigh and up my skirt. His hands are on fire.

"Tell me to stop," he murmurs before his tongue loops my earlobe into his mouth, his fingers inching up. "Open up for me," he demands in a voice that has me doing exactly that.

I shouldn't, but I'm weak when it comes to him.

Fingers graze me right where I'm purring.

"Killian," I whisper. "Not here."

But he's already slipped a finger between my wet lips, pushing deeper, finding my entrance so fast that I'm panting.

"I'll stop when you tell me to." His tongue is on my neck again, my whole body engulfed by him curling around me, his finger working into me.

"Oh, Killian." I breathe the words, my body quivering, stomach tightening. How in the world did we get to this stage in the middle of a busy room? My body seems to have already made a decision before my mind can catch up.

His assertiveness, bringing me to such a fast high, has me rocking my pelvis with each plunge. Every instinct is telling me to stop... but I just can't bring myself to say the word when I'm buzzing, the sensation so tight I'm about to explode.

"Fuck," he growls in my ear, that rich sound winding through me, going right down to my core.

My pulse flares between my thighs where he's pressing his thumb against my clit, rubbing me and sending me straight over the edge.

I buck in my seat, shuddering, my climax hitting me so fast it vibrates savagely through me.

Those sensuous lips are on my mouth, stealing my moans, inhaling my breaths. He never once relents from fingering me until I'm completely undone, having come all over his hand.

I'm flushed from head to toe, my heartbeat echoing loudly in my ears.

"Absolutely beautiful," Killian murmurs, his breath still warm against my skin as he pulls his finger out and straightens his back.

I pat down my skirt, ensuring it's covering my legs. When I lift my gaze, I catch the waitress standing across the table, staring at us with a wide, venomous stare. My cheeks heat up further, if possible, and I don't know where to look—away from her glaring scrutiny or back at Killian, who seems utterly unfazed by the interruption.

"We're done here. You can clear the dishes," he instructs her casually, dismissing her with a wave of his hand before his intense gaze locks back on to mine.

The waitress moves stiffly to clean the table, her attention swinging between us one last time before she retreats. I sit there, feeling embarrassed and still on my high.

"She... she saw that, didn't she?" I whisper, hardly believing the situation.

"Of course she did." He gives a nonchalant shrug. "And now she knows you're with me and will back off."

"Wait, you did that on purpose? For her to see us?"

"I had to show her I was taken." His smirk grows, a devilish gleam twinkling in his gaze. "Female Shadowfen are super territorial once they set their sights on a male. And yes, I might have wanted to mark my territory a bit by showing her I've claimed you, too."

My shoulders pull back as I process his decision. "You... you can't just use me to make a point!"

His laughter rumbles deep in his chest, soothing yet somehow provocative, and I hate how he makes me melt for him when I'm mad at him.

"Don't pretend you didn't enjoy our moment just as much as I did," he teases, leaning in closer again. "You were incredibly sweet, your cunt so soft and wet, my pretty little one."

As we stand to leave, the waitress reappears, holding a small white bag with a rather serious expression. "Your order, my Lord," she says, her response losing any previous warmth as she hands it to Killian. Then she leaves us.

"What's that?" I ask, curious, as we move toward the exit.

"A little something for later," he replies with a secretive smile.

"Later?" I echo, my curiosity piqued.

The vessel gives a subtle shudder.

Killian takes my hand firmly in his. "For dessert," he adds, leading me into the elevator.

Soon enough, the doors slide open. "Wait, this isn't my floor."

"You're staying with me tonight," he declares, not as a question but as a fact.

"Are you sure?" There's a comforting gentleness in the way he stares at me, saying that I'm not staying alone during the storm.

He smirks at me just as another tremor from the ship sends me instinctively closer to him.

"My point is proven," he says, amusement all over his face.

"Can we at least check in on Nyko while we're on this floor?" I negotiate.

He nods, and we detour to Nyko's room down the brightly lit hallway. He knocks lightly and opens the door. Wolfe is asleep on the oversized couch. From the other room, Nyko's steady snores confirm he's resting.

Wolfe stirs as we enter. "You're finally back," he rasps.

"Not really," Killian begins to explain, but I cut him off, stepping fully into the living area.

"How's Nyko?"

Killian flicks on the light, causing Wolfe to squint and shield his eyes.

"On the mend. He needs more sleep and to keep up with his medicine." He stretches his arms into the air, his back arched.

"Amazing news. I feel so much better. If something happened to him, I'd die," I say, moving to pour a glass of water from the tray that seems to be Wolfe's dinner remnants. Handing it to him, I notice the thanks in his nod as he accepts it.

"Thank you, beautiful," he murmurs, downing the water in a few gulps.

Exhausted, I collapse onto the couch opposite Wolfe while Killian stands somewhat awkwardly by the door.

"What's in the bag?" Wolfe asks, studying the small parcel Killian grips.

"We're passing by," Killian responds evasively.

Wolfe grins, a mischievous grin on his face. "You better tell me those are Moon Puffs," he states.

Killian shoots Wolfe a deadpan stare as he clutches the small bag close. "These aren't for you," he declares. "Sage hasn't tried them yet, so would you steal that privilege from her?"

Wolfe chuckles, shaking his head, his eyes glowing with flames as he glances my way.

"See how sneaky he is with the Moon Puffs? He's always been like this—snatching them away and gorging himself when we were kids, so Nyko and I never got them."

I can't help but laugh along, watching them minus the usual seriousness, feeling more at ease with them than I ever thought possible.

"How many did you get?" I ask, curious about the contents of the mysterious bag.

"Only three," Killian states.

"Perfect, there are three of us," Wolfe says, already rising from his seat with a grin.

"Why only three?" I probe.

Wolfe's smirk grows. "So he can give you one and keep two for himself."

"Now I really want to try one of these popular Moon Puffs."

Killian glares. "If I knew I'd need more, I would have ordered a larger batch." He strides over and opens the bag, revealing the contents to me. Inside are bright purple, thick, sponge-like cookies sandwiching a generous layer of cream, with small, colorful bits sticking out.

I grab one out. "What are these little things in the cream?" I poke at another.

"They're made to replicate the essence of our moons, which are teeming with... let's call them lunar worms."

"Please tell me these aren't actual worms, right? And your kind has been to the moon?" I ask, staring at the worms' different-colored bodies, slightly transparent and covered in what looks like sugar.

"We have powerful telescopes that reveal a lot of

intricate details on our moons." Wolfe bites into one, his eyelids slipping closed. "Absolutely delicious," he murmurs between bites. "No worms here, only honey with a gelatin substance."

Encouraged by his reaction, I do the same. The puff is unexpectedly sweet, the honey worm candy adding a chewy, slightly sour flavor that's incredible. I find myself moaning much louder than I intended.

Just as Killian reaches for his share, Nyko calls out, "Did someone say Moon Puffs?"

I'm on my feet in an instant. "He's awake!" I rush toward him, Killian huffing toward me, hand outstretched, handing me his untouched treat. "Here you go."

"You're amazing," I tell him, then step into the bedroom to see Nyko propping himself up against the headboard.

He takes it greedily, staring at me while gorging on the Moon Puff.

Killian comes in, seeming to be stuffing some Moon Puff into his face, while Wolfe strolls into the bedroom behind him, hands in his pockets. He must have shared half his Moon Puff with Killian.

A streak of lightning snaps alight across the sky outside the balcony glass doors, quickly followed by the crashing roar of thunder. I flinch at how long it sounds.

"You're looking more alive," Killian states, licking his fingers, not bothered by the storm.

"I could do with more of the Moon Puffs," Nyko croaks, glancing my way and smirking.

"Guess I'm going back for more, then?" Killian's already heading to the door as Wolfe and Nyko say yes in unison.

"Get at least a dozen," Nyko calls out, then chuckles as Killian heads out. "I'm fucking starving."

"Means you're getting better," I say.

"I sure fucking hope so," Nyko groans. Sitting in bed, covered to his waist with the blanket, and his hair a mess, I find him so sexy... even when sick. "I've been having these confusing dreams," he continues. "Like I'm trying to count the fish in the sea. And it never adds up, just keeps going and going. It's maddening."

Wolfe comes and stands behind me, his hands around my waist.

The ship rocks at once, sending me into a stumble, but Wolfe catches me, holding me against him.

From behind me, Wolfe bursts out laughing. "I had crazy-ass dreams like that."

"My mother used to say when you have what she called fever-induced dreams, it means you've hit the worst of your sickness."

"Thank fuck," Nyko murmurs, his eyelids fluttering as if he's fighting to stay awake. "I'm ready to have my energy back."

Wolf rubs my arms, and I glance back around to him standing behind me, at the way he studies me. Sometimes, I can't always tell what mood he's in. Mostly because of the constant brooding expression he wears.

"Are you all right?" he asks.

"For sure."

Just then, a soft snore interrupts us, and we both turn to see Nyko, his head tilted back against the pillow, fast asleep again. Wolfe and I exchange a smile, and he gestures toward the door.

As he shuts the door gently behind us, he says, "I'm going to make you a soothing velary tea. It's from a local plant that brings relaxation. The same drink I've been giving Nyko to help him sleep more soundly." He moves to the door to chat with Grimm, his personal assistant, who seems to be just hovering outside the door. I still struggle not to feel unease at his spindly legs that remind me of spiders.

In moments, Wolfe's shutting the door on him and returning to me.

"Grimm's going to bring us tea. It'll help you sleep through this storm."

"I might need it." And as if on cue, everything beneath me shifts, and I stumble into a couch.

Wolfe's at my side. "Tell me about your day." He asks such a normal question when being on Howler is anything but ordinary. I appreciate him trying to instill some normality into my life, so I rattle off the events of the day.

There's something about this moment—the ease of being with Wolfe, with all of them. There's no awkwardness, only comfort and the excitement teeming in my stomach, loving the way he stares at me... as though I belong here.

CHAPTER
TWENTY-SEVEN
SAGE

As I stride down the dimly lit corridor after dinner, the echo of my footsteps mingles with the soft thuds of the monstrous bodyguard trailing behind me. His presence, a massive hound-like creature with scraggly fur and long legs, sends a shiver down my spine. Wolfe's insistence on assigning his personal guard to me should be reassuring, but the beast's fierce eyes and hulking form leave me uneasy.

Killian and Wolfe are tied up in a lengthy meeting with the captain, but they didn't go into details. I feel a tiny bit abandoned, even though I know they're not far.

Nyko, on the other hand, is finally showing signs of full recovery. It's been three days since I almost killed him with my power, and today's the first time I saw him walking around his room with ease. I'm relieved, though when I went to check on him earlier, he'd been asleep. I didn't want to wake him, so I left him to rest.

Over dinner, I was going over Clay's words from a

couple of nights ago. Along with the idea that I need to do something about my father first, Clay had implied that I should take action before it's too late and he comes for me. The idea scares me, but the longer I entertain the notion, the more it feels like the right thing to do. I just need to discuss it with Wolfe.

Sighing, I keep strolling down the hallway, when I notice movement in one of the art pieces on the wall.

Pausing to examine one, I realize that the scenes in them are not static. Closer inspection reveals the frames are actually glass-covered enclosures, each a miniature world with half a dozen tiny, fluttering bugs. Their wings, half the size of the butterflies in the village, glimmer with washed-out cream and burnt gold edges. They have no antennae but small round heads, beady eyes, and large mouths. Curiously, one creature flutters closer to the glass as I lean in, its movements eerily slow.

"Why are you in there?" I murmur.

I touch one of the framed displays, lifting it from its hooks. It's surprisingly thick, but it's still a cage nonetheless. A latch on the back suggests it can be opened. When I turn it around to the glass front, the little bugs inside gaze up at me, their eyes large and round.

I contemplate freeing them, feeling awful for them being stuck in there as ornaments, fiddling with the latch.

"I wouldn't recommend that," the bodyguard groans from a few steps away. "Those are Shadowwings, critters whose golden dust carries hallucinogenic toxins. Enough exposure can be lethal."

"Then why keep them locked up like this where anyone can open them up... if it's so dangerous?"

"They are unharmed in these confines. In their natural habitat, they dwell in dense burrows, far more cramped than this. But most of their habitat no longer exists, so we offer them refuge with us. Here, they are fed and kept safe from predators—and from causing harm. Besides, there are far more dangerous monsters who walk freely on this vessel to worry about than the Shadowwings." He makes a strange, choking sound that might be a laugh.

It's almost ominous and raises the hairs on my arms. Seems the bodyguard has a dark sense of humor.

I reluctantly return the frame to the wall. "Let's not poison ourselves tonight," I mutter under my breath, half joking, partially truthful.

Once inside my room, I quickly lock the door, turning just in time to see the guard assume his post outside. A bit paranoid, maybe, but you can't be too careful on a ship full of monsters. To make myself feel more secure, I wedge a chair under the door handle—old habits die hard. I often did this back home when I noticed the Barons in the village paying me a bit too much attention during the day.

Feeling jittery from the day's events, I decide a hot shower might help calm my nerves. I'm in the bathroom in no time, the steamy water washing away the tension.

Wrapped in a towel, with another turbaned around my hair, I step out feeling refreshed. I flick off the main lights, leaving only the soft glow of the starlike lights embedded in the ceiling and the moon carving on the wall that spills light across the room in a gentle, candle-like glow.

I love the calmness it creates.

As I cross the room, a flicker of movement catches my eye by the door.

I freeze, my heart picking up its pace, but I see nothing there.

It's probably nothing, just the shadows playing tricks. But as I reach for the towel to dry my hair, I see it again—a definite shift in the darkness. Spinning around, I'm met with nothing but the empty room.

"You're being ridiculous," I mutter to myself.

As I drop the towel from my hair onto the dressing table, there it is again—the unmistakable outline of a dark form, its green eyes gleaming at me.

Panic strikes me in the chest.

"Help!" My scream shatters the silence, and I'm expecting the guard to burst in any second, but the door remains shockingly still.

The figure advances, blending with the shadows.

I recoil, heart pounding out of my chest, and I'm frantically trying to recall how I summoned my power with the snake. With it comes the terror that I'll cripple Nyko again. And I can't live with myself if I knock him unconscious. What if, this time, I kill him?

The shadow disappears as quickly as it came.

Breathless, I scan the dimly lit room, needing to get out of here and see where the hell the guard is. Just as I take several steps forward, a force slams into my back, driving me up against the wall, face-first.

My scream turns muffled as all the air from my lungs swooshes out from the impact, from the fright. In a flash, a cool breath tickles my cheek, and a large, powerful body presses closer, with a ridiculously thick erection against my ass.

Dread engulfs me, and I push against them, but they're unmovable.

"Get off me," I shout.

"You wanted to see my monster form? Well, here I am, princess," a familiar, deep, husky voice whispers next to my ear.

My mind races, fear mixing with confusion.

"Nyko? Is that you?" I manage to gasp out.

He pulls back just a smidgen, chuckling.

I turn to face him and gasp at the sight.

A tall, shadowy monster, almost translucent, stands in front of me. I can still make out the curves of his muscles, even in this form. However, it's impossible to see his facial features except for those spectacular jade eyes.

He's overwhelming.

Intoxicating.

Dangerous.

Obsessive.

And he's smiling—that much I can tell from his jade eyes squinting at the edges. They seem to sometimes turn into shadows and vanish, too, as if he has complete control of when he shows them.

With my surprise comes anger at the way he decided to surprise me.

"You asshole," I spit out. "You scared the hell out of me."

"My monster likes to play," he growls. There's something so much darker about him like this; even his tone has deepened. "He's been dying to meet you."

"Why are you talking about yourself in the third person? You're a bit frightening, you know. A bit much at times."

"He calls me to do things… and he's been starved for you since you arrived." His eyes glint with lust, with hunger.

"I've decided I hate surprises," I snap, the pounding of my heart loud in my ears. "Especially the kind that involves being terrified half to death."

Nyko laughs, a sound that rumbles through the semi-darkness of the room, making the hair on the back of my neck stand up.

"But you have to admit, being a bit scared is exciting, isn't it? The thrill? The adrenaline?" His fingers trail the side of my face, his touch cool, and my skin's charged, electric.

That small touch sends currents through me, the kind that leaves me struggling to keep my head straight as lust curls deep in my gut.

"Exciting?" My response wobbles because here I am, clenching my thighs with my mind already in the gutter.

"You're mine, Sage, and tonight, I'm going to prove

that we belong together." The possessiveness in his voice is sharp.

My stomach flutters at his promise.

"No, it's okay. You don't need to do anything to prove that."

The corners of his eyes crinkle again, telling me he's doing that evil grin because he'll do as he pleases anyway, won't he? Hell!

The room feels smaller, his presence enveloping every inch of space. There's a part of me that wants to lean into that darkness, to explore the depth he's promising. Though with the way he stares at me, I'm starting to suspect he might not give me an option.

"You can pull back now," I say, lifting my chin, not letting him see how strongly he impacts me.

"I'm ready to play." His words are a whisper now, a promise or a threat, I can't tell, but they have me trembling.

"No," I answer abruptly, sending him into more laughter. He leans into me, closer and closer.

"You're so dangerous for me, princess," he warns, his shadowy lips tracing a path up to my ear, his cold breath tickling me. "You can make a Shadowfen like me lose control easily."

"M-maybe you shouldn't exert yourself. You're still healing. And I'm no princess."

He's making a tsking sound in my ear, his hands skipping down to my waist before he rips away the towel around me.

"You're my princess."

I whimper, an automatic sound that comes when I'm around these monsters, which makes me wonder if my body does it on purpose... show these huge beasts that I'm a wounded deer... Total betrayal by my own body.

"You smell like dessert," he purrs, his lips grazing my neck, then dipping over my collarbone, and I'm buzzing all over. "I'd love another taste of your sweetness." His words send another wave of shivers down my spine, but this time, it comes with a sharp pang of realization.

"Wait, *another* taste?" I repeat, my voice hitching as the pieces click together of when the first time had been... The memory of that dreamlike encounter in Wolfe's room flares in my thoughts, where every touch in my sleep seemed too intimate to be just a dream. Now, it pulses to the surface of my mind.

"That was *you* in Wolfe's place while I slept? I thought I was dreaming."

He purrs, a sound that vibrates deep in his throat, resonating with a primal part of me. His mouth lifts from just above the valley between my breasts, and he raises his gaze to me.

"Very little can hold a Shadowfen back from an impossible attraction of his intended mate. Did you enjoy it, princess?"

The thumping flare deep between my thighs heightens, yet his admission stirs a knot of frustration in my gut. I'm damn drawn to him, intensely so, but he doesn't seem to be someone who has boundaries. That both worries and slightly arouses me; the unknown shouldn't excite me, yet it does. I've never met anyone like him before. Someone who brings out the darkness inside of me. Perhaps I've been on my best behavior for so long in the village of Nightingale that now I'm curious to explore the dark things that will bring me closer to Nyko.

His mouth finds mine, his lips pressing against me in a kiss that's both a promise and a provocation to fill that emptiness I feel inside me. My head spins with lust, slick pooling in my core as I kiss him back impatiently, unable to control myself.

Cool to the touch, his mouth claims me with a possessiveness that has a purr rolling over my throat. I've never made that sound before, but around him, my body responds with primal hunger.

By some miracle, I find my sanity, and this time, I muster the strength to push him back, my hands hard against his chest, ripping from his kiss. I use that moment to slip free from the wall. I should feel emboldened that I'm standing up to this powerful monster, yet my insides are burning up, craving his touch. Adrenaline thumps with my growing neediness.

"You're mine, Sage. I told you that already. Are you scared of me? Is this why you pull away?" he whispers the words, only adding to the whole Nyko vibe.

"I'm not afraid of you," I answer with clipped words, lifting my chin.

He barks out a laugh, his head tilting back. "You can't lie to me." He loves the idea of frightening me.

I dart away from him, my feet carrying me fast toward the front door.

His presence envelopes me the moment I reach for

the chair I used to jam the entry, wrapping around me so fast I cry out.

Still no guard to give me an interruption.

I know if I'm left here, I'll succumb to Nyko's charm.

"What did you do with the guard at the door?"

His mouth is on my ear, his arms curled around my body, one across my breasts, embracing them, leaving me breathless.

"He's taking a nap."

"Nyko," I groan, writhing against him, needing to show him he can't just take what he wants.

"There's nowhere you can run, my little one," he growls. "In Blight, we are driven by deeper forces when it comes to those we are matched with. The more you fight me, the harder I'll chase you."

My knees tremble. He's pinching my nipple between two fingers, rendering me weak. Heat flashes through me, and I'm drenched, finding myself groaning. I shudder at how quickly I fall.

"Will you give in to me?" he asks. "Or do you want me to keep chasing you?" His mouth finds my neck again. That wicked tongue is so long. The coolness of it on my skin sends pinpricks of pleasure through me.

His fingers are on my breasts again, the tips tracing around my nipples in circles. I moan, arching my chest out, so desperate for him to stop teasing.

"What does it look like I need," I ask, arousal rippling between my thighs.

He's inhaling deeply. "You're so ripe, smelling like sex."

My throat's dry, the room tilting as fire flutters down my spine.

Suddenly, he spins me around, pushing me back up against the wall. He falls to his knees in front of me, barely giving me time to react. Shadowy hands slide up my legs, leaving behind a lingering chill, and he nudges them wider.

"Mine," he growls, looking up at me as I catch my breath. His mouth opens wide—a gaping darkness that seems to swallow the dim light in the room. His tongue, much larger than any I've seen, rolls out, hanging down past his chin, and seems to glisten. He licks his lips with a slow, deliberate motion. The monstrous size of his tongue makes my heart race. Thick and wide...

Now, I'm a bit afraid.

"Nyko," I say with a shaky voice, but he's already pushing his face between my legs. That tongue pushes right to my clit, driving deeper, spreading my lips. I'm afraid but so turned on that I'm shuddering.

My head falls back against the wall, hands there, too, as he drags the tip to my entrance, lapping at how drenched I am. A groan falls from my lips, shivers covering every inch of me. His one hand reaches up, grasping a breast, squeezing it, the other curled around where he's holding on to my ass.

"I'm going to make you scream until you forget everyone but me," he growls, sounding animalistic. "And I'm not going to be gentle."

"I—"

He's on me once more, and I'm shaking with desire at

how incredible that huge tongue feels. Then he presses it into me, and I cry out, shaking, feeling him going in deeper and deeper as he fucks me with it. He tugs on my nipple, his other hands slipping between my cheeks, fingertips teasing my ass.

I bite my lip, whining with unbearable heat. He pulls that tongue out, licking the length of me, sucking down on my clit.

Knees wobbling, I'm lucky I'm still upright.

"I can't get enough," he purrs, glancing up at me.

I look down to where his gaze grins at me. That tongue pushes out once more, spearing between my soaking lips, driving into me and curling upward. It keeps going in and in, and I'm slightly worried about how deep one can go, but I sense the tickle almost in my stomach, feeling him right there.

"Nyko," I'm panting. "Don't..."

When he starts flicking inside of me—no idea how he's doing it—I moan, sucking in air as I feel the intensity he's awakening inside me.

Body tense, I hold on as he prods my cunt, pulling out and driving back in, his thickness pushing me open. Then he finally releases me, and with the flat of that weapon, he strokes my whole pussy like he's eating ice cream. It flickers out and back, coming at me with a tiny slap across my pussy each time he darts it at me.

The wet sounds, his finger pushing into my ass, his fingers twisting my nipple.

A growl rolls in my chest, and that's new. The sound comes so fast past my throat that I'm not sure what to make of my reaction. It's impossible to think straight with the biggest tongue in the world flicking my clit, bringing me to a melting point.

Everything spins as the dense cloud of lust envelops me. Even my chest hurts from the heavy breaths, from tensing up. He's devouring me like an animal, going wild, slurping, and the moment he drives that wickedness back into me, I scream out, my orgasm ripping me to shreds. The emotions that had built up in my chest came pouring out. Holding on to Nyko's head, my hands fisting his shadowy hair, I come hard with a shuddering moan. I attempt to clench my thighs, but he won't let me, won't move. He keeps lapping me up hungrily.

My stomach tightens, and I feel like a Goddess in the aftermath that has me floating down from the skies.

When he finally comes up for air, meeting my gaze, he licks his mouth.

His tongue is huge.

So long.

And the whole thing had just been inside me.

He gets to his feet swiftly. "I'm going to fuck your brains out now. I'm going to fuck you deep." He takes me into his arms, and I'm a puddle, my body still wavering from the most incredible climax.

"Deep?" I moan.

"You want it, don't you, princess? For that tight hole to be stretched with my knot."

"Wait!" I stiffen. "What?"

CHAPTER
TWENTY-EIGHT

NYKO

Back to the wall and deliciously naked, Sage is panting for air, her eyes wide, staring at me. Those cheeks glow rosy under the dim light of her bedroom, her chest rising and falling quickly while I take in her body—the tightness of her nipples, her thin waist, the way the strip of violet hair between her thighs glints from her arousal.

I'm so horny I'm drowning in agony. I adore Sage. I'm fucking obsessed with her, thinking about her every damn second of the day, jerking off whenever I remember those gorgeous, big tits and licking her juicy cunt.

My cock throbs, close to crippling me if I don't release.

Her taste and scent engulf my senses, sinking into my blood, into my soul. I may hold a shadow form, but those sensations aren't lost to me.

On her shoulder, she wears a bite mark, I assume from Wolfe. Bastard's a biter.

I reach over and collect her into my embrace, my arms coiled around the delicious curve of her ass, lifting her off her feet so she's eye level with me.

"What did you mean by knotting?" she asks between breaths.

"Every Shadowfen is born different. Each of us is uniquely armed. *Me*... there's always been something more animalistic about me." I walk her across the room and lay her on the bed, but the moment she hits the mattress, she scrambles backward.

"That tells me nothing," she protests.

Her energy floods me, overflows through me, pushing me to claim her over and over. She has no idea that the more she runs from me, the more my shadow side starves for her.

"Never run from a monster," I teach her, but she glares at me.

My heart thunders, close to tearing out of my chest to see her naked. I'm unable to stop staring at her little pink slit, the one I'm fucking desperate to sink into and stay inside all night.

"Why?"

With a grin, I inch closer. "If you make me chase you, well... I may not be able to stop myself once I catch you. Do you want to find out what will happen then?"

Swallowing loudly, she raises her chin. "I'm putting distance between us. That's not running," she argues.

I adore the way she's fooling no one. Except, she's out of arm's reach, so she's too fucking far from me.

"Anyway, you're not answering my question," she continues.

"I will show you what I mean by being animalistic. It's the only way you'll really understand."

She narrows her gaze at me, coaxing a laugh out of me.

"And I'm a human who wants information before anything happens."

"Half-human," I remind her. "You are more Shadowfen than you are an earthling."

Her shoulders stiffen, head high, and those nipples pebble, teasing me.

"You still fight your true nature? Just like you fight me."

"Maybe my body doesn't know what it really wants."

"You're beautiful and smart but wrong in this instance. Your body knows exactly what it craves—me." I chuckle at her deluding herself. My thoughts drown on grabbing her and burying myself in her, fucking her in every damn position, slamming into her until she admits her true feelings for me.

Watching me closely, she might have picked up on my savage intentions from the growl in my throat with her intense stare.

"You're wrong." She squares her shoulders.

I love her fire.

She glances over to the bathroom door, which is closer than the exit, which sits behind me.

"What's my prize once I catch you?" I ask, my voice a velvet whisper as I can predict her next move.

"Thinking of claiming your prize already?" she taunts. "Maybe I should start thinking about what I'll claim when I win."

I'm barking a laugh. "Enlighten me."

She springs off the bed, but I'm faster... so much faster. I lunge across the bed after her, arms snatching her around the waist. Knees digging into the mattress, I resist the forward momentum and swing her back onto the bed with me.

She cries out, writhing against me.

We fall into a heap, her body bouncing against mine. I can't get enough of how soft she feels, how sweet she smells.

She's on her back, and I quickly roll half onto her, one leg draped over her hips, holding her in place, inhaling her slick and honeyed scent.

Gasping for air, she manages, "Get off me."

That glare on her face is everything to me. I've always dreamed of having a mate who pushed me, challenged me, fought me.

My little princess. She's my fucking world.

"Should I be insulted that you keep trying to escape?" I murmur, staring down at her as I slide hair off her face.

She's breathing heavily, those full lips parting, and she purrs, her chest pushing up against mine.

"I hate that my body craves you so much that I have no control."

I stroke her cheek, and she places her hand on mine, but she's not pushing me away.

"Mine's the same," I explain. "But I've long given in to my desires."

"Oh, I can tell." She watches me carefully.

I study her mouth, desperate to taste it again. The tension building in my cock intensifies as I press it against the side of her thigh.

She squirms beneath me, but I've already won. She's mine... all fucking night long.

Her hand reaches over to touch my shadow cheek, and her fingers gingerly trace my jawline, then across my ear and my hair.

"It feels real but also cold, yet my eyes are telling me what I'm feeling is wrong. Your monster form is so different from the others."

"We don't get to choose what destiny gives us at birth. Though, my beautiful one, I'm curious to see your form."

Her touch traces down my shoulder and pauses over my biceps, and I flex them instinctively.

"I want to know, but I also don't," she admits, giving me a lopsided grin. "Then it'll make this even more real that I'm an actual monster. The thing I feared most of my life."

"And you're still scared after arriving here?"

She's half chuckling. "So much more, but I'm getting used to it, I guess."

"You know what might encourage you to bring your other form out? To give yourself over to me."

She raises an eyebrow while my attention is hyper-aware of her fingers trailing across my chest, exploring my body, which is all hers.

The throbbing between us increases. She glances down her chest to where my erection is pressed up against her. She's curious? I roll onto my back for her.

"Feel free to explore," I tell her, my cock sitting up like a fucking flagpole—thick, huge, and black as the rest of my shadowy form.

She twitches against me, and for a moment, I expect her to run, but she never does. That raw hunger inside me flares to seduce her, but I can wait a bit longer if my princess wants to see who her true mate really is. I'd give her the world if she asked for it.

Hands behind my head, I lie there. Her curiosity about my shadow form has her tracing a hand down my chest, poking me in the ribs. Not sure if that's on purpose, but I grin at her.

She's completely focused on me.

"You're curious how I'm holding solid form while I'm a shadow?"

She nods. Her touch is intoxicating, sending my body into small shudders. She trails down my chest, and her warmth seeps through the cool film that layers over my transparent shadow.

"Very interesting," she murmurs.

"I can take solid form with a single thought," I explain.

"Oh," she mutters but hasn't taken her attention off my body.

With a flicker of my will, I shift to my transparent shadow form.

Her hand instantly sinks through my stomach, and she flinches back, yelping.

The sound is delicious.

I laugh and return to solid shadow form.

"Should have warned you," I tease, watching her with predatory eyes.

"Gods, you think?" she snaps. "My heart's pounding in my chest." Yet she wears a smile, studying me more intently now, poking at me. Her fingers linger lower, and my balls tighten at the promise of her touch. Her hand glides over my hip bones, tracing lines of fire on my skin.

It takes all my strength not to reach over and drag her onto me.

"I've never seen anything like this," she says quietly. Her attention is everything. She's mesmerized, her eyes growing into orbs. "Does it hurt to change?"

"No," I say, shaking my head. "It's natural. Like blinking, like drawing in a breath."

"It's strange, but it's beautiful. You're beautiful."

I chuckle, the sound dark in the silent room. "You're the first to ever call me that."

She doesn't respond but twirls her index finger lower, examining my massive cock without hesitation, the tip thick, precum glistening.

"Go ahead and touch him. He'll reward you."

"Haha," she answers sarcastically. "I'm sure he will." Despite the flushing of her cheeks, she wraps her fingers around my shaft as if testing me out.

I hiss as she tightens her grip, and with a single will of thought, my dick thickens in her hand and lengthens.

She gasps aloud, but never once does she let go, yet her fingers no longer touch around her thumb from my girth.

"You can change your size at will?" She twists her head to look at me, shock clear on her raised eyebrow, her constant blinking.

"Any size you desire. I'll blow your mind."

Her breaths speed up, and I adore that she's still holding on to me, her grasp slowly working up and down my shaft.

"So, I can pick the size?"

"Of course," I say, pulse on fire, arousal hammering into me.

Her hand slides down to my balls, and she's going to fucking destroy me. Her hand releases him, and she's gently cupping my balls, facing away from me once more. I'm tensing, my dick twitching.

"Take him for a ride," I tell her, short of not growling my desperation.

She offers me a sly grin, and I must be hallucinating things, or perhaps I misread her escaping from me as something other than wanting distance between us. Up on her knees, she turns to face me and throws one leg over my lap, straddling me.

She's a Goddess, naked, legs spread, the fire from her like a furnace against my groin.

A low growl spills from my lips. "That's it, princess, take what you desire."

"I have this need inside me," she begins. "Something so hungry that I'm burning up with wanting you inside me in shadow form. But a bit smaller as this size is a bit too much."

My cock pulses, and I don't touch her, as desperate as I am, until she asks, but I will my erection to scale down a bit. Her full, lush breasts bounce about as she wriggles to work out how to sit on me, not lifting herself high enough or grasping my erection.

She's so fucking stunning and has clearly never sat on anything like me before.

"Want a hand?" I ask.

Raising her head, she smiles bashfully, trembling slightly. "It really shouldn't be this hard, but I don't want to hurt you."

"Trust me, you won't." I reach down between her legs, grasping my cock. "Now, lift yourself for me." As she does, I push my tip between those silky lips, running it down to her entrance.

I can't tear my gaze from her, seeing the way she moans and her nipples harden. She's so ready, so aroused, and with my dick hard and aching, I say, "Now, sit on me, gorgeous."

Exhaling, she pushes down on me. Those violet eyes burn, her mouth shaped in an O.

She's so fucking hungry for me, two fingers remaining on her swollen clit, rubbing her, reminding her why she needs to be fucked.

"Look at me," I command. She lifts her head from

where she's staring down. "Let me see the lust on your face as you spread your cunt over my cock."

I'm salivating, a rumble in my chest at letting her take her time, and once she's ready, I won't hold back. She's mine to claim, to do with as I desire, to ruin as I crave.

Lying on the bed, I wait for her to fully embed herself on my cock, slowly working me into her, and those beautiful, lustful sounds she makes are killing me. The ache inside is unbearable, breaking me.

Breathing rapidly, she pushes down all the way, and I love feeling her drenched walls around me, dripping down my balls. I hiss at the tightness, at how incredible she feels.

She groans and leans over me, her hands on my chest for leverage.

"That's it," I encourage. My grip on her hips guides her to slide up and back down. I growl like a desperate fool, being squeezed by her, and I'm losing my concentration.

"Fuck me, princess. Show me how much you want me." My voice comes out husky.

She's moaning, moving those sexy hips, her hole sliding up and down on my erection.

Grinding my jaw, I growl. My fingers dig into her hips, moving her quicker, supporting her. I lift my pelvis, meeting her on each thrust.

"Fuck," I snarl as her tight, wet cunt hugs my cock. I feel every shudder she experiences, her groans escalating, and she's holding my stare. With my grip, I move her faster, and she's writhing, her eyelids fluttering like she's barely holding on.

"My gorgeous princess, want me to take over?"

"Please, but give me a moment." She gasps for air, yet she smirks as she comes down on me hard.

The pleasure of being rammed into her has me howling. The pain, the pleasure... She knows it and is loving every second of being in control.

A Shadowfen can only take so much when I'm used to being the one who takes the lead.

I lean in close, whispering, "It's my turn, princess. Hold on."

Her eyes widen, but before she can ask what I mean, I shift swiftly to my side, throwing my arm around her waist to keep her on my lap. As she starts to fall toward the bed on her side, I tighten my hold and roll us both over fast, using the bed to bounce on top of her. Now she's beneath me, and I'm about to go wild.

She whines, caught off guard.

Best part... I'm still deep in her sweet cunt.

"Nyko!" she gasps.

Heat tugs on my insides, and an inferno is building inside me.

"I promise that in the morning when we're done, you can ride my cock all day long."

"Morning?" she gasps.

"Keep those legs spread, princess." Desire thumps through me as her slick drips out. I push in so fucking deep I'm on the brink of bursting.

But not yet...

"Is it me, or do you feel bigger?"

I grin at her. "You're ready for a thicker Nyko now." Gradually, I expand just enough to give her the ache she's desperate for.

"Wait, no!" But she's moaning, those violet eyes huge, fingernails digging into my arms.

"Feel good?"

A glint of perspiration glows from her brow, her hair sticking to the edges of her face. I love that look of exhaustion from being fucked.

"So, this is your animalistic side?"

"Nope. That's my next surprise."

Her mouth drops open.

"You're so fucking sexy." I pull out of her halfway, then I rock back into her hard, her body, her tits bouncing. "I've been so patient, waiting to rut you."

"And," she exhales the word while moaning. "Now you're going to make up for lost time?" She holds on to my arms harder as I thrust into her. There's no pause, no mercy. Only the savage hunger that's lingered inside me for weeks now. The wet sounds of slamming into her, of her cunt sucking down on my shaft, is euphoria.

I can't stop. I take her rough, claiming what's mine.

Her fingernails dig into my arms again, but that only makes me go faster. She thrashes beneath me as I shove into her, and the whole damn bed shakes with my plunge.

Her cries are spectacular, and I'm seeing stars from

how fast I'm hammering into her, her walls clamping down around me.

I lean forward, my mouth on hers, kissing her like the mad Shadowfen I am, letting her experience my hunger.

She purrs against my lips, both of us in motion, my hips thrusting wildly. I drag my tongue down her chin to her neck, feeling the racing pulse of her heart in her veins.

Her hips are rocking with mine, her noises morphing into loud groans and cries.

She's so damn close.

I latch my mouth around the side of her neck, my mouth larger in shadow form, teeth pressed to her flesh.

"Nyko," she growls, but I can't stop.

That animalistic side of me craves her fear, wanting her to tremble while she reaches her climax.

I shove into her again and again, the pressure on my cock building, my balls heavy, aching. That raw, fierce need grabs me by the chest. Instinct takes me, and I fuck her while she's calling my name.

"Nyko. Don't stop. Don't you fucking stop!"

I press down a bit more on her throat, my tongue on her skin, and sink into her as far as I possibly can, just as she quivers beneath me.

Screaming.

Slick sliding from her.

Shaking ferociously.

The savage shudder I've been seeking collides through me. I roar in my chest, holding myself deep in her, my cock swelling at the base that's pushing against her walls.

"Nyko, what the hell?" She's shaking. "Something feels different inside me."

I release her neck, licking the skin where my teeth marks are red imprints on that perfectly smooth skin. Lifting my head, I'm shaking with arousal, my cock pulsing, threads of white cum spewing into her, filling her, never ending.

"It's a knot." I muster. "My dick swells into a knot at the base, keeping us locked together."

Panic twists her expression while she's still coming down from her own climax.

I'm not yet done, my arousal still pouring through me and into her. A growl rips from my throat, pumping more cum, unable to see straight at how incredible it feels.

When I can barely breathe, I finally collapse onto her, buried in her, spent, but I'm smiling ridiculously.

She's still looking frightened, so I roll onto my back, her resting on top of me.

"This was your surprise," she states breathlessly.

I lean over to her bedside table where I planted a small something earlier today for this moment.

"Because if I told you, you would have panicked. Not many monsters can do this."

She frowns. "I've seen so much weird stuff, but the fact that your dick swells inside me to ensure we're stuck together..." She pauses, her cheeks flushing. "No, you're right. It's freaking me out now! And what happens when your adrenaline kicks in from being with me?"

"It's going to be okay, and the knot won't last for too long. I adore you for caring, but leave that with me for both of us. Deal?"

But I doubt she's hearing me as she spots the black jar in my hand, hard to miss since it's as thick as my fist.

"What the hell's that?" she demands. "I told you before, I hate surprises, especially your kind, but you keep bringing them out."

"I would never hurt you." I laugh, a dark sound that reverberates around us. "You need to trust me."

"You're making that really hard," she retorts, wriggling on top of me, sending jolts of electricity through my body.

Having her tight around my cock, her breasts against my chest, I'm exactly where I intended to be.

I lift the jar. "I told you earlier, I'm going to prove that we're true mates."

"Why am I going to hate this?" she mutters, suspicion in her eyes.

I uncork the black jar and pour its contents over both of us at once.

Pink mist billows out, infused with a spark of magic from one of the market vendors. The mist flutters rapidly toward our faces, swarming our senses.

She whines, batting at it with a hand, but it's too late. I inhale deeply, letting the magic fill my lungs.

"Just take it in… don't fight the inevitable."

"It's that stupid ritual mist again," she gasps, but

before she can argue, the concentrated dose blurs her vision as it does mine. She blinks, shaking her head, the mist taking its toll on her.

The room spins, our breaths mingling in the enchanted haze.

Our world fades to black. The last thought that flickers through my mind is that this is everything I've ever dreamed of—to finally find my true mate.

CHAPTER TWENTY-NINE

SAGE

I'm standing on the shores of a rocky beach, a sheer cliff looming at my back. The sky above is a twist of deep, bruise-like purples, but my attention is caught on our vessel, Howler—the massive, round, glass-like orb—engulfed in flames.

Fire licks at the sky, and thick black smoke darkens overhead, turning the sea into a dark, churning mass that reflects the chaos above.

My heart lurches, breath trapped in my throat. Tears sting my eyes, streaming down my face as I watch the inferno consume the vessel.

Shaking hard, I push toward the lapping icy water, the urgency to find my three monsters, to ensure they aren't on their vessel, eating me alive.

A whimper falls from my lips...

Yet, I know this is a vision; I'm aware of it, just as I'd experienced with the last two. Except this one is different... I've never been so scared.

The pain is sharp, a knife twisting in my chest.

"Sage," *a raspy voice echoes from somewhere nearby, the sound almost swallowed by the roar of the flames and the crashing waves.*

I turn to Nyko, who's suddenly at my side, eyes wide, the reflection of the flames in his glassy eyes, and it grips my heart.

"Fuck, fuck!"

He's rushing into the water from the shore, desperate in his movements, heading for Howler.

I dart after him, snatching his hand, stopping him with a strength I didn't know I had.

"It's just a vision," *I choke out.* "We can't change anything here."

He stares at me, tears in his eyes, and it's the first time I've witnessed fear in Nyko. My own fright intensifies at seeing such a strong Shadowfen crumble... the home he's known for most of his life is alight, and maybe everyone he's ever known!

"This was meant to be our moment to show we're true mates, but this... What the fuck! Why is the Howler on fire?" *His voice breaks, the sound raw and filled with dread.*

"I don't know," *I whisper, clinging to him, fear skittering across my skin.* "My other visions with Wolfe and Killian were of the past kingdom, others of the present..."

"Fuck me!" *he mutters, the word laced with hopelessness.* "Is this our future?"

He draws me closer into his embrace as we watch the flames devour Howler. Despite the huge flames and heavy smoke, I don't smell anything. It's just a vision, us observing a moment. Dark smoke floats from the vessel, smudging the world. The sight of his home—our home—being consumed by flames is a nightmare I can't look away from.

"If this is our future, we can't let this happen," I sob into his chest.

Nyko's grip tightens. "A vision is just that, but this is like throwing a wrench into the wheel of events."

I nod, looking up at the fear twisting his expression. Dread sticks to me, a suffocating weight because deep down I worried I'm being shown this for a reason.

My arrival has changed the course these three monsters had planned. They've held back from giving me to my father, so is the result? I quiver down to my bones to think my arrival would result in such devastation.

Nyko's skin glows almost orange, the fire's reflection creating a haunting effect against him.

I look up at the jagged stone wall behind us and the long stretch of sea in front of us, and I feel utterly lost. I have no idea where we are.

Nyko cups my face, his touch grounding me. His gaze glistens more.

"This is a warning, a mission for us to prevent."

"I think so, too."

"You are mine now, Sage, and I'm yours," he murmurs his vow, and I nod in agreement. "You mean everything to me. I knew meeting my true mate would change my world, but this is so much deeper than I expected."

The flames crackle in the distance, the smoke thick in the air.

"I can't lose you," he admits, the words almost a whisper. "I won't lose you."

"It won't happen." My heart races at his touching words, the ones that coil around my insides, reminding me that I'm not alone anymore.

He leans down, kissing me, whispering, "I think I'm falling in love with you."

Tears well up in my eyes from the depth of his emotions, from our horrific surroundings, from the sickening ache in my gut that the flames are a result of me.

He leans in for a fiercer kiss, and I soften against him, never thinking I'd ever have someone tell me they love me.

I cling to him, the dread of the dark prophecy looming over us, but for now, we have time, I tell myself. But for how long?

As the world darkens quickly, fading, Nyko holds me tighter, and I shut my eyes.

His kisses bring me back, soft ones all over my forehead.

I open my eyes to find us back in my bed, me on top of him, us still stuck together.

I'm crying. Tears won't stop falling, and the fear, the darkness in his gaze—it's all still there. With it comes a profound devotion I feel for Nyko.

Maybe it's the vision that's shaken me or that he's confessed to loving me. Whatever it is, my insides are clenched, and I don't want to let go of him.

"It's going to be all right," he says.

"Everything feels surreal." My heart's throbbing. "I

think that Howler burning in my vision might be my fault. Maybe it's a warning for me to make a change before it's too late?"

He frowns, the shadows deepening beneath his eyes. "It's not your fault," he says firmly, holding me tighter. "Don't ever say that."

"But it is." I shake my head, panic surging through me. "Being your true mate, and Killian's and Wolfe's, has changed everything. Maybe that vision is showing us that not taking action against my father as planned has set us on the wrong path."

"We're not giving you to him." His frown deepens, and darkness seems to edge closer. "I can't emphasize that enough."

My heart thunders against my rib cage, the weight of his words comforting but terrifying.

"It took me a while to understand why I was so affected by you, Killian, and Wolfe. I didn't truly grasp what being a true mate meant. But now I feel it strongly inside me—the desperation to be with you three, the fear of losing you all, the warmth in my chest when we are together. Each passing day, this place feels more like home."

I pause, the emotions swirling inside me, forcing me to face the truth.

"I changed fate because now you don't want to harm me, either. That's why I know the vision of Howler burning is because of me."

He studies me, his shadowy face hard to read, but that captivating jade gaze holds me.

"We've been talking about alternate plans," he explains, but it doesn't seem concrete.

I want to cry, to pretend none of this is real, but I push on.

"I have been thinking of a way to maybe fix this."

"What is it?" he asks, his arms across my back, holding me securely.

"You need to take me to my father."

"Like fuck we are!" he growls. "We're not going to sit back if you think we'll let you sacrifice yourself. Your father's a son of a bitch, and once he has you, there's nothing stopping him from killing all of us and burning Howler."

I shake my head. "I'd never do that, but I have a different idea."

"Go on," he says, studying me carefully in the dim light of my bedroom. It feels strange having such a serious conversation while he's still buried deep inside me, but there's a comfort in his presence, the building pressure a reminder of our bond.

"If we don't act, that vision might come true," I press on. "We need to confront my father. Not to sacrifice me, but to change the course of events."

He studies me carefully, the shock giving way to grim determination. "How do you propose we do that?"

I take a deep breath, trying to steady my nerves. "I'm his daughter," I say, meeting Nyko's sharp gaze. "And as such, I have a claim to be the heir to his throne, right?"

Studying me, not saying anything, his gaze is locked on mine, and I can see his wheels spinning.

"And if you three are my fated mates," I continue. "Then you are, through our connection, bound to also claim that throne alongside me."

"He won't hand over his kingdom." His response is immediate, his voice a low growl.

"I don't expect him to," I reply quickly. "We say we're next in line once he's no longer around. Until then, all we ask for is land for your Shadowfen and peace. If we are rightful heirs, we deserve that much." I'm waffling, nervous, but the words keep pouring out.

"I have no idea if this will work, but if he knows I'm here—and if he doesn't yet, he will soon—wouldn't it make sense to approach him before he comes for me? If we do this, perhaps we'll change the destiny of Howler. I won't sit and do nothing if he's the one who ends up torching Howler."

His breathing quickens. "I don't trust the bastard not to kill us once we arrive."

"Well, you all said he's been searching for me, wanting to understand my power. I don't tell him anything until he agrees to our terms and we're safe. I'll take my time telling him anything. If he comes to take me first, we lose all ability to negotiate. He might destroy everyone to get to me."

"He can just as easily take you and still eliminate us once we approach him," Nyko counters, his tone darkening.

"But we can't do nothing! Having Howler destroyed and everyone in it will ruin me. We have to try something."

"Risky as fuck!" He grimaces.

"A massive risk." I nibble on my lower lip as nerves dance in my stomach. He shifts under me slightly, and his cock twitches inside of me. And I'm buzzing all over, squirming, trying not to think about how incredible it feels to have him inside me during this conversation.

The gravity of my suggestion pushes down on me, my own words echoing in my head, doubt curling around them.

"If we're proactive, we have a chance to create peace in the future. But nothing is a guarantee."

He studies me for a long pause, his hands against me giving a slight shake.

"I'll support you... do anything to keep you safe, but we don't rush into this. We have time."

"I know," I concede. "But after that vision..." I swallow hard, still feeling the sickness in my gut to think of the Howler being destroyed. "I feel we may not have that much time."

He isn't okay; it's easy to see the frantic look on his frowning expression. I've observed more sides of Nyko recently, but this one makes him appear unraveled. It reminds me of my arrival in Blight. My panic, fear, and the unknown all terrifying me.

"If we wait, we're at his mercy," I whisper in the silent room. "This way, we at least have a chance to fight back on our terms."

He's silent for a while, his grip on me tightening.

"We do this, we do it together, plus we need Wolfe's and Killian's agreement."

"Of course." I nod again, feeling a surge of determination tangled with trepidation.

Leaning closer, I meet his lips, and he kisses me softer this time but with a passion I hadn't expected from him. This isn't hunger or desperation but one of affection, and it tugs at my heart.

The reality of what I've proposed sinks in.

I have no idea how a passionate night ended up with us making plans to face my father—a plan that might very well end in our deaths—but the more I think about it, the more I feel this is the right way to go.

CHAPTER
THIRTY
SAGE

I woke up alone.

Instead of Nyko, I found two guards outside my door, insisting they couldn't leave my side at Nyko's instructions as he had to attend an urgent meeting. After the events last night, I must have fallen asleep on top of Nyko, yet I woke up curled up in bed, finding he'd cleaned me up, seeing there was no gooey mess between my thighs. Nothing stops him from doing as he sees fit, and I can't even hate him for it. He's my true mate.

Especially not after our vision that's still sitting on my mind heavily.

My stomach's growling again, starved for food, and that's my first port of call this morning.

After showering and dressing, the guards take me to a new location to try, as per instructions from Nyko. The moment I enter the hall, I know I'm going to like the place, mostly from the heavenly baked smells, even if the decor is a mix of the monstrous and the charming. Dark, gnarled wood forms the tables and chairs while luminescent vines cast an eerie glow over everything. I spot an empty table and meander through the busy room. The smells intensify with spices and something musky, making my mouth water and my stomach churn.

I spot Joa sitting alone at a table, the girl I met during my first ritual, and she's waving me over with a bright smile.

"Join me," she calls out.

"Morning," I greet her, sliding into the seat across from her, glad to be with someone else and not have just all these eyes on me from around the room. The guards hover nearby, but I ignore them.

"Morning yourself," she chirps, sipping from a metal goblet filled with a deep red juice. Her yellow eyes sparkle from her grin, and aside from her serpent-like gaze and pale-yellow scales that run up her arm and more along her neck, she doesn't have any other monstrous features. "I've ordered too much food for me and my two sisters, but they've both gone into work early. So, you can help me eat this."

"I'm starving, so yes, please." The table is filled with plates of food, and my attention is shifting past the strange, transparent, jelly-like bowls with tiny bones sticking out of them to the baked goods.

She glances at the guards at the wall farther behind us. "What's going on?"

"Wolfe's a bit protective." I don't expand as I don't know who's listening. "Anyway, how did you do after the

Veil Ritual?" I ask, tearing off a piece of what looks like a pancake but has an odd, mushy filling. It's sweet, and I decide not to question what it is.

Joa shrugs. "It didn't exactly work out. One of the Shadowfen chased me, and we spent the most incredible two days and nights together." She sighs, stirring her spoon in a bowl of green porridge. "Then I discovered he already has a wife and three children."

"Oh, shit! What an asshole."

She's nodding, one side of her mouth pinching. "So, I did what I could. I tracked him down and stabbed him in the chest. Now he's in the infirmary recovering. I regret not stabbing him a few more times."

While slightly shocked at her story, I'm also laughing at how casually she talks about attacking him.

"So, it's normal to seek revenge like that?" I pop more of the pancake into my mouth.

"Absolutely. You are frowned upon if you take no action when someone has wronged you. But I met someone new at the infirmary recently, which made it worth it. Destiny always has a plan for us."

Destiny... I'm starting to believe I'm meant to be here. It's my fate.

Joa's gaze flits to a beastly monster across the room. He reminds me of the Minotaur creature from my mom's old books. He's bulky, with horns that curve off his face, and he's surrounded by other monsters, but he keeps glancing our way. Or I should say, in Joa's direction.

"That's Brakar," she whispers, pretending not to

glance at him again. "The gentlest Shadowfen you'll ever meet. Every night, he massages me."

"So, it's official? You're living together and getting married?" I tease, smirking as I reach for a small transparent pastry pouch filled with what looks like peas in a sauce. Placing it on my plate, I tear it apart with the two-pronged fork. The contents spill out, and I scoop a bit into my mouth. Dirt. That's how it tastes. I scrunch up my face, trying my best to force it down my throat and not insult anyone.

Joa giggles at me, then looks over at Brakar, batting her eyelids.

"That was the ritual, silly. Once someone selects you, you're meant to be bound for life. If you're lucky enough to find your true mate, which is rare, then that's a whole different level of emotional connection. Because my connection wasn't a true-mate one, it was easy for him to leave me, and why I had a right to take my revenge on him. Customs believe this will discourage Shadowfen from leaving a relationship after the Veil Ritual." She takes another sip of her juice. "And you? You're the talk of the vessel."

"Me?" I raise an eyebrow. "Why?" After my attempted assassination, I'd prefer not to have such attention on me.

"Not only did you take Killian, but all three leaders of the Howler. The three most eligible bachelors. So many girls are jealous, but I'm proud of you." She grins, and I really like her.

Our conversation flows easily after that, talking

about life on the vessel, the strange foods, and the gossip that never seems to stop. Joa's lightheartedness is contagious.

"Oh, and did you hear about the strange vessel spotted in the waters this morning?" she asks, her tone dropping to a whisper.

I freeze, my fork halfway to my mouth. "What sort of vessel?" Please don't let it be related to my father.

She shrugs. "No one really knows, but it didn't come from us. Some are saying it's from the kingdom, which is absurd. Why would they come to check on us when they haven't visited before? Some are saying it could be another colony of Shadowfen we didn't know existed on one of the small islands."

My mouth goes dry, and I feel a sick twist in my stomach, convinced the lingering vessel is from the kingdom. And if they're here, it can only mean one thing.

We're in huge trouble. My father's coming for me.

I try to focus on Joa's chatter, but my mind is racing. The food now tastes like ash in my mouth. I push the plate away, my appetite gone. The guards nearby remain still, watching over me.

"What's wrong?" Joa's smile fades when she sees my face.

"Nothing," I lie, forcing a smile. "I'm just full."

But it's not nothing. It's everything. I worry my father might be coming for me, which will result in him attacking Howler. I keep replaying the burning vessel from my vision over and over. "I need to go," I mumble, trying to keep my voice steady. My heart hammers in my chest, and the room spins slightly as I rise to my feet. "I'd like to do this again. I don't have many friends on the vessel."

"Count me in." Joa nods, smiling. "See you later."

With my guards, I cross the eating area, unable to move fast enough. Once we're in the hallway, I glance at the nearest guard, catching his eye.

"Take me to Wolfe right away, please."

The guard nods, and without another word, we hurry through the hallways, in and out of elevators. The dark corridors twist and turn.

We pass several locals, their monstrous forms towering and intimidating, yet they pay me no attention. I follow the guards, my insides tight.

Finally, we arrive at the beastly hall I recognize, the one dominated by a set of double doors flanked by terrifying creature heads carved in intricate detail. The guards knock, and a deep, familiar voice calls for us to enter.

The doors creak open, revealing a room bathed in shadow and flickering light from torch-like faux lights set in iron sconces. My three mates—Killian, Nyko, and Wolfe—sit at a round table with Clay and several others I don't recognize. Their discussion halts as their attention turns to me. Killian's on his feet immediately, crossing the room toward me.

"Everything all right?" he asks, his brow furrowing with concern.

"I'm sorry to interrupt. I-I can come back," I stammer, turning to leave, feeling their intense gazes on me.

"No, it's fine," Wolfe states firmly, also on his feet. "We're done here. Stay. Everyone else can leave."

When he says *everyone*, he means everyone other than me and my three true mates. The others, including Clay, trudge out, their gazes lingering on me suspiciously. Clay gives me a strange look, one that I can't quite decipher. Is it pity? Resentment? I shake off the feeling and step deeper into the room.

"Join us." Wolfe gestures for me to sit near him. "We need to talk."

I take a deep breath, trying to steady myself. "It's about the vessel spotted near us, isn't it? That's why I'm here."

"They're from the kingdom, but they are now long gone," Nyko explains.

Silence follows his words. Killian runs a hand through his hair, the other at my elbow, guiding me to the table.

Wolfe remains still, his gaze fixed on me. "Nyko told us everything about your ritual vision."

CHAPTER
THIRTY-ONE
WOLFE

The moment Sage entered the conference room, her presence instantly caught my full attention—dressed in tight pants that follow those beautiful legs and a black shirt with buttons pulling slightly across her bust. Her nipples are hard, pressed against the fabric, and the sight leaves me breathless. Add to that the gaps between the buttons revealing a tiny bit of skin has me hyper-focused on her chest and the reality that she wears nothing underneath the shirt. I'm mentally willing her shirt to rip open, to have her tits bouncing out.

It's incredible how her entrance can completely change the mood of the room from a stoic, serious, tense situation to one where her scent floods the room, and I'm unable to think about anything but her.

At my command, the room clears except for the four of us.

Sage joins us at the table, sitting between Killian and Nyko, who immediately places his hand on her leg.

"I think that vessel is here because it belongs to my father. He knows I'm here. And that puts everyone in this vessel in danger."

A blade twists harder in my heart, the same one that had lodged there when Nyko told us earlier about their vision of the burning vessel and Sage's plan to deal with her father. The thought of her being in danger sharpens the ache.

"You're right," I state from across the table. "I had scouts swim underwater to the smaller vessel just before dawn. They confirmed it was the King's guards. We're still a day's travel away from the kingdom since we paused our mission."

"Howler in flames has been haunting me." Nyko glances at Sage, and she leans into him, her presence seeming to ground him.

My fingers itch to reach out and touch her, to pull her into my arms. It's been too long since she's been at my side.

"Our time has run out." There's a determination in Sage's eyes that wasn't there before. "I want your support to go and tell him that I am his heir, and as my true mates, so are all of you. And if he wants to find out anything about my ability, he's going to have to accept us into his kingdom." She's fidgeting nervously in her seat.

"I fucking hate that idea, but maybe you're right."

Killian studies her, his lips poised downward. He takes her hand into his, unable to keep his distance, either.

"We go armed and with backup," I explain, repeating what we'd discussed with the team earlier, but I don't expand into the tactical details.

I pace the length of the room, knowing Sage's plan puts her front and center to a danger we may not be able to completely protect her from. I'll guard her to my dying breath, but the risks are fucking enormous. I step closer, my eyes locked on her, and she grimaces.

"Are you sure you want to do this?" I ask.

She nods. "We're offering my father what he wants, *me*, and I won't reveal to him what he's dying to know—what my abilities are. That should keep us safe initially. I'll drag that information out for as long as possible to keep Howler and everyone else protected until we can determine if he's open to negotiating with us." She pauses, breathing heavily. "And who knows, maybe if I get him alone, I can use my ability against him?" She's smiling nervously.

Killian clears his throat. "There's no guarantee how the asshole's going to react, and you're not taking him out yourself. If he gets wind of what you're doing, he'll kill you." His lips pinch tight, glancing at Sage, his expression softening.

"We push him to consider a treaty as we've returned you, and now you are his heir," I add. "We just need him to let down his guard, and I'll take out the fucker."

"I want to fuck him over so badly," Nyko growls, then

looks at Sage. "Sorry for saying that. I know he's your father, but..."

"Don't." She squares her shoulders. "I have no allegiance to him. I don't owe the man anything, even if he is my blood. He's not family, as far as I'm concerned."

"Priority is Sage's safety, gaining a home for our people, and ensuring your vision never comes to fruition," Killian says.

"I guess we're doing this, then?" she asks, her voice steady despite the dread rippling over her face.

"I'm ready," I state, Killian and Nyko mimicking me at once. We've been waiting for this moment for years—to have a reason to approach the King without being killed on sight on his island.

"I mean, I'm scared out of my mind, but the fear of doing nothing is so much worse," she says, offering us a lopsided grin. Fuck, she's adorable.

Nyko pulls her into a fierce embrace. "That's my girl," he murmurs proudly.

I'd give my left arm to be him right now, taking her into my embrace.

"All right." I nod. "We need to prepare for departure. Sage, you'll be staying with one of us three at all times from now on, just in case. Nyko and Killian," I continue. "Get the warriors ready. I'll speak with Clay about the course for the vessel, and I'll send a message to King Bren of our arrival to avoid them attacking us for arriving unannounced. Our plan is to be there in just over forty-eight hours." I swing my attention to Sage, my hand reaching up to cup the side of her face. She leans into my touch, the admiration in her gaze for me unmissable. It softens my heart.

"I hate that you're going to be in the firing line, but we'll risk everything to protect you," I explain.

"I never expected anyone to risk themselves for me."

Killian leans in and kisses her on the lips. Nyko closes in behind her and takes her mouth the moment they finish. A growl rumbles in my chest at the sight, the jealousy that I'm across the table from them.

Then everyone rises. As we head out, I grab Sage's hand, feeling the warmth of her skin. "Have you got a moment?" I ask softly.

She gives me that small smile that has me falling for her. Killian and Nyko glance our way, then leave us alone in the room, shutting the door behind them.

"Are you sure about this? It's easy to get caught up in the adrenaline. I can't bear it if anything happens to you."

"I'm ready. If this is my fault, I should fix it, right?"

"It's not your fault." I grip her hand tighter, my eyes searching hers. "If we're going to play the blame game, it's us three for seeking you out and bringing you here."

She sighs heavily.

"You know, you're a very different girl from the one who arrived in Blight," I explain, trying to steady the storm inside me, my fierce attraction to her.

Reaching over, she curls her hand through my dark hair, draping it over my shoulder. The touch sends a delicious shiver down my spine, and I lean into it, my hunger for her intensifying.

"Maybe I just didn't realize I was this person all along," she says softly. "I was never given the chance in the village."

"I fucking love this strong side of you," I confess. "But it scares me, too. The thought of you getting hurt..."

"I know the risks, Wolfe." Her fingers continue to play with my hair. "But I want to stop thinking about them for a moment as I'm going to be a mess leading up to seeing my father. I'd rather focus on your monster form because it does something wonderful for me." She bites her lower lip as her breaths quicken.

My gaze dips to her mouth, then lower to where the buttons strain against her heaving chest.

In a heartbeat, my human form sheds, and I grow and expand, standing in front of her in my Shadowfen form. My pants and shirt, feeling too tight, will be coming off soon.

"My monster form doesn't scare you?" A growl rumbles in my chest, the hardness in my pants growing. I trace my fingertips over her collarbone, enjoying the heat of her skin.

"It did when I first saw you that way." Her hand falls from my hair to the hard planes of my chest. Her touch, even through the fabric, is fire, and I'll willingly burn in her flames.

"You have no idea what I'd do for you." I thread my hand through her hair to the back of her head, pulling her even closer. "Right now, it feels like an eternity since you've been in my arms."

She purrs softly, the sound vibrating through me. I

adore that sound she makes. My lips brush hers, inhaling her sweet berries and sex scent.

"Good, you should never be frightened of me."

Her hands clutch at me, her body pressed tightly against mine.

Her scent fogs my mind, drowning out every thought.

Irresistible.

Unbearable.

Our mouths clash, stealing my breath. The intensity of our kiss is overwhelming, a desperate mingling of need and fear.

"I missed you," I murmur, my hands gripping her waist. "You have no idea how much."

"Oh, I have an idea. It's just a fraction less than I missed you." She breathes, smirking, her fingers pushing through my hair, tugging it slightly, and I lean down to kiss her again.

Our passion deepens, becoming more frantic, more urgent. Her heart pounds in her chest, thumping against mine as her body molds to me.

I hadn't intended to end up with my tongue down her throat or my cocks aching for release, but trying to think of something else—anyone else, for that matter—in her presence is impossible.

Sage consumes my thoughts.

Reaching between us, my hand tugs at the buttons of her shirt that pop open easily. With the last button undone, her breasts bounce free. My cocks twitch, my gaze all over the dusty mauve color of her nipples. I've got my hands under her armpits, lifting her off her feet. In moments, she's sitting on the table, and my attention is on those beautiful full tits that have been teasing me from the moment she entered the room.

"I've been dying to see your breasts again."

"Oh, is that so?" She breathes the words. Leaning back on her arms, she sticks her chest out, offering them to me like a reward.

A shuddering exhale rushes from my lungs. My pretty little monster wants me to suck on them, and I'll give her what she craves. I lean over her, my hands on either side of her, resting on the table, my tongue licking her beautiful offering, circling them, not leaving a section untouched.

"Is this what you want?" I ask before taking one of her fully erect nipples into my mouth. It's hard yet soft as I roll it over my tongue.

She moans as my hand claims the other one, pressing and squeezing it fiercely. I lightly bite down on the one between my teeth, pinching the other, not letting her go. I'm in fucking euphoria.

She has a hand curled around one of my black, curled horns, the sensation buzzing down to my balls. I adore her aggressive arousal.

My greedy mouth tugs and sucks on her, her hips already starting to rock, her musky perfume blooming. I release one breast, loving the red markings I've left around her areola, then I take the other morsel between my teeth, drawing more and more into my mouth. I'm fucking greedy as my hands pull open the buttons on her pants.

Her moans escalate. "Wolfe, should we be doing this here?"

"I'm going to fuck you here, and nothing will stop me." I latch onto her breast again as she wriggles her pants down her hips, then her legs. My cocks pulse in need, my balls pulled in so tight that a growl presses on my throat. I help her, tugging them down her legs while my mouth remains full. She kicks them off, then spreads herself for me.

Fuck!

Heat pours from her.

Intoxicating perfume.

She's mesmerizing.

Desperation rips me apart, and I sink my teeth into her breast, the copper taste of blood in my mouth in seconds.

"Wolfe!" she cries out, shoving against my shoulders, but I can't let go. My hand dips to between her thighs, and the moment I press my fingers between her swollen lips, she's moaning for more.

I lick the bite that's around her areola, the perfect mark staking my claim. Just like the one I gave her on her shoulder, I assume the others on her neck are from Nyko or Killian.

She now bears the marks of our obsession.

"That hurt," she murmurs as I tease her clit.

"And incredible!"

She glares at me, her gaze fogged over from the lust

consuming her. Two droplets of blood roll down her breast, the red against her ivory skin calling to me. I lick them, loving the taste of her.

"The marks on a true mate's body are a real indication of how much she's adored and loved."

Her gaze flips wider. "You love me?"

I sink two long fingers into her, sending her body into shudders. Leaning forward, pressing my forehead to hers, still fingering her, I stare into those stunning violet eyes.

"I think I fell in love with you the moment you arrived in Blight. I knew instantly that I wasn't going to be able to stop myself from falling hard. I just refused to accept it at first. But yes, I'm so fucking deeply in love with you that I don't know where my emotions begin and end anymore. You consume my thoughts every second of the day and night. I dream of you, and I wake up with your scent in my nostrils. That's why I know you're mine."

She's mewling from how fast I'm thrusting into her, but her eyes glisten, a whimper in her chest.

"I-I never expected to find someone who would care so much for me. I've always accepted that I'm the outcast, the one most ignored, so this..." She gasps for air, and there's a tear in the corner of her eye.

I lean in, licking it as it rolls down her cheek.

"Only you can make me horny as hell while making me cry at the same time," she whispers. "I don't know what to say."

"You don't need to say anything. I didn't admit my

love to have you mimic it back. There's no rush, as I know this is a lot for you, and I'm a patient Shadowfen."

She half smiles, half cries out, but then she's kissing me, and I'm lost to her completely.

I work into her harder, and she inches closer to me, her hands tugging down on my pants, our mouths refusing to part.

In moments, I have her off the table, breaking our kiss and twisting her away from me.

"I've got my sights set on filling your ass today."

"Wait! I'm not ready for that, and no way are you putting two in there."

She rocks away from me, but I have my hand on the back of her neck, holding her in place.

"You're not going anywhere, and I won't force anything. Now, bend over for me and lean across the table."

She's shaking, making those purring sounds that turn me wild. Yet she follows my command, and I release my grip on her.

Ass high, she spreads her legs for me, and I step back, needing a view.

"Fuck!" She's dripping wet, her pink lips engorged, glistening with slick that spreads all the way up her adorable little puckered ass. More of it coats the insides of her thighs. When I reach over, running my fingers over her entrance, her cunt pulses in response, seeming to flutter at my touch. Her hole squeezes, more slick seeping out.

"Sexiest thing I've ever seen," I snarl, dropping my pants, my two cocks bouncing out, then rip off my shirt.

"P-please," she groans.

"Do you want me to fuck you in the ass?"

"Don't make me wait. The desire inside me is too much. I'm burning up."

"You didn't answer me." With my hand between her legs, I give her greedy cunt a small slap.

She flinches, freezing in place. "Did you just slap my pussy?"

I laugh. "Keep ignoring my question, and I'll have you over my lap, spread and raw."

She's quivering, a moan spilling from her lips. "Yes..." She's breathing heavily. "Fuck me in the ass," she murmurs, rocking her hips for me.

Is she getting turned on by the idea? Noted.

"My filthy girl, let me reward you." The lower cock in hand, I run it along her slickness, then push the head into her, the walls clamping down on me instantly, squeezing.

"Fuck," I hiss.

"You make me feel so dirty, and I can't resist you."

"That's my sweet girl." Taking my second cock, I enter that pink ass waiting to be fucked.

She stiffens against me as I work my head into her slowly, in and out, getting her used to letting me in, to getting her opening up.

"Don't resist me," I start. "Deep breath and relax." And just as she tries that, I press in deeper. She groans loudly, the tightness of her ass strangling me. But she's soaked, and I know she can take me.

"I want to hear you screaming for me." Inching in deeper, I take my time with her, my fingers sliding down on her clit, rubbing that adorable nub.

She's barely standing now with her legs wobbling, but I hold her and push deeper, spreading those gorgeous holes. I give a final shove, driving myself all the way into her.

"Is it meant to feel so full inside of me?"

I chuckle, then moan each time she wiggles. "That's when you know you're being fucked well. Now, let me give you my reward." Releasing her clit, I grasp her round hips, pull out of her, then lean back in a few times, getting her readier than she already is. Her walls are tight, her entrances squeezing me just how I love it.

Then I'm fucking her, unrelenting, my fingers digging into her flesh, my cocks buried so deep inside her that she's screaming her pleasure. I lean into her again and again; the friction is fire, and I can't get enough. Never enough.

"Do you like being spread?" I snarl. "Tied up and used by me? Taking it whenever I give it to you."

"Wolfe, yes, you're my God!" Her words are barely a whisper as she rocks with the table she's leaning against.

A guttural grunt rolls over my throat at her words, the climax I'm chasing, building and building, clawing at my insides.

"The fuck!" Nyko's abrupt voice slices through my concentration, as does the door slamming shut. I glance over my shoulder at him, my cocks buried in Sage down to the hilt.

"Either join us, or get the fuck out," I snarl.

Evidently, I didn't need to give him an option as he's already ripping his shirt off and undoing his pants.

"What do you think, my sweet girl?" I rub a hand over Sage's beautiful ass. "Feel like a third cock?"

She moans, lifting her gaze as much as her restraints allow, her attention on Nyko in his human form. Her lips curl into a grin.

"I can't believe I'm saying this, but yes, I do."

Nyko smirks, pausing alongside me. Staring down at the cocks inside our true mate, his breath catches.

"You've got her so spread; I fucking love this imagery."

He maneuvers closer to her, and in no time, he's sitting on the edge of the table, our true mate between us. Each movement she makes has my dicks throbbing, her insides close to crushing me.

"Are you ready for me?" he asks, his attention on her.

"I'm ready. I need this," she says. "Whenever I'm with you three, I turn into this horny monster."

"You're ours, just as you are," I remind her.

Legs spread, Nyko holds her firmly by the shoulders, supporting her weight as he leans down to steal a kiss. She has her hands flat on his hips, letting Nyko take all her weight. When he releases her, she shuffles to get comfortable.

Tilting my head to the side, I watch the way her hungry mouth takes his erection. My cocks pulse at the image, at the notion that my pretty girl has three cocks deep inside her now.

With how she feels wrapped around me, I'd agree to anything she desires, no matter what. I rub her ass as I start to rut her again.

We fall into a rhythm, all three of us groaning, the meeting room having turned into a sex marathon. She shifts her position, adjusting herself so I can slide deeper into her.

"That's it, take more," Nyko coaxes her, rubbing her throat, teaching her how to take more of him.

Just when we have a system in place, thrusting into her at the same time, a rush of cool air comes up my back, telling me someone's just walked into the room.

"What the hell now?" I growl, twisting my head to find that it's Killian.

He pulls the door shut, swinging back around. "You fucking assholes! Why didn't you tell me we were claiming our sweet girl."

"This wasn't a planned event," I hiss as Sage squeezes me, making me shudder.

"Take a seat, and enjoy the show," Nyko grunts just as Sage releases him and turns to Killian.

"Well, this is kind of embarrassing," she teases, but right now, she's dripping so much, shivering, she's close to bursting.

Killian's there, stroking the hair out of her face. "Mind if I watch?"

"Or..." She licks her lips. "I've never felt this way

before, and I want the sensation to last... but my nipples are feeling lonely."

I burst out laughing. "Our sweet girl loves it so fucking dirty that she's going to ruin us all."

Nyko chortles. "I can fuck you all day and night, princess."

Killian, never one to shy away from getting his dick out, gets on his ass and slides in underneath her.

"Look at these luscious tits." He takes one in each hand, squeezing, and Sage moans.

"Please, now fuck me, make me scream. I want to feel like I'm the most loved woman in the world."

"That you are," Nyko groans.

The moment Killian latches onto one of her nipples, Sage is purring, her body buzzing. She's covered in a sheen of perspiration, her body working overtime as we make her ours, over and over. I drive into her, breathless, needing more.

I've never met someone so aroused, and this is why I know she's my forever mate. The way she reacts to us is insatiable. It's meant to be.

"Just think, Killian," Nyko says between guttural sounds from his cock being sucked. "When our princess is pregnant, how luscious she'll be to fuck. I can't wait to suck on those tits, drinking her milk."

"I will never stop licking her swollen breasts," Killian snarls.

Sage groans her protest, but Nyko's not releasing her from his cock.

Now I can't get the image out of my head of my mouth full of her milk, having it sprayed all over my face.

Fuck! I go harder when she starts to convulse, her climax rushing through her, her cunt and ass squeezing me, igniting my own climax.

I howl, spent. Releasing into her, I flood her with my cum. Nyko roars and stiffens, his eyes rolling back, ejaculating down her throat. Killian's got his cock in his hand, too, his mouth full, and the longer we burst, the quicker he joins in, ribbons of his cum coming all over his hand.

My beauty pulls off Nyko, moaning, her body still quivering. I'm pressing into her, close to being cross-eyed at how hard I come.

Drained into her, I pull back. Her legs are barely holding her, but I've got her by the hips. I memorize this moment in my mind, of my seed dripping out of her cunt and ass.

"Hell," I murmur, knowing I'll never forget this. "The things you do to me... to us."

Killian's on his knees, taking her weight, helping her down to her knees so she's in front of him. I join them, as does Nyko. The four of us closer, touching her.

"I've never felt so turned on in my life," she murmurs, wiping her mouth with the back of her hand.

I reach over, wrapping my arms around her shoulders, taking her weight. "You are absolutely beautiful." Kissing her on the side of her face, I leave a trail down to her neck.

She giggles as Nyko and Killian press in closer, all of us holding her. "I know I should be blushing, but I never imagined sex could feel so incredible." She blinks at us, exhaustion on her face. "But now, I'm a mess."

Killian strokes her face, whispering, "It's a beginning, a promise of everything we'll share in life going forward."

Nyko's kissing up her arm, and I'm keeping her warm body against mine.

This is perfect.

Yet thinking of us going to her father soon feels like shards of glass in my lungs, each breath stinging. Instinct is to take her and run with her, hide her back on Earth so she can make herself forget this world. To save her the agony, the danger.

Except, now that she's seen it, met us, she won't leave. I know that much. She's feisty, determined, and so fucking loving; it's a blessing to have someone like her in our lives.

CHAPTER
THIRTY-TWO

SAGE

"We're here," Killian whispers, his voice a low rumble that sends a shiver down my spine.

We're in an open, oval-shaped vessel—more like a boat from back on Earth but sleek, black, and motor-powered. The captain is in a small cabin controlling the vessel, while the rest of us sit in a circular seating arrangement at the back. It should be comfortable, but my knees are bouncing uncontrollably, refreshing with the air rushing through my hair.

I'm too busy staring at the enormous island we're approaching to notice much else. My mouth might be hanging open. We're passing mountainous sheer cliffs that run along the pebbly beach like a stone wall, a fortress around the kingdom. The tops of the cliffs are jagged, and what I hate most about them is how much they resemble my vision of Howler on fire.

Nyko's got his hand on my knee to stop it from

jumping up and down, offering me a crooked smile, a gesture that has me softening against him.

"My heart's going so fast," I whisper. "Maybe I should have practiced my magic or something?"

Wolfe, who's on Killian's side, leans in, his hand reaching for mine.

"That's the thing... each of our abilities is so unique that even the way they come to us is special. It's something that can't be taught. But that's why you have us and them." He raises his chin to the ten guards at the front of the boat, hunkered down—monstrous beasts, fierce and looking like they could tear you in half with their bare hands. Animalistic, hairy, clawed, and with horns. Wolfe told me a large group of warriors were also in the water, approaching the kingdom, hidden out of sight. Should things go terrible on our arrival, we'll have backup.

"I'm really nervous," I admit.

"We all are," Killian replies.

Wolfe squeezes my hand, and Nyko has his arm around my back.

As we come around a curve on the land, we approach a break in the endless cliff wall with a grand entrance carved out of stone. An oversized arched entryway is high up on the stone wall, filled with a waterfall that crashes down into the ocean. Above it stands a stone statue of an oversized crown, glinting with jewels and two swords crossing through it. Behind it is another arch with more water spraying down behind it.

On the left-hand side, there's a curved set of stairs

made of stone that leads to a doorway. Two guards stand above it on a platform, lanky things with six thin legs that remind me too much of bugs but a thousand times larger and more terrifying. There's greenery growing around the entrance.

I swallow hard.

Suddenly, I'm feeling less confident about this mission. Even dressed in pants with hidden pockets for blades, a tight shirt, and leather straps on my arms hiding tiny blades, I still worry.

"I'm not sure I'm ready for this," I whisper.

"We're here now... no turning back." Nyko rubs my back. "Just remember that dream and what's at risk."

I glance at him, the strength behind his gaze grounding me. He's right. Gone is the time to be afraid. I'm no longer the girl I was back in Nightingale Village.

"You're right," I say, more to convince myself than anyone else.

We dock at the wooden pier and disembark. The closer we get to the entrance, the heavier I breathe. Pebbles crunch underfoot, and there are no enemy guards rushing at us, only the two standing tall over us, studying our every movement.

Killian steps beside me, his presence a steadying force. "Just breathe."

I nod, trying to follow his advice, but my mind keeps drifting back to the vision. The screams, the flames, the devastation. I shake my head, attempting to dispel the images. *Focus*, I tell myself. *Focus on the now.*

Fear still lurks, waiting to pounce.

My three monsters stand tall, not showing a sign of being worried. The guards with us remain close, vigilant, and there's comfort in having them.

We stop at the base of the stone steps, the sound of the waterfall splashing nearby. The guards above the doorway don't move, their eyes studying our group. My heart pounds in my chest, but I force myself to stand tall.

One of the guards steps forward on the platform, his beady eyes locking on us with a chilling focus.

"King Bren has been expecting you. Approach the door," he growls, the sound echoing off the stone.

Killian leads the way, his steps confident. Wolfe and Nyko flank me, the guards at our rear. Their closeness is reassuring, but my nerves come from what happens once we speak with my father.

As we climb the wide, ancient stone steps to the kingdom's entrance, I recall the three visions I experienced—the kingdom how it once appeared in its beauty, the destruction, and a future I'm hoping won't come to pass.

It makes me wonder if those nightmares I experienced growing up were my monster side calling for my home world, for me to return to Blight where I belonged. But what about my mother? I belong with her on Earth, too.

Sighing, I push those thoughts aside.

The sun is a relentless blaze overhead. Glancing at Wolfe and Nyko, I try to draw on their calm, but it's hard. Wolfe's arm tight around my waist is the only thing that feels stable. Nyko, with his smirk, seems like he's ready to face down anything.

"Stay by my side, okay?"

"Of course," I answer, as I have no intention of leaving their sides.

Before I can gather my thoughts, we reach the top of the steps, and the heavy door creaks open. It's slow, making my heart beat faster.

Then they're there—guards, if you can call them that. They're out of a nightmare, all too real—oversized heads, horns like spears, and eyes... too many eyes, all of them calculating. They're not just looking at us; they're sizing us up, figuring out how to easily crush us underfoot.

Grinding my teeth, I hold still.

The guards finally step aside, faces unreadable. As they clear the path, a figure approaches from the dimness of the dark passage behind them.

My breath lodges in my lungs.

Is that him?

Violet eyes are the first thing to catch my attention. He has a round face and bone structure too similar to mine to ignore the similarities.

It's him...

My father.

King Bren.

The monster of true nightmares. What did my mother see in him?

He's in human form, dressed in a dark robe that absorbs the light, one shoulder slumped lower than the other, white hair pushed off his face. My stomach knots further.

"It's been a long time, Wolfe," he states in a tone echoing around us. "And I think it's about time to meet after all these years."

Wolfe clenches his jaw, a growl burning in his chest.

My father's attention moves to me, and I'm struggling, facing the man who is supposed to be my dad. I try to steady my shaking hands, clenching them into fists at my sides. The emotions swell inside me. My heart races with an aching sorrow. It feels like my throat is closing up, choked with words I can't voice. All the years of wondering, of imagining who he might be, and now here he is, just a few feet away. The urge to scream at him, to unleash all the questions and hurt, is almost overwhelming. Yet, here I am, struggling to swallow down the lump in my throat, fighting to keep the tears at bay.

His mouth pulls into a taut smile, and he knows who I am instantly.

"Wolfe told me he had found you, my child, Sage, but I didn't believe it... until now." His tone is gruff, as if he's been chewing on rocks, but low and commanding.

"That's me," I manage to say nervously.

"I owe you a world of gratitude for bringing her to me," he states to Wolfe. "Your kindness won't go unnoticed."

He reaches his hand out toward me, palm facing up, rings on each finger. "Come, daughter, we have so much to catch up on." Despite his gesture of welcoming us, his gaze doesn't hide the coldness behind them. I don't move toward him.

Wolfe curls an arm around my back, drawing me against his side.

I stand rooted to the spot, my heart beating against my rib cage.

Wolfe's arm tightens around me. "We didn't come all this way to simply hand her over," he asserts.

The King's smile falters. "Then what do you want?" he demands, the bridge between his eyes creasing.

My response pours out of me immediately, like it's been dying to burst out. "I'm here to claim my rightful place," I declare with a surprisingly steady voice. "As your daughter and as an heir to your throne."

Wolfe steps forward, his posture menacing. "You need to understand that Sage is our fated mate, Bren," he states firmly. "And that alone grants us rights here, including claims to succession. We're not here to fight but to assert what's rightfully ours under the laws you uphold."

The King's face tightens, his eyes narrowing into slits. "You're playing games," he hisses. "You're wasting my time."

The air charges with tension, skating down my arms.

"We request a King's Oath," Wolfe adds, and I have no idea what that is. "As King, you know the significance of this request. It grants us safe passage and a fair hearing, then you must acknowledge our request. A privilege you stole from my father all those years ago. Now's your chance to do the right thing for a change." His posture curls slightly forward as though it takes every restraint not to lunge at the King.

My father regards us with a steely gaze. "Let's not be hasty, son. Your claims need verifying before any oaths are sworn. I need to verify her true lineage and if she is indeed your mate."

Wolfe's muscles tense beside me. This is something none of us discussed or expected. But of course, my asshole father is delaying things by insisting on proving who I am.

"Then let's do it," Killian commands through clenched teeth.

The King's lips twitch, the growing sign of his irritation. "Bring them to the verification chamber," he orders the guards. His eyes lock with mine again, piercing and icy. "If you are who you claim to be, come peacefully. Prove your worth, and I shall honor the King's Oath. My honor demands no less."

He pulls back, his cold dismissal hanging in the air as he leans heavily on a cane that materializes from the shadows. It's clear he's weaker than he wants to let on, his limp noticeable as he retreats.

Suddenly, the guards are upon us, their movements swift. "This way," one barks, gesturing with a gnarled bug arm toward an arched doorway leading into the kingdom.

The air grows cooler as we enter the passage, the dim light from the torches flickering against the damp stone walls, casting eerie shadows that dance just out of reach.

We've entered a corridor, and there's no sight of the kingdom yet.

I'm terrified that we're walking into a trap, that my father will kill my true mates. With each step, shivers race up my arms.

Killian's grip on my hand tightens. The shuffle of our footsteps is the only sound that fills the heavy silence. Every step takes us deeper into the bowels of the corridor, away from the light and into the heart of darkness. And the deeper my fear grows.

The corridor leads us into another doorway that opens into a large room with stone walls, lit torches on the wall, high ceilings, and barred windows far above. The air is damp and cold, sending a shiver through me. This isn't just any room; it's a damn holding area.

I spin around, all of us inside, but not the King or his guards.

A heavy door clangs shut behind us, and panic clamps around my chest.

"Fuck, please tell me we didn't just walk into a prison?" My breath catches in my throat as the reality sets in.

But Wolfe leans closer. "It'll be all right," he murmurs, his presence comforting. "We're not trapped here. This is just a formality, a show of strength."

"It is?"

Killian nods, his jaw set. "They use these rooms for unexpected guests to ascertain if they are safe to permit into their kingdom."

"We have one on the vessel, too," Nyko adds. "I've

been known to find myself in it when I drink too much." He chuckles while Killian rolls his eyes.

"Yeah, and I'm the one who drags your ass down there when no one else can control you."

Nyko's hand finds mine. He winks at me, and I somehow manage to smile. Our guards position themselves near the door as I push down the rising panic.

"We did the right thing coming here, right?" I find myself saying, staring at their serious expressions, not feeling much better.

"We follow through now," Wolfe notes. "We've come too far to back down."

A knot of anxiety tightens in my stomach. The waiting is the hardest part, and I keep replaying in my mind the eagerness of my father to get his hands on me. That part terrifies me.

Then, without warning, the door swings open, and I flinch around.

The room suddenly feels smaller, crowded, as bug-like guards enter on their six spindly legs, ushering in a young woman.

Her pale green eyes, matching her hair, glance around the room, landing on me. She studies me harshly, her gaze hardening. Pale green scales down her arms and neck shimmer under the dim light. The King gestures to the woman beside him, her eyes haunted, yet she smirks at me, leaving me covered in shivers.

"Sage, meet your half sister, Elara," he declares, and the floor beneath me might as well crack open.

CHAPTER
THIRTY-THREE
SAGE

"I have a half sister?" I mumble under my breath.

Stunned, I don't move, just stare at Elara as she meanders alongside my father. The lights on the walls glint against the green scales on her arms and down the sides of her neck and face. She's easily a few years younger than me, maybe six-and-ten years old. Her brilliant crystal-green eyes blink in my direction, her attention locked on me.

I'm lost for words.

"We had no idea you had a half sister, Sage," Killian whispers, and I have no reason not to believe him.

My father grins, as though he's achieved the shock he intended.

Elara had to know I existed because she doesn't look surprised to see me. She's just staring at me. Wearing a simple floral dress cinched at the waist with a belt and sandals, her green hair tumbles around her face in small curls, cut short to her jaw. She's cute, and I can see parts of myself in her face.

So many questions whirl in my head. I doubt my mother even knows about Elara, but what would she say if she saw her? Would it hurt her to find out the man who abandoned her had a child with someone else?

"Elara has been by my side since she was a child," my father begins. "After her mother passed from a sickness in her blood, which is a shame. Elara carries a psychic power that will confirm if you've been truthful." His gaze drills into me, lingering, leaving me wanting to glance away, but I refuse to.

Wolfe steps forward, shoulders square, his broad chest sticking out. I'm captivated by him, proud to be at his side. "How does her power work, exactly?"

"Sage won't be harmed. Stand down," my father assures. "Elara requires a taste of her blood to see the truth of what you claim." He glances down at the girl, grinning, his hand gripping her shoulder firmly. Her brow pinches, but she doesn't brush him off. "She'll reveal the truth, as she has done many times for me in the past."

My thoughts race—a half sister with mind powers. The whole situation feels surreal. I study her again, trying to read her expression, but it's impossible.

"Hello, Elara," I say, eager to get to know her. "I'm Sage."

She tilts her head to the side, eyes blinking a few times before she steps forward, her hand rising from her side. The glint of the blade in her hand catches my attention.

Killian and Nyko throw themselves in front of me; they must've spotted the weapon as well. Wolfe pulls me farther away from her by my arm.

"I won't hurt you," she says softly in a voice that is soothing, handing over the blade, hilt first. "This will be quick. You can cut yourself or have one of them do it for you." Her gaze flicks to my three monsters.

My father is chuckling. "Look at you, my daughter, three powerful Shadowfen throwing their lives to protect you. Who would have thought?" He's mocking me. I hear it in his tone, and I hate him more for it.

Nyko steps forward, his hand reaching for the small, curved blade.

I nod, swallowing hard and closing the distance between us. "All right," I say, my voice barely above a whisper. "How are we doing this?"

"Just a small cut on the fleshy part of your palm should be fine," she murmurs, her attention flicking up to meet mine.

"Quickly now," my father urges. "We don't have all day."

Nyko faces me, taking my hand gently into his. "I'll do the cut for you."

"Thanks," I say, shaking, a rush of gratitude flooding me.

"You can look away if you want," he encourages, lifting my left hand. He must be picking up on my nerves, seeing he's not making light of the situation as he normally would.

I shake my head at his offer. "I'm fine."

The room feels like it's closing in on me, everyone crowding around, leaving me overwhelmed.

Nyko swiftly swipes the blade across the meaty part of my palm. At first, I don't feel anything, then bubbles of blood appear along the line, and the sting surfaces instantly. I hiss under my breath at the sharpness.

Nyko grins at me. "I've had paper cuts deeper than this. It'll heal in no time."

I laugh at his attempt to lighten the mood, when Elara suddenly grabs my hand, bringing it to her face. Her mouth presses over the cut, and the sensation of her tongue lapping at my blood makes my skin crawl. It's strange, intimate, and deeply unsettling, leaving a strange sense of violation. My gut churns as I watch her, trying not to panic and rip my hand from her grasp.

Her eyes flutter closed as she keeps drinking from me.

Silence suffocates the room, broken only by the pounding of my heart and the throbbing pulse from the cut on my hand.

Elara's nails dig into my skin, causing me to wince. She's convulsing now. As she releases my hand, her legs give out, and she's falling.

Heart in my throat, I lunge for her, but Killian catches her, not our father. He simply stands there, staring at her with a look of almost disgust, as if her convulsions are an inconvenience.

Elara's eyes are wide and unfocused as she licks the drops of my blood from her lips. Killian helps her to her feet. She glances at me, her expression unreadable, while I'm panicking on the inside.

What did she see in my blood?

"And? Don't keep me waiting!" our father berates.

She turns to him, still teetering on her feet.

"It's true," she finally admits. "She's your blood-born, my half sister, and all three Shadowfen here are her true mates. She experienced a ritual vision with the three Shadowfen. Such a ritual can't be faked. They told you the truth."

I glance at my father, along with everyone else. He remains stoic, unmoving.

"You have your confirmation." Wolfe stands tall, his voice booming across the room.

"So, it's true," he admits, meeting my gaze, lacking any emotions. "You are my daughter and as the eldest, the potential true heir to my throne."

I nibble the corner of my lower lip as Killian, Wolfe, and Nyko press tightly near me. Why *potential*?

"So then, as per the King's Oath—" Wolfe begins.

"I know the damn oath," my father growls, his gaze darkening. For a split second, his monstrous form pushes forward—a row of horns curving backward like spiky hair, black eyes, sharp teeth, and long arms tipped with black claws. His body is shadowy and covered in spikes.

Then the imagery is gone, and shivers rush down my spine. Despite having seen so many monsters on the vessel, he is terrifying. The notion leaves me wondering if my mother had seen his true monster side, and that's why she refused to speak to me about him.

"Then abide by it. You have your proof," Killian commands. "Or shall we announce it in front of the people of this city? Your daughter has the memory now in her psychic ability for anyone to see the truth, as do all the guards who heard her confirmation."

My father's nostrils flare, his chest heaving. "I will not give my kingdom to just anyone who shares my bloodline, or I would have already assigned Elara to it. Sage and you three must first deserve it."

Ouch. His insult for my half sister stings. She lowers her gaze, and my insides turn.

"What the fuck? How?" Nyko barks.

"A quest to prove you're worthy," the King states, his gaze turning to Wolfe. "Because fuck knows, your father didn't deserve his title. He squandered it, never fought to merge the Shadowfen clans from around the world because he didn't want to upset anyone. He let war rage between borders, and hundreds were killed. And look where that got him."

Wolfe's clenched, his jaw rigid. He throws himself at the King. "You fucking murdered him!"

Killian and Nyko are there, wrestling him back by his arms. The King's guards dart in front of him.

I'm frozen, terrified, unsure what to do.

"Wolfe," Killian hisses in his ear. "Tread carefully. We've come this far. Don't give him any excuse."

Wolfe's face is burning with rage, and I feel sick to

my stomach at his agony. The room seems to spin as my father laughs.

"Are you falsely accusing the King, boy?" My father puffs his chest out, glaring at Wolfe with such hatred that I want to drive a blade into his chest.

I'm half startled by my rage, at my admission of wanting to kill him. Cold loathing floods my veins toward him. He's making us jump through hoops.

"What does the quest involve?" I ask in a strong voice.

My three monsters are ready to rip him to shreds, glaring at him like predators, shoulders curled forward, chests puffing. A battle could mean we all die, and my vision for Howler might become a terrifying reality.

My half sister studies me with the rise of an eyebrow, her eyes wide at the burning tension around us.

"You must perform a task to prove your loyalty." My father straightens his posture, chin high. "A mission of my choosing."

"What sort of mission?" I ask, skeptical that it will be something close to impossible to complete.

He gives me a toothy grin. "Will you commit to show your true loyalty by agreeing to the quest? Otherwise, you will be thrown out immediately, and count yourself blessed for not dying today. And you will be forbidden from ever setting foot on my land."

"We accept," Wolfe growls with anger, not even giving thought to the offer.

I huff that he never asked us about it, but it's done

now. Killian and Nyko don't seem perturbed, but then again, they look up to him as their leader.

"Good, you're finally making a fucking correct decision." My father claps his hands twice as if we're his entertainment. "You will begin at the crack of dawn. The information you need will be supplied at that time. Tonight, you and your guards will spend it in the city in secured quarters. You will be supplied with food and everything you need. But let's make it clear... if you try to escape, you will be killed. If you hurt any of my guards or Shadowfen, you will die. If you are seen anywhere other than your quarters—"

"We fucking get it... we'll be killed," Nyko blurts.

"Then we understand each other. I am a Shadowfen of my word, unlike *others*. But if the four of you fail the quest, Sage is mine, and you three will die. You succeed at the quest, and I'll honor the King's Oath and publicly confirm you four as my rightful successors to the kingdom."

My stomach drops as I lean on Killian's arm for support, staring at my father, who's grinning, loving every moment of this.

Wolfe clears his throat, his shoulders squared. "If we agree and we succeed, you will also supply half of your land for us and our Shadowfen to live on immediately until it's our time to claim the throne."

Meaning *until he dies,* we get to live on the island with everyone from the vessel.

Silence fills the room. My father's jaw clenches.

Is he fucking kidding? My monsters' lives are at stake.

Wolfe glances at me, and silence pulses between us. When Killian and Nyko nod in agreement, now they're all looking at me, and I'm feeling sick to my stomach. This is moving too fast. I'm not ready to risk their lives, but they are relentless and insistent that we're doing this, aren't they? My father is staring, smiling a toothy grin, and I hate him more with each passing second.

Swallowing hard, I feel the pressure. My skin is burning up, and I want to say no, but we've come this far, and we won't get this chance again. But...

Ah, fuck it! It's now or never...

So, reluctantly, I give my confirmation.

Wolfe faces my father. "Agreed!"

"When you're ready, my guards will wait for you outside the room and take you to your quarters." Without another word, he marches from the room with his guards.

Elara remains and approaches me. "Good luck." Then she reaches over, patting my arm. Her touch is a furnace, and her fingers feel like pins digging into my arm where she touches me. She pulls back, and my mind darkens, my vision blots out, and I'm suddenly convulsing. I hear Killian calling for me, but my vision flashes until I'm no longer in the room but somewhere else entirely.

· · ·

A vibrant rose garden surrounds me, flowers in every color possible, the sun warm on my shoulders. Elara's smiling, standing by a pond, feeding large golden fish. She glances up at fluttering bugs that I swear are Shadowwings, the toxic butterflies, but she's not afraid. They leave her alone. The smile on her face is contagious. She's so happy in this world, so content. The peace in her expression tugs at my emotions.

Then, abruptly, the vision is ripped away. I'm suddenly in a mess hall, waiters rushing around and bringing platters of food to my father. His face is twisted in anger, glaring at my half sister.

"Stop wasting my fucking time, Elara. You're so useless," he snarls, shoving her from him and the table. She stares at him for a moment as though she imagined him pushing her away, tears glistening in her eyes, then she darts out of the room.

My heart breaks watching her scurry away, head down, shoulders hunched. What the hell's his problem?

Another vision slams into me.

Elara at a grand hall, everyone dressed in glittery gowns, some in human form, others monstrous, drinks flowing, music playing, and lights twinkling overhead. It's breathtaking. She's wearing a blue flowing dress adorned with wings, her smile radiant. Absolutely stunning. Our father appears at her side, grabbing her roughly by the arm, hissing.

"I told you not to show your face at these events. I guess my wish of finally having another heir, hopefully not as useless as you, is finally in Blight now."

"Father... I-I mean, King Bren, my ability is growing and—"

He squeezes her arm aggressively, his fingernails breaking her skin, a droplet of blood running down her arm. She winces.

"You dare challenge me in front of others? You show such little respect for your King? You're an embarrassment. You taste blood and see who someone is—that's not impressive for a King's daughter. You're weak, Elara, and that's why I've never let you taste my blood to have power over me." He drags her out of the hallway and drives a hand into her back, throwing her out, where she falls to the floor. "Guards, take her to the dungeon. Maybe a few days without food will teach her respect."

My insides are shards of glass shattering at his mistreatment of her. The vision fades fast.

Then, I'm back in the room with my true mates, with our guards, stumbling on my feet as I see the last wisps of Elara leaving the room.

"What the hell was that?" I rub my eyes, feeling as though I've just woken up from a deep sleep.

"Are you all right?" Killian asks, his hand on my back, steadying me. Wolfe and Nyko are at my side, too.

"I-I'm..." I can't finish as tears fall. I keep picturing her agony, her being bullied, how she might not even know of the atrocities her father committed as he won't let her link to his thoughts. "I don't know how, but her touch just showed me snippets from her past. Our father's been mistreating her, torturing her... I think she's reaching out to me for help."

Wolfe stares at me, his expression serious, his gaze reflecting my own worry. "Your half sister formed a psychic link with you when she tasted your blood."

My chest constricts, making breathing harder, thinking of her stuck here with that *fucking beast*.

Nyko embraces me. "You think it's legit or some kind of game her father's putting her up to?"

"It felt real." I try to rub the chill out of my arms. "You saw the way he treated her earlier, his comments. He's taunting her, belittling her." It reminds me so much of those who bullied me back in Nightingale Village, where I felt helpless, as though nothing I did was good enough. They'd made up their minds and hated me. My father kept telling her she wasn't good enough, not strong enough.

Fuck him!

"I want to help her."

Killian steps closer, his hand gently squeezing my arm, standing close. "Of course we will. But we also need to survive first."

Nyko tightens his hug, his presence grounding me.

I take a deep breath, trying to steady my out-of-control pulse.

"My father's going to do everything in his power to stop us."

Wolfe cups my cheek, moving in closer. "That's why we're not going to fail," he whispers. "I'm going to fucking murder him before we're done."

CHAPTER
THIRTY-FOUR
SAGE

The door swings open to our temporary accommodations. I'm ushered through the threshold by the bug-like guards and keep my distance, as I don't want their spindly legs touching me.

Wolfe, Nyko, and Killian strut inside, practically bowling over the guards. They're pissed, fucking fuming, and I can't blame them. I've been clenching my teeth since we left the holding room. Our guards from the vessel had been escorted into their own quarters farther down the hall.

Inside ours, the opulence strikes me instantly, especially in comparison to the elevator and dark underground hallway we just traveled through to get here, to avoid seeing anyone or the city itself.

The walls, a pale blue, are adorned with monster skulls as decorative pieces. There's a round dining table, chairs made from what look suspiciously like bones, and rugs dyed in dark hues over the stone flooring. An Lshaped couch sits by the curtain-covered window, and spotlights overhead chase away the shadows.

A grunt from one of the bug guards, and the doors bang shut with finality. I flinch at the abruptness of it.

Killian strolls through the place, vanishing into a hallway to my left. Behind me, I spot the other two chatting, Nyko joking about our cozy family set up in prison. Wolfe isn't laughing but sighing heavily. He meets my gaze, and the sorrow on his face mirrors my own.

I turn and follow Killian to check out the rest of the quarters, finding him in a grand bedroom with a bed giant enough to fit four, but it promises we'll be plastered to one another. Curtains cover the windows here, too.

He glances at me, then the bed. "Might just work if the other two bunk on the couch."

I laugh. "That's not going to happen. We both know it."

He's still grinning, that adorable spark in his eyes.

"If any of us get any sleep tonight," I murmur. "What if we don't pass this quest?"

Quicker than I can take my next breath, he pulls me into his arms.

"Your father has always been a cruel tyrant, and he's not going to give in, but nothing comes easy. Anyway, fuck him because you're with the three of us! And nothing is too much for us to face."

His words, meant to comfort, only tighten the knot of anxiety in my stomach. I stare up at him, my heart pounding against my rib cage.

"I just wish I wasn't related to him... I feel guilty for all the shit he's causing everyone."

Killian's hand is warm on my back, his lips pressing a soft kiss to my brow.

"Being blood-related doesn't make him family. He just happens to share your bloodline, and that's where it ends. He doesn't deserve your guilt. He wears all the blame for his atrocities."

His fingers gently tilt my chin up, making me meet his intense blue gaze. The closeness of his body, the manly, seductive scent that has me leaning against him, distracts me but not enough to forget the ache deep in my chest.

"I have no idea how my mother even ended up with him. She told me nothing about him, and now I want to ask her so many questions." Thinking about her makes me wonder if she took her medicine when she woke up. Or was she too worried after reading my note?

He leans in, our noses brushing as he whispers, "Some things are better left unknown, Sage. All you need to know is that he's a bastard, and maybe your mother didn't have a choice."

The possibility coils tightly in my gut, nausea fluttering against the sudden rush of bile. It's a thought I've considered before, but I let it go; it's too painful, too brutal, if real.

"I miss her," I whisper, the admission squeezing painfully tight around my heart. "I hope she hasn't woken up too scared with me not being there."

"It would be later in the day in Nightingale Village. A

full day hasn't passed yet. You need to stay focused on the here and now. If we don't survive, she'll never see you again," he murmurs, trying to soothe me, yet it's leaving me more jittery.

I think about the hastily scribbled note I left my mother, wishing I had known then what I know now. I would have told her not to worry, that I'm safe with Viscount Killian. That night in the village feels like a lifetime ago—a different world, a different me.

Suddenly, Killian's lips are on mine, his kiss deep and consuming. It steals away my thoughts, my worries. I lean into him, letting the world fade, my toes curling in my boots. His hand slides around my waist, pulling me closer. I clutch his shirt, needing this connection, this moment of escape from the chaos around us.

Just as the intensity of our kiss deepens, a loud "Fuck!" rings out from the other room. We break apart, staring at each other with wide eyes. What the hell now?

Killian takes my hand, leading me quickly into the main living area. Wolfe has the curtains pulled back, and bright light floods the room, casting everything in golden and pink hues from the sun and the pinkish sky.

Wolfe and Nyko are both staring out the floor-to-ceiling window that takes up most of the wall. The sight beyond the glass steals my breath—it's a panoramic view of the kingdom. For a moment, the beauty of it grips my heart, squeezing tight with a promise of what could have been.

I step closer to the window, unable to tear my eyes away from the view. There's a river winding through the city down below, stone buildings with multiple floors, arched openings, and stone footpaths crisscrossing in every direction. Greenery and gardens add life and color to the place, and in the distance, grand mountains rise majestically, framing the scene.

To my right, the most beautiful castle I've ever seen stands over a long arched stone bridge crossing the river. Waterfalls cascade from its base, and spiked towers and crenelations give it a fairy tale–like appearance. Trees grow amid the building, adding to its enchanting look.

I press my forehead against the glass, absorbing every detail from the bustling markets below to the distant, dark woods that border the kingdom.

"Wow!" Stone, cliff-topped walls encircle the kingdom.

To the left, the landscape stretches into rugged mountains, their peaks lost in the clouds. But it's the castle that steals the show, drawing my attention again —a place so beautiful, yet I remind myself it's in the grip of my father's rule.

Below, Shadowfen are hurrying about, not stopping to chat or enjoy the view. It's as if there's an unspoken deadline to everything they do, or maybe they're all just trying to stay out of trouble. Guards are everywhere, their eyes sharp on everyone. Talk about oppressive.

"Look at them," Killian grumbles, pointing to the streets below, where the pace of life seems frantic. "No one's enjoying this paradise. It's all just them being frantic. That's not living."

"How can something so beautiful feel so wrong?" I murmur, more to myself than to anyone else.

"That's how tyrants work, Sage," Wolfe says softly. "They build beautiful things to hide the rot inside."

"He's built a kingdom of stone and fear. No wonder he's survived so long."

Killian, staring out beside me, shakes his head. "Not for much longer."

I stare at Wolfe, his face pale as he studies the kingdom. I can't imagine the pain he's feeling. This was his family's kingdom, destroyed and rebuilt by my father, who shoved Wolfe out of the way. The anger, the jealousy, the unfairness would eat me up, so I move closer to him, taking his hand in mine. I don't say anything but let him know I'm here for him.

"I never expected it to look like this," he says with a tight voice. "This... beautiful. I fucking hate your father for making it so perfect. For excluding us, for taking my father's life..." His arms are tense, breaths heaving.

My heart aches at his suffering. Seeing him like this, so torn, fills me with a sorrow I can hardly bear. "I'm sorry," is all I manage to say.

He glances at me, shaking his head. "Nothing for you to be sorry for."

I embrace him, wrapping my arms around his strong chest, knowing he needs me. "I'm not afraid," I admit. "I'm ready to face anything he throws at us."

Nyko and Killian stand close, their presence a comforting reminder that we're not alone in this.

"Well, if we're going to reclaim a kingdom, can we at

least do it after food, sex, and sleep? In that order because I don't fight well without those things." Nyko grins because, of course, he'd say that.

Killian snorts, a half smile tugging at his lips. "Always thinking with your stomach and cock."

I turn back to the window, watching the people below. Wolfe moves away and crashes down on the couch.

As I stare out at the city, I think of my sister's happiness in the gardens from the visions she sent me. The thought that we're sitting ducks crosses my mind, but I'm trying my best to find hope. With me here, I doubt my father will attack us outright... at least not yet.

Breathing heavily, I watch the people below. They're moving fast, too quickly to enjoy their surroundings. What's the use of having everything if you live in fear?

I sigh, pulling away from the window.

"I'm going to rest," I tell the guys as they discuss our next move. "I'm exhausted."

I leave them talking strategy and head to the bedroom. Pulling back the curtain, I'm greeted by a breathtaking view of the mountains in the distance. I crawl into bed, curling up and trying to stop the panic stabbing my stomach. The worry is almost unbearable.

Staring out at the mountains, the edges of my vision blur, just like before. In seconds, I'm thrust into a vision. This time, I know what's happening.

. . .

*E*lara stands outside an ajar door, peering into a meeting room. Inside, our father is pacing, angry, hands clenched into fists. He smacks his cane hard against the stone floor with each stride.

"That idiot thinks he can come here and demand land for him and those traitors on his vessel. They never supported me when I took over, so fuck them all. I'd rather burn it to the ground before I let those fools remain here."

"My King," a tall monster covered in white fur says. *"What of the King's Oath? It must be adhered to. Someone's already leaked their arrival and the call of the oath to the locals. They're asking questions, wanting to see a fair trial."*

"Who the fuck leaked it?" my father growls, gripping his metal cane like a weapon.

The monster doesn't respond.

"Find them. Find out who leaked it. Interview every one of those fucking guards, then kill them for betraying me."

The vision ends abruptly, and I'm back in bed. My head feels fuzzy, and my eyes shut as I try to make sense of what I saw. The dread and horror grip me.

I know your real reason for coming to our kingdom… to kill our father. Suddenly, Elara's voice echoes in my head.

My eyes fly open, my heart squeezing with terror. I'm alone in the room, searching for any speakers. "Elara?" I whisper.

I won't tell him, you know.

Wolfe said she has a psychic link with me because of

our shared lineage. Is she speaking to me through her mind?

"What do you want?" I say out loud.

You don't need to speak your response. Say it in your mind. There's a hint of mirth behind her words.

All right, I think. *So why are you telling me this?*

I never knew my mother. I saw in some of your visions that yours loved you so much.

Wait, did you see all my thoughts? You saw everything?

She laughs, sounding eerily like me. *I didn't have enough time to see a lot of your memories during the blood connection. Only a few, but I focused mainly on you and the three Shadowfen you're mated to. And how much they chase you.*

My cheeks flush, thinking of the intimate moments she might have seen. I'm uncomfortable.

Don't worry, I've seen far worse from a young age. Not much shocks me anymore. But now that we're connected, I can only see the memories you send. I can communicate with you when I open up the channel between us.

Can I talk to you when I want to?

Not really how it works.

So... why won't you tell the King about our real mission, then? I ask, unable to hide what she's seen in my thoughts. When she doesn't respond, I press, *Is it because he mistreats you? I know how it feels.*

You wouldn't, she snaps.

I grew up in a village where everyone hated me because I was different, so I know a bit about being pushed aside, never accepted.

At least you had your mother. I don't remember mine. I have a few friends, but they're too afraid of my father.

I'm sorry.

Silence.

Do you want us to help you get away from our father?

She laughs bitterly. *That's never going to be possible.*

Yet I hear a sliver of hope in her voice. Why else would she reach out to me to show me those visions if not a cry for help?

I will try to help, I promise.

Then, the fuzz in my head is gone. She's disconnected from our chat. She's gone. I lie on the bed, blinking up at the ceiling, set to help Elara. But first, we need to somehow survive my father's madness.

CHAPTER
THIRTY-FIVE
NYKO

After an enormous meal, more than I expected from the false dicknose King, I've been crashed on the couch, listening to Wolfe talking for what feels like an eternity about all the ways tomorrow could go, what quests we might face, and, most importantly, how we could use the moment to our advantage.

Now, he's up on his feet, staring out at the city, melancholy as hell, and I can't damn blame him. Being back here, reminded of what he lost, is gut-wrenching. I feel the sting twisting in my heart, too. I lost my father to the Great Desolation, killed in the destruction, my mother died while she gave birth to me, and it's taken me a damn long time to accept their loss. I'm not over it—never will be. So, being here, all I can think about is anger, wanting someone to pay.

I clench my fists, grinding my teeth.

That's when I realize that Killian and Sage have been in one of the other rooms for too long. They're way too quiet, which makes me suspicious. I leave behind the living area where Wolfe is lost in his thoughts and stroll down the long corridor. I hear a small laugh, leading me to the bathroom. I knock on the door, and it swings open—it wasn't shut.

It's a grand room with an enormous tub built into the floor, large enough to comfortably hold five to six Shadowfen in monster form. Right now, Sage sits upright quickly at seeing me as though she's been caught doing something. The tub is filled with a mountain of suds, the jets whirring as they shoot water around.

"You're looking suspicious." I stroll over to her and hit the button on the side of the tub to stop the jets. The sound was setting my teeth on edge.

She blinks at me, taking her time responding, her gorgeous little mouth hanging open. "I-I'm fine." She's grinning a lot, her breathing coming quickly, and I'm curious about what she's been up to. Something she's hiding, that's for sure.

Sitting on the edge of the tub, I scoop some suds and stare at my gorgeous princess, who's blushing immensely.

"Just having some time out?" she gasps.

"Is that so?" I reach over to push a wet strand of hair stuck to her brow. She releases a small moan, then quickly schools herself.

I notice her mannerisms—her flushed cheeks, her rapid breaths. I grin, seeing her so hot and bothered, and I dip my fingers into the water; it's hot but not scorching, so she might have been in here for a while.

"So, shall I join you?" I ask, already pulling up my shirt over my head.

"No, N..." Her voice breaks into a gorgeous moan, her body shuddering, head back, holding on to the edges of the tub, completely undone.

I laugh, knowing exactly what I'm seeing. My beautiful girl is having a damn orgasm, unraveling. She's fucking gorgeous.

Leaning over, I plunge my arm down deep into the water, my hand falling right onto a damn head. Of course, it's him.

I fist his hair and drag him to the surface.

Killian's head pops up, and he's grinning like a fool in his Shadowfen form, his forked tongue licking his lips as water rushes down his face. Suds are piled up on his shoulders, and his gaze is hazed over from his arousal. The stick-on gills on his blue neck open and close.

"You fucker," I growl, then burst out laughing. "I wish I would have thought of it first."

"I was hoping it'd take you longer before you came sniffing around." He leans over to Sage, kissing her all over her face. "You're so beautiful when you come."

She pinches her lips as though guilt is getting to her for being busted. "Are you just going to stand there or jump in?"

She's going to be the death of me.

I strip in seconds.

"These bubbles are hiding you from me." Killian rubs the suds off himself, then sweeps his arms across the surface, collecting a whole bunch more and driving it over the edge onto the tiled floor. The water easily reveals my naked princess. Those perky tits are calling to me—her full breasts, tiny waist, the mauve strip of hair between her legs, her curves, the promise of her thighs tightening against my head. If I'm going to die, there's no better way to go than having my face buried in her cunt. I want her desperately.

"That tongue..." She's reaching for Killian, her hand on his chest before sliding south.

A growl rips over my chest. "All right," I blurt out, a surge of competitiveness consuming me. "Enough. Let me show you how it's really done because I'm the fucking king of tonguing."

Killian chuckles and reclines against the side of the tub, as though accepting my challenge.

I reach for my pants on the floor and take out my stick-on gills—living on water means it's commonplace to carry them on us at all times. It feels gooey to touch but holds its shape. I slap it to the side of my neck, feeling the quick, sharp bite as it attaches to my flesh. The ache fades, replaced by the fluttering sensation at my neck as they activate.

I step into the tub, the water so warm it instantly soothes my nerves.

Killian rolls his eyes. "Well, go on, then. And if you're not good enough, I'm going again."

Sage laughs, and the maddening influence she has over me, her beauty, her lovingness, all bring out the primal beast inside me, rearing up, and I can't stop thinking about fucking her.

"I'd like to see you try," she teases.

Challenge accepted.

I slide into the water, its warmth enveloping me, and slip into my shadow form as I duck under the surface. Standing in the deepest end, away from the seat that juts out from the walls of the circular tub, the water laps up to my waist.

The water muffles their voices, but I'm already sliding my hands between her thighs, savoring the smoothness of her skin, spreading her, and she complies.

Reaching her waist, I draw her closer to me, my fingers tracing patterns on her hips. She's trembling, and it fuels my desire. I lean in, pressing my lips to her stomach, teasing her, then move lower, all while pulling her ass forward on the ledge in the tub she's perched on. My gaze focuses on her spread for me, the dark pink lips, her clit still swollen, and she's spectacular.

My tongue rolls out of my mouth, extended longer, thicker. Desperately, I lick her with the flat of my tongue, able to still taste her in the water while wishing for nothing more than to inhale her intoxicating scent.

She flinches at each stroke, her moans reaching me, and I grin.

I have no patience today, so I'm licking, sucking savagely. I'm a fucking lunatic when it comes to competition, and no way in hell is Killian doing better than me with Sage.

Hands slipping to her soft inner thighs, I spread her wider and push myself closer. I can't get close enough. I devour her like she's never been eaten before and press my tongue into her entrance, deeper, thicker, giving her what she desires. To have her cunt stretched, to make her breathless, to scream my name. I tongue her back and forth, wriggling inside her tightness, aggressive and deep.

I crave more of her, wanting it all. My cock's thick and heavy.

She trembles against me, and I tighten my hold, needing more. I suck on her clit and feel her hands on my head, fisting my head and pushing it against her.

I'm in fucking euphoria.

Suddenly, she's screaming, so I deeply lick, greedy as fuck to take everything she offers me.

She arches her back, those thighs closing around me. I can't let go, and I ride the wave with her, keeping me trapped here, taking starved strokes. Of damn course, I take my time, my tongue exploring every inch of her fluttering lips, knowing exactly how to drive her wild.

I hear her moan, the sound muffled but clear.

Then she collapses, her thighs releasing me. With a final lick of her quivering lips, I push to the surface, water sloshing everywhere.

"Feel like one more, princess?" I ask, leaning my body over hers, my cock resting heavily on her stomach, as I stare down at her. She's leaning back, her eyes half-closed, a satisfied smile on her lips. "I've never sipped and devoured someone who's so delectable that I'd give up my monster form if it meant I'd get it endlessly."

Her eyes are wide. "I'd never ask you to do that, and you never need to."

"But I'd do it for you."

Killian mumbles something, but I'm not listening to him.

I capture her lips in a hypnotic kiss, arousal pulsing through me, loving the feel of her body beneath mine.

A clearing of a throat from the doorway has me breaking our kiss and glancing over to Wolfe, standing in the entrance. Worst fucking timing. It's bad enough I have Killian stealing my time. Now, Wolfe's here, leaning a shoulder into the frame, legs crossed at the ankles, already in his monster form and completely damn naked. He's staring at Sage with fucking sex in his eyes, his cock hard.

I grunt, pulling back. "There's really no more space in this tub."

"Oh, yes, there is," Sage purrs, stretching out her hand to Wolfe. "Join us. If we're going to have a challenge for the best pussy licker, it's only fair he joins in."

"Pussy?" I groan, glancing back at her. "Like a human animal, a cat?"

Killian chuckles. "It's an adorable nickname humans use, among many others. But this is most appropriate. She purrs like a cat when we stroke her pussy."

I grin, loving the sound of the name.

"Then, the pussy challenge is on," Wolfe howls, wasting no time as he strolls over and climbs in, the water sloshing around the edges. He's palming himself, and I don't need to fucking see that.

"It's too fucking crowded," I complain, shuffling to the other side, across from Killian and our girl in the middle with Wolfe, who's already wearing his gills. Bastard. How long was he watching us, waiting for the perfect moment to interrupt?

I snort a laugh, thinking about it. I have no issue with sharing her, but getting alone time is becoming damn impossible.

"So, how long have you been lurking?" I ask Wolfe, who's not even looking my way.

"Long enough to know you two need to up your game." He's cracking his knuckles, stretching his mouth in preparation.

I eye him intensely.

Sage giggles. "I'm not complaining one bit."

Killian groans. "Yeah, yeah. We're all one big happy family."

Wolfe leans in, brushing a strand of wet hair from Sage's face. "Happy indeed."

I look at Killian, then back at Wolfe. "All right, enough chitchat. Let's see what you've got."

"Yes, let's see," she says, sitting up in the water, her smirk devious. "Are we doing this here, or am I getting out?"

Wolfe doesn't hesitate, and with a growl, he dives underwater, splashing us all, half the bathroom getting soaked. Sage screams with laughter, wriggling and half dipping under the water. I chuckle, staring over at Killian, who's shaking his head.

"Fuck him for showing off his two cocks," he growls, but there's a smile tugging at his lips.

I can't help myself, already approaching her, needing

one of those nipples that keep popping out of the water in my mouth... Killian has the same idea—we fuck her brains out tonight. And she'll energize us, ready for tomorrow.

But for now, I'm reminded of what we're fighting for, and I steel myself for whatever comes.

CHAPTER
THIRTY-SIX

KILLIAN

Today we're going to destroy this goddamn quest. Standing outdoors, the cold clings to me. We were escorted by a dozen guards early this morning and told to wait on the edge of the city where the woodland in front of us stretches toward the immense mountains that cast shadows over everything.

Dawn paints pink hues across the sky while the dual full moons hang low. The city behind us sleeps, though several dozen locals have gathered nearby, huddling at the rear of a stone building. They're watching us. I'm surprised that word about our quest has been released to the population. I had assumed the false King would have done everything in his power to conceal it.

Speaking of the fucker, he still hasn't shown up.

My gaze falls on Sage, who's pressed close to Wolfe. He's whispering in her ear, bringing a smile to those beautiful lips. Today, she wears tight black pants, boots, and a fitted long-sleeved shirt. Her long violet hair is pulled back into a long plait, and the look is breathtaking. She looks fucking fierce—clothes courtesy of her sister, who had them delivered to our quarters early this morning.

Wolfe, Nyko, and I stand in our monster forms, and I'm ready to start. Fuck! What's taking so long? Waiting only has doubts creeping in... doubts that we're being set up.

A rising chatter among the spectators has me glancing over to where Sage's father finally approaches with more of his guards in tow. His other daughter is nowhere in sight. A gold-and-red mantle flutters from his shoulders behind him, and he's putting on a show for the people who bow their heads as he passes. Cane in hand, his eyes are dark when he glances our way, his lips twisted in a smirk that makes my blood boil.

"I have kept my word, as I always do," he begins, pausing several feet in front of us, his voice loud enough to carry over the gathered crowd.

I reach over, taking Sage's hand, already missing her, wishing I could bundle her up somewhere safe, somewhere other than here.

Wolfe and Nyko stand tall beside us, glaring at the King.

The fast, rhythmic thud of my heart never slows.

"As the King, I would not be doing my job if I didn't ensure my successor would take care of my Shadowfen. So, are you four deserving of such a position?" He pauses for effect, always the dramatic asshole. "Therefore, you will partake in a quest to prove your worth." The steel is gone from his gaze as he looks over at the locals from the kingdom.

Partake is a far stretch when he gave us no damn option.

These theatrics irritate me. Nyko's fidgeting, and Sage just stares at her father, her brow furrowed. Wolfe nods, his arms tense by his sides, barely holding back from lunging at him.

"And the quest?" Nyko asks abruptly.

The King's grin spreads, almost touching his eyes, the evil behind them infuriating. "Your quest is to kill a Nythrax beast."

A great collective gasp comes from the gathered audience, and now I'm questioning if they're staged for effect.

"The animal resides in the woods, far up in the caves, as it has done since we moved onto this land. No one has been successful in slaying the creature, and more recently, it's started to descend the mountain, picking off my loyal Shadowfen. True heroes would risk anything to protect their Shadowfen. So, I'm certain you four can put an end to it." His gaze lowers to Sage, tendons flexing in his neck, a dangerous look surging over his face—one of destruction, of cruelty.

My fingers curl into fists. *Kill him.* That's all I can think about.

"Is that all?" Nyko barks, more angry than frustrated. He's shifting on his feet, cracking his knuckles.

A glint of anger burns in the King's eyes. "I'll take

that as you're ready, and we'll cease the formalities, shall I?" He claps his hands twice.

An older man in a white robe and with white hair rushes over, mumbling words as he raises his hands toward the ascending forest.

My skin bites from the magic, and the world before us seems to shimmer when a black circle of flames erupts to life ten feet away. The center is large enough for a person to fit through, and it ripples like the surface of water. In moments, it's clear, giving us a window into another place.

I lean in, studying the gateway. Are you kidding me?

"A portal?" Wolfe gasps my exact sentiment. "Since when can you wield such power?"

The King smirks, puffing out his chest. "You think you're the only one who has such abilities?"

The old man who summoned the gateway glances at us in a nonchalant way, as though he's completely disinterested in the King's politics. His arms remain outstretched, assumingly holding the entrance open.

"The portal is workable within a small distance of itself, only within Blight, and—"

"Let the quest begin," the King roars, talking over him and patting him heavily on the shoulder.

"So, are we doing this?" I ask my team. They all nod instantly, even Sage, and as much as I wish she weren't forced to join us, we're going to make it work.

"Let's move," Wolfe commands.

The false King stands tall, watching us with that same smug grin, thinking he holds all the cards.

We walk forward. Having stepped through so many portals, it's second nature to me. Nyko has Sage by the hand, and they walk through the portal behind Wolfe. I take one final glance at the King grinning, and I step through, fucking hating him.

Stepping through feels different this time. Normally, I sense nothing but a rush of darkness, like plunging into an abyss. This one, though, has a lingering buzz, like the magic's still working out the kinks. I stumble out—more like being spat out—and the portal snaps shut behind us.

Wolfe takes the lead, followed by Nyko and Sage, then me at her rear.

The air here is different—heavier, filled with the scent of earth and moss. Shadows dance around us.

"Well, this is fun," Nyko says.

We're all glancing around to find ourselves on a narrow patch of grass. An explosion of trees spread in every direction, and we discover we're standing at a higher elevation than the stone walls that surround the city, and far below, the city sprawls out. We can't see the King, the trees blocking our view, but we're far from him.

Sage is scanning the shadows, her hands clasped across her stomach. I can't blame her for being afraid. She's not a warrior and hasn't been trained to fight. I move closer to her.

"It's going to be all right." I wrap my arm around the back of her shoulders. "Just stay behind us when we encounter it. Find a hiding spot and wait there for us."

"Unless I find a way to use my ability, then I can help." She shrugs, uncertain herself.

"All the help will be needed, and I know you can do it."

She's giving me a lopsided grin, and I hug her, adoring her savagely. It's a cruel thing to have an ability that's playing recluse. When we come into our monster forms and abilities, it's at random ages, and sometimes, they linger just below the surface for years before they take full effect. We're born into human bodies, then we grow into our true forms.

Nyko turns to Wolfe. "You study creatures. Tell us what we need to know about these fucking Nythrax. What is their weakness?"

He's rubbing his chin. "There honestly isn't a lot of research on them as they are loners and extremely territorial. Plus, nearly impossible to destroy." Wolfe's amber eyes grow fiery. "They're also rare, and their only known enemy is the flying Dryvolith because its claws are strong enough to tear through the hide."

"So we're fucked is what you're saying?"

Wolfe scowls, and I'm grinding my teeth because this is going to test us to our limits.

"We're going to have to get creative. Get it trapped, tied up for starters. Now, let's get moving." His hand flicks to farther up the mountain where there's a cave peeking out through the dense forest.

"I need to tell you something," Sage suddenly announces with a sense of urgency in her tone, pausing us.

We all turn to face her.

She takes a deep breath. "My sister spoke to me in my mind yesterday. She showed me visions... our father hurting her, threatening to kill us before letting us move into the kingdom."

Wolfe's brow furrows. "What else?"

Sage swallows hard, her breaths deepening. "I saw him shoving her, calling her useless, and saying something to the effect that he would rather see us dead than allow us to take over. If he finds out she told us, he'll likely kill her. I didn't say anything because we knew he'd be this way, but my sister's been on my mind a lot."

My jaw clenches, and I tighten my squeeze on her. "Fucking bastard."

Nyko laughs bitterly. "Of course he did. No surprise there."

"That's why he's going to die. Only way this will work." Wolfe pauses and reaches out to take her hand in his. "Now, let's move quickly and get this done."

We climb a steep slope, using low-hanging branches to pull ourselves up. I'm at Sage's side, an arm around her waist, practically carrying her.

"You have a huge heart," I whisper. "You barely know your sister, and you care so much for her."

"How can I not? She's stuck in a shitty situation, and I know she's reaching out to me for help."

We reach the cave, and a great guttural roar escapes from within.

Wolfe places his hand over his mouth, making a hushing sound.

Sage presses against my side, staring into the gaping black cave, and I push her to stand behind me, keeping her close. I don't feel safe leaving her outside on her own.

Staring at the cave, Wolfe and Nyko take the first steps inside.

I draw my swords.

When I move into view of the cave, I catch a sudden movement in the cave up ahead. Shadows shift, and I hear the crunch of stones. Something stirs.

"It's here and has seen us," Nyko murmurs under his breath.

None of us move.

It rushes at us—a shadow, a monstrous figure roaring, paws slapping the ground.

Panic surges, and I recoil, gently nudging Sage out of the way. "Quickly, hide."

The glint of teeth is the first thing I see as it emerges. We all scramble back, darting to the side. My gaze flicks to a fear-stricken Sage, who is several trees away, behind a trunk, staring at us.

I swing back to the cave frantically as the beast bursts outside.

It's enormous, four times our height, and completely black. Sharp spikes run down its back, and it has a thick, spiked tail. Rows upon rows of teeth glint menacingly as it snarls, snorting from flaring nostrils. Covered in leather-like skin that glints in the early morning rays, the Nythrax beast is a fucking nightmare brought to life.

We back away farther, the ground trembling under

its weight as it stomps in our direction. This isn't going to be a quick fight.

"Stay hidden," I shout to Sage.

"We do this!" Nyko commands.

In a heartbeat, we're charging, moving with lightning speed. I throw myself forward, my swords swinging across his flank, but they bounce off its hide as if it's made of stone. It swirls on the spot, growling and swinging its spiked tail wildly. I leap over the tail, then attack again, slicing my swords into its side because I don't fucking give up, but nowhere I hit breaks skin.

"I can't cut its hide," I call out.

Wolfe scrambles on its back, claws and teeth ripping into the thick skin at the back of its neck. No blood spills... fuck! The beast roars, shaking Wolfe off like he's nothing. He lands in a heap of bushes and jolts to his feet.

Nyko expands his form, dark shadows blotting out the rising sun as he charges the beast. He hits it with the force of a battering ram, knocking it off its feet. We use that moment to attack, knowing that for most animals, the underbelly is usually the weak spot.

I dart in, my swords slashing at it. The beast roars, thrashing wildly. Wolfe is back up, leaping onto the beast's back, claws digging in. Nyko's shadows wrap around its legs, trying to hold it down. It's a chaos of motion, all of us moving with deadly precision.

The beast thrashes, tossing Wolfe off again. He hits the ground hard, but he's up in an instant, a growl rumbling from his chest. I keep slashing at the beast's underside, but it's like trying to cut through steel. I'm not piercing through.

Nyko tightens around his legs as the animal attempts to get up, unleashing a shrieking sound, its claws swiping in our direction. I duck them and attack, but my swords just bounce off the skin.

"What the fuck is this thing made of?"

It loosens its arm from my hold and swings into me, throwing me off, then rakes at Nyko. He flinches away, missed by inches.

I skid across the ground, every inch of me aching from the impact.

Wolfe is back on his feet, leaping at the beast's head, claws outstretched. He rakes across its head, trying to reach for its eyes, and the beast shakes violently. Nyko and I charge again, that fucking tail coming out of nowhere and whacking into us, the sharpness of the barbs catching me across my side. Not deep, but it damn scratches me across my abdomen.

Bellowing, I stumble out of reach, willing my blades to vanish as I reach for my injuries. Blue blood rolls free from the gashes, and it goddamn stings like acid.

It swings its massive tail, hitting Wolfe and sending him flying. He crashes into a tree, the trunk splintering under the force.

I push myself forward, my body screaming in protest. As I glance up, I spot the beast staring in Sage's direction. She's backing into the woods, whimpering.

"No!" I shout, my heart thundering.

The beast snarls, charging after her.

I force myself to my feet, every muscle protesting.

"Sage, run!"

The beast roars, its jaws opening wide.

We're out of time.

"Fuck you," I groan, trying to push myself up, rushing toward him, Wolfe and Nyko doing the same. Fear pummels into me that it's turned its attention to her.

"You're not taking her from us," I bellow.

Not now, not ever.

CHAPTER
THIRTY-SEVEN
SAGE

T eeth and claws flash as the Nythrax beast rushes at me, blazing red eyes and rows of knifelike teeth coming my way.

Screaming, I scramble backward, trying to get out of its way, but it's coming too fast. My heart bangs in my ears, drowning out my cries. I call to my ability, but nothing happens—only the fear beating into me, paralyzing me.

It's going to kill me. Frantically running away, I keep glancing back, and suddenly, my three monsters fly at the creature's side with such force they send it reeling sideways. It loses its footing, stepping into a ditch, and tumbles down a small ravine.

Wolfe is at my side in an instant, dragging me against him, and we all move away from the creature, me panting for breath. Killian is staggering, with huge gashes across his torso, and he's bleeding blue. He glances at me, pain etched into his features as he scrunches up his face as though he's barely holding on.

"Killian... shit, shit!" I cry out, rushing to his side. He leans against a tree, and fear tumbles through me.

A guttural shriek comes from the ravine, where already I see the creature climbing out, and my skin crawls.

"I need to find you somewhere to hide." My voice wobbles. "We're not going to win against that animal."

"We have no option," Killian groans. "Don't you see? We walk away, we're dead. So, we fight to the end. To save you, to keep you safe... that's our mission."

"Are you insane?" I yell. "You're going to die saving me, then leave me here at the mercy of my fucking father? Don't you dare leave me or die, or I'll come for you in whatever afterlife Shadowfen have and haunt you. I'm serious!" I'm breathing so fast, hyperventilating, and dread consumes me.

Killian reaches over, his hand heavy on my shoulder. "I love your fierceness. I love everything about you, my pretty little monster, but I won't let you die."

I'm tearing up, tears falling freely now, feeling like my world is collapsing.

"Don't any of you leave me," I whisper, voice breaking. "Now, we need to get you somewhere safe. Lean on me."

A brutal roar slices through the morning, and my attention snaps back to the dark beast on all fours, staring at us amid the trees between us, his gaze blazing with fury.

Wolfe and Nyko are already stalking toward the beast while I'm desperately scanning the woods, spotting more exposed rock, for gaps, anything we can hide in.

"All right, let's move."

Killian's bleeding badly, but he still pushes along with me, refusing to place his weight on me, the stubborn ass. He staggers, wincing with each step. We pick up our pace when shouting comes from behind me. I glance back to Nyko and Wolfe charging to the right, away from us, from the galloping beast behind them.

Except, when the creature doesn't take the bait and has its gaze on us, my stomach drops.

"Oh, fuck! We need to run!" I call out.

Killian grunts, and he tries, but the moment the other two catch up, they practically carry him between them. We madly run for our lives. The forest is a blur of dark shapes and filled with snarls. Branches snap, paws pound the ground, and I hear the damn thing crashing through the underbrush behind us, getting closer.

"Faster!" Wolfe shouts.

Reaching the open rock face, we run alongside it, and I'm scanning it when I spot a lofty fissure in the wall, a black gap beyond it.

"Here," I call out, already shoving myself into the hole in the rock, fitting through easily, and I pop out into a cave. It's cold and musty, and I pray there's nothing else here.

Seconds later, my true mates are desperately shuffling through sideways to fit in. Wolfe's last, and he bursts out, stumbling as an explosive roar bellows from the gap. A shadow falls over the opening where the beast pauses, scratching at the wall with those huge claws.

I rush over to Killian, who's propped up against the wall, looking ready to fall over. Every inch of me shudders at his injuries. My heart is still racing, my breaths coming in ragged gasps. Wolfe's there, as is Nyko.

"Fuck, that looks bad," Nyko states the obvious.

"Please tell me Shadowfen have fast healing or something," I murmur.

Killian shakes his head, clutching at his wounds while Wolfe's getting him to lean on him.

"Let's get you to lie down. We need to stop the bleeding." His hands are already on Killian's wounds to apply pressure.

"Stop fussing. I'll survive," Killian groans, panting for air. His brow glistens with sweat from the sliver of light coming through the crack in the cave.

I rip off my shirt, thankful I wore a tight sleeveless shirt underneath. All eyes are on me, but I'm too busy folding the fabric and using it as a makeshift bandage. Applying it to his wounds, I press lightly to help stop the bleeding. The sight of so much blood makes me slightly nauseous.

Killian grimaces, and Wolfe's sitting next to him, doing the same on the other side of him with his bare hands. Nyko's pacing near the entrance, watching the Nythrax.

It slams that spiky tail against the cave walls, the impact making the ground tremble beneath us. Dust rains down from the ceiling with every hit.

"How the hell are we supposed to defeat it when we haven't pierced its skin once?" Nyko roars.

"Unless..." Wolfe begins. He's staring at me, and I know exactly what he's about to say. "You're so powerful, so strong. We've seen it, and you need to remember the energy you used to tap into it. Use me, drain me, whatever you need, because right now, your power might be our savior."

I nod, trying to steady my breathing, but the fear is suffocating.

The beast roars outside.

"I tried before, but it's not working."

"Try again," Killian croaks. "You've got this."

I attempt to center myself, feeling my true mates' energies humming around me, their strength. Closing my eyes, I concentrate on the feelings I experienced when facing the snake creature back on the vessel.

The ground shakes, and all I can think is that the Nythrax beast is coming for us.

My insides are on fire, my mind screaming, and that light, familiar sensation wraps around me as though I'm floating... as if I can walk on water. I recognize the power. It's there but so faint that it's barely there. I reach for the power swirling within me, but it's like trying to grasp smoke.

My hands are shaking, my thoughts spiraling. "I can't... I can't do it," I stammer, tears stinging my eyes.

"Yes, you can," Wolfe insists firmly. "You have to for you, for us, for your sister."

A spark, a flicker of power blooms inside me, and I cling to it. *Please work... please.*

Killian stares at me, his eyes filled with pain and desperation. "Is there anything unusual you remember when it happened the first time?"

Nyko joins us, kneeling beside me, back in his human form.

"Well," I begin. "The snake was attacking me, and I freaked out. Next thing I know, it's there—the shadow. I'm so scared right now that I can't feel much else. Just the fear of losing all of you, and there's nothing I can do about it."

The world seems to be pressing in around me, not just in this cave but in my own mind. Every growl outside, every tremor around us from the beast outside, is a reminder of how much trouble we're in. The thought of losing them, of seeing them torn apart, is unbearable. That's when I know I have to make my power happen.

A tremendous roar comes from outside as the beast slams its tail into the cave with such power the walls begin to crumble. The noise is deafening, and I sense the vibrations in my bones.

Nyko embraces me, his lips on my ear. "You're beautiful and so strong, my princess. Focus on how much we adore you, how much we love you, not the fear."

The beast's tail smashes against the entrance again, and cracks spiderweb across the walls. The sound of rock grinding against rock fills the air, and the cold grip of fear tightens around my heart.

"I have a plan." Wolfe's voice is barely audible over

the chaos outside. "Nyko and I are going out to draw the beast away from the cave. Sage, you and Killian are going to start your descent down the mountain."

"No, I'm not leaving you." I stiffen.

Killian groans. "Look, I already feel better." He goes to move but winces from the ache, and a tremor races down my spine, shuddering all the way down to my stomach, knowing he's going to struggle to make it out, let alone face the thing outside again. I reach over and grip his arm, staring at the hard lines of his jaw, at those captivating blue eyes, at the scars on his body. He's not a monster to back down from a fight, no matter his injuries—which is what worries me.

"Sounds like a plan to me," Nyko says in an unenthusiastic voice. "Let's do this."

"And then what?" I ask.

"We'll come up with something," Wolfe says, glancing over at Nyko. I see the ache in both their eyes, the fact that they're willing to sacrifice themselves to save me and Killian.

Are they insane?

"No, I'm not going anywhere without you two," I cry. "Don't do this. I'm going to try harder to reach my power. Please!"

Wolfe's eyes glisten, and he glances at Killian, who, in turn, reaches over and clasps my hand. "I think it's a solid plan."

I rip my hand from his and turn on them, fury rising through me. "Sacrificing themselves for us is not a fucking plan!" Shaking from anger, I reach for Wolfe once more, clasping his hand. "Please, I can't lose any of you. I just need a bit more time to work on reaching my power. Give me that." I'm frantic, my emotions tugging in every direction.

"Then we try again," Nyko suggests instantly, grinning at me, and I know he hates the plan, too. "What do you say?"

Wolfe finally nods, getting up, breathing heavily. "Of course. I'd do anything for you, Sage, and that means ensuring you aren't hurt. No matter the cost."

His words strike hard, and I hate that I love him even more for them.

I look at them, my heart aching. We're beaten, bleeding, and exhausted. The beast is relentless, and I have to reach my powers. The weight of our situation crushes me, and the walls of the cave seem to close in, trapping us worse than before.

The two of them climb to their feet, and both lean down, stealing a kiss.

"I know you can do this," Wolfe whispers.

They move to the entrance, waiting for the beast to pass, then they slip out.

Sick to my stomach, I turn to Killian. "Hold my shirt to your injuries."

He's wincing, paling faster, but he reaches over and does as I ask.

"I never thought I'd find my true mate," Killian starts. "But here you are and more beautiful, more powerful than I ever expected. You just need to believe in yourself."

"That means a lot because I doubt myself often." I stand up and lean against a wall that's cool to chase away the fire I'm feeling. Closing my eyes, I search for that light sensation. I know it's there.

You need to get back, Elara abruptly cries in my mind.

I shudder, almost losing my footing, and slide off the wall.

"You all right?" Killian grunts.

"Yeah."

Elara, what's going on? I need your help with the Nythrax beast. It's got us trapped.

Fuck! Why aren't you using your ability? I've felt how strong you are. Why haven't you destroyed it yet?

I'm tired of being told that when I feel anything but strong.

Stop letting your fear block you. You have the power inside you.

I'm trying, but it's not working, and I don't know how to stop being scared when we're going to die. I don't have control of my ability.

You need to be at your full power to defeat it. She sighs. *If I'd known you couldn't control it... Shit! Let me help.* In an instant, a sharp pain jolts through me, electricity snapping down my arms. I collapse to my knees, heaving for breath, but something else stirs inside me. That light sensation from earlier—the power that lingers just beneath the surface.

"Sage?" Killian asks.

My heart's racing, my mind is in overdrive, and I feel different, lighter, as though I'm floating.

With a growl, I stagger to my feet, and instantly, the power flares through me, an explosion of electric energy rippling down my arms.

"Shit, Sage, are you—" Killian's getting to his feet, but I need to move, knowing what needs to be done.

"Stay here," I call out, rushing out of the cave and scanning the forests.

In the distance to my right, the beast has one paw pressed down on Wolfe beneath him as Nyko relentlessly attacks it.

I scream from my terror as the beast lifts its paw to finish off Wolfe.

In a heartbeat, I summon a shadow Nythrax beast, and it's here in the blink of an eye, right next to the real one. As I did back in the vessel when I faced that snake, I'm punching and kicking to indicate I want it to attack the beast.

My shadow lunges at the real one, their bodies clashing with a force that shakes the ground.

Nyko swoops down, grabs Wolfe, and they rush back to me. They're saying something, glancing my way, but I don't have time, not when every bit of concentration remains on the battle I can't lose.

The real beast roars, swiping its massive claws, but they pass right through its opponent's body. My shadow mirrors its moves, parrying every strike. It snarls, biting into the real creature's hide, using its solid form, just as the snake had done back on the vessel.

Green blood sprays, and I'm cheering that it worked. My shadow is savage and relentless, tearing into the beast with unmatched ferocity. It latches onto the back of its neck, ripping away a huge chunk of flesh.

I cringe as Nyko and Wolfe call my name, but I'm too busy punching the air to control it. I have no idea if my motions are needed, but it feels like I'm actually fighting.

The Nythrax pivots instantly and brutally bites down, fangs sinking into my shadow's side. It slices through me, the agony, the pain. I'm screaming, falling to my knees.

Shit, I experience its pain?

I reach to my side, expecting a hole, but instead, my body is airy and cold. Glancing down, I notice I look different. I gasp, my head spinning as I stumble back onto my feet.

My entire form resembles a void, as though I'm staring into space at the stars through myself. I have my body shape, but it's a dark, star-filled expanse. Against my fingertips, my body feels cold, and there's no substance I can reach into the void. I have no idea how I did this.

Wolfe and Nyko rush to my side.

"Princess, you finally turned into your monster form," Nyko coos.

"Fucking hell, you're everything." Wolfe smiles, shaking his head. "But how about you destroy the beast now?"

I swing my gaze to the animal who's attacking my shadow form again, every swipe of its claw plunging right through the body. Steeling myself, I prepare for the fight. The energy flares through me, a strange, exhilarating power.

I take a deep breath and reach out with my newfound power, and my shadow rises from the ground.

The Nythrax lunges, and this time, I meet it head-on, both of them clashing head-to-head. I lash out, striking the beast with claw after claw, tearing into its hide. It's reeling, bleeding, but I don't back away, knowing if I don't remove the creature, it'll come after us.

The beast stumbles, legs wobbling. I can see bottle-green blood, the wounds I've inflicted finally taking its toll. With a final charge, the shadow slams into the animal, teeth to its throat, and rips it out.

I flinch. Did I just do that?

"Sage, you're savage. I love it," Nyko says behind me.

The creature crashes to the ground, letting out a deafening roar as it thrashes in its death throes.

I stand there, panting, my void form flickering with the remnants of the battle's energy, then it's gone, and I'm back to normal.

I stumble, breathless.

Nyko and Wolfe are there, catching me.

"My princess," Nyko admits, smiling with his eyes. "You realize what this means? I'm not dying because you didn't drain me. Neither is Wolfe or Killian. You're taking the energy from the universe, from the world, like all of us do."

I laugh, shocked, overwhelmed, scared. "I can't believe I did that." But ever since my sister helped me finally unlock my ability, it flowed so easily, like it has always been a part of me.

Wolfe kisses my face. "I knew you would be incredible in your true form. And we're going to celebrate, but now we must face the real monster. Your father."

Nyko darts into the cave and emerges moments later, carrying Killian, who's still conscious but barely.

I rush to his side just as bells are tolling loudly from down in the city.

In a flash, my vision blurs in and out, the edges dark, and the world in front of me vanishes.

I'm on a balcony in the kingdom, where the bells ring louder. Screams echo in my ears as I clutch the railing, my body shaking.

Below in the streets, everyone is running around frantically, screaming and crying. The sky is deep purple and pink, almost bruised. Smoke rises from several burning buildings, dark plumes twisting into the air.

A deafening explosion rocks the air, and I stumble on the balcony. I whip around just in time to see my father's elaborate castle engulfed in flames. Pieces of the structure crumble and fall.

"Fuck!" I scream. "What's going on?"

My breath catches in my throat, and panic flares within me. I'm suffocating, the smoke and heat pressing down on me, even from this distance. Tears blur my vision as I watch the rising flames and the Shadowfen yelling on the streets, running like mad.

My heart feels like it's being torn apart, the weight of everything crashing down on me. So, I'm swaying on my feet. My thoughts are a frantic jumble. The castle is gone. Everything is falling apart.

Suddenly, my vision darkens, and I'm no longer on the balcony. I'm standing in the middle of the street, the sounds of the bells now mixed with the cries of the injured and the sharp clash of weapons. The smell of blood and smoke permeates the air. My stomach churns, and I fight the urge to retch.

People run past me, their faces filled with fear and agony. A woman stumbles, clutching her bleeding side, crying for help. I rush to her to help, but she runs right through me.

My heart shatters.

Then I see them—armed Shadowfen surge forward from the castle in the distance, a wave of monstrous figures savagely cutting through the chaos. There have to be dozens of them, and the locals are rushing away, terrified. As they get closer, I recognize the leader.

Clay!

Our vessel's captain.

My mouth drops open, shock ripping through me.

His blade glints in the dim light, and here I assumed him to be frail in his birdlike monster form.

What the fuck is he doing?

More monsters follow him, their roars mingling with the screams of the fleeing locals, and I recognize some faces from the vessel... they're attacking the kingdom. Does Wolfe know about this?

Why is no one stopping them while the castle burns behind them?

I flinch, stumbling back at their approach.

Eyes locked on to Clay, I spot what he's holding—a head with white hair.

My father's head.

The sight is like a punch to the gut, and I stagger, my vision swimming. He holds it high, a trophy, a symbol of their victory. My father's eyes are wide, his mouth open in a final, silent scream. I hate him for what he's done, for the pain he's caused, but seeing him like this... it's too much.

"What the fuck?"

The streets are chaotic, his men slaying anyone they pass, including people trying to escape them. I can see the dark purpose in Clay's eyes. He's not just here for revenge. He's here to destroy everything. To take the kingdom by force. To kill them all.

I scream at him to stop, but my voice is lost. I try to move, to do something, anything, but my feet are rooted to the spot. I can only watch as the Shadowfen carve a path of destruction through the city.

Suddenly, the vision flashes again, and I'm back in the mountains, bursting into tears.

CHAPTER
THIRTY-EIGHT
SAGE

My vision blurs from the tears streaming down my face.

Anger strangles me, but it's more than that. It's grief, it's fear, and I can't stop crying from the devastation I just saw in the city.

I'm instantly surrounded by all three of my true mates in the woods. They hold me, staring at me with confused looks.

"What's going on? And why the fuck is the castle on fire?" Wolfe's voice trembles, his hand gripping mine.

Their gazes search mine for answers, but I'm staring over the tops of the trees in the distance at the flames claiming the castle, remembering that devastation in the city.

Despite his injuries, Killian holds me tighter, more concerned with me than himself, while Nyko's brow furrows, and he pushes strands of hair out of my face.

The wind that's picking up just pushes it back, and he keeps brushing it aside.

"It's Clay," I finally say. "He's rampaged into the kingdom, taking over, killing the locals, and he was..." I pause to catch my breath, my body shaking. "He was carrying my father's decapitated head around, parading it."

Silence. It's as though they're all processing what I just said. Then Wolfe stiffens, snarling like a beast.

"I'm going to fucking murder Clay," Wolfe shouts, his fists clenched. "Who the fuck does he think he is?"

I can't concentrate on the three of them bursting into anger over Clay. Right now, I hate myself for crying over my father's loss, but it's not just about him—it's about everything I never got to ask, everything I'll never know about my past, my monster side.

Nyko fiercely pulls me into his embrace before the other two get a chance, hugging me. "Princess, I'm so fucking sorry. I know your father's an asshole, but you didn't deserve to see it the way you did."

Killian's embracing me, too, as is Wolfe, our breaths heavy and fast.

"Sage, I'm so sorry," Killian murmurs, his voice thick with emotion.

I cling to them, shaking my head. "I'm worried about my sister," I choke out. "And I can't stop seeing his severed head."

"You shouldn't have experienced any of that," Wolfe murmurs, his brow heavy with furrows, his shoulders bunching up in fury.

Nyko exchanges a quick, grim look with Wolfe. "I never trusted that bastard."

Wolfe's heaving for breath. "He kept going on about making those who stuck with the King pay for their betrayal, and now it appears the fucker is trying to start a rebellion, and we need to stop him." His expression darkens.

"Fuck him," Killian swears under his breath, his jaw clenched. "We need to get back to the city... now!"

Wolfe and Nyko practically carry Killian, who's struggling to keep up, his injuries slowing him down. My adrenaline numbs my pain and terror. Branches scratch my skin and tug at my hair, the dense underbrush making every step a struggle. The descent is brutal.

Wolfe grunts as he slips on the wet ground, his arm shooting out to steady himself against a tree trunk. Nyko curses under his breath, one hand on me so I don't fall.

My breath comes in ragged gasps. The forest is dense and oppressive, the canopy above blocking out most of the light, casting everything in eerie shadows. We move as fast as we can, but it feels like a slow-motion nightmare.

Fear for my sister gnaws at me. I can't lose her. Not after I just found out that I have an extended family.

"We're almost there," Killian grunts, his face pale from the effort. "Just a bit farther."

I nod, swallowing hard. The terrain is treacherous, the ground slick with mud and leaves. I slip, my feet sliding out from under me, but Wolfe's quick reflexes catch me before I hit the ground.

"Careful," he coos, helping me back up.

"Thanks," I whisper.

The forest begins to thin out, the trees giving way to open space. Shouts and screams reach us, the smell of smoke heavier. My heart sinks as we burst out of the woods, the city sprawled out before us in utter chaos. People are running desperately in all directions, their fear cutting into me.

Far across the city, the castle is falling apart under the flames.

Wolfe's grip tightens on my arm, his eyes scanning the scene with grim terror. "Where the hell is that motherfucker?"

Nyko nods, his expression hard.

Killian, despite his injuries, stands tall, his eyes burning at the sight. "Let's move," he commands. "We have to stop him before he destroys everything."

As we push forward, I scan every person, every home we pass for Elara's familiar face. I lead them to where I roughly remember seeing Clay last, though in all honesty, the streets look alike, and I have no idea if I'm going in the right direction.

We enter a center square, an open area surrounded by flowering trees and benches, with a platform on one end for performances or announcements. The area is large enough to fit several hundred Shadowfen. Now, it's marred by chaos, with locals frantically dashing across it.

Then I see him across the open space.

Fucking Clay.

He stands there with a sickening smirk on his face

with only half a dozen guards. Back in my vision, he had dozens following him... are they all scouring the city for us now?

But I forget them when I find my sister, Elara, chained around the neck, being tugged along like a dog by Clay. She's clawing at the chain in her monster form, crying to be released. I'm caught by her appearance as it's my first time seeing her true form—skin shimmering with a translucent glow, almost like moonlight filtering through water, her eyes a deep purple, her hair matching and flowing down to her thighs. She has a human figure, yet she looks more ethereal, especially with the sparks of sunlight bouncing off her body, almost giving her a glow.

Seeing her struggling with the chain, being shoved to keep walking by a guard from behind, has fury boiling inside me. I feel it radiating off my true mates as well. Wolfe's growling under his breath like a hound about to attack, Nyko's chest heaves rapidly, and Killian suddenly materializes swords in his hands.

"Clay, you fucking idiot!" Wolfe roars across the square.

Elara's eyes lock with mine, and I see the terror in her gaze. Clay turns to smirk at Wolfe, his expression mocking.

"My Lord, I have done your duty for you," he says sarcastically as he gives an overexaggerated bow.

I tremble with anger, my hands shaking.

"What the fuck did you do?" Wolfe snarls, stepping forward. "Who gave you instructions to invade the kingdom? To kill the locals? Look at all the dead!"

We move toward Clay, and the spindly, spiderlike guards following him move in our direction, covering him from either side.

Around us, several bodies of fallen monsters lie scattered, their blood staining the ground. My heart shatters at all the loss.

"They betrayed us, or have you forgotten what happened to your father? How you watched him murdered in cold blood," Clay barks. "And I did what you couldn't." He points to my father's head, being held up by one of the guards.

I struggle to stare at it, grimacing.

"You have no idea what you've done." Wolfe's fists are trembling, his eyes locked on Clay. "We lost so many people during the Great Desolation, and there are so few Shadowfen left. And you butcher more? You fucking maniac!"

Nyko's face twists with anger. "Can I kill him now?"

Several more guards step closer to Clay as we close the distance between us and them.

"These Shadowfen betrayed us when they took the false King's side, and you appear weak by accepting this," Clay keeps arguing. "And now his daughter will pay the same price."

He glances at Elara, who tugs against him. My fury blinds me, and I step forward, my heart pounding in my chest. I stare at my sister.

Don't do anything crazy, or he's going to kill me, she pleads suddenly in my mind.

The ache in her voice leaves me trembling.

No, he's not, I reply firmly. *You're not going to die, Elara. But Clay will. The moment we make a move, you tug from his grip and run to us. I'm not going to lose my sister. Not going to happen.*

Thank you, she says, her voice filled with a mix of relief and fear. *Whatever happens, thank you for being kind to me. Not many have been.*

I'm getting teary, and I want to hug her. It kills me to see her chained up. At the same time, I sense my monster lingering inside now, like a growing emotion; it's a part of me.

Just hold on. I promise they won't hurt you.

I trust you.

I nod subtly. The sight of her chained and helpless fuels the fire inside me, but I need to stay focused. For her. For us.

The argument with my true mates and Clay returns me to the present.

"You might reconsider having her on your side," he snorts, glaring at me, his tone dripping with disdain. "Because you're sleeping with the enemy, Wolfe. She will backstab you. I should have tried harder to get rid of her when she escaped the Sylar." He scowls at me.

I'm burning up. "You asshole, tried to kill me!"

Clay chuckles, sounding more like an annoying bird squawking.

Killian snarls dangerously in his direction.

All while Elara's eyes plead with me, and I can't stand the thought of losing her. My mind races, trying to come up with a plan, a way to save her and stop this madness.

"Enough of this!" Wolfe roars, his voice echoing through the square. "Let Elara go, and we'll discuss this... you and me. Enough blood's been spilled."

Clay hesitates, his gaze flicking between Wolfe, Nyko, Killian, and then me. We're standing only a couple of feet apart from him now.

For a moment, the world seems to hold its breath. The tension is so thick it's suffocating, and the weight of everyone's stares on me is unbearable.

Clay suddenly shoves Elara to the ground with his foot and lunges at Wolfe, his blade flashing in the light.

Nyko and Killian charge in at his back, Killian wincing, but it doesn't stop him.

Wolfe meets Clay's lunge head-on, wrestling to force Clay's blade away from his body. To my surprise, Clay is a lot stronger than he appears. At that same moment, two guards charge at Killian, who's already injured and struggling to stay on his feet. He parries the first strike but is knocked back by the second, blood seeping from his wounds.

Nyko, in his shadow form, moves like a wraith, his figure shifting and blurring as he attacks the guards targeting Killian and the four coming for him. He wraps his shadowy tendrils around one guard's neck, yanking him back and slamming him to the ground. The other guard swings wildly at Nyko, but his blows pass harmlessly through the shadows. Nyko materializes behind him, delivering a swift, lethal blow to the back of the head.

I can't look away, not when my true mates are in danger. Wolfe shoves Clay to the ground, lunging after him while ripping the blade from him, wielding it himself. There's no pause, just sheer savagery. Clay snarls, his face twisted in rage, kicking him in the gut. It's enough time for him to roll and scramble up, snatching a blade from a fallen guard.

My attention swings to my sister's cries. Her leash is held by a huge furry Shadowfen, and he's raising a blade behind my sister, who's staggering up to her knees.

Terror grips me.

I burst with a power that buzzes down my arms, and instantly, a shadow double of the guard materializes behind him. It wields two swords, and without pause, he sinks the blades into his back. He grunts, crying out, trying to reach his back while falling over.

I duck and run to my sister, who's now screaming from the guard who tumbled half on her, shoving her back to the ground. Frantically, I move my shadow to roll the man off her. I desperately grab her arm, drawing her to her feet just as my shadow falls away to the wind like ashes.

"Sage!" Elara sobs, her cheeks red. "Take it off me, take it off."

I fumble, trying to find where the chain on her neck is connected. At the back, I unlock the latch, and it falls to her feet.

She's sobbing, and I hug her, quickly rushing her away from the fight, needing her safe.

"I was going to die."

"It's all right. You're safe now. I promise," I whisper, bringing her to a bench at the corner of the square, far from the battle.

"I saw them kill Father," Elara murmurs, choking on her words. "It was horrific... I hated him, but I didn't want to see that..."

"I'm so sorry," I say, my heart breaking for her, for us. "But you're with me now." Her cries continue, and I try to comfort her, but I need to help my true mates. "Give me a moment."

When I glance back, I find all three of them standing from the fight, splattered in blue and green blood.

Clay lies on the ground at their feet, broken, twisted, his head snapped backward and in a pool of his own blood.

He's dead!

A few enemy guards survived, and they've dropped their weapons, heads bowed. Locals from the city are gathering around us; they must have watched the battle, seen it all. More of our guards and those belonging to the kingdom emerge, and there's no hesitation from them in falling to their knees for Wolfe. Clearly, they weren't loyal to my father or Clay at how quickly they give in.

"Anyone who stands with Clay does not belong here," Wolfe growls. "I do not condone his actions, and for that, he paid with his life." His breathing is heavy.

I stare at him, loving him more than I thought possible.

Nyko has Killian leaning on him, and he's walking him over to a bench where he sits him down. He lifts his gaze in my direction and blows me a kiss, leaving me swooning, then he returns to Wolfe's side. Elara and I get up and quickly move to join Killian, my sister clinging to my side.

"You're hurt," I say, taking in how much more blood he has on him, but not all of it is his.

"I'll be fine. I mean, that hurts like a bitch, but it's worth it," he mutters, wincing as he shifts and tries to twist toward me. "Besides, we can't leave just yet."

I glance over at Wolfe, who stares at those surrounding the square.

"King Bren is dead. His torment and tyranny end today. My family and I..." He glances at Nyko, then over at us on the bench, directing everyone's attention our way. "We will restore order to this kingdom, but we need everyone's help. We're here to protect you, not to harm you."

His words are met with murmurs and nodding heads, along with a few skeptical glances. The Shadowfen in the kingdom must have seen my father's brutality... I recall seeing them running around the city terrified, guards at every corner. That's not a peaceful way of living but one of being controlled.

After a moment, Nyko steps forward, his presence commanding.

"The true King from Silvercrest Kingdom, the son of

King Roan, has returned to claim his throne." He steps aside, casting a hand toward Wolfe. "Wolfe Roan will take his rightful place on the throne of Blight and will now lead us into a new era! We will hold a coronation to make his title official and give the city a much-needed celebration. Soon after, there will be a royal marriage to arrange." Nyko and Wolfe are staring at me, and I'm flushing all over. Did I just hear right?

Marriage?

I might be swooning.

Crying.

Killian's laughing, an arm around me.

"We've been planning when to best ask you," he says. "Seems this is the perfect moment." He chuckles, and I lean against him. Reaching up to kiss him, I blow my other true mates a kiss each. I have so many questions about what that entails, but there's time. First are the city and the kingdom.

Even more Shadowfen begin to gather closer, some clapping, others cheering, the shock giving way to realization. Someone shouts out that they recognize the old King in Wolfe's face and that they look alike. That he wants the old ways returned. And slowly, one by one, they start to bend a knee to Wolfe, bowing their heads in submission and respect. The weight of their acceptance is beautiful.

Killian's swaying on the bench. He's going to pass out soon, and he can't wait any longer.

Elara moves to his side. "I know who can fix your injuries, but we need to go to the medic room now!"

Killian just smiles, even though he's pale and bleeding blue everywhere. He looks up at her, his smile widening. "I finally feel like I can breathe easy," he admits. "It hurts like a son of a bitch, but I haven't known this kind of peace since I was a kid."

"Peace?" my sister asks, her brow furrowed in confusion.

"We're off the vessel, on land we'll make our home. I have my true mate, and the two assholes in my life are dead. It sounds like a perfect day to me."

I giggle, unsure how I'm even laughing, seeing so many others who lost their lives. Death is all around us. The sight of the fallen, the blood-soaked ground, infuriates me.

More guards and other locals start to emerge from their homes, chattering, eyes wide with shock. Some ask Wolfe and Nyko questions.

Killian's whining, and I can't even tell if he's bleeding more or is covered in blood from the battle.

"All right, let's go get you healed." I get up, and my sister and I help him up.

As we start to move, the crowd parts for us. I glance back at Wolfe, his gaze meeting mine with a determination that has me grinning to see him take back what was always rightfully his.

Finally, we reach the medic room in a nearby building, and Killian heaves himself up on the bed, groaning in the process before he flops onto his back.

Elara's liaising with the doctor, who's already

studying Killian's wounds, before quickly getting to work.

I'm at his side, clasping his hand, staring into those deep blue irises. "You better heal," I tell him. "We have so much to do in this kingdom." I watch as Elara tends to Killian, my heart aching with gratitude and love for my true mates, who've fought so hard for us.

"I'm proud of you," I whisper to Killian as he winces under the doctor's care. "You've been so strong when I know you're hurting."

He chuckles weakly. "Takes more than a few scratches to take me down."

"The injuries will need stitching up," the doctor states. "They're deep, and you've lost lots of blood."

"See? Told you," Killian gloats. "I'm perfectly fine." But the moment the doctor starts to clean up the wounds with a liquid he sprays across his stomach and chest, Killian flinches, shouting, "Fuck, that stings!"

"It'll stop you from getting an infection," the doctor says, continuing to work. Killian's hissing. "I am going to have to put you to sleep as there are plenty of scratches, and you might pass out from the pain once I glue you back together."

"Pain doesn't scare me." Killian's sweating and tries to shrug but cringes from pain instead. "But... I could do with some sleep."

I chuckle, as does Elara. The doctor gives Killian a light sprinkling of blue dust over his face. Within seconds, Killian's eyes flutter closed, and he passes out, his body finally relaxing.

I move to the corner of the room, giving the doctor space, Elara at my side.

"I never thanked you for saving me in the mountains."

"I should have done it earlier," she replies, shrugging. "But I didn't know you needed my help. I assumed you knew your power."

I pull her into a quick hug.

"I should thank you," she says. "You saved me, so we're equal. Actually, you saved me twice... from our father and death just then." She's grinning as we pull back, and she looks exhausted, her face smudged with soot from the fires, her breaths ragged.

I can't believe how everything turned out. It's all surreal, like a dream that hasn't fully settled into reality, yet I know it's real. Reaching this point of success was brutal, but I'm not sure I'd change a whole lot. I've learned a great deal and discovered that I have a bigger family now. It hits me that this might mean I'll get to see my mother soon. I'm desperate to see her, having so much to tell her.

Two days later, my true mates, my sister, and I hurry through Silvercrest Kingdom, heading toward the open front gates. So much has passed since the day we arrived.

Cleanup of the city and castle has commenced.

We welcomed the Shadowfen from our vessel to their new home. Finding them accommodations has become a chore in itself, but the locals have been so embracing, offering to share their homes until repairs to the city begin and more homes are developed.

Now, we're emerging onto the shores outside the kingdom, where we stand on the rocky shore of the ocean. The beach is packed with Shadowfen all the way down the edge of the sea in the curved bay where we'd first arrived.

The dual moons hang high in the sky, casting a pinkish hue over the landscape.

We follow Wolfe to the steps in front of the crowd, where the soft water laps close to my feet, and my gaze lifts out at sea, like everyone else.

Our vessel is floating in the distance, partially destroyed as a result of Clay's rampage. He sabotaged the ship to ensure Wolfe couldn't leave.

The horn suddenly blows, its sound deep and mournful, echoing across the water. Someone shoots an arrow into the vessel, and the moment it strikes, it bursts into flames. The explosion is fierce, flames licking the sky, reaching for the heavens. The vessel, already battered and broken, splinters further, pieces of it crashing into the water below.

No one says anything... it's eerily peaceful from the Shadowfen. The heat from the flames reaches us, even from this distance, and the smell of burning wood and metal fills the air. The fire reflects off the water, more beautiful than it should be, considering what it represents.

Once a home, it's now a ship of the dead, a farewell to everyone who passed in the recent tragic event. Even my father is there and Clay, all of them being sent off in the blaze.

My sister clings to my arm at my side. Killian, now completely healed, holds my hand, Wolfe's at my back, and Nyko stands close at my shoulder, his hand on my arm. We stare at the flame as the horns blow a few more times to send them off.

I hate seeing it burn, but Wolfe had said they've salvaged everything from it, including Howler's technology, something he'll add to our castle once it's rebuilt. That part about living in a castle is still surreal to me.

Killian leans in, his voice a soft whisper in my ear. "In Shadowfen customs, it's believed that we are born from the universe, and when we pass, we return there. I believe that's why your monster form is revered by so many now, why many are talking about you. You are a window into our past and our future, into where life begins and ends." He kisses my cheek.

I smile, loving his tenderness, though his words surprise me. Locals are talking about me, but most importantly, does my monster form have significance? I'm not going to lie to myself… I love that!

"It does feel amazing when I'm in my true form, but it also still feels strange," I whisper as I'm learning so much about myself, even while in my human shape at the moment, I'm still getting used to having two sides to myself.

"There's time," he whispers in my ear. "We have all the time in the world now."

We stand there, the five of us wrapped in each other's warmth. Wolfe, Nyko, and Killian, all close, forming a protective circle around Elara and me.

The fire roars, the heat washing over us, and the smell of smoke and ash fills the air. The flames leap higher, consuming the vessel piece by piece.

I glance at Elara, her eyes reflecting the flames. She's been through a lot, yet she stands strong beside me.

In this quiet, powerful moment, I realize how much my life has changed. From a village outcast to a Queen, from a girl who never felt like she belonged to a woman who has found her true family. Sure, the Queen part will happen at the coronation, but that will take place once the kingdom is built... which is a while away. It gives me time to practice, to learn how to be Queen.

"We're finally home," I whisper, my voice filled with conviction. For the first time in my life, I feel comfortable being just me and truly happy.

It's a strange, bittersweet feeling, knowing that we've lost so much but gained even more in return.

CHAPTER
THIRTY-NINE
SAGE

Two Weeks Later

I'm spit out of the portal, stumbling in the dark, landing in Nightingale Village in a field near the pond. Night encases everything, and it's surreal. Nausea churns in my stomach from being back here. A lot has happened, yet I feel like I'm back to that night Killian found me in the garden and took me to Blight. Now I don't feel like the same Sage I was before.

I'm no longer naive.

Not as afraid.

And I've embraced that I'm different. I love who I am now, and I understand why I never fit into this village. This whole time, I was a monster pretending to be a human.

Even though only about four-and-twenty hours have

passed, the world feels different... almost smaller, more back in the times, but also cozy and familiar.

I steady myself, straighten the backpack on my shoulder, and try to shake off the dizziness and the overwhelming sense of traveling through the portal.

Killian leaps out of the portal with more grace than I managed, landing softly beside me. He stretches, his muscles rippling under the moonlight in his human form, dressed up fitting a Viscount. When I glance at him now, I'm no longer afraid of him. Killian is my true mate. A Shadowfen who saved my life, who loved me so passionately it left me with marks, and someone I absolutely love. Besides, we're going to get married, so technically, he's my fiancé.

"Ahhh, this place," he groans, making it clear he's not a huge fan. "Let's move. It's best if no one sees us and asks questions."

I nod, my heart pounding with a mix of excitement and anxiety.

"I can't wait to see my mom again. It's been so long, but for her, I know it's more like four-and-twenty hours. I just want to stop her worrying about me and let her know that I'm all right."

Killian glances around, ensuring the dark field is clear.

I try to steady my nerves, and start strolling quickly toward the village. My mind races with thoughts of my mother. What will she say when she sees me? How will I explain everything that's happened? The anticipation is almost too much to bear.

As we near the first few homes, the reality of what we've been through hits me. When we reach my house, I turn to Killian, who gives me an encouraging nod.

We're in the shadows, outside what used to be my bedroom.

"I won't be coming inside with you since I have a few things to settle," Killian says. "I promised to take care of this village before I left, and that's what I'm going to do, but first, I need to visit the Elite City."

It makes me wonder if my friend, Alina, actually made it there, but I don't want Killian to ask about her in the Elite City, not wanting to draw attention to her just in case she doesn't want to be found. I smile, telling myself that, just like me, I hope she's found her happiness.

"So, what's in the Elite City?"

"It's a who," he says with a grin. "The Elite City King offered me the position of temporary Viscount in Nightingale Village, which I took to come and learn more about you."

I grin shyly, realizing how things had been set into motion by him way before we ever met.

"And I'm going to gain approval for our regular returns to Earth from Blight to visit your mother and notify him that I won't be spending time in the city any longer."

"Unless my mother wants to join us?" I ask, hopeful though worried she'll struggle there. "However, before she fell sick, she loved the simple village life."

He shrugs. "Sage, that might be difficult, seeing as

approval may be needed from Cain, and it may not be given since that could raise a lot of questions. I have something else in store to help your mom, but initially, I have to speak with Cain. Something that could go either way."

I swallow hard. "Should I be worried?"

He laughs softly. "Never with me." Then he places something in my palm, and I glance down to find a small clear bag with powder inside. "Give her this to drink with water, and her chest infection will completely go away. She'll be healed in a few hours."

My throat thickens. "Really?" I throw myself into a hug with him.

He threads a finger under my chin, lifts it, and in the dark shadows of my house, his mouth meets mine. It's fire, passion, an explosion of carnal pleasure. With it comes a memory of the way he adores my body when he claims me. He's a dominant lover, enjoying me being tied up, and I've grown to love it. I'm planning to surprise him next time with a trick of my own—binding his hands. The thought excites me, and I kiss him back deeper, leaning against him, pushing myself on my tippy-toes to reach him fully.

I almost laugh, thinking about how those girls who used to bully me in the village would react now if they saw me kissing the Viscount.

Killian pulls back. "All right, my pretty little monster, now head inside, and I'll return as soon as I can." He walks me to the front of the house, takes a quick kiss, then whispers, "I love you more than stars sparkle in the sky. I'll see you soon." And he's gone.

I'm buzzing all over, my lips slightly sore from his kiss, my insides swooning from his words. I watch him vanish into the dark.

The familiar creak of the front porch has me covered in goose bumps from excitement. There's a soft glow in the window, telling me the kitchen light is on. She must be up, probably worrying about me.

Taking a deep breath, I gently knock on the door, not wanting to just barge in and scare her. Hurried footsteps rush to the door, and moments later, the door swings open. My mother stands there, her face pale with shock and relief. She's suddenly crying, and I burst into tears.

"Sage?" she gasps, pulling me into a tight embrace. "Oh, my sweet girl, you're home!"

I hug her back, the warmth and love of her embrace bringing me back home.

"I've missed you."

I pull from her and move inside, closing the door quickly behind me, then I hug her again.

"You have no idea how much I wanted to contact you, but I couldn't leave the monster world at first. It's complicated."

We move into the kitchen, where it's warm, and she's just made herself a hot tea. She's in her robe, her hair messy. She breaks into a rough cough that has her trying to clear her throat several times. Then she stares at me, smiling as she wipes her tears.

"Where have you been? What happened? After I read

your note, I suspected the worst... that I'd never see you again." She examines me, smiling yet uncertain. "You look different, your hair, it's more violet. And your eyes." It's as though she finally sees me now.

I grin at her, and she sighs heavily.

"You know what I am, don't you?"

She nods almost reluctantly.

My insides tighten to think that she knew this whole time.

I set my bag down on one of the chairs at the kitchen table. "We have so much to catch up on, but first, here." I give her the small bag of powder from Killian. "Mix this with water and drink it all in one go. In a few hours, your chest infection will be completely gone."

She looks at it skeptically but trusts me enough to say, "All right, but you need to sit down and explain everything. I'll get you a hot cup of tea."

I'm not sure how to begin as I flop down in a chair. She hurries about the kitchen, setting the hot water kettle on an already burning stove that keeps the house warm. She then prepares her own concoction, the liquid in her glass turning a vibrant violet. She stares at it carefully, then looks at me.

"Are you sure?"

"I am. I promise it will heal you," I reassure her.

She takes a sniff, her face relaxing slightly.

"So, anyway," I begin. "You knew my father was a monster the whole time? And that I was different?"

She sighs, setting the glass down on the table, the memories clearly weighing heavily on her.

"Yes, Sage. I knew. I was working in the field late one evening. I was younger then, and since I lived alone with my parents long gone, I had to finish my quota to get food. So, I worked late that evening." Her voice softens, her eyes distant as she recalls the past.

"I met a man who I didn't recognize. He was the most beautiful man I'd ever seen, and I should have been scared of him, but I wasn't. Especially as he was much older than me, but his presence was mesmerizing, and I couldn't look away. After he approached me, we talked for hours. He was charming and kind, and I found myself drawn to him in a way I couldn't explain. Then he blew sparkling dust in my face, which was so strange, but it made me relax. He told me I'd be okay... then one thing led to another and..." She glances at me, her cheeks flushing. "Well, nine months later, I had you."

I listen intently, my heart aching for my mother. "What happened next?"

"I never saw him again," she continues, her lips turning downward, and I can tell she really felt something for my father, while I hate him for everything he's done to her, to Blight. "But I think of him often, wondering who he was. Before he left, he whispered to me that he was a monster who had snuck into our world behind someone else from his world as it was Monsters Night, and he had to return soon. Then he left."

Tears well up in my eyes. "Mom, why didn't you tell me?"

"I wanted to protect you, Sage. I thought if you didn't know, you could have a normal life. But as you grew, I saw the signs. I knew you were special, that you were different, and I figured one day I'd tell you."

I reach across the table, taking her hand. "I know you did the best you could." I can't be mad at her, not after all she's gone through, too, being the outcast in a town for getting pregnant by a man who left her. A monster. And she could never tell a soul.

"I'm sorry for keeping it from you." She squeezes my hand, her eyes glistening with tears. "I thought I was doing the right thing."

The kettle whistles, and she's on her feet, returning moments later with my cup of tea. She's brought a small pot of honey as well, and I put a few swirls in my tea before sipping the chamomile brew.

The room falls into a comfortable silence, the weight of our conversation hanging in the air. Thoughts of my father spins on my mind, of the darkness that runs through my veins. But I also think of my new family—Wolfe, Nyko, Killian, and my half sister.

I notice she hasn't drunk her concoction. "Mom, drink it up so you can heal."

She starts sipping and then gulps it all down in one go. She makes a scrunched-up facial expression, saying, "Tastes like grass. Not pleasant."

She coughs again, and I hope that's a sign of it being effective. If I've observed anything about powders from the monster world, it's that they work almost instantly.

"I've got something else for you." I open my backpack and pull out a bag of Moon Puffs, opening it to reveal half a dozen, some slightly crushed. "These are delicious monster treats."

She stares at me. "So, you survived a monster world? How did you get out and return home?" She stands and collects a small plate from the kitchen, and when she returns, I set the puffs on the table.

"It's a long story, and I've got all night to tell you everything. But do try these; they'll take the grassy taste from your mouth."

She studies one and takes a bite, then makes a moaning sound. "Oh, what is this? It's so delightfully sweet, and those little candy pieces are so chewy and fruity."

"They are meant to replicate lunar worms."

My mom pauses, staring at me, scared.

I laugh. "They aren't real worms. Trust me, I asked."

She eats it quickly, then takes another, and I join her.

"You know, I met my real father."

She stops mid-bite, her eyes widening. "You did? What was he like?"

I take a deep breath, trying to find the right words.

"He was... complicated." A fucking asshole. "Powerful." A bastard monster. "Ruthless." A murderer. "And terrifying."

My mom's hand trembles slightly as she reaches for another puff.

"Did he hurt you?"

"No," I reassure her. "He tried, but no. He's not someone you can easily trust but not someone to worry about ever again."

Her brow furrows, and she catches on to what I'm saying. I reach over and squeeze her hand as I sip my tea.

"Anyway... Let me tell you everything from the start."

"Please." She settles comfortably in her chair, taking another Moon Puff.

"I met Killian first," I begin, my mind racing back to the night that started it all. "He told me that I'd been selected to be offered to monsters. So, he took me to his world, Blight. The vessel, the monsters, the mind-blowing world—it was all so surreal." I explain it all in detail, and my mother's eyes grow huge. Her hand grips mine like she's scared for me.

"Sage, that sounds terrifying. And wait, so Killian, the Viscount, is a monster?"

I nod. "Yes, he is. Anyway, I wasn't alone in the world. I had three Shadowfen who looked after me." I go on about the devastating state of the old kingdom and how my father killed the old King, knowing I can't shield her and she deserves to know the truth.

She gasps aloud. "No, he wouldn't!"

"He did." My voice wobbles as just thinking about everything brings up so many emotions, so many memories. "Someone even tried to kill me." My mother looks pale, but I quickly say, "I was saved by the three Shadowfen, who turned out to be my true mates."

"True mates?" she mimics, the bridge between her eyes bunched up.

"It's a perfect match for life. Like soul mates," I say. "There's Wolfe, Nyko, and Killian. Each one is different but amazing in his own way." I go into more explanation about each one's personality and how they spoiled and protected me. "And they had a plan to take revenge on my father," I continue. "Wolfe is the son of the King my father killed. It's so twisted."

"I don't even know what to say."

I go into everything else, and finally, I reveal, "I have a half sister."

She's almost crying, and my heart breaks. I reach over to her, embracing her. "I can't tell you how happy that makes me. What is she like?"

I pull back smiling. "Elara is amazing, younger than me, and we get along so well," I say, feeling a warmth at the thought of my sister. Then I add, "I can't stay here in Nightingale Village. I think you know that, right?"

She nods, understanding. "I know, Sage. I see that now. I'm so sorry for everything you went through, my baby."

I hug her back, having missed her so much. "It's all right because I feel stronger now, as though I am who I was meant to become all along." I break away.

"Killian is going to the Elite City to ask their King about getting approval for me to come back and visit you more often, unless..." I stare at her. "You want to join me in the monster world?"

She shakes her head almost instantly, her shoulders back. "Oh, I don't think I can do that. I won't like it. This is my home, where I feel safe, where I have a close friend next door..."

"But I can't stay here," I say, feeling the weight of the decision.

"I know," she says softly. "But now that you're safe and you have three men looking after you—which is a little bit strange, I must admit—I can stop worrying. Especially if you keep visiting me and bringing me monster treats. And maybe one day, I can meet your half sister."

"Of course," I say, hugging her again, feeling exhausted from talking so much. "When I say it all, it sounds like a crazy, made-up story."

She chuckles, and I notice that she hasn't coughed since she took the drink.

Outside, the roosters are already singing, and I keep wondering what Killian meant when he said he had something in store for my mother.

The late afternoon sun is shining brightly on the horizon, casting long shadows across the village. My mother is making supper, and my mind is far away. I can't stop thinking about the weeks I've missed back in Blight. How terribly I long for Wolfe and Nyko and wonder how they are doing, how my sister Elara is managing. The ache of not being with them is a constant throb in my chest.

A firm knock sounds at the door. My heart leaps, and I rush to open it. There stands Killian, looking as strong and handsome as ever. My excitement explodes, and I drag him inside, shut the door, and throw myself into his arms.

"So happy to see you're back!"

He catches me, his arms wrapping around me. He kisses me deeply, his lips warm and familiar.

"I missed you so much," he murmurs against my lips. "I've been experiencing such dirty thoughts about what I plan to do to you once we get back home."

I laugh, and he sets me back on my feet.

He lifts his head as my mom approaches, and she pauses, slightly uncertain about seeing a Viscount in our house. But he's so much more.

"You must be Sage's mom. I'm Killian," he says, offering his hand.

Instead of shaking his hand, she moves forward and hugs him tightly.

"Sage told me everything," she says, her voice trembling slightly. "Thank you so much for taking care of her."

Killian laughs, a warm, hearty sound that has me close to purring. Who would have thought that our distance would make me so hungry for him?

"Well, that makes it easier," he murmurs.

We move to the kitchen table and sit down, and Killian turns serious as he faces my mother.

"My role as Viscount was temporary," he begins. "I now have permission to appoint someone new permanently, and I want you to take over the village."

My mom's eyes widen, her hands flying to her chest.

"No, I don't know what to do..." she gasps, clearly shocked.

I stand next to her, rubbing her arm for reassurance.

Killian smiles. "But you're no longer sick, right? I've spoken to others in the village, and even though they treated you as an outcast, many have admitted, even reluctantly, that they see how much you love the village, how hard you work. You care for anyone who comes to you in trouble. So many from the village can learn from you. And this is the chance to show them they were wrong about treating you that way and teach them to better accept differences."

Her eyes fill with uncertainty.

"You will be amazing at it," I say, taking a seat next to her.

"Will you take the offer?" Killian asks. "You will receive great benefits that will make your life more comfortable, and no one will ever look at you as anything but the Viscount they should respect and abide by."

"Mom," I say, my voice soft but encouraging. "You said yourself you love it here. Think how much you can help others and change the way the village has been treated."

She glances at me, a smile teasing her lips, her eyes glistening, then back at Killian.

"You think I can do it?"

"Yes," we both say in unison, and I giggle while Killian grins deliciously.

"All right, I guess I can try," she finally agrees.

"Excellent," Killian says, shuffling closer, and I do the

same. He begins to detail that he will return in a day or so to go over everything with her, about who she reports to in the Elite City, and how it all works. "I have been given permission to come and go as I please, along with bringing Sage with me, which means you will see a lot more of her. But first, we will return home. Our kingdom is being rebuilt, and I would hate to discover what decisions they've made for my quarters in our new home. You know, one day here is a month back home, and Wolfe and Nyko will be crazy with worry over our Sage. Maybe one day, we can bring you over to see the kingdom?"

She's not saying anything but staring at Killian.

"Mom, are you all right?" I ask.

She turns and drags me into her arms, sniffling tears. "I think this might be good for me," she admits. When I break away, she faces Killian. "I accept all of those offers."

"That is exceptional news," he answers. "Once I return, I will make an official announcement to everyone in Nightingale Village about your new role, and I will help you settle into it. I will also notify everyone that Sage was selected as a late monster Offering and has already left the village. That way, there will be no questions you need to answer."

"Thank you," is all she says, and I hug my mother, loving her so much.

"And not sure if Sage has told you, but you will receive a formal invitation to our wedding, plus she will officially be Queen of the Silvercrest Kingdom."

"Oh, Sage, that's amazing news!" my mother shouts.

We hug again. I'm still coming to terms with the whole thing, but I welcome it.

My mother suddenly makes a face as she pulls back and says, "Just don't start making everyone call you 'Your Majesty' now."

I burst out laughing, not having given that even a thought.

I'm so proud of her and knowing she's getting healthier eases my stress. Yet, a part of me also aches to be back with Wolfe and Nyko, my true mates. I miss them horribly, and I know they must be worried about me.

I feel like, finally, I can start a new chapter in my life. And I'm more than ready.

EPILOGUE
SAGE

Three Months Later

I'm a bundle of nerves.

The grand hall falls silent as Wolfe and I stand at the front, facing two golden thrones intricately crafted from interconnected bones that gleam in the light pouring in from the arched windows. The thrones sit atop a platform a few steps up, and everything feels like a fairy tale, that it's not really happening.

Behind us, a crowd of at least a thousand Shadowfen remains hushed, their gazes fixed on us. I glance back quickly and see the crowd, their eyes gleaming. In the front row, I spot my mom and sister next to Killian and Nyko, who are blowing me kisses. I'm blushing crazily.

Mom's smiling, though she occasionally glances around nervously at the numerous Shadowfen in their monster forms. But she's been surprisingly embracing since she arrived in Blight this morning.

Seeing them together, I'm ecstatic, and my heart swells with emotion. I smile at them because it means the world to me to have them here, witnessing our coronation. This moment, surrounded by those I love and those who believe in us, is more than I could ever have dreamed.

"Your father would be so proud, Wolfe," Eirik says.

I turn back around to see an older monster, who looks like a legendary warrior from ancient tales, standing several feet in front of us. He's broad and huge, with white hair and aging lines etched deeply into his face, and he's wearing a mauve robe. Wolfe told me Eirik is one of the closest friends of Wolfe's late father, the old King. His smile is wide, genuine, and filled with happiness as he looks at us.

"Both of you, rightful heirs, standing here today, it's a sight that is overdue."

With my father taking over the kingdom—through him killing the old King—it means that as the eldest, I was also considered an heir to the Silvercrest Kingdom under Blight law. Which would have meant that Wolfe and I would be required to fight for the position to the death... that's if we weren't getting married and taking the thrones together.

Somehow, all the tragedy and chaos have brought us to this perfect ending.

Wolfe grins, standing tall in his monster form, his tailored black pants fitting him perfectly. It took some convincing, but I insisted he wasn't completely nude—especially with my mother attending—and now he looks every bit the royal he deserves.

I'm wearing a mauve-pearl gown, holding my human form for my mother to avoid frightening her more. The dress's delicate fabric shimmers in the light. The gown is more elaborate than anything I've ever worn. Its semitransparent material hints at my curves but doesn't reveal anything. The bodice is fitted and adorned with silver embroidery that traces swirling patterns over my torso. The skirt flows out in layers of gossamer, trailing behind me in a long, elegant train. Tiny, enchanted spiders made of silver thread sit on the train, their presence apparently customary as they symbolize the powerful web of connections and responsibilities that come with ruling a kingdom.

I try not to think about them as it's slightly creeping me out. Every time I shift, the spiders seem to come to life, their legs glinting as they weave their way through the fabric.

"Today, we honor not only the past but also the future. You both have fathers who were Kings, and while the past is the past, today you begin your reign as the rightful heirs." Eirik's voice booms across the extravagant hall, only recently built.

The ceiling is lofty and arched, and the walls are white but painted in dark gold with artistic drawings that depict the scenes leading up to this moment. From the collapse of the first kingdom to the vessel in the water, our battle with the Nythrax beast, to me in my monster form, and Wolfe, Killian, and Nyko in theirs. It leaves me giddy to think I am part of this world's history.

The coronation is already well underway, and I'm almost bouncing on my toes. It's overwhelming standing here next to Wolfe, about to be crowned in this magnificent hall.

Two monsters in mauve robes, similar to Eirik's, step forward, each carrying a soft cushion with a crown resting atop. The crowns leave me breathless as they catch the light and sparkle brilliantly. The crown that I assume is mine is a masterpiece of mauve pearls, the radiant amethyst set in the center casting a soft purple glow. Smaller diamonds and pearls are encrusted around the band, forming delicate patterns that glint with every movement. It matches perfectly with the pearl necklace Nyko gave me. My eyes sting, but I promised myself I wouldn't cry.

Wolfe's crown is set with a large, dark sapphire at its center, surrounded entirely by gleaming diamonds, and is stunning. As the crowns are brought closer, I blink away the tears. Wolfe's hand is in mine, and I glance over at him. He's smiling at me like I'm the most amazing person in the world. My knees are weak, and I curl my fingers around his hand, needing his stability before the emotions engulf me.

Eirik lifts Wolfe's crown first. "With this crown, we honor your lineage and your right to rule as our King." He places it on Wolfe's head.

Then, turning to me, Eirik smiles warmly. "And with this crown, we welcome a new era, guided by strength and unity as you rule as our Queen." He carefully places the crown on my head. It's a bit heavy, but I feel like a Queen standing here with Wolfe.

A tear slips out from the corner of my eye, my chest so tight from the overwhelming happiness flaring through me.

Eirik steps back, addressing the crowd. "I present to you your new King and Queen of Silvercrest Kingdom, rightful heirs to the throne!" Then he waves for us to go to our thrones.

The applause is deafening, the room filled with cheers and roars of approval.

"I call forward Killian and Nyko," Eirik continues. "From this moment on, let it be known that Killian and Nyko, loyal and true, are now appointed as Princes of the Silvercrest Kingdom. Together, they will lead us into a new direction of prosperity and strength."

I glance back and see everyone, including my sister, Elara, and my mom, on their feet, clapping. I'm full-blown crying now, unable to stop my tears. My mom looks so proud, tears glistening in her eyes.

Killian and Nyko stroll toward us, both in their monster forms.

Wolfe's hand grips mine a bit tighter, grounding me in this moment.

"Look at you," Wolfe says softly, his eyes shining with pride. "You look like you were born for this."

I smile, my heart swelling with love and pride. "I couldn't have done it without you," I whisper back.

We're now standing in front of the thrones that are

made of gold with violet cushioning. Wolfe and I take our seats, Nyko and Killian standing on either side of us. The whole crowd roars. I'm shaking from this moment, something I will never ever forget.

I reach over and squeeze Nyko's hand, feeling like I'm living a real fairy tale. I glance at Wolfe, who is sitting tall and proud, his presence commanding and strong, just as I imagine he'd seen his father sitting on the throne. Killian and Nyko are smiling and, surprisingly, not saying anything. Though I can tell it's killing Nyko, as his shadow form can't stand still.

Eirik steps forward once more. "This is a new beginning, a new chapter in our history. With our new King and Queen and their loyal Princes, we will face any challenges that come our way. Long live the King and Queen!"

"Long live the King and Queen!" the crowd echoes, their voices united in celebration.

As I sit here, tears rolling down my cheeks, I know that this is the happiness I've always sought... I just never knew I was destined to be a Queen with three soon-to-be husbands at my side.

I'm laughing, trying not to cry out as Nyko licks my neck. We're in a dressing room, as I've come here to change out of my gown from the coronation into my wedding dress. The wedding won't be a traditional ceremony, but there will be an exchange of vows and blood in front of everyone, which officially makes the four of us married. Down in the main courtyard, the celebrations are about to begin. So many people are there already, including my mother and half sister.

The moment I arrived upstairs to change, Nyko found me... in his shadow form.

"You're tickling..." I whisper, half giggling, half moaning.

"Only because I'm being gentle. Fuck, I almost died being next to you but not having you against me. We might as well have been worlds apart." His lips drag across my collarbone, his cool shadow arms looping around my middle, pulling up my dress. "I'm going to help you get changed, then I'm going to fuck you," he purrs in my ear. "If I don't do this, I'm going to steal you from the celebration because I can't stand another second without having you."

I giggle, unable to get enough of him. "But everyone's outside... and..."

"There are guests waiting, My Lord and Queen," Howler's sudden interruption fills the room, to which Nyko groans, and I'm grinning. I love that we salvaged him from the vessel, and now he lives in our kingdom, connected to all royal buildings.

"Go away, Howler. Not now," Nyko growls, his gaze on me. "I need this. They can wait."

"Of course, My Lord, I will play a different round of songs to get everyone up and dancing."

"Thank you, Howler," I say, then turn my attention on Nyko.

In moments, he has the gown off me, and it's a slight relief to have the spider dress off me. His huge tongue drags across his lips, and I'm instantly wet for him, my thighs squeezing together.

"You're so fucking beautiful, Sage. Every time I see you, it's like the first time."

He has me in his arms, walking me to the couch, just as the door barges open to both Killian and Wolfe entering.

I flinch, watching their expressions.

They eye us, grinning, and with the door rapidly shut, they rush over to me, undressing.

"Good idea. I need her before the celebration, or I'll go insane," Killian states.

"The way you looked in that dress," Wolfe adds. "You were destroying me in there, as I tried so hard not to get a hard-on."

I'm laughing as they stroll toward me, and I flop onto the couch. They watch me, hungry, gazes lowering to my breasts, to me spreading my legs.

"I guess there's no other way but to serve my men." I try to put on a royal voice but sound anything but, and I giggle.

Then they fall to their knees, Wolfe reaching for my hand.

"Anything for our Queen."

They come at me, and I feel so loved that I can't remember what it was like to experience anything but adored.

Nyko's tongue trails down my stomach, sending shivers through my body, his head dipping between my thighs. His touch, though shadowy, is solid and cool against my skin, and when his tongue laps my pussy, I cry out with exhilaration. Wolfe's strong hand curls over a breast, and he leans in, his breath hot against my ear.

"You make me so fucking aroused, Sage. I can't wait to fill you with my cum every day."

I gasp at his words, but I'm distracted by Nyko's tongue and by Killian's fingers tracing over my other breast and pinching my nipple. His lips find mine, and we kiss like we're on fire.

"You are everything to me," Killian whispers against my mouth.

I wrap my arms around him and Wolfe, pulling them closer. My legs curl over Nyko's shoulders, and I moan. My body buzzes, floats, while my heart pounds with love for my monsters.

I can barely breathe, overwhelmed by the sensations and the emotions from today.

"I love you all," I cry out. "So much..." I lose my words to my cries of desire as my body spills into a climax. I shudder against them, adoring how they never let me go but enjoy my pleasure with me.

They pull back, and to my surprise, they are getting to their feet.

"You know, it's customary," Wolfe begins, "that

before a ceremony, the new bride is rutted by her intended husband in view of the audience."

I gasp. "Shut up, that's not true, and we're not doing that, ever!"

Killian chuckles, while Nyko has an expression on his face as if he's contemplating it, then says, "It could be so easy to go on the balcony, bend you over and fuck you so hard, make you scream, and the Shadowfen will cheer you on."

"I can't think of anything worse. That's an awful tradition, I'm sorry to say. And my mother and half sister are out there." Normally, when it comes to sex, I've given in a lot to their requirements, but this is where I draw the line.

"Which is why we're in here and not out there," Wolfe explains with a cheeky grin, taking my hand and pulling me against him.

I can hear the sounds of the celebration outside, laughter, music, and the murmur of voices, but right now, I'm surrounded by my future husbands, naked and pressed against me. Four cocks for a Queen like me seem fitting... I glance at them all.

"Well then, show me how my King and Princes truly adore their Queen."

They take me in their arms, and I'm at their mercy, I know I am, but the sense of arousal, of peace, of fulfillment, is a reminder that this is it.

This is my perfect ending.

MOON PUFFS RECIPE

Ingredients:

1 1/2 cups AP flour

1/2 cup cake flour

1/2 tsp baking soda

1/2 cup salted butter, softened 1 cup packed brown sugar

2 tbsp instant vanilla pudding 1 large egg, room temp

1 Tbsp vanilla bean paste

1/2 cup buttermilk

2 Tbsp purple food coloring

Filling:

Monster Moon Puffs

1 block of room temp cream cheese (8 oz pkg) 1 stick (1/2 cup) salted butter

1 tsp vanilla

3-4 cups powdered sugar (taste preference) Purple food coloring (have fun with the color!) Optional : add in lunar worms (gummy worms)

Directions:

-Preheat oven to 375 F (190 C) and line baking sheets with parchment paper or silicone baking mats and set aside.

-in a medium bowl, whisk the dry ingredients together and set aside.

-In a large mixing bowl, use a hand mixer and beat the butter on medium speed for 30 seconds. Then add in brown sugar until light and fluffy. Add in egg and vanilla.

-Next alternate adding dry mix and buttermilk mixing after each just to incorporate ingredients. Next add in your food coloring (gel food coloring makes more vibrant colors)

-Using a medium cookie scoop (about 2 Tbsp) place batter 1 inch apart on a baking sheet (macaron baking mats are great for these!)

-bake for 9-11 minutes or until the tops are set. Cool completely before assembling.

Filling:

Add in softened cream cheese, butter, and vanilla to a bowl or stand mixer. Cream together the add in powdered sugar once combined, add in food coloring. Scoop into a piping bag and pipe filling onto one cookie and top with another cookie.

Enjoy

BIND ME
IMMORTAL VICES AND VIRTUES

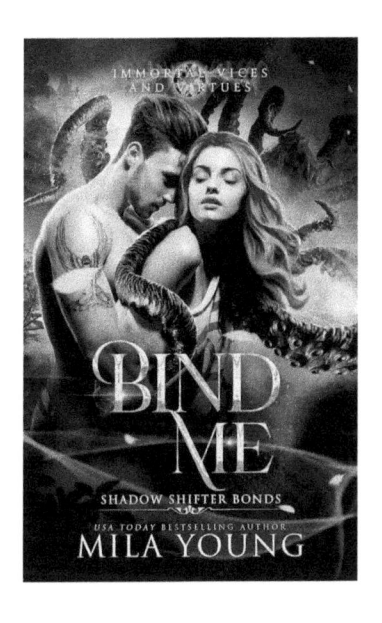

Fate shattered my world in a heartbeat.

As a bounty hunter, I've pursued the supernatural, yet nothing prepared me for the truth about my own bloodline.

Exiled by a harsh twist of fate, I'm thrust into the cold heart of Norway. Here, amid ancient forests and icy waters, I'm supposed to start over. But shadows from my past cling tighter than ever.

On a mission that was supposed to be my redemption throws me into the path with *him*—a man as dangerous and mysterious as he is infuriating. He's hiding secrets that will get me killed, revealing he's my fated mate.

Unbelievable!

His touch sparks a flame inside me, leaving me questioning everything.

Together, we stumble on a dark conspiracy, centuries in the making, binding our fates together. As truths surface, we're forced to work together.

As lines blur between us, I'm faced with a choice: Can I trust the man who awakens my soul but might be my ultimate undoing?

Bind Me *is a spicy standalone fantasy romance set in the Immortal Vices and Virtues Universe. It's a guaranteed happily ever after with a satisfying ending and no cliffhangers.*

THEIR LETHAL PET
A MONSTERS NIGHT NOVEL

Discover Alina's story in Their Lethal Pet...

Run. Hide. *Fight*.

It's Monsters Night, the annual event where the portals to other realms and realities open, and monsters flood the streets to search for their potential mates.

And I'm one of the candidates.

Why?

Because I broke all the rules. I fought back against the elitist system hellbent on enslaving humankind. And f-ck if I'm going to let one of these monsters claim me. Let alone three of them

Orcus.

Reaper.

Flame.

They saved me from a compromising situation. But that doesn't mean I *like* them. I don't care how gorgeous they are or how well-endowed they seem to be—I kneel for no one. And I have no interest in becoming their lethal little pet.

"Try to tame me," I dare them.

"We have no interest in taming you, sweet pet," they say. "We want to make you ours."

"Ours to worship."

"Ours to love."

"Ours to keep."

THEIR BLOOD QUEEN
A MONSTERS NIGHT NOVEL

Three sexy vampires haunt my dreams and they love to make me scream.

For all the right reasons.

The nightmares started on Monster's Night. I figured my overactive libido was just tripping out because of all the literal monsters on the news. Some portal opened up and they were terrorizing women, in particular.

But seriously, what female hasn't thought about that monster under the bed once or twice in a sensual light? There's just something about danger, about fangs, about long tongues...

So, I let the dreams happen. I ***invite them in.***

But one night, when I open my eyes and they're literally feasting on me... I realize it's no dream.

This is real.

A FREE STORY JUST FOR YOU ....

Did you enjoy Savage Sector and want more? Sign up for my newsletter at www.subscribepage.com/milayoung and you will receive a free novella from me as a thank you gift your joining my newsletter.

In addition, you'll be given special access to deleted and bonus scenes, new release announcements and so much more!

About Mila Young

Find all Mila Young books at www.milayoungbooks.com

Best-selling author, Mila Young tackles everything with the zeal and bravado of the fairytale heroes she grew up reading about. She slays monsters, real and imaginary, like there's no tomorrow. By day she rocks a keyboard as a marketing extraordinaire. At night she battles with her mighty pen-sword, creating fairytale retellings, and sexy ever after tales.

Ready to read more and more from Mila Young?
www.subscribepage.com/milayoung

Join Mila's **Wicked Readers group** for exclusive content, latest news, and giveaway.
www.facebook.com/groups/milayoungwickedreaders

For more information...
mila@milayoungbooks.com